ARRIVAL

ARRIVAL

MANABOUND BOOK 1

TRAVIS ALBRECHT

ARRIVAL

THE FLASH

No matter how much Sloane Reinhart tried to keep her on a schedule, her daughter danced to the beat of her own drum. There was something timeless about the scene of a parent waiting on their child. It was a dance Sloane struggled with daily. Nearly every morning, her daughter, Gwyneth, had to rush to get ready to leave the house. Gwyn was not a morning person. She never had been.

Sloane tapped her foot as she stood in the kitchen. "Gwyn! It's time to go. What are you doing?" she yelled across the house for the second time. *Ten-year-olds…*

With a sigh, Sloane leaned on the island and focused on the living room TV. She grabbed the remote and flipped through various news channels before settling on one. The current segment featured two anchors as they discussed the first successful orbital launch of the rocket named Starship.

The blasé attitude of the Italian news anchors belied the significance the missile would have on spaceflight, at least according to her. The fact that it could potentially take the first humans to another planet? That was important.

Sloane had always enjoyed hearing about the progress of the company and its goal of putting humans on Mars. While her focus was more on things within the world than outside of it, she had always imagined what it would be like to step foot on another planet for the first time. It was just a thought—the passing dream of a woman who had once lived for adventure. She'd had her fun traveling the world and seeing new things in her early twenties, but that life was behind her. Now, at thirty-four, Sloane experienced those adventurous feelings within the pages of a good novel.

Still, as her daughter's footsteps finally pounded down the hall, she considered that maybe the adventure she craved had just taken on a new phase.

Dismissing her reverie, Sloane looked at the clock as she waited for her daughter to appear. They had to leave soon to get Gwyn to school, and then Sloane had to drive into Milan to get to work.

I don't even have time to stop for a cappuccino now. She sighed.

Her patience had worn thin by the time Gwyn rushed into the kitchen, sliding across the hardwood floor in her socks. She wore black pants and a gray jacket, looking as if she were ready to go hiking. It was only early autumn—the gelato shops hadn't even closed for the season yet.

"Gwyneth Reinhart, you are taking far too long this morning," Sloane said, exasperated.

"I'm putting my boots on!" Gwyn protested.

"I told you to get your shoes on ten minutes ago. What were you doing?"

"I had to put my socks on, Mom." Gwyn rolled her eyes.

And there's the eye roll. This girl. "Well, we need to go if you want to go to the café before school."

"I know, Mom," Gwyn said, as Sloane hurried her daughter out of the kitchen.

"Don't forget, tonight we have to—"

"I know," Gwyn interrupted, cutting her off with exasperation before she could finish.

Sloane closed her eyes and took a deep breath. "Gwyneth…" she began but stopped after opening her eyes and seeing her daughter standing there ready. "Ugh, fine. Let's go."

Sloane collected her things as her daughter hefted her brightly colored backpack—a rainbow checkerboard patterned thing that she had begged and pleaded for—onto her shoulder, and together they walked to the door. Sloane looked around one last time before leaving, certain that she was forgetting something.

"Mom, you forgot the watch."

Sloane let out an exaggerated groan. "Oh, yeah! Thanks, Gwynnie!"

"Of course, Mom. You're welcome. Let's go!"

Sloane went and grabbed the case that held one of the prototypes for a revolutionary smartwatch she had a key part in designing. Her team was nearing a crucial point in the last stages of its development and, currently, it was all hands on deck. She and several of her engineers had begun wearing them off-campus for real-world usability tests. Even though it was not that fashionable yet, she enjoyed it. The usability and software were far more important to her job than the experimental looks of a product still in development.

That wouldn't be a concern for long because the release candidate model was scheduled to be built soon in preparation for mass production. Life would get much easier for her after the team reached that point.

For the time being, Sloane was crazy-busy, but it wouldn't be much longer until everything was calm again. She just had to keep at it and not let the stress get to her, or affect her relationship with Gwyn. Perhaps things weren't as bad as they seemed...

Sloane took the watch out of its charging case and fastened it to her wrist. She glanced at her daughter, who smiled at her, then shut the door. Yes, everything was alright.

Sloane waited outside Gwyn's school at the end of the day. Work had gone surprisingly well, and she'd managed to ensure a bunch of tasks were completed. She was excited that she was able to leave and spend the evening with her daughter, instead of having to drop her off with the nanny before heading back to work.

Her mind drifted back to work as she waited for school to be released. Their new hardware required a radical redesign of the operating system to make use of the increased capabilities enabled by her team's revolutionary chipset architecture. Her hardware team had to be on hand to work out any issues that arose during the software team's tests and integration.

Before the redesign, it had been years since she last dealt with any system coding, so thankfully she didn't have to worry about that. Luckily, they were still on track for release the following year. They just needed to work out how to mass-produce the new chip design with the manufacturer they contracted. It would require some improvements in their nanometer lithography process, but the factory had assured them that it could be done.

She sighed. *It's only going to cost us millions of investment funding.*

Sloane looked up at the school as she heard the unmistakable sound of a hundred kids streaming out, chatting and laughing, and excited to be free of their classrooms. She walked toward the gated entrance as she saw her daughter crossing the courtyard, and waved once Gwyn noticed her.

"Hey, Gwynnie! Ready to go?"

"Yup! Gelato?"

"You know what? Sure, let's get some."

Looking over Gwyn's outfit, Sloane asked, "So, why'd you end up getting all dressed up today? I didn't see anything about your class going on a hike."

"I knew we'd be out and about today. Wanted to make sure I'd be okay walking."

"So, you just knew we'd be walking to get gelato and I wouldn't have to go back to work?"

"Yup!"

With a laugh, Sloane took her daughter's backpack and put it in the car before they headed toward the local gelateria a little more than a block away.

Gwyn reached over and grabbed Sloane's hand as they started to walk.

Sloane smiled down at her and squeezed her hand. "So, how was your day?"

"It was okay. I got hurt again, and Miss Alberta asked why I'm always getting hurt so much. I told her that it's just my life."

Sloane laughed. "She really put you on blast, didn't she?"

"Yeah, it was my knee this time. I fell kicking the soccer ball away from the boys. They were being mean."

"I'm sorry, sweetie. You okay?"

"Yeah. I just played with my friends after."

They continued to talk about Gwyn's day as they crossed the bridge over the canal that surrounded the town's center. Sloane glanced up and gasped as she did a double take of the blues, purples, and reds mixing in the afternoon sky. Gwyn immediately looked up too.

She squealed lightly and brought a hand to her chest. "Mom! That's so pretty! What is it?"

"Looks like an aurora, sweetie. It's really weird, isn't it?"

"Yeah, but it's cool! Look. Everyone's looking at it."

Sloane looked around and noticed crowds of people also staring and pointing up at the sky. Instinctively, she grabbed Gwyn's hand and pulled her close. A loud burst of noise resounded everywhere, almost as if a jet had broken the sound barrier above them.

Sloane whipped around, trying to ascertain what was happening. People nearby, startled by the seeming sonic boom, screamed. Children stopped midplay and stared upward. Couples held each other. One older woman smacked a younger man and pointed at a young child who was starting to move away. The man rushed to grab and pick up the child before returning to the woman.

Sloane gripped her daughter's hand tighter. "Gwyn, stay close."

"What's wrong, Mom?"

Sloane tensed, trying to figure out what was going on. Everyone around them wore panicked looks. Her heart raced as she scanned the area for any other sign of danger. "I don't know, sweetie. Just stay close to me."

Gwyn quickly moved in just as the sky suddenly flashed blue.

"Mom!"

"Gwyneth! St—"

Sloane was blinded by the flash and hit by a huge gust of wind. She felt Gwyn jerk her hand away in fear as she screamed. Sloane reached out for where she thought her daughter was, but then suddenly felt as if she were falling. Her last thought was of Gwyneth as everything turned black.

*　*　*

The high elf merchant Onas Fenren relaxed as his wagon rolled down the dirt road as they traveled to the next stop on their route. The day was clear, and the scent of grass and trees sat in the air. A nice breeze blew through to solidify the day as a good one. It would not take them long to arrive at the village where they would deliver some goods the headman had requested through one of Onas's other employees.

He reviewed his ledger and inventory list. Onas preferred to keep himself busy, but sitting inside the wagon could be such a bore. Luckily, he did not have to worry about driving as he sat on the front bench with one of his three guards. The other two rode horses along either side of them. At least here he could converse or just listen to his guards talk.

The horse on Onas's left moved forward a bit as the rider looked over at the rest of them. "Boss, how much longer until we reach Larton?" asked the sun elf guard with a bit of mirth.

Not this again...

Onas shook his head as he smiled. Their overall route passed through six villages, three towns, and, finally, back to his home city of Strathmore. The town of Larton would be the last stop before returning home.

He couldn't wait to get back and be with his family. His wife and children were managing the storefront they maintained. This annual route was merely tradition at this point and not something that actually had a noticeable effect on his family's business. That said, he would not complain when he was able to both stock and sell any surplus he made from his travels. Plus, making connections and meeting new people was always a worthwhile investment. The trip this time had been quite lucrative so far, and he was interested in reinvesting some of the profits in upgrades to his company's caravans.

He glanced back at the guard who had asked the question.

The guard had a hint of a smirk on his face, as if he knew exactly what he was doing. There was a rugged look about him, one that hinted he was used to a fight. Which he undoubtedly was. He had close-braided, dark brown hair, and his dark skin, which was common among the sun elves, was contrasted by his bright yellow-orange eyes.

A recent addition to Onas's merchant company, the guard had the enviable ability to switch between humor and calm professionalism when required. The man himself was well worth the additional expense. The presence of additional guards also helped deter any would-be bandits.

Taenya Shavyre, Onas's head guard, leaned forward on her saddle so that she could see the guard on the opposite side of the wagon. She did not look amused.

"Raafe, do you insist upon asking so many times? You know it's a week. Same as five hours ago when you asked. You should pay more attention to your surroundings. We'll be reaching Hilshen soon, where we'll be staying for the night. Watch for any bandits," she stated in an exasperated tone.

Taenya had been working for Onas for eight years now, and at twenty-nine she was well used to the route the merchant traveled, and its dangers. She sat atop her horse with a steel gaze set to her hazel-green eyes, constantly scanning the distance for any threats. Her blond hair, which normally fell to her shoulder blades, was pulled up into a bun that complemented her face. Her race, the telv, looked similar to the high elves—the only differences were the shorter points on their ears and softer jawlines. The telv people were native to the continent on which they resided—Ikios—unlike the Loreni, which consisted of the high, sun, and moon elves.

"Oh, come on, give him a break," Keston, the high elf guard, interjected from the wagon's driving bench. "You know he's always been a bit bad with his numbers. We've all seen him need to use his fingers to add. Actually, come to think of it, that might go for you too, boss. Obviously, it's not quite a week if five hours have passed."

The man was clearly not thinking very hard for his weak attempt at getting a jab in on Taenya as well. Onas looked at his guards and smiled as they continued bickering. During his annual route, he sold various odds and ends, basically anything of sufficient resale value. Sometimes, he simply sold anything needed by people on the route. It always paid to make positive connections, even if the profit margins were smaller in trades meant to build relations.

Right now, he had various goods from the previous towns and villages he thought would sell well in Strathmore. He was also delivering a shipment of swords ordered for Larton's town guard by the local baron. The baron, who was actually a valued partner and friend, was working to grow his guard. This meant they needed to supplement the meager stock of supplies their few blacksmiths were capable of producing. It seemed they were wary of the recent actions of the nearby Duchy of Edimiss. This, Onas thought, was a bit of a knee-jerk reaction that might even further encourage the duchy. In fact, he would probably end up telling his friend to go petition the duke of their duchy, rather than focus on it himself. However, as it didn't really affect him directly, he wasn't going to argue against making good coin. Even if it was a friend. *I'll give him advice, but he did already commit to the purchase.*

Onus started thinking about what he would do when he got home as they followed the road toward Larton at a steady pace. He glanced up as something caught his eye. The formerly clear sky was now filling with a shimmering wave of light.

It looked like the sky lights seen around the coastal regions to the northeast. They weren't common this time of year, during the day… or even in this region. It was a beautiful sight, though, especially the way they hung in front of the Sister Moons. *It seems the Family is smiling down on me. This is surely a boon.* Perhaps he would be able to use this to his advantage in Hilshen.

He turned to say something to Keston when he was pulled from his thoughts by Taenya as she called for a halt of the wagon.

"Onas, look at the sky. Perhaps we should stop here for a bit?" She hesitated slightly before continuing, "I have a bad feeling about this." Taenya's voice held a hint of concern as her gaze focused on what lay above them.

"It's just some sky lights, Taenya," Onas said. However, as he glanced up again, he noticed the sky was starting to turn an unnatural shade of blue as the lights grew in size. Soon, they obscured the Sister Moons that shared the sky with their Father, the sun, who should have been lovingly gazing down at the Mother from their celestial home. Instead, the sky was growing dark.

"Actually, Taenya, you may be right. Let's take a second and rest. Maybe—"

There was a bright blue flash in the sky, and Onas, in surprise, almost toppled from his seat. He opened his mouth to speak just as everything turned black.

CHAPTER ONE

ARRIVAL

All across reality, magic and mana were thought to not really exist. A thing of fantasy and legend, stories told to children. That changed one day in a way that no one could have predicted. Mana is different than imagined. It is a natural existence filled with intent and purpose. A purpose that changes and enhances everything it touches. When mana burst into existence within our reality, it created a cascade of effects that tore everything asunder. One of these events caused families and individuals to be ripped from their worlds and transported to others.

A History of Mana. 184 SA

Sloane awoke to a strange sight. She blinked—there were moons hanging in the blue sky above her as she lay on the grass. Not just one... but two. She rubbed her eyes and looked again.

They were still there.

"What the hell?" she groaned. Then she remembered her daughter. "Gwynnie? You okay, sweetie?" She turned her head to look at Gwyn, and her breath hitched. Her daughter wasn't there.

"Gwyn?"

Sloane shot up and looked around, eyes darting over the scenic landscape that was obviously not home. She was on a small grassy hill near a dirt road alongside fields. A line of trees stood about thirty meters in the opposite direction. What she didn't see anywhere, however, was her daughter.

"Gwyn!" she yelled, panic swelling in her chest.

Her stomach dropped and her mind hazed as she jumped up and started searching in earnest. Seeing nothing but nature, she found herself at a complete loss; she had no idea where she was, no clue where her daughter was. She had been right there next to her.

"Gwyneth! Answer me!" she shouted between quick, short breaths, her lungs beginning to burn with the strain of hyperventilating.

She had to get a handle on herself. *Breathe, damn it. Standing here panicking will not find Gwyn.* Determination settling in, Sloane pushed herself to count to three while taking deep breaths, then all but shoved herself into action, knowing time was of the essence.

With her mind finally slamming into overdrive, she tried to think of what had happened, where her daughter could be, and where she should look first.

First, the fact that there were two moons in the sky meant something absolutely insane had happened. She was no longer on Earth, couldn't be. Second, her daughter had been within a meter of her just before… Could Gwyn have been left on Earth? She'd be all alone but in her hometown. The police would help her get to Sloane's family.

No. She thought it more likely Gwyn was here, too—they had both been enveloped by that light. If that was the event that had brought her here, it gave credence to the possibility that Gwyn was here, too. So, finally, where the hell was she?

Maybe she'd landed in a different place. Maybe she hadn't woken up yet. Maybe she'd woken up and had walked away to see something. Yes. Sloane had to assume that her daughter had been transported as well. She just needed to find her. Studying the grass, she looked for any disturbed areas that would signify where her daughter might have moved. But the only indications of movement were the ones she'd made herself.

"Think, damn it. Sloane, think. Where is she?" She looked around one more time and made a choice. She started running down the hill toward the road. After reaching it, she immediately started looking it over for any sort of tracks. She looked along the side of the road, searching near bushes. Anywhere that could be hiding her baby girl.

"Gwyn! Baby, please answer me! Where are you?" she screamed as tears began to stream down her face. Her heart was racing and she felt as if she were about to start hyperventilating again. There was nothing—not even a sign that her daughter had been there.

Sloane ran back up the hill and looked toward the tree line, seeing no tracks or trails that would signify movement. She ran toward the trees anyway, looking around for any kind of sign. Something. Anything that would give her a clue as to where her daughter could be.

She searched for what seemed like hours, desperately hoping her daughter had been simply transported somewhere else. Yelling out her daughter's name so much that her voice was hoarse. She found nothing and no one.

Sloane walked back to the road, ready to start following it, but instead, she collapsed to her knees and started sobbing. Overwhelming dread slammed into her like a train. She could not even move, her very soul aching at the possibility that her daughter was gone. What would she do? It was her job to protect her. Gwyn was so young; she couldn't fend for herself. Especially not alone in the wilderness like this. What if something terrible happened? Or had already happened?

Sloane felt a hollowness invade her as she clenched her knees to her chest. She was supposed to be able to protect her daughter... always. Tears slowly fell as time slipped forward, her mind cycling through each and every worry for her daughter. Where had Gwyn landed? Would she be able to find something to eat? Water? Would she be able to find help? Someone to take care of her until Sloane found her?

How am I going to find her?

Sloane was unsure of how much time had passed, but when she slowly started to regain her senses, the reddish sun had started its descent toward the horizon. She had gone catatonic, her mind looping through all of her worst fears. She was pulled out of it eventually as she heard what sounded like horses coming. She looked up through red, tear-soaked eyes and saw a large, enclosed wagon with supplies attached to the roof and lanterns hanging down at the corners. It was pulled by two horses. Another four surrounding it came toward her on the road. What confused her the most were the people riding the wagon and horses.

The six people looked like... knights. Wearing some type of iron armor. They didn't have helmets on and what she saw of their faces surprised her even more. There were four variations of what she could only describe as elves, with their long, pointed ears, lithe figures, and angular facial structures. Of the four, two were picturesque pale elves with one blonde who looked just as haughty as she expected an elf to be. Another had dark brown skin, while the last seemed slightly different with shorter ears and a mane of curly red hair..There were also two others that could be orcs if the tusks and green skin were anything to go by, but maybe more half-orc-like with their more graceful features.

Yes, she knew what elves and orcs were. She was an avid fan of the fantasy genre. She had dabbled in a bit of everything—books, games, and even a bit of tabletop RPG'ing. She'd watched a plethora of movies and TV shows—hell, she'd even gone to a convention once. Seeing the actual real deal in person was a shock, and solidified her belief that she was in some fantasy world. A realization she thought Gwyn was ill-prepared to handle on her own.

Looking over the group, she noticed there was a mixture of sexes, and it was one of the females, an orc, who noticed her first.

When they got close, the female orc, with short tusks and a muscular build, held a hand up and the group stopped. She dismounted and walked toward Sloane. Sloane stared at the fantasy woman come to life.

The orc crouched down in front of her, and Sloane was able to look into her deep gray eyes; there was a kindness in them she hadn't expected. Two rows of braids ran parallel from the front to the back of her head. The rest of her short hair fell to the sides, framing her soft face. She wore a suit of armor that covered her vital parts, blue fabric clothing underneath, and a flowing piece of the same blue fabric draping down from her waistline.

"Greetings. I am Gisele, knight-captain of the Order of Haven's Hope." She glanced around the area, then seemed to give Sloane a once-over. "Have you been harmed? Do you need assistance?"

"My… daughter," Sloane croaked out.

Gisele's light green face instantly filled with concern and she gestured toward the others. "What is your name, miss? Where is your daughter?"

"S-Sloane. I don't know. I can't find her." The feeling of loss threatened to overwhelm her once more, and Sloane started crying again.

"Sloane, I need you to focus, please. What happened? Where were you when she went missing?"

Sloane wasn't sure if she should say, but she was at the point where she didn't care. She was weighed down by emotion, and anything to find her daughter would help.

"We were together at home," she tried to speak coherently. "Earth. There was a blue flash and then I woke up here, on that hill." Sloane pointed over at it. "But when I looked around, my daughter was missing. I've searched for hours all around and can find no trace of her. I know she's here. I know it."

Gisele tilted her head in thought. "Sloane, we too were affected by this blue flash you speak of. Were the sky lights in the air before the flash?"

"You mean the aurora? Yes. Why do you think that's relevant?"

"Sorry, sorry. Just trying to understand. My fellow knights and I can help you search for your daughter. One of my men, Ser Cristole, is an adept tracker. Can you please explain to him where you have searched already?"

"Yes, please, help me find my daughter."

"Don't worry, we will." Gisele turned back to her people. "One second, let me call someone else. Ser Maud! Come here, please. I need you to help Sloane to the wagon while I talk to Cristole."

The elf with shorter ears named Maud climbed down from the wagon and came over, stopping at a respectful distance before addressing her. "Greetings, miss. May I help you stand up?"

Sloane nodded and Maud gently reached below her arm and assisted her to her feet. Holding her firmly but with care, Maud led her over toward the wagon where Gisele and another elf—Cristole—she assumed, were talking.

Gisele turned her head toward them as they approached. "Sloane, this is Ser Cristole. Please tell him what you told me and everything you have done since you arrived."

With a respectful bow, the elf man with long pointed ears and angular features spoke. "The more information you can give me the better, miss. Any detail, no matter how small, may be of assistance."

Sloane nodded. "It started when I picked up my daughter Gwyn from school…" She proceeded to tell them everything that had happened that day. Recalling the timeline, Sloane began with picking Gwyn up from school and ended when she had collapsed by the road. She didn't know how long she had sat there.

Gisele and the others looked at each other. Cristole opened his mouth but immediately closed it. The orc woman stared into the distance as she considered what Sloane had related. Seemingly coming to a resolution, the knight's face became serious as she committed to a decision.

"First, Cristole, can you take Ismeld and Deryk with you and start searching the area? Maud, please grab your kit and check over Sloane here for any kind of injury. Ernald, keep watch of the area and stay here with us and the wagon."

Sloane watched as the darker-skinned elf sat up on the wagon and the other orc, Deryk, and the two male and female elves with long ears and light skin tones started about their given tasks. As they walked away, Gisele looked back at Sloane.

"Alright, Sloane, I'm going to be honest. Your story sounds completely unbelievable. However, you don't look telv and you're certainly not one of the Loreni. You'd be a giant to a dwarf. Your clothing is absolutely unusual. If you pardon my bluntness, what are you?"

Sloane blinked, surprised, realization sinking in that these people were completely different races. "I—I'm human. Are you an orc? Where am I? What planet am I on? How can we speak the same language?"

Gisele gave her a sad smile, her short tusks accentuating the gesture. "Easy there, Sloane. Let me answer what I can. I am an orkun, although I am surprised at how close you were. We are both speaking Common. Is that not the language you thought we were speaking?"

Sloane had no idea how they were speaking the same language. It shouldn't be possible; the differences there would be in cultural and societal development, not to mention the linguistic drift that occurred over time, should have precluded it. There should have been no way they were speaking the same language, and yet, here she was, perfectly understanding what looked like a fantasy medieval knight.

It hurt her head to think about it, but she had far more to worry about. That could come later. She slowly shook her head. "No, I am speaking what I know as English. I… it doesn't matter, as long as you understand me."

"I do not know any more than that," said Gisele. "As far as 'planet,' I am not entirely sure what this word means. If you mean the land, it is Ikios. Currently, we are in the Kingdom of Westaren, near the town of Valesbeck. We are traveling knights, on an… errantry of sorts. Now, please let Maud look over you while the others conduct their search."

Hearing the knights in the distance calling out for Gwyn, Sloane nodded. She tried to remember how a female knight was addressed. She went with the first thing that came to mind. "Thank you, Dame… Gisele."

Maud started looking over her with care. Gisele chuckled. "We use the honorific 'ser' for all knights here in the western regions of the continent. At least, in the majority of orders that you may interact with." She paused, then bobbed her head side to side. "Some of the orders that are nations in their own right may have different rules regarding titles. These titles are also something that changes depending on the nation. However, you are typically safe if you use the common title if you are not a noble yourself. You… aren't a noble, correct?"

As Maud checked over her hands and arms, Sloane shook her head. "No, there are no nobles in the nation I'm from."

"Oh, something like our republics or federations, yes? Interesting. They are not especially common; the Lymtoria Republic is probably the largest, while the Ilsaldi Confederation is the most reputable. The republic is about half of the size of either the Kingdom of Avira or the Empire of Vlaredia."

Sloane missed most of what Gisele said. "Sorry, I—"

"No… no. It is alright. I'm just trying to get your mind off of the situation," Gisele reassured her. She turned and looked at Maud, who completed her examination.

Nodding, Maud addressed them both. "Physically, she seems fine. She's got the health of a Lady. So definitely better off than either of us. I cannot be certain, however, because I am using a telv as a baseline. Although, she seems similar enough. That said…" She took off her waterskin and handed it to Sloane. "Drink. You need water."

Sloane started drinking, quickly realizing she was much thirstier than she had thought.

"Thank you," she said after drinking her fill. Sloane scrutinized the redheaded elf woman in front of her. She could almost be human except for her more pointed ears. Maud actually reminded Sloane of a half-elf, from the fantasy she knew.

"What is a telv? Aren't you an elf?" she asked, trying to ask in a way that wouldn't seem rude.

The woman tilted her head. "I am a telv. My people are not elves. Physically, their muscle and bone structure are different. Yours seems closer to mine or even Gisele's to an extent."

The orkun woman snorted. "Well, she isn't a shade of green, nor does she have tusks, so I'd say she's closer to a telv."

Maud rolled her green eyes. "Your body structure is not that much different. Only your lower jaw."

Sloane looked between the orkun and telv women. It was clear that the telv knew what she was talking about. Something to explore later.

Maud gave Sloane one more quick scan before nodding. "Anyway, she is fine. I will search the immediate area for anything that looks off." She placed a hand on Sloane's shoulder. "It is nice to meet you. I am sorry it is under these circumstances. We'll keep searching."

Sloane thanked the telv woman and watched her walk away toward the others.

Gisele patted her shoulder. "Now, let's see how the search goes. It's getting late, and we will need to set up camp soon. Your hill should suffice."

They spent the next hour joining the knights in the search, to no avail. In the end, the knights had to call it off for the night so that they could set up camp. They were efficient, each evidently having pre-assigned roles and tasks to perform.

By the time the reddish sun had descended beyond the horizon and the twin moons lit up the night, there was a fire set up in the center of the camp on the hill. Sloane sat off to the side, trying to stave off the thoughts of despair. Thankfully, the knights let her have time to herself. Attempts to rein in her tears were unsuccessful, and thinking of anything other than her daughter proved impossible.

After another hour, Sloane noticed the knights had started eating and quietly talking among themselves. She noticed Maud grabbing two bowls and heading toward where she sat alone.

Maud stopped in front of her and looked down at the log that Sloane had been using as a seat. "May I sit with you?" Sloane nodded and gestured to the empty spot next to her.

The telv woman sat down and barely waited a moment before she held out one of the bowls of stew in front of Sloane. "Here, eat. You will do your daughter no good if you are too weak to search for her."

Sloane nodded, grabbing the bowl so that Maud could start eating her own stew. Taking a bite, Sloane noted its salty yet bland taste. She didn't mind though, she was hungry.

"Thank you. All of you, truly. I don't know what I'm going to do. I need to find her. I am going to find her. I just hope that nothing—"

The telv stopped eating and set her wooden spoon in the bowl. She turned her head so she could look Sloane in the eye. "None of those negative thoughts now. Ser Gisele and the rest of us discussed it. We will do some more searching tomorrow, and after, if need be. We will help you find your Gwyn." Maud paused for a moment and took a deep breath. "Ser Gisele didn't mention it, but the six of us? We're it. All that remains of our Order. Helping you is a worthy cause for us." The telv woman nodded as if she were reassuring herself at the same time. "We'll help you," she repeated.

They sat in comfortable silence as they ate their dinner, each contemplating the future. One of the other knights came over to take their bowls and clean up once finished. Maud placed a hand on Sloane's shoulder. "Come, you can bunk with me in my tent. Get some rest."

They went to the small tent that Maud pointed out. Inside, two cots stood side by side, and they could stand only if they hunched a bit. Sloane took off her jacket to use it as a pillow and lay on one of the cots while Maud removed her armor. The telv closed and tied the tent's opening flaps, and fastened her voluminous, curly hair into a bun before she also lay down. In no time at all, the redhead settled into a calm, peaceful sleep.

Sloane was still awake. How could she sleep not knowing where or how her daughter was? It wasn't that easy. She was scared. More scared than she had ever felt before. More than she had ever imagined. Sloane could only imagine how scared Gwyn was at that moment.

Her emotions cracked as she tried to process it all. *I have to find Gwyn.* She shoved her face into her jacket, her body convulsing as she let loose full-body sobs.

Her daughter, the one thing that mattered most to her in the world, was gone. With no traces of where to find her or whether she was even still alive. She didn't know what to do. Yet, she knew that nothing would stand in her way of finding Gwyn.

Sloane would turn this world upside down if she had to.

CHAPTER TWO

ONLY A SLIGHT DELAY

Onas awoke to Taenya gently shaking him and calling his name. He slowly opened his eyes. He was still on the bench of the wagon, but instead of Keston, Taenya was next to him. Exhaling, he took note of how Taenya was reacting—it would tell him how he should feel. She was clearly nervous, constantly glancing around at their surroundings. Onas looked around and wondered if he was the only one who had passed out. Warily, he turned to his trusted head guard and friend.

"Taenya? What happened?"

"I'm not sure, Onas. Everyone passed out, but it does not seem like we've taken ill. I was waiting for you to wake up before we did anything. But I'd like to take Raafe and scout ahead to see if we see anything."

He waved her away as he sat up. "Yes, yes. Of course. Go."

"Thank you." She turned to look at the high elf guard. "Keston, take ten minutes, then start heading toward us. Be on the lookout for anything suspicious. Keep your eyes on the tree line."

"Understood." Keston tilted his head toward Onas next to him. "Don't worry, sir. Everything's going to be fine."

Keston and Onas waited the ten minutes a bit anxiously—or at least Onas did. As they began to move ahead in the wagon, the merchant knew it was times like these that he should avoid talking. Taenya had shut him down after the first few times he had tried to talk too much during a tense situation.

About fifteen minutes later, Onas heard a horse galloping toward them. Raafe rushed around a bend and forced his horse to make a sliding stop.

"Boss, there's something you need to see just up ahead. Taenya is there,"

Raafe informed him, but before Onas could respond, the sun elf turned around and sped off back toward Taenya.

"Alright. Keston, let's go see what's got them in a huff."

He could only hope it wasn't something that would delay his return home.

Onas wasn't sure what he had been expecting. But when Keston brought the wagon to where Taenya and Raafe were, he knew a young telv girl had not been it. As they drew closer, Onas got a clearer look at the girl.

What have you got us into, Taenya?

While at a distance she had looked telv, now he could see she was different. For one, her ears were rounded. Her clothing was most unusual: it looked of high-quality material and craft, and he was curious to know how it was made. Keston stopped the wagon.

Onas got down, and walking toward them, he heard Taenya talking to the girl.

"Gwyn, you said you were… what was it? A human?"

The girl nodded, her face still flushed from crying. Her chocolate-colored hair was pulled up into a messy bun on the back of her head and the top looked frizzy and loose, as if she had been rubbing her hands through it. The chocolate color turned to bright pink at the ends of her hair, and Onas wondered how that happened. She was tall for a child, about one hundred and fifty centimeters. She was thin, with long legs that accounted for an appreciable portion of that height. Speaking to Taenya, her intelligence was exposed through her piercing blue eyes as she struggled to stay calm so as to absorb and analyze her surroundings, remaining wary of the telv in front of her.

"Yeah, I'm human. You're an elf? Right? Like from TV? You're not going to hurt me? You're gonna help me find my mom?" The girl, Gwyn, was trying to be brave, but Onas could see she was on the verge of tears again and very scared. It was a testament to Taenya's personal skills that she had helped the girl calm down and talk.

The telv guard looked at Onas, raised an eyebrow, and gave him a slight head gesture in the girl's direction. She looked back at the child and then crouched down in front of her. "Gwyn, of course, we're not going to hurt you. We want to help you. My people are called the telv. The others with me are of the Loreni, but more specifically, they are high elves, and Raafe over there is a sun elf."

Gwyn's eyes narrowed. "If they are elves, why are you also calling them Loreni?"

Taenya smirked. The girl was quick.

Onas tilted his head. "Do you not have different races where you are from?"

"No, silly. There are only humans," Gwyn said with an eye roll.

That caused both Taenya and Onas to pause. Only one people? How?

"Have there ever been other people? Different races?" Taenya asked.

Gwyn squinted. "I remember going with mom to a museum and learning about Neanderthals. But they were just different types of humans... I think?"

Taenya couldn't help but shake her head. What would the world be like if there were only telv? She sighed. Just like it is now. Nations fighting nations.

Onas seemed to be lost in thought. Taenya decided she would have to answer the girl. "Loreni is the collective name for the people that originated on the continent of Loren," she explained.

Gwyn nodded. "That makes sense! It's like when we say European. What about your people, Taenya?"

Onas watched her, clearly expecting her to continue. Taenya smiled sadly. "The telv, raithe, and orkun originated from this continent. Its name is... Ikios," she said.

"So are you... Ikiosan... Ikiosi?"

Taenya shook her head. "We are simply the telv."

The girl seemed a bit confused but nodded. "I understand."

Taenya wasn't sure that she did. She extended her arm toward the merchant. "This is Onas. He's a really good friend of mine, and he owns that big wagon over there. What do you say we set you up on the bench behind the horses and you can explain to him what happened to you and your mother?" She glanced over at Onas, then back to the girl, and added, "Is that okay?"

Gwyn nodded again. "Yeah, okay." She turned toward Onas, raising her hand in a small greeting. "Hi, Onas. I'm Gwyn Reinhart."

The girl impressed him with her ability to stay in control of her emotions; it wasn't common for one so young. There was something about her that he couldn't quite pinpoint, almost an aura about her.

He got his best, as his wife described it, customer face and voice ready. "It is a pleasure to meet you, Gwyn! I am Onas Fenren, the owner and patriarch of the Fenren Trading House. I am very glad that Taenya here was able to help you. One your age shouldn't be wandering the roads in between towns by themselves, it's very dangerous." He glanced at Taenya, and his smile faltered when he saw her hand over her face.

Gwyn seemed to instantly take on a look of fiery defiance. "I'm not wandering around! My mom picked me up from school, and I was in my town with her, and we were walking to get gelato. On the planet Earth! I'm human! Not an elf! There's only one moon. Not two like here," she said, pointing up at the Sister Moons. She lowered her hand to her hip. "Then, boom!" Her fingers splayed as she threw her arms out dramatically. "Everything went blue, then I felt dizzy, and then I woke up here!" Taking a second to catch her breath, she seemed to think of something else to say. "And, and... our roads are better!" she stated with finality.

Onas was taken a bit aback by her spark, but perhaps he should have let her start.

His telv guard's reaction seemed to make more sense now.

Trying a different tactic he added, "That is quite the journey. What do you say we get you over to the wagon where you can rest? Then you can regale me with your tale, little miss, and perhaps you can explain what a planet is."

"You don't know what a planet is? Ugh! Fine. Let's go," Gwyn said in an exasperated tone, throwing her hands up and starting to walk toward the wagon. As she passed, she mumbled something in what sounded like a language other than Common that Onas didn't catch. He looked at Taenya one more time to see her suppressing a laugh, likely at his expense.

No. Definitely at my expense. He would definitely be the focus of some joke later.

Onas paused as the girl walked away, and tried to gather his thoughts. There were significant indicators of the girl's status.

Taenya glanced at him but he gestured to wait for a moment.

He closed his eyes and recalled everything she'd said.

This child was much more headstrong than his own two children, and they were older. Perhaps she was a noble wherever she hailed from. He considered the evidence thus far, mentally ticking off points as he went. Her clothing was certainly high quality. Her speech was refined, without any noticeable accent that he was aware of, and her education level was high. She looked well-fed and fit for what he assumed was eleven years old or more due to her height. The ability to speak a second language. While he wasn't sure if she was fluent, the fact that she had smoothly shifted to it led him to believe she was. Her control over her emotions, and that she wasn't afraid to speak her mind to him, a stranger and an adult. She had even added extra emphasis when she described her town. Yes, he would undoubtedly need to change tactics. She was clearly a noble.

Onas rubbed his hand through his hair, then started heading toward the wagon with Taenya where Keston was sitting on the bench with the young girl. "She's something else, isn't she, boss?" Taenya was undoubtedly getting at something. "She's going to need help. Raafe is out looking for her mother, but we didn't see any evidence of, well… anything except Gwyn. She's all alone, Onas."

"Did she tell you what her mother looked like?"

Taenya shook her head. "She tried to, but then she started getting upset. Raafe is looking for a round-eared woman who resembles the girl."

He couldn't argue with that. "Alright, let's have her tell her story again; it may just be a flight of fancy for her. She's young, and the young have quite the active imaginations."

"Onas, she's not a telv. She is not one of the Loreni. I guess she could be some weird-looking dwarf, but I highly doubt it. We're pretty far from Dirn Loduhr, and her build isn't the same as theirs. Plus, she's young and already taller than most of them."

"I get the hint, Taenya, but we can't just abscond with her. She's likely a noble. None of us have the clout to handle that kind of situation if they want to say we kidnapped her." He looked up to see Keston talking to Gwyn, showing her the horses and how he would drive the wagon.

"I don't know," Taenya said. She gestured toward the scene in front of them. "You may be outnumbered in the end."

As if to prove her point, Keston turned his head as they stepped up to the wagon. "Hey, bosses! Can we keep her? She's great!"

Next to him, Taenya started chuckling. Onas sighed again. "Keston, let's have Gwyn tell her story again for us, shall we?" He gestured to her. "Gwyn, could you kindly repeat your story for me? I'd like to make sure I have all of the facts as you present them."

"Right, right. Okay, Mister Onas. This is what happened today. First, Mom and I got ready for school…" Gwyn started telling him all about her day. He had to ask her many clarifying questions. Like, what were her mother's name and profession? What was a watch? What was a car? What was this "science subject" she was learning about? On and on it went, and they talked for over two hours as Gwyn told him all about her day and tried to explain everything she knew about her world. She mentioned what she called an aurora, which, when elaborated upon, seemed to be what he knew as sky lights. She talked about how there was a flash of blue light that surrounded her and about how she then woke up where they'd found her.

As she was finishing up, Raafe returned from his search, looking at Taenya with a solemn look and shaking his head. Onas watched as Taenya's shoulders dropped and she took a breath.

Raafe raised his hand slightly as he tried to get everyone's attention. "Miss Gwyn? Could you please describe what your mother looks like again? I want to make sure I have it right as I search for her."

Gwyn exhaled. She nodded. "Okay. My mom's tall, like really tall." The girl quickly sized each of them up. "She's taller than all of you. Well, maybe about the same height as you, Mister Raafe. She has pretty blue eyes and she always says I look like a mini-her. She has dark curly hair just like mine, but she doesn't have pink tips like I do." She grabbed at her hair and pulled it out of the bun before finger-combing the ends.

"Mom is pretty athletic and strong. She likes to run and work out a lot. Um… uh…" The girl started sniffling as she tried to think of more things to say.

"I—I can't remember what she was wearing. I'm sorry. Why can't…"

Taenya quickly stepped forward and pulled the girl into a hug. "It's alright. It's not your fault. It's not your fault."

Gwyn started crying softly.

Onas sucked in a breath of air. *I can't imagine what I would do if this happened to one of my children. Kerala would be fine, she's an adult. Relas, that boy could likely handle it as well… but Kalen? He's about this girl's age.*

Taenya seemed to force a smile on her face as she pulled away. "Gwyn, what do you say we take a moment to go clean up? It's getting a bit late in the day. Come along, I'll assist you." Taenya reached out her hand to help Gwyn get down.

Wiping her eyes, Gwyn nodded. "Thank you, Miss Taenya." She took Taenya's hand and climbed down from the wagon. She paused, looking back at the area where, Onas assumed, she had arrived. Taenya held Gwyn's hand and gently tugged at the girl. Gwyn turned her head and followed the telv woman.

As they walked away, Onas reflected on all the girl had told him. It was quite a tale and filled with material she couldn't possibly have fabricated. Some of the things were frankly almost too fantastical. A wagon with no horses? One that went far faster than any horse could run? A location to teach children her age subjects more advanced than many of the academies that the larger nations hosted nearby. His own Kingdom of Avira's Royal Academy came to mind. He supposed the girl could have embellished some of the facts, but when she talked about what a planet was? That seemed almost too much, but if she really did come from another one of these… worlds, it made sense.

How the blue flash had done such a miraculous feat, he wasn't even close to qualified in making a guess. Surely, a miracle of the gods. His own experience with the event was simply passing out. He supposed now he should feel lucky that he hadn't been taken somewhere else.

He didn't realize how muhc time had passed until he looked up and noticed Taenya and Gwyn were already back and talking quietly.

When did they…

He caught Taenya's eye and the woman rolled her eyes at him.

She clearly noticed I was in my own world.

Keston and Raafe walked to the wagon with stew and bread. He glanced over and saw the stew pot sitting over the fire on its stand. The wooden handle of the ladle sticking up over the side. Onas wasn't even sure when they had started a fire or begun to cook anything. He looked around, noticing the sun was already going down. Raafe handed him and Taenya two wooden bowls with some food while Keston handed Gwyn hers.

Gwyn immediately started to eat as if she hadn't in days.

Keston smiled. "You look pretty hungry there, Gwyn. How is it? Is it similar to what you're used to?"

She took a moment to consider her response. "This is good, but it's a bit bland. Needs more seasoning." She went back to eating, the taste clearly not inhibiting her.

Onas started. "Seasoning? Do you mean herbs? Spices are expensive, Gwyn. Are you telling me your mother has food cooked for you with them often?"

Gwyn took a second to look up from her food. "We have herbs that we get from the store. I know what herbs are, Mister Onas," she admonished. "Mom has lots of seasonings, something for every type of food we make. Stuff for when we have beef and rice, different ones for when we have pasta. Oh, there's the really good seasonings she puts on steak and lamb, and not only salt. Mmm, I love lamb. Mom has an entire cabinet just for spices. It's right next to the rack where she keeps her wine. But..." she quickly looked at the high elf guard, "you cook well too, Mister Keston. Maybe you just need to tell Mister Onas to give you more spices and herbs."

Keston instantly smiled. "Yeah, boss, I think she's right. We need more spices for our food. And salt!" His smile grew even more. "An entire cabinet full, Master Onas." he added with a flourish.

Onas couldn't help but chuckle. "Fine, Keston, absolutely. Anything for my most loyal and respected employees."

Keston seemed to perk up a bit in surprise. "Wait, really boss?"

Onas got a glint in his eye. "Most assuredly, Keston. However, due to us not having the same level of means that Gwyn's mother clearly has, I will simply have to deduct the cost for the seasonings from your pay."

"That is a most glorious idea, and we thank you for your contribution to the rest of us, Keston," Taenya said, obviously not wanting to be left out of this japing session. "What do you think, Raafe? Maybe we can even have lamb if you contribute your pay as well."

"Oh, I am quite fine with bland, stringy stew and bread, boss. Don't put me down for any type of pay cut," Raafe quickly added.

Gwyn laughed. "I'll show you what you need to cook, Keston, it's okay." She giggled again. "You guys are funny." She paused and stopped smiling, her face taking on a grave expression. Looking between the three of them, she asked them what they all knew she wanted.

"Will you help me find my mom?"

Keston, Raafe, and Taenya all looked at Onas, expectant looks on every one of their faces. Onas sighed; he'd known this was coming for hours now.

He looked between each of his people one more time before settling on Gwyn. "Gwyn, I am unsure of where to start exactly in searching for your mother, but—" Gwyn opened her mouth like she was going to say something, but he raised a hand to stop her. "But you can join us on our journey back to my home in Strathmore. We will ask in every village and town we pass through if they have seen or heard anything about your mother. Sloane is not a name I have ever heard of, so it should help us find her if someone has heard it."

The girl nodded weakly and seemed to be on the verge of crying.

"I'm sure my wife would be honored to have you stay with us until we can find your mother for you," Onas assured her. "Once we get back to Strathmore, we can determine a plan to assist your search. In the meantime, I request your aid in the journey. If there is anything you could contribute, it would be greatly appreciated. Taenya will be here to assist you with anything you require. She and the other two will keep us all safe. Please, do not hesitate to ask for whatever you may need."

Onas took a deep breath. He wasn't sure he really wanted the answer to what he was about to ask. "I do have one question that I believe I must ask, however. Gwyn, are you and your mother members of the nobility?"

Gwyn seemed to get a mischievous look in her eye. "Nobility? No, Mister Onas."

He felt his small tension ease ever so slightly, just before Gwyn performed a curtsey and exclaimed, "I'm a princess!"

Onas's breath caught in his throat as his eyes bulged. Taenya's breathing also hitched.

This was definitely going to cause a delay.

CHAPTER THREE

ORDER OF HAVEN'S HOPE

Sloane woke to the sound of several people laughing. Groggily, she rubbed her eyes and looked around. Maud's cot was gone, likely packed up for the day. With a groan, Sloane sat up and searched for her phone to see what time it was—only to notice it was gone. She tried to remember if she'd had it when she arrived but came up blank. She started taking inventory of what she had.

She had her clothes and shoes. Her watch was there... But everything else was simply gone. Her phone, belt, earrings, purse, wallet, and even her earbuds were gone. She would have noticed a pile of accessories around where she had arrived. It was as if they had just vanished. Which could very well be likely.

So, that left her watch and clothes as the only possessions she owned. No money. Nothing. Not that euros would be accepted here...

Looking at her watch, Sloane noticed it wasn't working and the screen was swirling with a dark blue nebulous material. She took it off and tried examining it, but she couldn't figure out what it was. It was as if the screen had been damaged in the transition but was still somehow doing something.

"Weird. I don't really have time for this right now. But...wait..." She tapped her head with her fist—thinking for a moment—then continued talking it through to herself. "Why would the watch make it if everything else didn't?" She racked her brain for a reason.

Such thoughts kept her sane. When overwhelming problems arose in her life, Sloane knew she could count on tinkering. Whether it was engineering a random contraption or designing a new robot—a hobby she enjoyed—there was something calming to focusing on the logical. And of course, the universe had to throw magical teleportation into the mix.

That's not logical at all!

Unless I make it logical.

She shook her head and returned to the problem at hand. "Okay, so, metal. Sure. Let's go with that… The watch has minuscule amounts of it in this version. Mainly just the solder and battery. That's the only reason I can think of. Everything else had metal in larger quantities." *At least it's a theory.*

Sloane cursed. *That is such a stupid theory…*

"Why would that be… Magically flung to another world and all I got to keep was this damn watch." She looked around again and groaned. The inside of the tent was lit by the sunlight creeping through in small rays of light. The bedroll would need to be put up, along with the wool blanket Maud had provided her. The tent itself, she had no idea how to take down. It seemed deceptively easy. She'd need Maud's help.

What Sloane needed to do was get up and make a plan of action. The watch and all that entailed could come later. She needed to find Gwyn. She needed money. There was no way she could rely on the knights for everything—they'd done a lot already, and they'd already pledged to do more. Sloane wasn't one to take advantage of those who provided assistance. *Never mind that they can't provide their help indefinitely.*

The tent flaps shifted, causing Sloane to look up as Maud stuck her head in.

"Good morning, Sloane! I hope you don't mind. I heard you talking. So, I wanted to see if you'd like to get something to eat before leaving. There won't be many more stops until we get to Valesbeck, so now's the best time. Just some bread and cheese, I'm afraid."

Putting on her best approximation of confidence, Sloane smiled. "Thank you, Maud. That would be lovely. I'm going to freshen up and I'll be right over."

The woman nodded and her head retreated from the tent.

After using the water left behind by Maud to clean up, Sloane headed to the woods to relieve herself. She still felt pretty gross by the time she got back to the camp, but at least she was ready to go.

Surprisingly, the knights were nearly packed up and ready to go as well. She looked back to where she came from wondering just how long she was gone. She didn't think she had been gone long enough for almost the entire camp to be cleaned up and stowed.

Shaking her head, she mumbled, "Knights. Got it."

As she walked up, Gisele turned and lifted her hand in a wave. "Sloane! Good morning, we are about ready to start traveling to Valesbeck. Are you ready? We can ask around there if anyone has seen or heard anything about your daughter, Gwyn. We should arrive by tonight, and we can stay in the inn there."

Looking at the orc-like woman with green skin and short tusks, Sloane realized that she didn't look quite like the orcs she knew of from stories, but more like some type of half-orc. Gisele was actually rather pretty, even with her more muscular physique. If anything, her build made her even more attractive—she carried herself with such surety.

Sloane nodded; it was good that they had decided on a plan. *I would wander aimlessly if I had to do it alone. At least until I can learn more about this world.*

"I'm ready. Ser Gisele, may I ask if we can get together after we arrive to determine a course of action from there? I like to have a clear plan of action for a task. Also, if there's anything I can do to help, please let me know. I may not be a knight, but I like to think I can pull my weight. At least until I can find a way to earn some funds."

Gisele smiled. "Glad to hear it! Of course, we will discuss how we go forward. Here, I have a spare sword. You may hold on to it until you can acquire your own." Gisele handed her a sheathed short sword, which for her was probably a backup blade, compared to the longswords they all seemed to prefer, except Maud and Ernald. "You can use the straps to attach it to your back, as I see you don't have a belt to attach it to. I know it's a bit awkward, but I'm sure you'll get used to it quickly. There will be shops where we can find you some clothes in Valesbeck. Anything more and we will need to wait until we arrive in the city of Thirdghyll."

Sloane slung the straps of the short sword over her shoulders and tightened the sheath to her so that it didn't shift too much with movement. It was angled so that she could grab it over her right shoulder. A bit of an awkward angle, but she could get used to it. Her eyes fell on the six knights, and she teared up a little. "Thank you, all of you. I will repay you for your kindness, and I will strive to not be an undue burden."

Gisele straightened a bit and the knights all looked at each other. Gisele had a look of… pride? Sloane wasn't entirely sure. Perhaps it was something between all of them that she'd missed. Whatever it was, the orkun woman clearly cared about every one of the others. It wasn't quite motherly, but it was a level of familiarity that Sloane had never known with someone who wasn't family.

The only other orkun in the group, Deryk, straightened. "The honor is ours, Lady Reinhart. You have given us a worthy cause," he said.

Nodding, Gisele walked forward and then turned to address the group. "Haven's Hope, let's get going. Maud, Ernald, you two are on the wagon first. Take turns driving and let Sloane sit up front. The rest of you, let's mount up and head out. Cristole, I want you riding scout. Be on the lookout for any bandits or undesirables. Frankly, be on the lookout for anything strange. Sloane is proof enough that strange times are afoot. Ismeld, you'll be riding rear-guard. Let's move, people."

Once again, Sloane appreciated the efficiency of the Knights of Haven's Hope. She got up on the bench at the front of the wagon, and Ernald, who was driving first, sat beside her. He looked her way as he grabbed the bridle. "Ready, Lady Reinhart?"

She tilted her head. "I am, Ser Ernald. But you can just call me Sloane. No 'lady' or last name necessary."

Ernald chuckled. "It's only proper, milady. You are clearly from a privileged household. Perhaps we can discuss the intricacies of your society and etiquette as we travel?"

Sloane let herself show a small smile. "Of course, Ser Ernald. Don't think I don't know what you're doing, though," she gently reproached him.

Ernald held a hand over his heart. "Me, milady? I would never dare attempt to keep your mind off any past or present events that may burden your heart and soul." Overplaying the theatrics, his face alight with mirth, he continued, "Why, I am but a simple scholar, ever in pursuit of knowledge." He finished with a melodramatic flourish.

Seeing her raised eyebrow, he chuckled and took on a more serious tone. "Perhaps first you could explain what it is you wear upon your wrist?" He inclined his head toward her watch as he spoke.

Sloane smiled, letting him distract her from her thoughts as the wagon started to move down the road. "Of course, Ser Ernald. This…" she held up her wrist so he could look at the watch, "is a watch. That is, it is a device that allows me to track the time of day, check the weather forecast, track my heart rate and distance traveled, maintain a schedule of appointments, make payments, and many other useful functions."

Ernald's brows scrunched up in thought. "You can do all of those things, in that little piece of glass and strap? How?"

Sloane frowned a bit. "Well, for now, the watch is currently not working. Something to do with how I arrived here, I suspect." She perked up a bit, thinking about the difference in technology in their respective societies. "But Ser Ernald, let me tell you all about the wonders of electricity and silicon. I do believe we have plenty of time."

She took a deep breath, centering herself. Luckily, the sun elf knight did not press. *Keep strong, Sloane. Distract yourself. Ignore the thoughts of all that could have gone wrong. Maintain the facade. Fake it till you make it.*

She proceeded to regale the dark-skinned elf over the next few hours with the history of electricity and various inventions and uses for it. He was highly inquisitive and insatiable in his desire for more knowledge. He asked so many questions about things she took for granted, like How do you catch the lightning to use it for all of the devices? She chuckled thinking about it. She enjoyed the conversation, and admittedly, it did distract her.

Sloane looked around at the knights she could see. They were good people. It didn't matter that they weren't human. They had dropped everything to help her. She wasn't sure how long they would remain with her, but she knew she had gotten lucky. Sloane had zero knowledge of this world, and she needed allies. Learning about it and how to navigate it would be paramount. And an order of knights were a great first choice of allies, even if they were, as she suspected, either exiled or running from something. Their past didn't matter—she would work with them if they helped her find Gwyn. Any knowledge exchange she could facilitate would be extremely beneficial to her.

Eventually, Maud traded spots with Ernald. The kind half-elf, or telv, was happy to sit and talk to her about her chosen profession of healing. Maud was about a head shorter than Sloane and had long curly, red hair. One look into Maud's vibrant eyes, coupled with her excitement and sunny demeanor, was enough to take one in completely.

Maud's green eyes shone in the midday light and seemed to almost sparkle as she spoke of her profession. There was something about her. She had an approachable demeanor and way of speaking that was endearing. Maud seemed to genuinely care, and Sloane was taken aback by the level of empathy the telv expressed.

Sloane wasn't extremely knowledgeable in medical sciences or biology, but she had a basic understanding that she believed far surpassed a medieval society. She sat patiently, listening to Maud's interesting personal story.

"So, once I completed my surgeon apprenticeship, I joined the Knight Order of Havensway in a support role. However, as time went on, I joined my fellow knights more and more in their martial training. Eventually, Knight-Captain Gisele sponsored me before the order commander. It took another two years of training and schooling, but eventually, I was dubbed a knight by the local lord at the behest of the commander. I have been a knight-medic for eight years now."

Havensway? An older name, maybe? There seems to be more to that...

"Wow. The process to join a knight order is a lot more in-depth than I had imagined," Sloane said. Although, she'd done only cursory research into knights in the past. She tilted her head. "So, the six of you are far from home now?"

Maud got a far-off look in her eye and gave a slow nod. "Yes, we hail from the island kingdom of Blightwych. We were a small order of knights, and we had a compound that acted as our headquarters near the coast. Our—" she paused, composing herself, before continuing. "Our order was called upon to defend our port town of Havensway from a large group of Ve'rokan Raiders from the southeast. From a nation whose ambition should have been checked by our kingdom's pact with the Lymtoria Republic."

Sloane noticed Maud's fists clenched so hard her knuckles were turning white. She waited, not wanting to interrupt her thoughts and what was undoubtedly a difficult topic for the telv.

Maud briefly closed her eyes and then reopened them. "The raiders were well-informed. Havensway was never meant to stop a coastal raid that may as well have been an invasion. The raiders numbered nearly two thousand. Our order had fewer than two hundred, including support personnel. The town guard combined with the small guard the local lord kept for his own manor as we attempted to hold off the raiders. Our order made a stand to hold a breach at the eastern wall of the palisade. We fought over three times our number in just that part of the fight, and in the end, we successfully managed to force them back to their boats and retreat. But not without cost: our knight-commander, dead, felled while personally holding off ten men. Our order was shattered. Of the seventy knights there, fewer than twenty survived. The others wanted to stay and join the lord, as they had families they did not wish to leave behind. The support personnel either moved on or joined the town as well."

Sloane listened with a heavy heart as Maud recounted the tragic events that led to her and her fellow knights being far from home. Sloan couldn't even begin to imagine the pain and loss they must have felt.

"That's... that's terrible," she whispered.

Maud nodded somberly before continuing. "The six of us formed the Order of Haven's Hope in remembrance of our fallen brothers and sisters. We have been traveling—looking for causes to help not just others but also ourselves. To regain our honor and pride. While it may not seem like a cause that requires six knights to any outsiders, we understand your search for your daughter is everything to you. This resonates with us. Family. We all lost people that day. People we knew for years, whom we grew up with. We will help you find Gwyn, Sloane, and maybe... maybe somewhere along the journey, we will find ourselves again too."

Sloane knew it wasn't the time to ask, but she couldn't help but wonder how and why they thought they had lost their honor. And what exactly they believed they needed to accomplish in order to regain it.

Maud started tearing up, taking slow, deep breaths.

Sloane reached over and put her hand on the telv's shoulder. "Thank you, Maud. I know we have known each other for barely a day, but I think you and your fellow knights are some of the most honorable people I have ever met. I'm sorry I brought up such traumatic thoughts for you."

Maud nodded. "It felt good to say it aloud."

They fell into a contemplative silence. Eventually, Maud thanked Sloane for the discussion and switched places with Ernald.

Hours passed. As they continued onward, Sloane got to know the sun elf more. The man was filled with curiosity and loved to read. He was in charge of the ledgers and all the documentation of the small order. In fact, he'd been the one who had maintained the records and library for their former order as well. His own recollection of the event that saw their former order's demise came out as a morbid surprise that he'd even survived.

Sloane changed subjects quickly after that.

Ernald spoke of all the various things they had to keep track of, especially as they crossed borders. Inside the wagon was a bookshelf and chest dedicated just to his function.

The more they discussed it, the more interested Sloane became. She spoke of ways humans tracked information and found that her reliance on digitalization ran deeper than she could have imagined.

Ernald also mentioned how he'd had to juggle all the education he had to go through with his martial training to be a knight. She got the hint that the man was not really a fighter but maintained proficiency traveling with the others.

It made Sloane hum in thought. "So, you're a combat administrator, essentially. I feel like that could be the name of a military job back home," she said with a chuckle.

Ernald laughed. "Combat administrator? That sounds like I'll be sitting at a desk with a stack of paperwork before I have to grab my sword and rush the field! Actually… huh, I don't suppose that would be much different than a planner or general."

Sloane raised an eyebrow. She had forgotten that officers in militaries were more directly involved in combat during the Middle Ages.

"How are you at strategy?" she asked.

He lifted a hand to his chin. "You know… I don't think I'm too bad. Maybe you are on to something—"

"No, Ernald, she is not. Do not let him fool you, Lady Reinhart."

A horse strode forward until Sloane saw the blond high elf woman, Ismeld, pull alongside the wagon.

"We learned long ago to not let Ernald come up with any of our plans. Lest we die," she deadpanned.

Ernald put a hand over his heart as if holding on to the shaft of an arrow. "You wound me, Issy. Here, I thought you were my closest friend," he replied.

The serious woman rolled her eyes.

Sloane laughed.

The two bickered back and forth for a bit. Ismeld clearly had a close relationship with the rest of the knights, but she seemed a bit standoffish with anyone not from their group.

Ernald, on the other hand, was an extrovert. The man was fun and well-intentioned, and all the little jokes he made were playful rather than biting.

Their fun was interrupted by Cristole calling out from ahead. Gisele rode forward to meet him. Ernald called out to the horses and slowed the wagon. Ismeld glanced back and waved—presumably to Deryk.

The wagon came to a stop, and Ernald set the brake before getting down. Maud appeared from inside and Sloane hopped down to follow everyone.

The knight-captain and the high elf were standing over something in the middle of the road.

Sloane's eyes went wide. *Is that...?*

It was. A horse lay dead, a saddle still strapped to it. Sloan immediately started looking around but saw nothing else. No indication of what could have done it.

"What did that?" she asked, causing the knights to pause and look at her.

Gisele exhaled. "It looks like an attack by some animal—"

Ernald shook his head. "Look at the bite marks... that is no normal-sized animal."

Cristole nodded his agreement. He got up and moved toward the brush, pushing it aside and looking for something Sloane couldn't see.

Ismeld and Gisele spoke quietly as they walked ahead along the road. Deryk stood away with his back to them, keeping watch.

Cristole stepped out of the brush and shrugged. "Nothing here. Anything over there, Maud?"

Sloane turned her head and saw that the redheaded telv was on the opposite side of the road looking around. Her curly hair was pulled up into a ponytail, and her lips were pursed as she turned and shook her head.

"No. There are no tracks, either..." she said with confusion.

Cristole looked back at the ground near the carcass. "Strange. There aren't any tracks other than a horse's here. It seems it walked back here, turned around, and then fell."

"There's some here," Gisele called out. "More horse tracks. And something else. Looks like a bear in size, but similar to a wolf?"

Ernald jogged over and knelt down. He shrugged. "I'd say it is a wolf's paw, but it's easily two or three times the size it should be."

Maud sucked in a breath as she and Sloane approached. "That doesn't seem right... Let me see?" Maud asked.

Sloane peeked around the telv as she looked down. After a moment, the redhead stood up. "I am not sure, either. It is definitely something large. It's not a reptile. Perhaps one of the northern wolves somehow made it down here? A poacher lost their catch, maybe?" she posited.

Wait... Did she say reptile?

Cristole shook his head. "It's still bigger than even those. I can't think of anything regional that could have done this. Perhaps you are right and something got loose," he said with a shrug.

What kind of animals do they have here? And why aren't they more surprised by the size of the track?

Gisele glanced around before settling her gaze on the scattered group. "Back to the wagon. Let's move, and keep an eye out for anything strange or out of place. There are enough tracks here for three horses, but there are no signs of struggle. Maybe it is just a single wolf or some other predator in the area. Hopefully, it has moved on."

Everyone agreed and they were soon back on the road.

Sloane was worried. *But wolves are pack animals...*

CHAPTER FOUR

A WHOLE NEW WORLD

Seeing the dead horse had put everyone on edge, but nothing had come of it so far. While the knights were wary, Ernald seemed to be focusing on keeping Sloane distracted. The sun elf had been chatting with her on and off for some time—primarily small talk to fill the silence once it started dragging on. After about an hour, Sloane noticed him staring at her wrist.

She tilted her head. "Everything alright, Ser Ernald?" she asked.

"Lady Reinhart, what does that signify on your watch? Is it one of the functions that you spoke of before?"

Confused, Sloane glanced down at her watch.

The swirling mist under the screen was becoming a brighter shade of purple. It seemed to gravitate toward the left side.

"That's odd. I'm not sure what it's doing, Ser Ernald." She moved her hand around and noticed the mist kept pointing in the same direction and was getting brighter yet. "Weird. It's almost as if it is pointing over there." She moved her hand to indicate the woods on his side of the wagon. The mist coalesced at the front as she did, and his eyes narrowed as he examined the watch.

Ernald followed her hand to where she was pointing and looked out into the woods. He shifted to get a better look. "I agree, that's strange. I do not see anything, but there are a lot of trees. We'd likely have to go into the wooded area itself to see anything."

Sloane kept scrutinizing her watch and was startled when suddenly the mist formed into seven separate points along the edges. Whatever it was indicating was all around them and moving in the woods on either side of the wagon. Thinking back to the horse, her stomach dropped.

"Ser Ernald, I think something is out there," she said with building trepidation.

To his credit, he didn't hesitate to heed her warning. Ernald immediately wrapped the horses' bridle strap to the post meant for it in between them and stood up, looking around.

The sun elf called out to the orkun woman ahead of them. "Knight-Captain, be aware, something may be near us."

Gisele, who was riding ahead and to the right of the wagon turned in her saddle. "What do you see, Ernald? Did you hear something?"

Ernald glanced back at Sloane's watch and then focused on the area where the brightest point was indicated. "I'm not sure... I don't see—"

A gray blur flew out from the tree line and barreled into Ernald. The sun elf cried out in surprise as he was knocked off the wagon in a massive crash of iron and flesh.

"Ernald!" Sloane cried out. Lifting from the bench, she looked down at where he had fallen. Terror filled her as she took in the sight of an enormous wolf standing over the fallen knight. Sloane screamed.

Gisele was quick to react, drawing her sword as she yelled out, "Knights! To arms! Beast attack!" She turned just in time to make a swift slice at another jumping wolf aiming for her back.

As Gisele tried to keep her target back, Deryk was knocked from his mount by yet another wolf.

Sloane suddenly understood what the mist on her watch was showing her. "Ser Gisele! There are seven of them in total!"

Gisele swung her sword at the wolf that was attacking her. The thing was larger than any wolf Sloane had ever seen or even heard about outside of movies and television. Each was about half the size of the horses. Gisele let loose a shrill whistle, and yelled again, this time as loud as she could. "Ismeld! Cristole! Rally to the wagon!"

Sloane looked down at Ernald, lying on his back on the ground and fighting to hold off the wolf. His face had gashes from where the beast had clawed him.

Determined to help him, Sloane pulled her short sword out of its sheath and jumped off the wagon. She put all her strength into an overhand swing, but the wolf noticed her at the last moment and tried to evade her. She still, somehow, managed to catch it in the shoulder. The sword bit down deep into the beast's tough flesh. The wolf yelped loudly as it jumped backward, the blade pulling out in a spray of blood as it did.

Keeping her body and the sword between Ernald and the wolf, Sloane quickly redirected her focus to Ernald.

"Are you okay?! Can you stand?"

He nodded, rolling over to push himself up. "I'm fine. Thank you for the aid. Now, get behind me!"

He brought up his sword and charged the wounded wolf, intent on finishing it off. The wolf held its injured leg off the ground, weakly growling as Ernald rushed it. It tried to lash out one last time with a bite, but Ernald was able to dodge and then end its life with a swift slice to its neck.

A rush of adrenaline filled Sloane and she bounced on her toes, ready to charge another wolf. Gisele was not far away, holding off two wolves while standing over Deryk protectively. One of the wolves surged forward only to jump to the left of Gisele at the last moment and lash out at her, forcing her to turn and put her sword in between it and herself.

The second she turned, the other wolf pounced on Deryk and made to bite down on the orkun's throat. Deryk managed to dodge the wolf's maw just in time. He pulled out a dagger and plunged it into the side of the wolf. The oversized beast cried out, jerking away.

It was then that Sloane heard hooves rushing toward them from the front. Cristole came galloping toward them on horseback. The high elf knight unstrapped the bow he had attached to his horse's saddle and pulled it up. In a swift, practiced movement, he retrieved an arrow from the other side of the saddle, nocked it to the bowstring, and drew back.

He sighted in on the wolf standing over Deryk and released. The arrow flew through the air and deeply embedded itself in the wolf's neck. A final, pained yelp sounded as it swayed.

Deryk shoved the beast to the side as it began to collapse, and struggled to get up. Ending one threat, Cristole immediately sighted in on another. Before he was able to do anything, however, Sloane noticed him snapping his focus to her face in alarm.

"Sloane! Look out!"

She didn't even think. She turned and lashed out with her sword at whatever was coming from behind. Resistance to her swing came almost immediately as it met flesh.

A moment later, something very large and heavy smashed into her. Pain shot through her side and the world turned sideways. The breath was knocked out of her as she landed in a thud. A rush of energy filled her as her primal instincts to survive clicked in her head. Screaming with rage, Sloane kicked and punched the wolf that lay on top of her.

It felt like an eternity, but she did everything possible to end the threat to her life. Scared that any moment the beast's massive maw would clamp down on her throat, Sloane tried stabbing at its side but wasn't able to get a good angle.

Then the wolf rolled off her and Gisele was there.

The woman's face was filled with concern as she looked down at her. "It's okay, Sloane. It is dead. You got it."

Sloane nodded quickly, her pulse racing, adrenaline pumping. Gisele reached out her hand. Sloane grabbed it and the knight yanked her to her feet. Sloane glanced back down at the wolf and saw a large gash through its throat. It had been dead the entire time.

Gisele seemed to quickly scan her for injuries. "Are you hurt?"

Sloane shook her head, breathing heavily. "No, I'm fine. I thought it was going to kill me. Shit. Is everyone okay?"

Gisele nodded, but Sloane's eyes darted around anyway. She noticed Ernald and Deryk standing together, holding each other up.

Wait! She immediately looked toward the back of the wagon. "Maud! Ser Maud. Is she—"

Maud stepped out from behind the wagon with Ismeld. "I am fine, Sloane. Ismeld and I worked together at the back. She got there just in time to help me. You are well?"

Sloane bobbed her head and Maud nodded back. "Good. Let me attend to Deryk and Ernald."

Gisele was still staring at Sloane. "You did well, but I think we will need to get you some armor. Your garments, while of high quality and apparently quite durable, do not seem to provide much protection."

Sloane's eyes fell on her clothes, which, to her surprise, were still clean and not damaged at all. "Huh, that's strange. Yeah, I guess so. I didn't think we would actually be attacked. Let alone by wolves that size. Why were they so large?!"

Cristole looked at one of the wolves. "I have no idea. I have never seen or heard of wolves this size, especially not roaming this close to villages. They were larger and stronger than even the bears back home. After we killed five of them, the last two ran off into the woods."

Gisele nodded. "We will need to inform the village. They need to be aware of the danger of these wolves. They were clearly not ordinary specimens. Hopefully, Valesbeck will have hunters who can end the threat they present. I will admit that I had not considered the horse we found to be more than a single unfortunate circumstance. Good reactions, everyone."

After that, they all dispersed to perform various tasks. Ismeld and Cristole set to the task of harvesting the wolves. Meanwhile, Gisele checked the status of the horses and wagon, and then the two wounded knights. Deryk soon came out of the back of the wagon to retrieve his horse.

Sloane walked up to the impromptu "clinic" that Maud had established in the back of the wagon. The knight-medic was kneeling next to Ernald and looking at the gashes on his face. "Hold still, you big baby. Let me get a good look at them."

"I am not a baby! *You* have a horse-sized wolf leap over a wagon, knock you to the ground, and then claw your face. See how you feel!" Ernald complained.

"They were big, but not that big. Perhaps everything just looks bigger when you're on your back," Maud teased him. "Now. Hold. Still."

She gently examined his wounds. Sloane suspected Maud wanted to see how deep they were. Suddenly, Maud gasped. Sloane started.

"What? What's wrong, Maud? Is he going to be okay?"

Ernald also tensed. "What's wrong? What did you do?"

Sloane moved so she could see their faces. Maud was looking at her own hands with wide eyes. Ernald's wounds looked like they were starting to close.

Sloane's eyes widened. "Maud, what did you do?"

Maud just kept staring at her hands. "I… I don't know. I just touched the wounds to see if I would need to stitch them. I felt a… a rush of something going through my hands, and the wounds… they… started closing," she stammered.

Sloane's eyes popped. Could it be?

"Maud, try it again. Focus on healing him. Whatever you did before."

The knight-medic's eyes darted to her, then back at Ernald. "Alright, I'll try."

Sloane got an idea as Maud placed her hands on Ernald's face. She focused on her watch. It started glowing bright green on the entire side that pointed to Maud.

"Holy. Shit. It's magic," Sloane whispered to herself.

She turned her head up and watched, slack-jawed, as the redhead's hands glowed. A subtle green was emitting from them as Maud gently touched Ernald's face.

Slowly, the gashes started closing themselves.

When they were nearly healed, Maud gave a grunt and sagged. Sloane quickly reached out and grabbed hold of her.

"Maud? Are you okay?" Sloane asked quickly, uncertain what could be wrong.

Maud, moving sluggishly, nodded. "Yes, I just feel really tired. I don't think I can do it anymore."

Sloane tried encouraging her, "You did amazing. You performed actual magic! And my watch was able to read it happening!"

Ernald's eyes darted between the two of them as he slowly touched his face.

"Maud. This is a miracle! This is amazing." He reached up and gently cupped Maud's face. "Thank you, my friend. I will never forget this."

The telv smiled weakly. "It is my duty to keep all of you safe. To care for my friends."

He smiled widely. "Eona be praised, Maud. This is… it's a gift from the gods. You've been blessed. The others need to know about this!"

Maud's eyes fluttered. "I'm sorry, Ernald. I am just so tired."

Why is she tired? Did she use too much magic?

"Maud, you should sleep. You may have just strained yourself," Sloane suggested.

Ernald tilted his head toward the cot in the corner of the wagon. "Lady Reinhart is correct. You must rest. I feel well enough to drive the wagon."

Maud nodded. "Alright. But only for a little while. Come get me when you need to switch. Deal?" Even tired, she looked determined to help.

Ernald smiled as he started to get up. "Of course. Rest, our sweet healer."

Letting Maud lie on the cot to sleep, Ernald and Sloane stepped out.

The two of them shared a glance. "I—"

"She used magic, Ernald. Do you know what this means?" Sloane said excitedly.

"I suspect that what we are thinking are two different things, Lady Reinhart," he said quietly.

He glanced around. The others were working and checking over everything. He hesitated, before steeling himself. "I need to tell the others."

Sloane agreed. It was too important not to. She walked back to the front of the wagon with Ernald. She pulled herself up and sat on the bench as the knight-scholar explained what had happened to a stunned Gisele and the others.

As for herself... Sloane was flabbergasted and amazed. She'd witnessed actual magic. In the flesh. Literally.

She grinned and peeked down at her watch. The watch's purpose had clearly been altered during her transportation to this world. By what, she had no clue. She wondered if there was anything else the watch could be used for. What other magic could be performed?

Gisele walked to the back of the wagon where Maud was. The quiet male orkun, Deryk, took over the harvesting of the wolves from Ismeld. The high elf woman stopped and looked over Ernald's face and healing wounds. Sloane heard her comment on how it might actually help him find a woman. The sun elf laughed.

Ismeld grabbed her water skin and stared at Sloane for a moment. Sloane nodded at her. The high elf just turned her head and walked away.

As everyone else busied themselves to leave, Sloane's mind raced. She knew what she would do now. Learn magic. She had a wealth of knowledge she could utilize. Knowledge that could be used to make things—potentially things that would help the knights, and in the process, her.

Of course, she had no idea how magic worked. But she did know that everything was just something waiting to be studied. Another obstacle to overcome. Human ingenuity knew no bounds. She would learn how it ticked. How it functioned. Then she would use it. Anything to give her an edge.

Anything that would help her find Gwyn.

Sloane shook her head. The thoughts seemed so unreal. As if she were in a dream. Who woke up and thought, "Oh, I'll practice magic today"? She wasn't Hermione Granger.

Glancing at the wolves—and ignoring the queasiness from seeing what remained—she knew this world wasn't some fairy tale. There were real dangers. Focus on them too long and she risked spiraling with thoughts of Gwyn having to overcome them.

Suddenly, her eyes went wide. *Wait a moment...*

She had always been a fan of fantasy, but the possibility that magic could really exist had never even crossed her mind. *The knights were as surprised as I... What did Ernald say? Something about having different thoughts on it?*

Had magic not existed before? Or was it just rare? Sloane had been brought to this world by magic—that was the only answer. Her breath caught in her throat. Possibly, brought there by the *emergence* of magic. It had been a short time since she had arrived, and Maud was already using magic. If the Flash had brought magic, what all could be done with it? Clearly, healing magic was a thing. What else? Fireballs? Her eyes widened again. Scrying? That would be useful in her search.

What if I can't use magic?

Sloane grunted. If she couldn't use magic, she'd simply create tools to give her the ability. How did the saying go? *Where there's a will, there's a way.* And Sloane had all the will in the world. She had no choice. Gwyn was counting on her.

An immediate goal had appeared. Learn magic. Use it to gain an advantage. *And magic will help me get to Gwyn.*

Sloane sat with renewed hope and strengthened determination as the wagon and group resumed their journey to Valesbeck. She didn't stop thinking of all the ramifications and possibilities of magic until she heard Gisele call out. She looked up.

Past the fields of vegetables, wheat, and corn, a small town sat under the setting sun. Even in the distance, Sloane could see that despite the late hour, there was a swarm of activity around a palisade that was being hastily raised. Bonfires dazzled around the perimeter of the town proper.

CHAPTER FIVE

VALESBECK

Sloane and the knights reached Valesbeck at twilight. The frantic wall construction they had observed while approaching the town showed no signs of abating. As Gisele led them toward the gate, Sloane noticed just how many armed people there were. Most were telv, with their short, pointed ears and rounded faces. There were also some Loreni, the elf-like races with angular faces, long pointed ears, three different skin tones, and, she suspected, other subtle differences that denoted which particular race they belonged to. A decent number even had a bluish tone to their skin, which amazed her.

Frankly, the armed people couldn't be considered more than simple militia. Most of the militia wore a gambeson and were armed with a spear and wooden shield. A few, who she assumed were officers or squad leaders of some sort, wore chain mail and had the same wooden shield but reinforced with iron. There were two makeshift watch towers she could see with archers that looked very on edge watching the fields.

Before they even approached the gate, the militiamen were gathering on either side of the road, waiting for them. They looked especially twitchy. Sloane heard Ismeld speak to Gisele. "Gisele, something's happened here. They're particularly tense. I suggest a calm, friendly approach."

Gisele slowly nodded. She took off her helmet and raised her hand in greeting while urging her horse forward. "Hail! We are looking for lodging for the night. We are just traveling through on our journey to Thirdghyll."

A grizzled man with purple-hued skin and short ears like a telv stepped forward. He reminded Sloan of a type of half-vampire, half-elf race she had seen in various fantasy media on Earth.

He also wore chain mail, but instead of a spear, he had a longsword strapped to his waist and an iron-reinforced kite shield on his back that seemed entirely impractical. He frowned as he gazed over the group.

"That's far enough, orkun. Hop down off that horse and let's chat. You may bring one with you." He regarded the group, looking at each member. Sizing them up.

Sloane leaned toward Ernald to her left. "What race is he? Telv?"

Ernald shook his head. "No, he's a raithe. Similar, just different skin tones, and they have fangs."

Sloane looked back at the raithe, seeing that his eyes had settled on her. A small smirk appeared on his face as if he had made some great decision. His fangs jutted out over his bottom lip. Pointing at her, he made his choice. "Her. She can join you."

Sloane was surprised. "Why me?" she blurted out. Ernald raised his hand slightly, motioning for her to wait.

The raithe smiled, his fangs gleaming in the dimming sunlight. "Because you definitely look like it would require the knight here to focus more on protecting you than to fight my people or me. I have better things to do than to tussle with an orkun knight."

Gisele looked slightly irritated. "Friend, we are just travelers. My fellow knights and our charge are weary from a beast attack only a few hours ago. We simply wish to rest and purchase provisions before heading toward Thirdghyll. There does not need to be any trouble. If you do not wish for us to enter your town, we will simply move on." She turned and started to move back toward the group.

The raithe hesitated and seemed to be warring with himself over something. Finally, one of his people leaned forward and whispered in his ear. He turned to look at the other before giving a slow nod. Having come to a decision, which in Sloane's mind had taken far too long, he let out a heavy sigh and looked up at the sky. He shook his head.

Turning again, he whispered something to his man, who straightened and assumed a stance that clearly conveyed he was ready to take action. Others around him took up a similar posture.

The raithe clapped his hands once, hyping himself up, and then walked toward Gisele. She shifted in her saddle, wary, and glanced at Cristole, who backed up his horse, creating distance from any of the spear-wielding militia. Ismeld slowly lowered her hand to her side, resting it on the hilt of her blade.

The raithe seemed to notice this, and spoke quietly to Gisele. It required Sloane to strain just to make out what he was saying.

"There's no need to be like that, lass. *Ser.* Look, I'm Melchior, pleased to meetcha. I have the dubious honor of being in charge of this here town militia." He sighed again. Sloane noticed just how tense he was.

"Look. My boys? They're a bit on edge. I only wished for you to come chat so that they could see you don't mean any trouble. What do you say we start over, milady knight?"

Gisele took a moment before nodding. "Fine, but only because we have some who should have a proper rest tonight. Do you mind telling us what has all of your people on edge and rushing to build a crude palisade?"

Melchior looked around before settling on one of his men and calling him over. The young man jumped in surprise and pointed to himself. The raithe sighed but waved him over with a bit more urgency. "Come here, lad. I want you to show them your little trophy."

The young man ran over and reached into his pocket. He pulled out a claw almost as big as Sloane's palm. She instantly knew what it was from.

Gisele let out a slow whistle and then addressed the militia commander. "You were attacked by the wolves too?"

Melchior looked surprised but hid it quickly. "Yes, about forty of them hit the town last night, they seemed way too coordinated and precise to be simple beasts. Some have suggested that the wolves may have been trained and used to target us. We don't know how many or what else is out there, but we lost eighty-six people, including children, before we rallied."

He paused, composing himself. "Wait. What do you mean 'too'?" He looked around, then answered his own question. "Your people who need rest. The beast ambush. How many?"

"Seven. We were lucky they targeted my people on the wagon instead of the solitary members away from the group." She sighed in a way that came across as practiced. "We got lucky," Gisele repeated. "But it was still a difficult fight. We killed five, the other two ran off. We didn't see any evidence of more. That said, we had thought we were bringing news of them to you."

Melchior ran his hand through his hair, his bearing relaxing slightly. "Do you have proof of what you say?"

Cristole tossed him a bag, which Melchior opened. He pulled out wolf fangs. Nodding to himself, he closed the bag and threw it back to Cristole. "Alright," he said in a loud voice, likely for his men's benefit. The previous tension noticeably left his body, which had a ripple effect on his men. "I believe ya. Let's get you inside. If you give me a bit of time to get my people organized for the night, I'll meet you at the inn. A round on me for your troubles."

Gisele gave him a nod. "Thank you, Melchior. We appreciate it. Perhaps we can discuss your issue over ale as well. We may be able to give you some suggestions or insight. As outside observers, of course."

The town's head of the militia nodded and turned to another of his men, waving him over. "They're good to head on in. Show them the way to The Giggling Bugbear. Let them know that they're clear."

Gisele motioned the rest of the group forward, and they moved on, slowly heading through the gate. By the time they entered the town proper, the sky was turning dark. Townsfolk were bringing last-minute supplies to the militia and workers outside the wall. Others were boarding up doors.

Looks of fear and uncertainty were painted across every face Sloane saw. She felt bad for them. The wolves were massive, and having that many get into the town? She could only imagine the chaos that had occurred. It seemed that everyone within Valesbeck was contributing to the efforts.

They traveled for roughly ten minutes, slowly weaving through the crowded street that seemed designed to make their trip even longer. They even passed by several inns on the way toward their destination, including a few right inside the gates. However, the ones that she saw were all boarded up with no lights on. It was as if they were directing everyone closer to the center.

Groups of militia moved past them occasionally, some looking at the knights with both envy and hope, as if they thought the knights were there to save them.

As much as Sloane felt for them, if Gwyn was not in the town, she preferred to leave. *If these wolves are around, I need to quickly search all the places I can. And hope she made it to a village or town...*

Once they finally arrived at the inn, Gisele tasked Ismeld and Cristole with stabling the horses and securing the wagon. The rest of the group entered the door behind the man Melchior had sent as an escort.

The inside of the tavern looked as though it had been ripped straight from a fantasy movie. There was a bar that looked like it also served as the front desk for the inn. A female high elf stood behind the counter. She looked up from a book as they entered.

She was thin and about the same height as Sloane, who was already pretty tall. Though Sloane supposed she didn't exactly know the average heights for the various species in this world. Squinting her eyes and looking at Gisele, she guessed the orkun was about half a head taller than herself. Perhaps using humanity as a standard wasn't a good idea.

Sloane looked back at what she assumed was the innkeeper. She had light brown hair and a fair complexion, freckles lining her cheeks. Her high cheekbones and narrow jawline gave her face an angular appearance. What drew Sloane in most, though, were her eyes, an unnaturally vibrant green color. Even more so than Maud's, which were more of a natural green, like Sloane was used to. Their uniqueness fascinated her and Sloane found herself distracted. She noted that the woman's lithe features contrasted with the other beings she had seen. Even the elves in Gisele's group were of a larger build. Although, maybe the knights shouldn't be used as a standard, either.

Sloane redirected her attention to find she'd missed the conversation between Gisele, the militiaman, and the woman behind the counter.

The woman shrugged. "The doors will be boarded up at night. We expect all guests to provide any aid in case of another attack."

The knight-captain easily agreed, setting the woman at ease. Sloane expected no less from a group of honorable knights.

Gisele turned. "Alright, we have rooms for the night, but there are only three: two larger rooms and one small. So, good news. Sloane, you get your own room for the night. The rest of us will split the other two."

"I would like to stay with Sloane. With the attacks, I do not feel comfortable leaving her alone," Maud said.

Gisele nodded. "A sound decision. Thank you, Maud." Handing keys to Cristole and Sloane, she continued, "First, let's get out of this armor. Then we'll all meet downstairs for food. How's that? I don't know about you all, but I am hungry." She paused. "Keep your weapons within reach. Just in case," she added.

Everyone quickly agreed. No one wanted to try and fight those wolves without weapons.

"After dinner, we'll get back into our armor and set up watches. But I know we all want to get clean, so let's hurry and eat."

Sloane let Gisele know that she would remain downstairs, and handed the room key to Maud. Soon, she found herself alone and standing in the tavern. She looked around. The mood in the room did not seem festive. In fact, no one actually seemed to be drinking much. She wondered how many had lost someone.

Seeing as how she didn't have armor on, Sloane elected to choose a table for the group. She found a large table in the back corner that would accommodate the seven of them.

As she sat down, a telv walked over and greeted her with a larger-than-life personality, which surprised her.

"Welcome to The Giggling Bugbear! You're new around here! What can I get for ya?"

Sloane looked around uncertainly. The man's tone did not fit the room and she was worried that it would draw attention. Fortunately, not a single person turned their head, so perhaps the man's personality was known.

She also didn't have money, so she didn't want to just get something under the assumption the knights would provide for her. "Uh, I don't know. I think I will just wait for the moment. Just until my companions come back downstairs."

He gave her a sympathetic look and a sad knowing smile. "Oh, dear. Honey, it's alright. I'll get you something. On the house."

Honestly, Sloane thought it a bit condescending and she resisted the urge to lash out. "No—you don't have to. I am just saving the table for my group as they freshen up."

The man patted her hand. "I promise. It is fine. In these times, we have to all stick together. I will just get you something small if that assuages you."

She sighed. "If you really do not mind. I would appreciate it…" She left off, hoping he would catch the implied question.

"Oh, sorry! Where are my manners?" He smoothed out his doublet and then straightened his back, adopting a dramatic pose. "Welcome to the Giggling Bugbear. I am pleased to be your host tonight. Lazy songwriter by day, inn waiter by evening, and a mediocre musician by drunk. I mean, night!" he exclaimed with a laugh. He ended with a bow and a flourish. "At your service milady!"

Sloane couldn't help but chuckle at the man's theatrics. Perhaps that was why he did it. To bring a bit of cheer in an otherwise dreary scene.

"It's a pleasure. I'm Sloane." She gave him a small bow with definitely nowhere near the same level of enthusiasm.

"My, my, what an intriguing and serious name you have there, Sloane. Where do you hail from?" He seemed genuinely curious, which Sloane liked, but of course, it may have just been an act for the customer. She was bad at telling those types of things.

She also did not want to give much away. Her curly hair was down and covering her ears, so thankfully she did not have to explain how she had appeared from thin air. She settled on obfuscation.

"I am from far away. Truthfully, I'm looking for someone—my daughter, Gwyn. She and I got separated and I am trying to see if she passed through here in the last day or so?"

He crossed his arms and tapped his chin. "Your daughter? I have to say, I think you and your group are the first travelers I've seen pass through town in the last two days. The town has been a bit preoccupied with the attacks that happened last night… I'm sorry."

Her face fell, but she nodded and thanked him. She supposed it was too much to hope for, but she had to try.

A voice from the kitchen yelled, and the telv glanced over at the source. He yelled back before letting out an exaggerated sigh. He winked at her. "Now, let me get you that drink. Maybe we can help take your mind off unpleasantness."

Sloane nodded and stared at the man's back as he strode away.

She settled in to wait, for both the knights and her ale. She hadn't been a big beer drinker in many years. A glass of wine with dinner was about all she partook in. Maybe an aperitif if she were out with friends in the piazza.

Now felt like a good time to start up again.

During that time, people came and left. When the waiter finally brought her ale, he was also holding up a big tray of food. He was apologetic and dropped off her mug before quickly moving toward a nearby table with a group of militiamen.

Sloane took a swig of ale and winced at the taste as she eavesdropped on the group. She stole glances their way in between sips.

"Did you see that group of knights?" a raithe asked his companions.

A telv sitting across from him grunted. "Yeah, we all did. They're stayin' here, you nimrod. What of 'em?" the man said.

"Are they here to help us?" the first asked. Was that tinge of hope?

Sloane glanced over as the group paused. A woman, one of the moon elves, was shaking her head. "Those knights aren't Westari. The leader is an orkun. No, I'd put money on them leaving as soon as possible."

A bunch of angry murmurs and comments that she couldn't make out overlapped each other. The first man slapped the table, quieting the group.

"Then why don't we kick them out? We may need the food, the rooms… If they're not going to help, they don't need our generosity!" the raithe angrily stated.

The moon elf woman tutted. "They aren't worth the trouble. We do not want to waste energy on anything but the beasts. I say that this is our fight, and we don't need any gods-spurned knights to protect our homes. Their coin is as good as any others', and when our town is safe, we can spend the coin."

"Hear! Hear!" the rest of the table called out.

Sloane ducked her head. The waiter returned and gave her a look when he saw how she was sitting.

"Don't worry about them, hon. They're just worked up. They mean well. Are your people going to want to eat?"

She nodded. "Absolutely. I don't know what they like to eat, though."

He nodded sympathetically. "You poor dear. How did you meet them?"

Taking a deep breath, she considered how to respond. "They happened upon me on the road. I was alone, and they have been helping me look for my daughter ever since."

His eyes softened and he sat down next to her. "When will your group leave?" he asked quietly.

Her eyes darted toward the group of militiamen. She lowered her voice. "Tomorrow, I believe, is when Ser Gisele wants to depart."

The telv man nodded slowly and leaned closer to her. "Tell you what, Sloane. I'll ask around about your daughter for you and I will see what I can find out for you tonight. Describe her to me."

Sloane did.

Just like the people of the town, she couldn't help but have a bit of hope.

CHAPTER SIX

HARD DECISIONS

By the time the knights returned from their rooms, Sloane had nearly finished nursing her ale. It was not that good, if she were being honest. The beverage was only slightly cooler than room temperature, and was cloudy and thick with dregs that had not yet settled. Essentially, it was almost like a modern British ale. She smirked at her own joke, slightly disappointed no one was around who would understand what it meant.

Ernald's eyes fell on the mug she was holding. "Already starting, are we? How rude!" the sun elf jested.

Maud glanced at him as she moved to sit next to Sloane. "Ernald, if anyone here deserves a drink, it's her. You could probably do without one."

Ernald faked an injury to his chest. "You wound me, Ser Maud, and here I thought you were on my side."

Deryk, the orkun knight, smirked. "Come now, Ernald. If it wasn't for your mind, I'm not sure anyone would stand your tongue to be on any side but the back one."

The look of betrayal on the sun elf's face was priceless.

Sloane huffed a laugh. "Ernald, for as often that your closest friends 'wound' you, I do not know how you survive your enemies," she added.

"Not you too!" He shook his head. "And we only just met. Which of these cretins influenced you?" the knight-scholar asked, feigning seriousness.

That got everyone laughing, and the others decided they wanted to join in on the fun. Walking up, Cristole smacked Ernald's back, then laid a hand on his shoulder. "Ah, lay off him, everyone. We all know each traveling troupe needs a jester!" He shook the sun elf a little, adding, "I certainly appreciate your quick wit and sharp tongue, Ernald. Don't let these uncultured sots bring you down!"

Ismeld raised an imaginary mug as she sat down at the table. "Hear, hear!"

Maud looked at her and grinned. "So Sloane, how'd you get the ale? Did someone buy you a drink?" she asked, waggling her eyebrows.

Sloane rolled her eyes. "Yeah, definitely nothing like what you're suggesting. The server was nice and took pity on me is all." She smiled. "But hey, at least you are all here now. Let's eat!"

The group of militiamen not far from them fell into whispers and kept stealing glances at the knights. Sloane thought they would say something, but she caught the raithe man at the table saying that he had lost his appetite. The rest of the group seemed to agree because they promptly got up and left after putting coins in the waiter's hand.

I'm just glad nothing came of that, she thought. *A bar fight felt almost inevitable.* She would not have been any help in a bar fight.

The knights settled into light conversation after they ordered their drinks and food. Finally, the waiter brought food to the table on platters so that everyone could share. A selection of roast meat, bread, cheese, and some fruits Sloane couldn't quite identify was spread in front of her.

Deryk looked over to her from the other end of the table. "Lady Sloane, how does a normal dinner from your world compare to this?"

Sloane thought for a second. "Honestly? It's not vastly different. We usually eat a type of meat, a starch—that is, potatoes, pasta, or rice—and some vegetables as the main course. The biggest difference is the way our food is prepared and stored. We also use more spices, as they are more commonplace, simply because we shifted from a local economy to a national and global one where we could affordably get produce or other food products from other nations without spoilage." Sloane met the blank stares, blinking. "I guess that was a more extensive answer than you wanted?"

The group laughed, and Deryk responded, "No! It was fine. I didn't expect you to give more than a passing answer. Thank you."

Cristole swept his gaze around the table. "Actually, there was something I wanted to ask everyone. When I killed that wolf, I felt something. Almost as if a rush of energy ran through me, invigorating me. I thought it was just because I had managed to fell the beast, but that feeling hasn't gone away." He formed a fist and peered down at it. "I feel a bit stronger and better than I have in a while," he added.

Ismeld looked up from the food she had been focused on. "You too? I had thought it strange and figured it was just me. It reminded me of the feeling of a burst of heat that rushes out at you when you throw alcohol onto a fire. I thought it was just the thrill of combat, my arms prickling in anticipatory glee at the fight."

Sloane looked at Ismeld, taking her in fully for the first time. She seemed about Sloane's age, in her mid-thirties, but had a wary, serious look from constant martial training and fighting. She was tall like Sloane, though a hair shorter, but with the build of an MMA fighter. Ismeld had neat, shoulder-length blond hair that framed her angular jawline and slightly pointed chin. Her ridiculously perfect eyebrows seemingly had the requirement that one must be raised at all times. Her narrow, golden eyes assessed the room, constantly on alert for threats. Sloane thought she seemed as if she had a chip on her shoulder, almost as if she were honor-bound to prove herself. There was likely more there, and perhaps Sloane would be able to get the woman to warm up to her.

Sloane contemplated what was being said. Had she felt something after killing the wolf? She had originally attributed it to an adrenaline rush, her body reacting to a highly tense moment. Now having had time to think about it before, she realized that the feeling hadn't really gone away. She wasn't on edge anymore; she didn't feel anxious. She just felt a little stronger. After adding her thoughts to the conversation, she noticed something and said, "Was it only those who killed a wolf who felt this?"

Everyone looked around. Maud spoke first, "I didn't feel anything like that, although when I healed Ernald…" She nodded toward the sun elf. "I felt something and then a surge through my hands."

Sloane looked over at Deryk, who had also not landed the killing blow on one. "Ser Deryk, what about you? Did you feel anything?"

He slowly shook his head. "No, I did not. You think it is because everyone else managed to land the final strike to fell the beasts?"

Sloane believed so. Or perhaps those who didn't get the killing blow simply weren't affected as much. Testing that would take time and effort. Either way, the rush they felt was something new. She was not sure exactly how it was related, but Sloane wanted to find out.

"I think so. I have a theory, but I would prefer not to mention it until I have formulated my thoughts. We will need to do some tests after we leave Valesbeck. That is, if you are all amenable to such a thing," Sloane said.

She smiled as she took in all of the nods. "So, Ser Gisele, with that said, I believe you stated we would come up with a plan of action once we arrived at the tavern?"

Gisele glanced over at Cristole, then back at Sloane. She seemed almost… guilty. "Yes, I have an idea of where to start. Realistically, we cannot search the entire land, so what we need to do is try and hit all the villages on the way to Thirdghyll and inquire about Gwyn in each of them. Thirdghyll has a smaller branch of the Royal Westaren Academies, named the Ghyll Academy, and is the primary place of learning for this region of the kingdom. Also, many travel there from the local sovereign cities like Goosebourne, Swanbrook, and Marketbol.

What is little known is that the Ghyll Academy is also the headquarters for the Westaren Order of Secrets. The group is tasked with maintaining both general news and secrets of all potential threats to the kingdom—which they interpret as any nation or city that isn't Westaren. If anyone knows anything, it will be them."

The others nodded, Sloane slowly understanding the thought process of the knights that pledged to support her. "So, you will take me to this order and vouch for me in hopes that they have information regarding my daughter? Is that where we will part ways? Not to sound unappreciative, because I really am, but what if they don't know?"

Gisele's face was solemn. "Sloane—" She paused to take a breath. "Sloane, the travel from here to Thirdghyll will take some time. Especially if we encounter more enraged beasts and stop at all the villages we can along the route..."

She hesitated, and Ismeld stepped in for her. "What Ser Gisele is saying is that we may need to accept that if there is no news at that point, either your daughter did not arrive with you or something occurred. Your daughter is young, so many things could have—"

"No, my daughter is alive. I know it. I will find her. I appreciate your aid in traveling to this city of secrets you spoke of. If we must part at that point, just know that I am grateful for the assistance you have given me." Sloane pushed back from the table and stood, holding back tears of frustration. She looked over the group one last time. "If you'll excuse me, I'm going to rest for the evening."

She turned and walked away, hearing Maud speak sternly to the others as she did. "Great job, everyone. Really, good job. The woman may have lost her daughter and you threaten to strip away the only hope she has?"

Sloane paused by the stairs, out of sight from the others, listening.

"Maud, it is highly unlikely her daughter has survived if she arrived away from any village or town," said Cristole. "If there is no news by the time we arrive and inquire at Thirdghyll, I fear the worst."

She was just about to rush upstairs when she heard Deryk's voice. "What if her daughter simply arrived farther away? Perhaps not even in Westaren?"

Sloane's eyes widened. *Why hadn't I thought of that?* She leaned against the wall and listened for a response.

"That's certainly possible, Deryk," said Gisele, "but if Gwyn did arrive elsewhere, how will we find her? Will we escort Sloane around the entire western half of the continent? What of the rest? At what point do we stop, Deryk? Maud?"

Maud shifted tactics. "Until our conscience is clear. Sloane saved your life, Ernald. Would you give up so soon in helping her after that?"

"Maud, I am deeply grateful for what she did for me, really. I..." Ernald trailed off. Just when Sloane thought the conversation was over and she was about to head upstairs, he continued. "I would be agreeable to escorting her to a port after Thirdghyll, possibly Swanbrook. This would allow her to charter a ship to Avira. The Royal Academy of Avira has some of the greatest minds anywhere in the region. Maud, you used actual magic to heal me. If anyone understands what is going on since the blue flash, it will be them."

"So, Swanbrook. We will help her find a ship to Maireharbora in Avira. It will be there that we part ways with her," Gisele clarified.

A mixture of unintelligible responses came from the group all at once before they went silent.

With the conversation ended, Sloane made her way up to her room. She felt frustrated by the situation. While intellectually she had understood their parting would come, it was to be much sooner than she'd expected. Even if the journey took a while.

I should have known.

Soane pulled out the key Maud had given back to her and unlocked the door. Entering, she took in the quaint room. Two single-framed beds, each with its own ornately decorated trunk, were placed at the foot. A small bag sat on top of one. Maud's things, she noted.

Leaves the other bed for me.

There was also a single desk with a stool, a small vase of flowers, and an oil lamp providing lighting. A small water basin was set up on a table in the corner next to the door, with a pitcher next to it already filled.

Sloane took off her shoes and sat on the bed, considering her course of action for a moment. She needed an edge.

Edge.

She had an idea. Sloane stood back up and started taking off the sword and sheath the knights had given her. She placed them on the trunk. Ernald had also given her a knife after the wolf attack on the way to Valesbeck. She removed that from where she had strapped its sheath to her right shin. Pulling the blade out, Sloane looked over it, considering its edge.

Nodding, she sat at the desk, set the knife to the side, and pulled off her watch. Finally getting a chance to closely examine it, she noticed the changes that had occurred. For one, the watch's plastic was much stronger. Almost like a type of metal, but not quite like the stainless steel the end product would have been. She wasn't exactly sure what it was made of now, but it definitely wasn't the same material the test device had been. The watch face seemed to have changed too. Before, it was a strong glass-like material similar to the type used for smartphones. Tapping on it with her fingernail, she tried to get a sense of what it was.

She walked over to the water basin and filled it up with the pitcher. She dipped her finger into it and then let a small drop fall onto the watch screen. The water remained in a drop shape, signifying that it was likely a type of crystal glass, instead of mineral-based, as it had been originally.

She felt along the edge at the seam. It was a tight fit, but she thought the face was removable. Carefully, she used the knife edge to pry the watch apart at the seam, wishing she could use a heat gun, suction cup, and pick to not chance damaging anything. Slowly pulling off the face did not reveal the cable connections she had been expecting. Checking where the battery should be also showed an anomaly. Instead of the tiny lithium battery she expected, she saw what looked like a small rectangle of crystal glowing in a swirling purple color. She gently removed the crystal where it was inlaid and looked below. Everything inside was different than she had expected.

Instead of a motherboard embedded with various processors, modules, and sensors, she saw what looked like a central gem where the processor would be, followed by a few others in key locations. The ones that stood out were the diamonds, rubies, and sapphires. An emerald too. There was some type of glowing metallic substance that formed pathways connecting the gems. Small engravings ran along both the pathway and the gems themselves. The pathways looked almost like silver, but the glow confused her. The various engravings were precision-etched on their surfaces and the arcane language shone softly with an almost ethereal light. They appeared to be some sort of alphabet.

Sloane would need a set of jeweler's loupe glasses to see it clearly and manipulate any tools she would need. Not knowing what else to do at this point, she carefully put the watch back together.

Thinking about the implications of the change, she was starting to think the blue flash had been some sort of magic. It was just so far beyond any possibility she knew that it was hard to digest. Something had definitely happened, but her watch magically changing was the least of her worries. She would figure out how it worked and use that knowledge to whatever benefit she could. Thirdghyll would hopefully have the tools she needed.

She also needed a way to test anything she came up with. If Sloane couldn't find new allies by the time she reached this port city they had mentioned, maybe she could convince the knights to stay with her a little longer by making things for them. She thought this plan had a greater chance of working than meeting and convincing completely new people to help her find Gwyn.

The plan devised, she figured she would look at making something for Maud first. Maud had already displayed magical ability. Sloane's watch was ostensibly using magic, so maybe the first item could be something that enhanced Maud's healing magic.

Sloane put her watch back on, blew out the lamp, and went to bed. She thought about all the fantasy movies and books she had grown up with. All those magical tools, weapons, and items that had appeared fantastical on Earth now seemed completely within reach.

* * *

A light knock on the door woke Sloane. Groaning, she rolled over and sat up. Light from the moons shone through the small window. It was enough to let her see around the room. A soft snore announced that Maud was asleep in the other small bed in the room. Sloane peered closer at the woman and had to cover her mouth as she held in a laugh. Maud had a strand of hair stuck in her open mouth.

I didn't even hear her come into the room. I must have passed out hard.

Another knock sounded and Sloane groaned as she walked to the door. She unlatched the lock as quietly as possible, careful not to wake Maud. The telv waiter stood before her. He seemed to breathe a sigh of relief as she popped her head out.

"I apologize for the late hour, milady, but I have some news," he whispered. "Not exactly what you are hoping for, but it's not necessarily good or bad. Well, it is bad, but I hope not for you personally." He fidgeted slightly. His entire posture seemed restless and on edge.

It made Sloane wary. She glanced around, but the hallway was empty and it was completely quiet. The two of them were the only ones awake, it seemed.

"What is it?" she asked, hesitantly. *I should have grabbed the dagger.*

The telv man glanced at the side of her head. "Frankly, Lady Reinhart, it didn't register earlier, but you're not a telv are you?"

She narrowed her eyes. "No, I'm not. Why?"

"Well, you see, I asked around and the militia found another person that had ears and a similar complexion like yours. It was a man, though, a little taller than you."

That surprised her. "Oh? Another human? Where is he? What did he say?"

The waiter's expression turned far more serious than it had all night. "That's just it, Lady Reinhart. He was found dead. He had been killed by the wolves."

She gasped and her eyes went wide. "Did you find out any information about my daughter?" she demanded.

He lifted his hands and shook his head quickly. "N-no. This man was the only other... person like you who was seen or found."

She had a thought. "Have any other telv passed through recently?"

He paused. "Yes, actually. I had forgotten earlier because they did not stop here at the inn... On the day of the Flash, there was a group of telv that passed through. They had several children with—"

"Did any match the description I gave you?"

His eyes went wide and he sucked in a breath. "I think so. Yes. There was a young girl who had dark curly hair. I did not get a good look at her, so she could have had her ears hidden."

Sloane's breath caught in her throat. Could it be her? Gwyn?

"Where did they go?" she hissed.

"I—I do not know… They left soon after. Tunstead, maybe? They were also heading toward Thirdghyll."

She nodded. "Thank you. Thank you."

His expression softened. "I hope it turns out that it was your daughter and that you find her, milady."

Her eyes started tearing up. She had a lead. "I do too. I appreciate this. Truly."

As far as she knew, they were leaving the next day. She needed to make sure they stopped in Tunstead.

CHAPTER SEVEN

AT OUR CORE

The next morning, Sloane woke early and ready to get the day started. She had a rough plan and just needed to start executing and filling in the blanks. Step one? Food. She strapped her knife back to the side of her shin and covered it with her pants. She slipped her back scabbard over her shoulder and tightened it down, and looking around one last time, she left the room.

She had barely stepped into the taproom before her name was called out.

"Lady Reinhart! Over here!" Ernald hollered from a table in front of the bar. He was sitting with Ismeld and Cristole. Sloane waved and made for the last chair at the table.

Ismeld was the first to speak as Sloane sat down. "Good morning, Lady Reinhart. How are you? You missed out on some good fun and drinks after you stepped away."

Sloane gave Ismeld a curious look. That was the most she had said to her yet. She decided to go slow with what she wanted. Bursting out with the lead she had might not be the best choice after the conversation from last night. Seeming desperate—even if she was—would be a bad look.

"Honestly, not well. I received news last night from the waiter. Before you guys came down, he offered to ask around for me. Well, he did. He came to my room and told me that another human, like me, had been found dead. A man. Apparently, he had been killed by the wolves sometime in the last day or so," she replied.

Cristole's eyes widened slightly. "I am sorry to hear that, Lady Reinhart." He paused and tilted his head. "However, while tragic, perhaps you should take a portion of this as good news. It means that other members of your race besides just you and your daughter were transported to our world."

Ernald looked at Cristole in thought. "That is a good observation, Cristole." Turning to look at Sloane, he added, "If a significant number of your people made it here, the news will spread. It may make it easier to search for your daughter based on her description."

She considered this line of thought. "There is potential there, but it's too early to say whether it will help. Still, it's better than searching the whole continent for Gwyn with zero direction." Looking between the three of them, she pushed, seeing how much they would tell her about the decision the night prior. "Speaking of direction, after you leave me in Thirdghyll, do you have any suggestions for where I should next direct my travels?"

The group froze and their eyes darted between each other. Finally, Cristole sighed. Ernald covered his face with his hand. Ismeld's face scrunched up as if she were constipated.

Cristole looked at Sloane. "You heard it all, didn't you?" he said wryly.

Sloane squinted her eyes, debating whether to play off the fact that she had completely failed in her tactic. She supposed she had never done well manipulating a conversation to get what she wanted. *I'll probably need to work on that.*

Accepting the loss, she told them the truth. She fidgeted slightly, then continued. "But I wasn't sure if you all would tell me. I was a bit disappointed in the decision, but it makes sense… I guess. At least in hindsight. This is only day three since I arrived."

"We…" Ismeld began.

Sloane waited for her to continue but the high elf just looked away. Sloane wasn't sure she'd ever get along with that woman, but it was still early in their relationship. *I've overcome worse odds.*

Ernald audibly groaned, "Fine, alright, Sloane. How much did you hear?"

Sloane raised an eyebrow. "Escorting me to Swanbrook, tossing me on a boat, and pointing to somewhere called Avera? Apparently, they have an academy that is more likely to have information than the one in Thirdghyll, if that one doesn't pan out?"

Ernald nodded. "Okay, so you got most of that, and it's Avira, by the way. A large kingdom that believes it's better than everyone else, which leads them to think they can push their opinions and laws on the rest of us."

Sloane squinted. "Will we be passing through a village called Tunstead on the way to Thirdghyll?" she asked.

Ismeld tilted her head. "Yes. We will be staying there for a night. Why?"

That was good. It would not be as difficult as she thought. *Hopefully, they believe me.*

She sucked in a breath. "The human man wasn't the only thing I learned from the waiter last night. There was a girl who came through town that he believed matched Gwyn's description. At the time, he had thought her a telv, but—"

"He did? Where? Sloane, why didn't you lead with that?" Ernald asked, sitting up in his chair.

Sloane closed her eyes and exhaled. Tears welled up in her eyes. "I didn't think you would believe me. You all just had those talks… I thought you would think I was lying just to convince you to keep helping me. You can ask him, though. He—"

"You do not have to worry. I do not believe you would deceive us on something so important to you. We will be leaving later today. Gisele is still provisioning supplies this morning. We will follow this lead when we get to Tunstead," Cristole said with surety. He glanced at Ismeld, and she nodded.

The blond high elf took a moment to examine Sloane. Blue eyes scanned her face. Searching.

Sloane could only think that Ismeld found her wanting. She wasn't a knight. She wasn't a noble. *I will prove her wrong.*

"Sloane, you should be prepared. You may get many false leads in your quest. I say this not to discourage you, but to ensure you do not lose hope if this lead does not pan out," Ismeld said.

I… did not expect that. Sloane nodded. "I understand." And she did. It did not matter how long it took. No distance would be too far. She would find her daughter.

She closed her eyes for a moment. Collected herself. When she opened them, the three knights were staring at her. She did not want them to walk on eggshells around her, so she preempted by changing the conversation.

"What else did I miss from the discussions? Maud didn't come to the room until late," she said. "Speaking of, does she always snore so loudly?"

Cristole and Ernald laughed and Ismeld's lip turned upward.

"Yes, that woman sounds like a lumberjack sawing a tree," Ernald said.

Sloane shook her head. "The first night must have been a good one then. She didn't snore that night."

Ismeld sniffed. "She stayed up nearly all night for your sake. If Maud is not snoring, she's just relaxing. She slept the next day in the wagon while you rode with Ernald."

She heard me cry myself to sleep, then…

"Oh… So uh, what else came up? Sorry…"

Ernald squinted his eyes but decided not to address whatever it was he was thinking. "Concerning news or anything important, not much. Melchior finally came by and talked about the situation. Their scouting parties were hit by the wolves last night, and they lost six of their people. They did manage to kill another fifteen though. So, that's a plus. It's basically a small attack force of… wolves. No one has even an inkling of why there are so many. It's highly unusual," the sun elf knight explained.

Sloane nodded. "I agree, that is frightening." It reminded her of an event on Earth, a late-night Wikipedia rabbit hole she'd gone down. Also a good distraction. Moving from one distraction to the next seemed to be the only way she could function at this point. Perhaps there was something there, though. *And maybe it will distract them from the looks of pity they're giving me.*

"In a nation far from mine, in a cold tundra region, there was an especially harsh winter. The temperature was extremely cold, and due to this, the usual prey of the local wolves was depleted drastically," Sloane started.

She noticed they were transfixed on her as she recounted the Russian event she'd read about online. "The lack of a reliable food source compelled the wolves to focus on one particular area. A town. Around four hundred wolves besieged this town. Luckily, they only targeted the horses and other livestock out of hunger and desperation. In my world, the average size of a pack is only around ten to fifteen." She watched for their reactions as she spoke.

Cristole actually seemed fascinated. Ismeld and Ernald just sat with wide eyes.

Sloane smiled, then administered the coup de grâce. "And that doesn't even come close to the man-eating wolf attacks from eighty years before that. Where, in the same nation, over two hundred packs of wolves terrorized a city intermittently for over ten years. Hunting and devouring mainly children who walked the streets alone or even in small groups. Over the course of four years, hunters and organized groups killed over two thousand wolves."

She had them.

Cristole looked utterly speechless, just opening and closing his mouth as if he couldn't figure out exactly what he wanted to say. A shocked expression was plastered on Ernald's face.

Ismeld was the first to come to. "Your world sounds terrifying."

Sloane realized she might have gone too far. "The wolves of my world are nowhere near the size of the ones we fought," she said. "Plus, these were very peculiar circumstances, which is why I mentioned them. Something is agitating these wolves. They're larger than normal, more aggressive."

She turned to Cristole. "Was there anything out of the ordinary when you stripped down the wolves we killed?"

Cristole thought about it, then snapped his finger. "Yes! There was! I will return with haste." He sprang to his feet and rushed upstairs.

Ismeld spoke for him. "We did find something abnormal, something in each of the wolves' chests." The high elf woman paused, looking up as she considered how to explain. "At first, we thought it was only an abnormal growth, but it was hardening in our hands. There were a bunch of nerves branching out from it. However, as we grabbed hold of it, the nerves seemed to just fall away." She thought for a moment, then added, "Further, when we touched it, it seemed to spread a feeling of... I can only describe it as a... tingling? It was undoubtedly a strange experience. It appeared to also react to the knives. The feeling seemed to travel through the hilts into our hands."

Sloane was about to respond when Cristole came charging back down the stairs, leaping down the last five. She smiled. The sight of the tall elf, with his angular jaw, long sharp ears, and body of an athlete, in this super-excited state amused her. His normally calm, stoic demeanor was missing as he held up what looked like a rough orb about the size of a golf ball.

"This is it. When we found the first one, it felt like any other organ. It was slowly hardening, but that sped up once we removed it from the wolf. Now it feels like a stone." He handed the petrified object to her, sat down, and looked at her expectantly.

She rolled the orb around in her palm, feeling for soft areas or something that would signify where the nerves Ismeld described would connect.

"Oh, okay. Wow. This is really strange. It's almost as if nothing had been attached to it when it was in the body. I can definitely feel something coming from it too."

Cristole nodded. "I know! It's fascinating. The growth was in the exact same location on each wolf, just like you would expect any other organ."

She placed it on the table in front of her and stared at it, thinking.

Ernald drew her attention. "Sloane." She looked up at him as he pointed at her wrist. "Your watch. Look."

She peered at the device and witnessed the mist collecting on the side closest to the orb, taking on a slight green tinge at the very edge. Moving her wrist until the watch was just over the object forced the mist to move back into the center. Even more turned green.

"You're right about one thing. Fascinating. The... core... is emanating magic. A magic core? No, that's not right. This is probably what's causing the wolves to be so large." Handing the core back, Sloane considered the implications. Her mind tried to think of multiple things at once and she was barely able to formulate a complete idea.

She became only vaguely aware of the conversations continuing at the table. The core... She knew it was magical in nature. If the wolves had it, then that led her to believe that maybe people did too. That might explain Maud's new ability to heal. *What tests could we do to prove this? Maybe it's something native to Eona? No. This is new to them as well.*

Sloane's eyes widened. It had to be the Flash. *Wait... does that mean I have a core now too?* Her hand moved to her chest and she considered what it could mean. The new vein-like things snaked through the wolves' bodies. Is that how magic affects the body? She squinted as she tried to figure out what those would do. Magical conduits? It would explain the adrenaline high that never came down. *Can everyone use magic? Or just Maud?*

She heard someone say her name. A hand materialized in her face and snapped her thoughts back to reality. Sloane jerked in surprise, seeing Ismeld waving at her when she glanced up.

"You all there?" the blond high elf asked.

"Yes, of course. What was the question?" Sloane inquired.

Ismeld sighed. "What are you thinking about?"

"Oh, yes." Sloane straightened her back. "So, this—we're going to call it a core… I suspect it is what allows the magic that is everywhere to improve the wolf. Or improve anything, actually. I cannot verify, for obvious reasons, but I suspect that we have one of these as well."

The others looked both surprised and skeptical at her revelation. Ernald narrowed his eyes as he considered her thoughts. "Explain."

Sloane shrugged. "It all goes back to how each of us felt after we killed the wolves. We felt a rush, and now there is a minuscule but noticeable improvement in our bodies. I believe that was our cores taking on the magic from the wolves and then distributing it within us."

Ernald crossed his arms and started stroking his chin, considering. "This has merit, but the implications are, frankly, terrifying. This would mean that each of us was physically changed by the flash of magic."

Sloane nodded again, "Yes. This is huge. Perhaps we can perform an autopsy on someone? I have zero clue how to do that. I'm unsure of the specifics. I do believe this merits additional investigation, though. I believe this core is what allows us to utilize magic. If anything, Maud lends credence to this, as she clearly performed magic."

Cristole tapped his chin, then lifted his finger. "If we have this core, does that mean we could learn magic? I did not see Maud's magic, but I can see the effects on Ser Ernald's face."

Ismeld, who had been staring at her hands, looked up. "If the cores allow us to do magic, and the cores are still filled with magic, could we do something with them?"

"Actually, let me try something," Sloane said as she pulled out her knife. "So, I know you mentioned it, but I want to see how this feels myself."

Experimentally touching the dagger's tip to the core, she tried to channel the feeling through the weapon. Concentrating, she focused on the core, moving the blade forward slightly so the flat of it was resting on the object. Slowly, she began to feel something, definitely a force of some sort. It reminded her of… nature or maybe life. It was very strange, and she was certain it was magic. It made her excited to think of ways to use the core.

Sloane's remembered something from her world's fantasy stories and ideas. "Wait, is there a blacksmith nearby?"

Cristole nodded.

"Then, yes, I definitely think there is something we may be able to do. I may need money, but can we head there now?"

Ernald looked around. "But you haven't even eaten. What of—"

"We're leaving later, and I do not want to delay us. However, this may help us on the road if we are attacked again. So we should hurry."

Sloane glanced at his plate, which still had a hunk of bread and a couple of pieces of cheese. She smiled and snatched them up as she stood. Taking a bite, she said, "There, now I have. Let's go!"

Cristole laughed as he stood up. "Sure, let's go. We have some money we can use. Just please make sure it's for a good cause! Ser Gisele will kill me if you spend it all for nothing!"

CHAPTER EIGHT

THAT WHICH BINDS US

Sloane followed the knights as they led her to the blacksmith. In the morning light, Valesbeck was already bustling with townsfolk doing whatever activity they could to help the construction and defense efforts. They passed the market square, which was filled with people purchasing goods, while militiamen spread out in groups along the outer edges.

Mostly, she saw various foods and small household items. There were some basic clothing items, but nothing that she would need at the moment. It seemed Gisele's suggestion of obtaining clothing and armor in Thirdghyll would hold.

Soon enough, they arrived at a large building that looked about two and a half stories tall with a single chimney attached to an overhang that held an outside forge and bellows. Three anvils of various sizes were arranged nearby with racks of tools. A young telv boy seemed to be cleaning up the area.

Cristole called out. "Boy, is the smith available?"

The boy jumped and quickly turned around, eyes widening upon seeing the three knights and Sloane. "Yes, milord, I'll get him at once!" he said with exuberance. He ran inside the building, slamming the door in his rush.

Ernald looked amused. "You think he'd never seen a knight before. He was quick!"

"He's just excited. You're new, and he may bring the smith a new customer. He'll be happy he got to help. More so if we purchase something. First, hand me the core please?" Sloane said offhandedly.

Cristole pulled the object from his pouch and handed it to her. "What are you looking to do?"

"I'm looking for either a staff or a scepter. I would prefer a scepter, as it's smaller, but a staff could work. Whatever we can get, it needs to have a setting that can fit the stone," Sloane explained. "I'm unsure if it should be polished, but I think the safest bet is to not damage it too much for at least our first attempt. I also think there will need to be some type of metal going all the way from the setting to the grip. That way there is always a connection flowing to Maud—but I'm not sure of that." Sloane paused. If this were to become a thing, she would have to come up with everything she needed to augment the other knights' equipment. Then to improve her own.

"Thinking about it, I'll need to get tools to do this kind of work when we get to Thirdghyll if the city is everything you guys mentioned. I'm no blacksmith, but I should get everything I'll need to fabricate tools and other objects."

Ismeld nodded, then tilted her head in confusion. "Wait… Maud? I thought this was going to be for you?"

Sloane shook her head. "No, Maud is the only one we can definitively say is able to use magic. It has to be her to establish if it works." She thought she saw a hint of approval in the way the high elf looked at her. "If it does—"

The smith came out before she could finish, interrupting her thoughts. He was a telv, and if he had been human, he would have been of average height and slightly above average weight. His long, dark red hair was pulled back into a ponytail. His round face and short, pointed ears were also red—likely from standing in front of a furnace. He had a close-cropped beard that gave the smile he sported a good-humored appearance.

The smith reached out to her but quickly noticed his hands were dirty. Instead, he wiped them on his apron and crossed his arms in front of his chest. "Good morning! What can I do for you?"

Interesting. He's the first person I've met who wanted to shake my hand.

Sloane smiled and got right to it. "I'm looking to purchase either a staff or scepter that has or can accommodate a setting that can securely fit this stone," she said as she held it up, not wanting to confuse him by calling it a core.

He reached out his hand. "May I?"

She nodded and handed him the core. "Absolutely. Oh, and one more thing: we would need this today, as we are trying to resume our journey."

The smith scratched his beard with one hand as he held up the core and looked it over. "I think I have something that can fit this. Come on in, let's take a look."

They entered a room filled with various pieces of armor, weapons, and objects on display. Sloane heard Ernald and Cristole speaking in a low voice about the selection of wares. There seemed to be a level of concern and confusion in their voices.

At the back of the room, the boy they'd met earlier was sitting at a desk. He had a ledger in front of him and his excited face showed he was ready to process any transaction.

Cristole let out a slow whistle. "This is a lot more weapons and armor than I expected in a small town."

The telv blacksmith shook his head sadly and looked over his shoulder at the group. "Times have forced me to redirect my efforts toward more... martial requirements. What you see here... let's just say that I have the militia arriving later. Now, I don't think I have a scepter or a staff that will accommodate that stone. However, I have something I think will fit. The user, they're another knight?"

Sloane nodded. "Yes, she is the knight-medic for the Order's squad here." She noticed Ismeld giving her an appreciative smile, which she suspected was because of the subtle suggestion that the Order was larger than it actually was.

The telv smirked. "Great. Then yes, this will be perfect." He walked over to a case and pulled out a beautifully polished steel mace shaft with an intricate design. Next to it lay a seven-flanged head shaped with complex indentations and projections. A conical finial at the tip capped off an opening to fit a decorative stone or gem, good for accommodating the core. The smith picked up the head and slotted the core into the setting. Sloane gaped at how perfectly it fit.

"Would you like the stone polished?" the smith asked her. "It will take me a few hours to complete the forge weld."

Ernald looked at the mace and then at Sloane. "I know you said we should try without, but that mace is too beautiful for such a rough sphere. You may as well see if it retains its properties after polishing."

Sloane nodded. The mace would be both beautiful and functional as a weapon instead of just a magical focus. "Yes, I agree. Let's do it." She turned to the smith. "Could you also sell me supplies to do polishing on my own?"

The telv showed a toothy smile. "Of course! I have some spare supplies I can add in for free. Will you need a mace frog as well?"

Sloane looked at Cristole, who answered for her. "Yes, we will take one. Thank you."

Nodding, the smith started collecting the items they wanted and setting them aside. "Very well! Please pay my boy at the counter there and return in, say... three hours?"

Sloane and the others thanked the smith and Ismeld settled up the cost of their order.

They stepped out of the smithy and started heading back toward the market. Cristole and Ismeld wished to purchase supplies for the next leg of their journey, which would take about two weeks.

As Cristole and Ismeld shopped, Sloane discussed potential ways Maud could harness her mace's power.

"So, you believe she just needs to focus on pushing her magic into the core and it should amplify the effect?" Ernald asked.

"Yes, I suspect that's what will occur," Sloane replied with a nod. "Or maybe she can instead pull magic from the core to empower her own magic."

Ernald pondered her words. "You know, I'm not fond of using 'magic' to describe both the action and the substance."

"Yeah, that will get confusing, won't it?" she concurred, already thinking of other ways to describe it. "I'll consider different terminology to define the process. Hopefully, it will suit your most prodigious mind." She winked.

Ernald chuckled. "I appreciate that, milady. I shall mention your contributions when I present my research to the scholars of the Orlême Université in Blightwych."

Sloane's laughter caught Ismeld's attention. "Sloane, if you are done, come," she ordered. "Let's get you a set of traveling attire and a pack."

Sloane smiled, unable to help herself as she remarked, "Girl time shopping for clothes and I don't have to spend a cent? Count me in."

Ismeld raised an eyebrow. "I am unaware of what a cent is, but yes, over there," she said, pointing. "We can find clothing for you in that store."

As they entered the shop, a small bell chimed, announcing their arrival. Sloane observed an extensive array of attire, including dresses, tunics, and pants. A shop employee approached and welcomed them.

A striking raithe, she had meticulously styled teal hair and dark grey skin. She was nearly a full head shorter than both Ismeld and Sloane, with a much more slender frame. She offered a dazzling fanged smile, and her bright pink eyes sparkled as she addressed the pair.

"Good day! Welcome to Dashing Tailors! How may I assist you, miladies?"

Ismeld immediately took the lead. "We need a set of traveling clothes for my companion here. A tunic, breeches, some boots, a cloak, and a belt. Some underclothes as well. A hip pouch and a pack she can wear on her back. It needs to be durable and maneuverable in case of any hostilities."

Sloane couldn't help but chuckle, earning a glare from Ismeld.

"Is there a problem?" the blond knight asked.

Sloane shook her head, covering her mouth with her hand. "No, Ser Ismeld. I just find your no-nonsense approach to clothing endearing."

The high elf nodded in response, turning her attention back to the shop assistant.

The girl gave them a moment to ensure nothing else needed to be said, then addressed them. "Wonderful! If that's all you require, we can certainly accommodate you! Please, follow me so I can take some measurements." She glanced at Ismeld, who promptly shook her head, indicating that she had no intention of joining them.

Sloane followed the raithe to an open area near a divider she assumed was for her to get dressed behind. The young woman introduced herself as she grabbed what she required. "May I have the honor of knowing your name, milady?" the woman asked as she looked at her with expectant eyes.

"My name is Sloane. It's a pleasure to meet you. What do you need me to do?"

"Not much, Lady Reinhart! Please just allow me to maneuver you and obtain the measurements I need to ensure we get you clothed properly. We have many items ready to adjust to nearly any size."

Sloane nodded and the girl instantly went to work measuring her in every possible way. That was interesting to Sloane. In her world, ready-made clothing would not have been available during similar time periods. Clearly, the textile industry was more robust here. She would be interested in learning more about how it was possible.

"Where did you get your clothing? It is… unique. And very well-made," the raithe said, her face filled with curiosity as she pulled and prodded Sloane's shirt and pants.

"Oh, I just got them back home. These are common there," Sloane stated a bit hesitantly.

The seamstress's mouth dropped open for a moment and she paused. "Common? H-how?" she asked after coming to herself.

"I'm not sure, to be honest. I don't really know how they're made. I just like them. That said, I'm aware it isn't what the people of your nation wear. I'll be happy with whatever you can provide. All of your clothing looks fantastic," Sloane deflected.

"May I ask where you're from, milady?"

"I hail from a nation far from here. It is of no importance."

The young woman got the hint and stopped asking more questions as she went back to obtaining the measurements required. In a few minutes, it seemed the raithe had what she needed. She showed Sloane to a nearby chair and left to gather the items Ismeld had requested.

After about ten minutes, the raithe woman returned with an armful of clothing. "So, milady, I know your knight friend has some ideas of what you should wear, but I think I have just the thing for you."

Sloane grinned. "I'm happy you took initiative. Let's see what you have."

Sloane stood in front of a mirror looking at the long-sleeved forest green dress she wore that fell to the middle of her shins. It was made of a rugged, medium-weight material with outdoor travel and hiking clearly in mind. A thin short-sleeved undershirt kept her more comfortable. Looking down, she examined the waist corset, which she ensured wasn't too tight—she didn't want to end up breathless if she had to run. Below sat a belt with a hip satchel attached and a place to attach her short sword.

Draped over her shoulders was a blue cloak with a beautifully stitched silver border that came together with a pewter clasp formed in the shape of two little dragons. She wore breeches underneath the dress with a pair of boots sporting hard soles and laces down the front. Her dagger was strapped in a way that hid it within her boot. She loved the outfit. Sloane smiled, thinking about how much it would fit in at a fantasy convention back home. She finally felt as if she could stop standing out in a crowd, especially if she hid her ears under the hood of the cloak.

She looked over at the seamstress, who noted Sloane's goofy grin. "Like it, do we?"

"I do, thank you. Could I get my companion to see what she thinks?"

"I'll go grab her for you, milady," the raithe girl offered.

After a few minutes, she heard steps and turned to see Ismeld and the woman walking up to her.

She beamed at Ismeld as she approached. "What do you think?"

Ismeld squinted her eyes and crossed her arms, looking her up and down, then nodded. "Turn."

Sloane huffed a laugh as she slowly turned to allow Ismeld to see the back of her outfit.

"It will do. It is suited for travel. Like what I would have to have worn back home. Unfortunately."

Sloane turned back to face her. "You don't like this style?"

"No. I worked hard to become a knight so I did not have to wear it anymore. Do you have everything? Did you get a pack?" Ismeld asked, short on details of her past.

Sloane shook her head and looked at the raithe woman. "May I wear it from here?"

The raithe smiled. "I will need to do a few quick adjustments, but it won't take long. I'm delighted you are happy. I do agree with the lady in the armor: you need a pack. We have a few that have straps to wear along your back. Let's look at them and choose one, and then we can meet the lady knight at the front to finalize the transaction."

Ismeld nodded and returned to the front, while Sloane followed the woman to look for more accessories and get the adjustments required.

Forty minutes later, they finally emerged from the shop. Cristole and Ernald were sitting at a table with empty mugs in front of them as they waited for the women. Cristole looked up as they came out, scrutinizing Sloane's new look as they walked over.

"Wonderful! Lady Reinhart, you finally look as if you belong. With that hood up, you can undoubtedly pass as a telv. We could easily walk into any town or city without unnecessary questions as to your origins."

Ismeld nodded. "While it isn't what I suggested, it does perform the function intended. One benefit is that it allows you to appear more fittingly for one of your station. So, I believe this will benefit us as well. Especially in the villages."

Rolling her eyes, Sloane smiled. "You all know I don't have a station. Especially not here."

Ernald tilted his head, looking at her. "It matters not, milady. You have the appearance and intelligence of a noble. I believe I can speak for all of us when I say that it's only time before it's noble in truth. The first step will be to establish some means for yourself." He stopped and took in her appearance again. "I must say, you look stunning, milady. Positively breathtaking."

Sloane blushed slightly under the attention. "Thank you, Ernald. Now, I believe it's time to retrieve Maud's new weapon and then return to our companions at the inn so we can be on our way."

Cristole nodded. "You are correct. Let us go!"

The telv blacksmith was waiting for them at the smithy. "Welcome back, sers and lady. I completed your order." He took out a small box and opened it. Inside lay the fully assembled mace. The polished core was a striking marbled green color that reminded Sloane of malachite. The core glowed with a soft shimmer of green mist that seemed to be just below the surface. The color and glow contrasted with the engraved steel designs of the mace beautifully. The requested mace frog was next to the weapon, the leather dyed black with a steel ring that would hold the mace to Maud's waist.

The smith glanced between the mace and the knights. "I can tell there is something different about the orb you gave me. It started glowing after I polished it, and then the mist started swirling after I finished attaching the head of the mace to the shaft. I am not sure what it is, but I know when I should keep my mouth shut."

Sloane nodded, choosing not to respond. She was thoroughly impressed, and when she picked up the mace to examine it, she gasped. Turning to the knights, she said, "I can feel it even in the handle. This is going to be perfect." She handed it to Cristole. "Here."

His eyes widened as he held it. "Yes, this will do." Turning to the smith, he dipped his head respectfully. "Thank you, Master Smith. Your work is excellent and will serve our sister well. I will endeavor to seek you out for more work if we pass this way in the future."

The smiling smith returned the nod. "I thank you, milord. Your words bring me joy, and I am deeply honored to be able to provide my craft to ones such as you. And you, Lady Reinhart, please, if you are passing through again, come see me." He reached onto the counter and grabbed a small leather sack. Handing it to her, he added, "I have the supplies you requested here. Again, thank you for your patronage."

Sloane smiled. "Thank you! I will definitely come to see you if I am in the area again!"

The group left the blacksmith and headed toward the inn. Sloane was excited to see how Maud liked the new weapon and, hopefully, just how much it would improve her healing magic.

She nearly gasped as she remembered something from her world. Something she should have thought of immediately when considering the magic. "Ernald! I got it!"

"Got what, Lady Reinhart?"

"The magic terminology! I think I know what we should call it!"

Ernald perked up as his interest grew. "Oh? What is it? Something you know from your world?"

She nodded. "Yes, it's not in our world, but we have a name for it. It's what gives you the ability to do magic." She waved her hand around. "Or rather, it is what allows magic to happen at all here. My watch can manipulate it to a small degree and can certainly detect it in some manner."

Both Ismeld and Cristole stopped and focused on her, listening as well. Ernald motioned for her to continue.

"I believe the substance that Maud is using for her magic—" Sloane took a deep breath, excitement bubbling as she got a little bit closer to understanding what was happening in the world around her, "is mana."

The world around them seemed to exhale, making the hairs on her arms stand on end as if it agreed with her assessment.

Sloane shivered as a chill ran down her spine. She smiled.

It seems that I am right.

CHAPTER NINE

LIFE

They arrived back at the inn, finding the wagon parked in front. Both the side and rear doors were open, and Maud and Gisele were loading supplies. Deryk came out of the inn carrying a crate. The orkun man handed it up to the knight-captain, who loaded it onto the roof and tied it down with some rope.

Gisele jumped down and looked at the group as they approached. "Nice of you all to join us," she said with an unamused tone.

Her gaze swept over everyone before settling on Sloane. "I see you got some travel clothing. That's good. That will be helpful." Looking at Cristole, who held the sacks of food and supplies, she added, "At least you did not return empty-handed. What else did you manage to purchase?"

Cristole lifted the two bags. "More rations and other various supplies to help us get through the journey to Thirdghyll." He hesitated. "I got you some cheese I know you'll love too."

Gisele sniffed. "Of course you did. Like you always do when you know you managed to get out of doing most of the work."

Cristole chuckled. "Better to get you something as an apology than to show no remorse, yeah?"

Gisele tilted her head. "I suppose that's true."

Taking that as his cue, Cristole headed toward the stables to retrieve the horses. Ismeld took in the scene with a scowl.

Ernald opened his mouth but the orkun woman lifted a hand. "No. It's not the day to mess with me, Ernald. Do you have anything important?"

The sun elf shook his head.

Gisele nodded, focusing on her last two knights. "You two good?"

Ismeld nodded. "We are. Are you?"

Gisele shrugged. "One of those mornings…"

Ismeld gave her a sympathetic look. She turned to the sun elf. "Ernald, hand Sloane the package. We will go assist Deryk. With your leave, Knight-Captain."

Gisele hesitated at Ismeld's tone but then shook her head with a sigh. "Not today, Tenera…" Sloane heard her mutter. Gisele forced a smile and addressed the elf. "Of course. I suppose I have you to thank for taking Sloane to purchase clothing. Ernald, we'll talk more later."

Ismeld and Ernald nodded, the latter handing Sloane the box with the mace before they went to help Deryk finish loading up the wagon.

Sloane called out to Maud. "Ser Maud! We got something for you. Come here!"

Gisele looked confused but seemed content to wait for an explanation as Maud walked over.

Handing Maud the box, Sloane explained, "So, the wolves we killed had what we are tentatively calling a core, or mana core, within them. A new organ that emanates mana, the substance that allows you to perform magic. Upon death, a mana core seems to solidify about as hard as stone. The cores we took from the wolves appeared to have properties that I believe will work with the magic you demonstrated. Thinking of a way to harness that core for your magic, we went to the local smith and purchased you a new weapon."

They followed her to the wagon as she talked. Standing next to the side door, she finished with a bright smile and hands clasped in front of her. "Please, open the box."

Maud's face went through a range of emotions before settling on her usual excitement as Sloane finished her explanation. She placed the box on the steps leading into the wagon and opened the lid. With a gasp, she looked at the beautiful mace that lay inside.

Her piercing green eyes darted to Sloane. "Really? This is for me?" Maud asked as she carefully hefted the mace from the container.

Gisele's eyes widened as she saw the mace. "That is gorgeous. You said it should enhance her healing magic?"

Sloane nodded. "Yes, I believe so. Maud, do you feel anything as you hold it? Can you try both pushing your magic into it and pulling magic out of it?"

With a look of pure concentration, Maud tried manipulating her magic with the help of the mace. At first, nothing happened, but then after a couple of minutes, with sweat dripping down her brow, the knight-medic jerked as if something seemed to click. Slowly, the mace's head and the orb contained within began to glow a light green color.

Gisele and Sloane watched Maud intently as she cast her spell.

Maud focused on them, raising the mace to point it at Sloane. Her face scrunched up as she worked at whatever internal struggle she was going through, and after a second, a subtle green flash washed over Sloane.

The healer lowered the mace and looked at her two observers. "How do you feel?" she said between rapid breaths.

Sloane looked down and took stock of herself. Where she had been tired before from being gone all day, now she was utterly refreshed.

Realizing it only by their absence, aches that she hadn't paid attention to were also now gone. She felt as if she could run a marathon.

She looked up at Maud, who had a smile on her face. "I feel amazing. How do you feel? It looked like you were concentrating pretty hard."

Maud nodded. "Yes, it took a bit to figure out exactly how to perform what you suggested. However, I think it will go easier next time... Actually..." She looked at Gisele, raised her mace, and performed the same action as before.

With the same light green flash, Gisele immediately straightened, gasping as she did so. She felt her lower abdomen. Her eyes widened and a broad smile spread across her face. "Maud, this is amazing. I also feel perfect. Do you think this would help heal a wound like Ernald's?"

Maud considered the question. "Yes, I do. But I feel that performing the same action on a wound will not be as easy or widespread as what you are feeling now."

Gisele nodded. "You, me. We are talking more in private. To discuss... other uses," she told the healer.

The redheaded telv nodded. "I understand. I am happy it worked. You did not look comfortable." She turned to Sloane. "Thank you, Sloane. This is an absolutely wonderful gift. I will treasure it."

Gisele smiled. "I agree, Sloane. The benefit we will gain from this weapon alone will be indispensable for our group. Thank you."

Sloane tilted her head toward her, a smile tugging at the corners of her mouth. "I'm glad I could provide something beneficial to all of you. I'm looking forward to doing more on our journey." She paused. "I also received some news. There has been at least one other human transported here to your world. And there was potentially a girl who matched Gwyn's description heading with a group toward Tunstead."

Maud gasped. "Why didn't you lead with that?"

Sloane shook her head. "Something Ismeld said. I don't want to get my hopes up—at least, not yet. When we get to Tunstead, we'll get more info," she explained.

"We are almost ready to leave. If this group has a lead on us, we will need to hurry. However, if they are heading to Thirdghyll, we will hopefully be able to catch them there. This is big news, Sloane. I too am surprised you are not more excited," Gisele said.

Sloane took a deep breath. "Don't get me wrong: I am excited and hopeful and filled with so many other emotions, but if I get my hopes up too much, I risk spiraling if I am disappointed. All I know is that there was a young girl who matched Gwyn's description but may have even been a telv girl."

The two women nodded and spoke briefly with her about the conversation with the waiter. Maud seemed mildly surprised she had not been awakened, which made Gisele chuckle.

Sloane paused, breathing deeply. Keeping it together was important.

Gisele stepped close and placed a hand on her shoulder. "Thank you for not giving up on us, Sloane. I know our decision for the journey wasn't exactly what you hoped for but—"

"I heard the plan last night, Ser Gisele, and talked to the others today while we were gone. It's okay. I understand where you are coming from. That said, it doesn't downplay the help you have given and will be giving in the near future. If this is Gwyn—"

"Then we will help you get settled somewhere safe and secure for both of you. It is the least we can do. Thirdghyll will not be the proper place for that, however. But that is a discussion for after. For now, if you'll excuse me, it seems the others are nearly done packing. We need to leave soon if we are to catch that group you spoke of." With a slight bow, Gisele turned and walked to where the others were gathering.

Sloane looked at the cheerful redhead with a smile, her ears poking out from her long curly hair that seemed to have a life of its own. "And then there were two. Will you drive the wagon first, Maud? Maybe we can talk and I can tell you about my world and my daughter?"

Even Maud's eyes smiled when she replied, "I would love that, Sloane. Let's finish up here, and then we can be off." She started to turn, then stopped. "Sloane?"

Sloane tilted her head slightly. "Yes?"

Maud rushed forward, grabbing and holding her in a tight hug. She whispered into her ear, her voice catching. "I hope this lead holds true and we find Gwyn. I understand why you don't wish to get your own hopes up, but sometimes, a little hope is good." She gestured to her mace. "Thank you for the mace. You have no idea what this gesture means to me. I hope that one day you will."

Sloane hugged her back, and they stood, embracing, emotions threatening to overtake them both. With one last squeeze, Maud stepped back, dropping her arms to her side. Grabbing Sloane's hand to pull her along, she said, "Come. Let's go."

Five hours later, Maud and Sloane sat on the wagon's driving bench as they traveled on the road toward Thirdghyll. They would be stopping in seven villages and two towns along the way. All told, Gisele expected the trip to take weeks, more if any unforeseen delays occurred. After everything that had happened so far? Something was going to pop up—it was inevitable.

It took two more hours, just two, before one such event occurred. Sloane felt as if she needed one of those "Days Since Last Incident" workplace safety signs. The group came across a merchant wagon that had been attacked by what the knights assumed were bandits. The wagon's goods had been looted and there were three bodies tossed in a nearby ditch. They didn't stay long, but the knights did provide last rites to the deceased and buried them under stone mounds.

She learned a bit about the religion after that. Sitting with Maud in the wagon while Ernald had taken over the driving, Maud explained, "I sometimes take for granted that there's even a possibility of someone not knowing who the gods are."

That made Sloane sigh. "Well, I am from an entirely different world. We have our own religions."

Maud looked surprised. "You have more than one?"

Sloane smiled. "We do! Perhaps I can tell you about them sometime," she deflected. The religion of Avira was relevant, but she didn't wish to get into a theological debate with what was essentially a person who lived in their world's Middle Ages. She wasn't sure how religious the people here were, but she felt it was a bad idea to potentially debate or introduce such volatile concepts from her world.

"Could you tell me what I should expect here? I noticed a temple inside of Valesbeck, but was that to all of your gods or just one?"

Maud nodded. "Of course. So, temples. Villages usually have a shrine or two that are typically places to venerate and worship at a personal level to a specific god. Some villages have dedicated services on specific days around the shrine. Meanwhile, towns like Valesbeck host a Temple of the Celestials. This is a dedicated temple to the entire pantheon. Depending on the size of the temple, it may be broken down into separate chapels for each of the four major gods. There may also be a hall of shrines dedicated to the minor gods."

Maud took a breath. "Whew. That's a lot. Okay, so next we have the cities, like Thirdghyll. They also have a dedicated temple for the Family, but it's typically larger, as it potentially hosts entire wings dedicated to one of the major gods. Larger cities may even have smaller temples for specific minor gods. However, if you're lucky, they'll simply have a single temple dedicated to the lot."

Sloane took it all in. "Sounds pretty reasonable. So, there are major and minor gods. Are there, like, good gods and bad gods?"

Maud raised an eyebrow. "No. What? The gods are just gods. They are neutral in the affairs of mortals. First, we will talk about the major gods. There are four of them in the Celestial Family. Alos, the Father Sun: he provides light for the day and heat to keep out the cold. His domains are Justice, Righteousness, and Law. His avatar is a sun elf, signified by their dark skin and fiery eyes, like Ernald. Alos protects."

Pausing to ensure Sloane was still following, she continued. "Next we have Eona, our Mother World. We reside upon her, and she gives us life. With her husband, Alos, she ensures that nature provides. Her domain is life in all its natural forms. Her avatar takes on the form of any of her children but is usually her high elf form. Our world is called Eona, and, as a healer, she is my patron goddess. Eona provides.

"Next, we have the Sister Moons. Relena, the larger Moon, was given the honor of presiding over the Afterlife. She ensures that all souls are able to make their way to her and find their redemption or peace before rejoining the cycle of souls. Her avatar is a raithe. The other sister is Tenera, she is the goddess of the night and vengeance. Her moon shines the brightest in the night sky, as a light to comfort us in our darkest moments. Her domains are change and vengeance. She manifests her avatar as a moon elf. The Sisters bring redemption and retribution."

Sloane hadn't expected that turn. "Wait... Vengeance? That came out of nowhere."

Maud nodded solemnly. "Tenera's Father realizes that true justice may not always be possible in its purest form. Therefore, he charged his Daughter with ensuring those who have been wronged in the worst ways are guided toward their righteous vengeance—their retribution. So that they may do so with purpose and maintain their honor."

"Finally, we have the Stars, the minor gods. There are nine of them, and not all are equal, however, perhaps we can discuss them at another time? I do not wish to overwhelm you." Maud said considerately.

Sloane appreciated the thought. "Thank you for all the knowledge, Ser Maud. This will help me immensely. Now... could you explain some of the cultural faux pas I should be aware of?"

Maud smiled. "Of course! I'd be happy to help you. First, let's start with verbal and nonverbal communication."

Sloane had to force herself to not cringe, realizing she may have inadvertently asked for more than she had intended. She resolved to sit through her instruction and learn; it would only help her in the end.

The next day, Sloane was sitting up front with Ernald when Ismeld, who had been riding ahead, came rushing back. "Maud! You are needed!" she called out.

Gisele looked at her. "What happened?"

Maud jumped down and hurried to the group from the back of the wagon where she had been sitting. "There's a wounded merchant ahead," Ismeld explained. "He's been walking for hours—he was part of the caravan that was attacked. He's not going to make it to the next village."

Gisele looked at Maud and made a decision. "Deryk, give Maud your horse. Maud, take Sloane. She may be able to help you with any of the magic."

Sloane and Maud looked at each other, nodding, then she hopped off the wagon and hastened to the horse that Deryk was holding for Maud. Maud climbed up and Deryk assisted Sloane on behind the knight-medic.

Maud turned her head to try and peek behind her at Sloane. "You ready?"

"Ready."

Ismeld nodded. "Follow me." She instantly spurred her horse forward, galloping back the way she had come. Maud rushed to stay close while Sloane gripped Maud tightly, not used to riding a horse at such speeds.

Soon enough, they came upon an armored sun elf crouched next to a male telv, who was sitting against a tree. It was clear that the telv was not in a good shape. The elf was pressing his hands against the other man, applying pressure to what Sloane could only assume was a stab wound. The guard looked up as they approached.

"You've returned. Thank you, milady. Please, help Master Raolin."

Maud handed her bridle straps to Ismeld. She jumped down from the horse, pulled out her mace, and rushed to the wounded merchant.

Sloane took a bit longer to get down, but as she walked over, she looked at Maud, who had taken over from the guard. "What can I do?"

Maud looked up at her. "This will be confusing. Please take—" She stopped and then turned her attention to the guard, who glanced between the telv and Sloane. He hurriedly introduced himself.

"I'm Averet, milady. What can I do?"

"Go with Lady Reinhart. I need some space, but I will save your employer," Maud stated with conviction.

Averet nodded hesitantly and looked at Sloane with a worried expression. She gestured to him and then to an area a few meters away. "Come, let's allow her to work."

Giving Maud the space she needed, Averet pressed. "What is she going to do?"

Sloane looked back at Maud. "You are about to see something that is, frankly, miraculous. Please do not interrupt Ser Maud after she begins, no matter what you see."

Averet seemed to become concerned. "But, that doesn't really—"

"Wait. She's starting. Watch," Sloane interrupted.

They watched as Maud, holding her mace in her right hand, held her left over the wound. Much quicker than she had demonstrated before, her hand took on the soft green glow that Sloane was coming to associate with, at the very least, life magic. After a few seconds, the area surrounding the wound was lit up with that same green before it flashed brightly. Maud lowered her hand and slumped slightly. Determined, she started examining the wound.

Sloane gestured to Averet. "Come, let's see if she needs further assistance."

Maud looked up, a proud but tired look on her face. "I did it, Sloane. The wound is closed. I felt around, and it seems as if inside was also healed."

Raolin was looking down at the hole in his tunic, which showed nothing but smooth, healed flesh. He looked up at Averet, who had tears in his eyes as he dropped to his knees next to the telv.

"You're okay!" Averet said. He looked at Maud. "Praise Eona. You performed a miracle, milady!"

"Eona provides," said Raolin. "Milady, you have my undying gratitude. I would have died if not for you. I owe you a debt."

Maud bowed her head. "Eona provides. I simply did as any healer should," she said. "Please, take it easy. Our wagon will be here soon. You should not try to walk to the next village on foot. Allow us to escort you."

The merchant guard scanned the group before him. "You knights are as honorable as I had imagined," he said. He turned to Raolin. "My friend, I believe we should accept their offer. You still need rest."

Sloane gave Maud a reassuring shoulder squeeze. "You're doing an excellent job, Maud. You didn't even need me here."

Maud turned to Sloane and placed her hand atop hers, squeezing it gently as she looked into her eyes. "Maybe, but having you here while I do all of this helps me remain calm. Your confidence rubs off on me, and then I know I can do it."

It wasn't long before Gisele and the others caught up with them. After getting the merchant and his guard set up inside the wagon, they continued their journey. Maud sat with them to keep an eye on her first true patient. Gisele had given her horse to Ernald and was driving the wagon, sitting next to Sloane.

"Maud's ability is improving. Others will hear about it, and they'll come to her," the orkun woman said.

Sloane nodded. "Maybe. At least, at first. I believe we all have the potential to learn magic. Maud simply has a strong affinity for what I am currently calling the life element. I feel like I'm getting closer and closer to connecting with my mana too."

Gisele looked surprised. "You are? That's very good, Sloane. I shall work on it myself, then, if you truly believe any of us can learn it."

"I do. If Ernald and I are correct, we all should have a new organ that connects us to the mana. We simply need to learn how to utilize it. What I've been trying to do is meditate whenever I can, trying to feel the mana around us and connect with it. I'm learning, though. I could be wrong," she explained.

"We will soon reach the village of Tunstead," Gisele announced. "We need to inform them about the bandit attack and seek their assistance for our two new companions. Additionally, we can inquire if there is any news regarding the arrival of your people. However, I suggest that you wear your cloak with the hood up as we enter the village, to avoid drawing unnecessary attention."

A few minutes later, Sloane noticed Gisele had a far-off look on her face. The knight-captain sighed, leaning back against the bench they sat on, deep in contemplation. She seemed almost weary.

"The world really is changing isn't it, Sloane? It seems... that you may be one to heed if others want to stay at the forefront of everything that is happening. I look forward to the possibility of gaining my own magic for both my people and myself... but I also am curious in observing your progress."

Sloane simply nodded in agreement as she sat there, daydreaming about all the magic she could potentially learn.

She wondered if Gwyn would also learn to utilize all of the mana surrounding them.

CHAPTER TEN

INCOGNITO

The arrival of the Displaced threw everything into uncertainty. The new people seemed similar enough, in that they were not much different than the telv. However, their very existence and connection with the Flash shook the people of Eona to their core. These people were not welcomed with open arms. They were met with uncertainty and confusion. As time passed and knowledge of the Displaced spread, that uncertainty turned to curiosity and, in some cases, greed.

These new people represented opportunities, and some sought to exploit these scattered individuals. Those with more forethought took advantage of these opportunities to mutually rise in influence and power.

The Displaced, A History. 241 SA

Hilshen was a fairly large village, as far as such things went. Which meant that it was smaller than any place Gwyn had been to. No towns in Italy had looked like... this. There weren't even paved roads. The buildings were all made of wood or stone and had a roof that looked like the ones she remembered seeing in England. Tach? *Thatch.* That's it.

It was early in the evening and the sun was starting to go down. If she had to guess, it was nearly dinner time.

Gwyn noticed that there weren't many people out and about in the village, but those she did see were lively. They came to watch as Mister Onas's wagon made its way toward the center of the village, where a large building sat.

It looked to Gwyn like a really big two-story house with an attic, but there was a small sign over the little covered entrance. A store? The bottom floor was made of stone, while the top was made of wood. There were a few tiny windows on the second floor, each with a pot of plants outside of them. Overall, the place looked really nice compared to the rest of the town. In fact, it was the only place that had shingles. They looked poorly made and were wood instead of what she was used to, but the roof wasn't made of straw. Which was a plus.

Gwyn glanced up at Mister Raafe, who was driving the wagon currently. "What is this place, Mister Raafe?" she asked.

The man pulled on the reins and slowed the wagon to a stop. "This is the Traveler's Inn. It brings most of the coin to this little village. It was built by the local lord specifically to entice traveling merchants and people to stop here," the sun elf explained.

"Oh. That's interesting."

Mister Onas stepped into view on the ground next to her. He must have heard their conversation, because the high elf man had more information.

"The lord is hoping to entice more people to move and build here. By building this inn, he's basically planting the foundation for the village to eventually grow into a town. We will set up the wagon here and allow the villagers to come see our wares," the merchant said.

Raafe glanced down at her. "That's my cue to help the boss, Your Highness. I have to take the horses to the inn's stable for the night."

Gwyn perked up. Seeing where the horses would stay sounded really fun! She opened her mouth to say so, but then Miss Taenya called her name. Or rather, she called out, "Princess Gwyn!" Gwyn thought it was funny. They were treating her like someone important, and she had to say, it felt really cool.

She waved to Raafe, hopped down from the wagon, and rushed over to Miss Taenya, who was grabbing a few things. The two of them made their way, and Gwyn got her first look at the inside.

The ceilings were low. No one stood behind the counter. As Miss Taenya walked up to the desk and called out, Gwyn heard people talking through the entryway to her left. She stuck her head through the doorway and looked into the next room.

It was a decent-sized open area with three long tables and benches that stretched the same length. A large fireplace was centered in the wall. A big pot hung inside, a fire burning underneath it.

Gwyn was mildly surprised by the number of customers in the room. There were at least fifteen people in there, including some kids! As she looked around, she saw that almost everyone was either a telv like Miss Taenya or a high elf like Mister Onas and Mister Keston.

Gwyn stepped in, and it wasn't long before one of the kids noticed her. The boy said something to who she thought was his mom and pointed at her. Gwyn smiled and waved, and the room went silent as everyone turned and looked at her. She hesitated. The attention made her feel uncomfortable. Quiet whispers broke out.

"You poor girl. What happened to yer ears?"

Gwyn turned and gasped.

A woman stood there, about the same height as Gwyn but with a broader build. She had light brown hair in a long braid, and piercing brown eyes. There were beads intertwined with her hair, which Gwyn thought looked really pretty, and she had more stitched into the top of her dress. That looked… really itchy. It was a flowy green top with a brown vest. The woman's billowy white skirt looked like the same material some curtains were made of. A small satchel sat at her waist, where Gwyn noticed a small knife was also strapped.

Gwyn instantly knew what she was from all of the movies she and her mom watched.

"You're a dwarf!" she said.

The woman's eyes narrowed and her broad nostrils flared. She did not seem amused. "Never seen a dwarf before? Don't ye think it's rude to say it like that?"

Gwyn straightened and narrowed her eyes right back. "Don't you think it's rude to point out my ears? I will have you know that my ears are perfectly fine. They're cute."

She may have snapped a bit, but that made her mad! How could that woman say something about her and not expect Gwyn to say anything in response?

The woman huffed and crossed her arms. "I suppose ye got a point there, girl. Now, what can I do for ye?"

Gwyn was still on edge and ready for a fight, but she shrugged. "I think we are trying to get a few rooms for tonight?"

"Ah, your parents are at the counter, then? Why di'n't ye say so?"

Without another word, the woman stepped past Gwyn and headed toward the front, nearly barreling her over and forcing her to quickly move to the side. Giving the room one last glance, Gwyn followed the dwarf woman to where Taenya stood patiently.

The telv guard frowned slightly as she saw Gwyn with the woman, but she did not comment.

The dwarf huffed as she walked around the counter. "Yer daughter took after her father, then? Poor thing. Yer pretty enough."

Gwyn's brows shot up. She was pretty sure the woman had just called her ugly.

"You're really rude," Gwyn stated. She felt something inside of her moving about. Anger?

The woman scowled. "I don't like children. Especially ones who do not show proper respect."

"Maybe you'd get more respect if you were nicer and not a jerk," Gwyn snapped back.

Miss Taenya lifted her hand. "Please, Your—Gwyn, Miss. First, this is not my daughter. Second, if you insult her again, we will have issues. Understood?"

The woman scoffed, but then Taenya's voice lowered dangerously. "I asked you a question."

A thickness seemed to fill the air, and the woman nodded slowly. She reached under the counter and pulled out a big book. "Fine. How many rooms?"

Gwyn felt satisfaction fill her as Miss Taenya quickly put the mean woman in her place. *I knew I was a great judge of character. Miss Taenya's awesome.*

"Three," Miss Taenya informed her.

The dwarf opened the book and flipped to a page near the front third. She wrote things down as she asked Miss Taenya questions. Finally, the woman handed over keys and gave directions to their rooms. Gwyn would share a room with the telv guard.

As they walked away, Gwyn heard the dwarf woman mumbling insults about her. Her blood boiled. *Adults should be more mature. That woman is a bi—*

She glanced around to make sure she hadn't accidentally said anything out loud. Ms. Taenya raised a brow at her frantic movements, but nothing else. Gwyn let out a sigh of relief. *Mom would get me in trouble so fast if I cursed.*

Her heart fell when she remembered that she had no idea where her mom was.

The princess was with Onas as he showed off his wares out of his wagon. Keston and Raafe had helped convert the wagon into a small stall suitable for any market—not that the village had one. The merchant had wanted to get started right away, at least while daylight remained.

Taenya walked back inside the inn. The sound of a lute playing reached out from the tavern. The dwarf woman stood at the counter working on the inn's ledger in silence.

Choosing not to interrupt the woman, Taenya decided to try and secure food for the others.

The dwarf woman cleared her throat before Taenya made it three steps toward the tavern area.

"The girl isn't a telv, is she?"

Taenya paused. She slowly turned toward the too-curious woman and tilted her head. "Why would you think that?"

The woman narrowed her eyes. "I can tell she's different, lass. I know what it is like to be different within the kingdom. Where are her parents? She said her ears were normal. Only dwarves have ears like that. She isn't one of my people. That's clear enough..."

Taenya breathed deeply. She wasn't sure why the woman was so stuck on it.

Was it just curiosity? It made her wary. Her hand instinctively fell to her waist where her sword lay. "Why are you so curious? This is more than passing interest at this point."

The woman closed the book and pointed toward the tavern. "It's all anyone can talk about, lass. That blue flash that made everyone in the village pass out, then your merchant arrives with a girl wearing strange clothing, hair touched with an unnatural pink. The most vibrant blue eyes I have ever seen. And round ears. I've heard the way she talks and the way your merchant speaks to her. I heard him call her princess. I don't want to see trouble in Hilshen. Are you bringing trouble to our village?"

Taenya would need to tell the others to be careful about how they addressed the princess in public. Gwyn's best protection right now was her anonymity. Taenya wasn't sure how much she should say to the woman, so she decided to simply be vague and reassuring.

She sighed. "We aren't bringing trouble. We were all affected by the Flash as well. The girl more than most. There won't be any trouble from us," she reassured the woman.

"That tells me next to nothing. I can respect yer privacy, lass, but something tells me that your companions, at least, are completely out of their depth. You seem to have a bit of sense about you, so let me give you a piece of advice… Fix her appearance."

"I do not—"

"Lass. She stands out like a sore thumb. If you want to keep her… status hidden—which I can respect—you need to make her seem more…" she shook her head side to side, "normal."

That got Taenya thinking. What could they do to help keep the princess safe? It clicked. They needed new clothes, and to cut her hair—at least the ends. That was the easiest thing. The logical thing.

The realization must have been plastered on her face, because the innkeeper smirked. "Had an epiphany did ye? Good. I already spoke to some of the other women. Now, we aren't like those fancy towns with their clothiers—we still make our clothing ourselves. We have a seamstress who did move here from the town, though. The lord gifted her with cloth so that she could make his people clothing every now and then. She will sell enough to make two dresses for the girl. It will take a few days."

That was not ideal. Onas did not want to stay more than a day or two here; there were only a couple hundred villagers, and those who wanted to purchase anything would get what they could either by that night or the next morning. But she could probably convince him.

He seemed to be coming up with some sort of plan regarding Gwyn. She just hoped he did not let his ambitions get the better of him. She laughed internally.

Not that his wife would let him. She couldn't wait to see the woman again. Being back in Strathmore would be a relief.

While Taenya was lost in thought, the dwarf nodded. "We'll cut the girl's hair here. Get rid of that pink. Not much else to do except have her wear it down."

That brought Taenya back to the present. She stared at the woman with a confused expression. "Why are you offering to help?" she asked.

The woman sniffed. "We're not doing it for free, lass."

There it was. She knew that Gwyn was a princess and wanted to milk them for all the coin she could. Taenya couldn't help but sigh. It solidified the fact that they needed to have Gwyn travel incognito.

"Fine. I'll grab her and smooth it over with Onas. Then we can get started."

The woman nodded and Taenya made her way outside.

Onas shouldn't mind spending a bit of coin. After all, he always told me, you have to spend money to make money.

She just had no idea how they would make money from helping Gwyn. Perhaps that was what had the man lost in thought so much.

The next day, Gwyn walked with Miss Taenya through the village. The dwarf woman had apparently given the telv directions to a seamstress who had retired to the village. On the outskirts, they finally found a small cottage surrounded by a small wooden fence.

Miss Taenya knocked on the door and an old elf woman appeared. She barely took one look at the two of them before gesturing for them to come inside. As they walked in, Miss Taenya introduced them and discussed their need to have some dresses made. The woman nodded and looked Gwyn over before saying she had enough for two dresses.

Gwyn, however, frowned.

She hated dresses.

What surprised Gwyn was that Miss Taenya did not mention anything about Gwyn being a princess, as the others had been doing.

The seamstress had kind eyes and a gentle smile. When Miss Taenya requested the two dresses for Gwyn, the woman was more than happy to help. She led them through her cottage and showed them the materials she had.

Gwyn was surprised to see how simple the materials were compared to what she knew, just as Miss Taenya had informed her on the walk over. Then, the woman pulled out blue and gray bolts of fine linen that she had been given by the local lord.

Gwyn smiled. Blue was her favorite color, so at least the dresses had that going for them. She would have been miserable otherwise.

Okay, let's be honest. I'll just be slightly *less miserable.*

She was hesitant at first, but the woman put her at ease, assuring her that the dresses would be beautiful and fit her perfectly. The woman, who had introduced herself as Marris, made Gwyn feel safe and comfortable. She even felt a little eager to see what the dresses would look like. Marris measured her, took note of her preferences, and went to work.

While Marris worked on the dresses, Gwyn and Taenya explored the village. They met many friendly villagers and even visited a few people who had set up tables in front of their homes to sell various items. They bought sweets. Gwyn was having the time of her life, despite the fact that she was still far away from home and her mother.

By the end of the day, much to Miss Taenya's surprise, Marris had finished the two dresses. Gwyn was excited to try them on. When she saw herself in the simple mirror, even though it wasn't quite clear, she was speechless. The dresses were beautiful, just as Marris had promised. They were simple yet elegant, and they fit her perfectly. The one she liked best was dark blue but had a pattern of gray stitching along the edges that looked like interlocking circles. The sleeves were fitted but then billowed out at her wrists so that she could hide her hands if she wanted to. Down the middle of the skirt, the blue material split to reveal a triangle of gray underneath that reached the bottom of the dress.

Gwyn twirled around, feeling like a real princess.

Miss Taenya was also impressed with the dresses and thanked Marris for her hard work. She offered to pay her extra for her speed, but Marris refused, saying that the joy on Gwyn's face was enough. Gwyn hugged Marris, thanking her for the beautiful dresses, and promised to never forget her kindness.

As they made their way back to the inn, Gwyn felt more confident and ready to face any challenges that lay ahead. She was grateful for the new dresses and the wonderful experience she had that day in the village.

When they returned, Mister Onas was speaking with several villagers as they looked over the wares in his wagon. The side of the wagon had a big window in it, and it was opened with the shutters spread wide. They did not want to interrupt, so they continued toward the inn.

Gwyn was feeling nervous and excited as she walked into the inn with Taenya. She was about to get her hair trimmed by another dwarf woman, who was apparently known for her skill with hair. The rude innkeeper had arranged for the appointment and Gwyn was curious as to why the woman was being helpful. When asked, Miss Taenya just grunted.

They walked to a room at the end of the hall on the second floor.

The dwarf woman, whose name was Dori, was seated at a table in the corner of the room. Dori had curly gray hair that was styled in a short bob, and a friendly smile. She welcomed Gwyn and Miss Taenya with a nod of her head.

"Hello, little one," Dori said in a gruff voice. "I hear you want a trim."

Gwyn nodded eagerly. Miss Taenya had already explained that the pink in her hair made her stand out too much, so they needed to cut it off. Gwyn could understand that.

"Yes, please."

Dori gestured for Gwyn to sit in a chair in front of her. "Let's have a look."

Gwyn sat and Dori took hold of a strand of her curly hair. "Your hair is lovely," she said, examining it. "But it's a bit of a mess. What do you think about cutting it to just below your shoulders and letting your beautiful curls stand out?"

Gwyn smiled. "That sounds perfect."

Dori brought up some of her pink tips so Gwyn could see. "This pink is gorgeous and vibrant, but I can understand the need to not want to draw attention to yourself."

That got a look from Miss Taenya, but the dwarf woman just gave the telv a wink. "I heard about your little tiff with my daughter downstairs. Don't mind her, she's just a tad overprotective of this here village."

Miss Taenya chuckled and relaxed. "Thank you for helping us, Miss Dori."

The woman waved her off. "Think nothing of it. This wee girl is beautiful, and she deserves to be reminded of it with a proper hairstyle."

Gwyn smiled.

Dori gathered her hair tools, which looked somewhat like the things Gwyn was used to, and started working. She told Gwyn about the village and the people in it. She spoke of the dwarven city she was from, which was where she had obtained the tools she used. Gwyn was fascinated by the stories and soon forgot about her nervousness. She was surprised by how gentle the dwarven woman was in removing her tangles.

When Dori finished cutting, she braided Gwyn's hair and then held up a mirror so she could see the results. Gwyn gasped with delight. Her dark brown hair was beautiful. Her natural curls were no longer frizzy and a mess of tangles, but soft. Braids were woven throughout to just below her shoulders as pretty accents. Dori had tied her hair loosely at the base of her neck and drew it together in a way that covered the tops of her ears.

Gwyn was somewhat sad about the pink highlights that she had only recently gotten done with her mom, but maybe one day she could get more.

"It's beautiful," she said, admiring her reflection in the cloudy mirror.

"I'm glad you like it," Dori said, putting away her tools. "It suits you."

Gwyn turned around to face Dori and gave her a big hug. "Thank you so much."

Dori hugged her back and let out a breathy chuckle. "You're welcome, little one."

Gwyn and Miss Taenya headed back downstairs to eat. Gwyn was excited to show Onas and the guards her new hair and dress. And she couldn't wait to show her mom when they found her.

As they sat down at one of the long tables, Gwyn reflected on her day and how Marris and Dori had been so helpful and nice. It made her realize one thing: old women were just as kind here as they were back in Italy.

She smiled.

CHAPTER ELEVEN

INQUIRIES

Raafe walked into the inn behind Onas and Keston. The day had gone well enough, but the high elf merchant hadn't sold as much as he'd wished. It seemed as though they would need to leave soon. Which was unfortunate. Raafe wanted to ask around the village for Gwyn's mother, Sloane.

The young princess was a genuinely happy and nice girl. He didn't wish what had happened to her on anyone. From what she had told them, her world was much different. Safer.

But maybe that safety was an illusion. Raafe knew that the young often had a very narrow view of the world around them. Her own situation may have been filled with comfort and safety, but it did not mean everything was. He knew how people could be. He'd seen how quickly the girl had taken to them. How easily she'd put her trust in them.

Onas Fenren was a good man. Perhaps a bit too focused on his business for Raafe's tastes, but he had faith he'd do right by the girl.

That said, the girl needed someone at her side. Someone who—

Actually...

"Boss, I will catch up. I'm going to do some looking around," he told the older man. He would also do right by the girl. It was the least he could do for her. There was ample time to ask around. See if anyone had seen any other humans like her.

The high elf turned around and gave him an inquisitive look but nodded. "We will be here eating with the pri—Gwyn." The merchant caught himself. Taenya had told them to be careful about how they spoke about the princess in public. Raafe found himself agreeing. There was no telling what spreading that knowledge would do. Especially if it got back to a noble of any sufficient standing.

They did not want that.

Raafe had intimate knowledge of the predations of nobles. It was one reason he had sought this job. His family had been targeted by a middle noble and it had driven them into debt. So much so that when the noble had bought out their debt, they'd been forced to become his servants to pay it off. They were then relocated to the capital to live at the noble's small manor there.

His poor sister had been forced into becoming the personal servant of the lord's young daughter. His brother, a stable hand. It made Raafe so angry, especially since there was nothing he could do about it. A family who had been in good standing and respected had their entire world turned upside down in a short amount of time. Raafe's hand gravitated toward his sword—his grandfather's legacy. His grandfather had been a brilliant cavalryman in the duchy's service. He'd passed away when Raafe was young, but it had always been his desire to see his grandson trained in its use.

And that was what Raafe had done. He'd been admitted to the Guard's Guild and given the opportunity to be trained. Guards who completed training with the guild were selected to join houses and cities regularly. He'd wanted to join the Strathmore City Guard. A respectable position that may have one day seen him join the ranks of a cavalry, like his grandfather.

In fact, that was the only reason he'd avoided joining his family. By the time they'd lost everything, he'd already left home and was on his way to create a new life for himself in Strathmore. Learning about what had happened to them forced him to do whatever he could to help them.

He'd tried to go to the duke, which ended in a misstep on his part. He'd argued with the wrong person and never even got the opportunity to meet the man. It ruined his chances of joining the City Guard. Which led him to take a job with Onas Fenren: a man who paid his guards well and was surprisingly supportive of his people. Raafe would save up to help his family.

He glanced at Keston. The high elf was all smiles. Constantly in a good mood, he loved to joke and banter with Raafe and the others. And he loved to cook. Something the man shared with the young princess. Those Raafe worked with were good people, but he was still new to the group. It wasn't the time to unload all of his issues on them yet.

Yes, he knew the dark side of the nobility. And Onas and the others did not need that sort of attention. *And neither does Gwyn. I need to protect her from that.* He would help his family in time. For now, he needed to help a young princess stay away from the evils of his world. She needed her mother, and she needed a guardian.

"Got it, boss. Be back soon," he promised.

Walking back outside, Raafe remembered seeing several other people setting up tables in front of their homes. Like most villages, Hilshen did not have shops or stores. The people sold their goods directly from home. The inn was the exception.

Onas had said that he believed the village would eventually grow into a town. The merchant had an eye for these things, so Raafe had no reason to not believe him.

Several people had started to pack up their things. He approached a telv woman who was putting away some knitted items into a basket.

"Pardon me..." he started.

She looked up at him and gave him a once-over. She swept her dirty-blond hair out of her eyes and placed the basket on the table. "Yes? Can I help you?" she asked.

"I was curious, have you seen many other travelers in the past few days? Since the Flash, that is?" he inquired.

The woman crossed her arms and looked up in thought. Her lips pursed for a moment but then she nodded her head. "Yeah, there was a group of folks that came through. Happened to be the same day the lord was checking on the village after the Flash."

He nodded. "Were they Loreni? Telv?"

The woman shrugged. "Some telv, some high elves. One moment..." She turned and yelled at a man across the street. "Oi! Remember them travelers what came through after that flash of light that had us all on our arses?"

The old telv man started walking over. "Yeah? What of 'em?" He glanced at Raafe. "Friends of yers?"

Raafe shook his head. "No—"

The woman continued, "What happened to 'em?"

The man tilted his head. "The lord invited 'em to the castle. They didn't come back through after leaving, or maybe they're still there. I dunno."

That caught Raafe's attention. He had forgotten about the local lord. While he would prefer to avoid him, if a human queen was passing through, surely she would meet him.

"There were telv, though? Do you know that for certain? Do you recall any identifiable things about them? Maybe weird ears?" Raafe asked the two of them.

The woman glanced at the old man, who shrugged. "Weird ears?" said the man. "Nah, lad. I don't recall any abnormalities about 'em. But I didn't talk to 'em. They didn't even stop by the inn before the lord whisked 'em away."

Raafe nodded. "Thank you. I appreciate your information," he said.

"That merchant sell anything worth a damn at a decent price?" the woman asked.

That made Raafe chuckle. Villagers like this were usually reluctant to trust merchants for all that they needed them.

"He has a few items. Most of our space is taken up by a shipment to Larton, but he reserves some crates for villages just like this one. Onas Fenren is a good man. He's not one to take advantage of people," he explained.

The old man grunted. "Fenren. I recall him from last year. I'd say he's a decent fellow." He glanced at the woman. "He's the merchant that comes through every year round this time. They're from the city."

"The city? Yer from Strathmore?" the woman asked.

Raafe nodded. "Yes. This is the annual route that Mister Fenren does. Apparently, it's the route that helped him get his start. He enjoys it."

The two villagers nodded.

"You say the Flash knocked everyone on their arse. Other than the travelers, has anything else of note happened?"

The man shook his head. "Not that I can rightly remember, lad. The lord got here quick enough. Good man, that. I can appreciate a lord who reacts to an event with haste."

Raafe grunted. "Rare. However, it is his duty," he said.

The woman chuckled. "Right you are. Usually, he doesn't get off his arse for anything. I was surprised to see him."

The old man huffed indignantly. "Now, the lord—"

The two villagers started debating the usefulness of their lord. Using that as an excuse to leave, Raafe thanked them for their help and made his way back to the inn. He needed to see if Onas would be willing to meet with the lord. From a distance, especially with her hair down, Gwyn did not appear to be anything other than a telv. Even close up, you could say she just had some weird ears. The thought that she could be from an entirely new people was not something that would cross most people's minds.

As he walked back, he paused by the village's shrine to the Family and said a quick prayer to Alos. The girl needed protection. Every little bit would help.

When he was young, Raafe always dreamed of becoming one of the Paladins of Alos. While he knew he would never be good enough to be one of those vaunted warriors, he would do all he could to protect the young princess.

After all, she did not deserve to be a target of the evil this world could produce.

He only hoped he could shield her from it for as long as possible.

The table where Gwyn and the others sat lay filled with various plates of food. Fish that still had the head was the centerpiece of the main course. Pieces of bread, cheeses, roasted vegetables, and a colorful mixture of small potato-like things were also present. Each of them picked at their food with a very basic set of iron forks and knives.

Raafe had joined them just before it was all brought to the table. The sun elf, with his dark skin and fiery eyes, seemed to be lost in concentration. His gold piercings along his lobes made him look every bit the part of a swashbuckler. If it wasn't for his professional-looking equipment, Gwyn would have thought he was one. His sword was curved and fancy, just like she thought one should have. It was a pretty thing.

Yet, even Gwyn's prodding didn't yank him from his thoughts. When Miss Taenya had asked him what was on his mind, he simply requested to discuss it in private.

Gwyn knew that the man was really nice, so whatever it was, it was serious. She'd resolved to try and be as nice in return to all of them. After all, they were helping her. If they liked her, they would be more willing to look for her mom.

I'm just a kid. It's hard to make them want to stay and help me. Got to act the part. I can do this.

Onas and Keston had complimented her look, and Onas said that the dress was exceptionally well made. He commented that he might want to talk to Miss Marris the next day.

"Gwyn, I will speak to the innkeeper after dinner about paying for a bath. Will you need assistance?" Miss Taenya asked.

She shook her head. "No, Miss Taenya. I am perfectly fine taking my own bath," she said as seriously as she could. *Help me take a bath? What am I, a toddler?*

The woman looked down at the table in thought. She squinted her eyes and looked back up at Gwyn. "Please, just call me Taenya. I think I speak for all of us when I say that."

The others nodded their agreement. Gwyn told them she'd try. Her mom and her *maestra di scuola* had always lectured about the importance of showing proper respect to adults. Well, her mom had always said to show it to everyone until they displayed a reason they didn't deserve it... so... same-same.

"Gwyn, could you describe your mother again for me?" Raafe asked.

Gwyn smiled. If the man's thoughts were focused on her mom, then that meant that he was trying to help her. *He really is a good guy.*

"Sure, Raafe!" she said and launched into every detail she could remember. The man pulled out a small piece of torn parchment and started writing on it with what looked like a piece of dark gray rock wrapped in rope. Almost like the stuff in a pencil?

She shrugged and kept going.

Gwyn remembered crying after thinking she'd started to forget what her mom looked like. It had been gut-wrenching. It made her feel like such a failure of a daughter. What kind of daughter was she if she couldn't even remember what her mom looked like after such a short time?

But now, she realized it was just nerves. After last time, she'd made sure to wrack her mind about it. Focusing really hard had helped. It was like something clicked in her head, and almost like magic, she could do it. It seemed all Gwyn had to do was use the thing in her mind that sang and helped her [Focus] and everything became clearer. The excitement at recalling the memory of the two of them walking down the sidewalk after school gave her such a rush. It felt like a burst of energy filling her, and it made her happy.

The rest of dinner went by fairly quickly. Gwyn joked a little with Keston and Raafe—whose mood had returned from the land of seriousness—and eventually, the men left to return to their rooms. Soon after, Taenya paid the dwarf innkeeper to help them set up a bath.

Gwyn didn't know what she was expecting, but it certainly wasn't the woman having two telv men carry up a big wooden bathtub to her room and set it up in the corner, then put up a wooden divider. She found herself in a very awkward situation.

"Gwyn, are you sure you're alright over there?"

Her teeth chattered. "Y-y-yes. I-I am f-f-fine!" she ground out as she continued to try and wash herself with the rough soap. The water had not stayed warm very long at all, and she couldn't just turn on a faucet for more. She had been so silly. She had begun to think everything here was fun and cool. But now the stark differences between their two societies slapped her right in the face.

Like jumping into a cold pool in the spring. Mom was so mad at me.

"Do you need help?" Taenya asked again.

Gwyn glanced at the towel, which did not look warm or comfy at all, that was draped over the divider.

"P-p-please. I'm s-so c-c-cold."

Taenya chuckled as she grabbed the towel and appeared. "Come on, dear. Let's get you dried off and warm."

Any embarrassing thoughts were a thing of the past as Gwyn rushed out of the bath and to the towel.

Taenya groaned and rolled over as a knock sounded on the door. She waited, hoping whoever it was would leave. Another knock killed any hope of going back to sleep.

"I'm coming…" she called out in a hoarse whisper as she sat up. She glanced around the dim room and saw that Gwyn was still passed out. Taenya grabbed her knife as she walked over.

She paused, swapping the blade to her other hand behind her, then unlatched the door. Opening it revealed Keston. The high elf was dressed and seemed ready to leave.

Taenya narrowed her eyes. "Why are you fully clothed?" Immediately, she winced. That had come out poorly.

Keston chuckled. "I will let that one slide out of a desire to live a healthy life. Boss had a messenger a bit ago. After the man left, he wanted me to wake you. The local lord has inquired as to whether Onas could meet over breakfast at his castle."

Taenya took a deep breath. That hadn't been part of the plan. She and Onas had discussed leaving. The merchant was ready to make for Larton. Clearly, he was planning something, and she had resolved to get to the bottom of it that day. She figured it had something to do with Lord Iemes. The man was a partner and friend of Onas. If there were machinations brewing in the high elf merchant's head, it likely involved that man.

Taenya sighed. "I thought Onas wanted to leave this morning."

Keston shrugged. "I just do what I'm told, boss. Is the pr—Gwyn still asleep?"

"Of course she is. Everyone should still be asleep," she stated.

The man chuckled. "It's not that early. There are people downstairs already."

She groaned again. "Fine. Let me get her up and ready. We'll be down soon."

Waking Gwyn up proved to be more difficult than she could have imagined. The girl slept like the dead. Then, when she got up and Taenya spoke of needing to hurry, the girl almost panicked. She said some words in that other language of hers and started rushing. Taenya had to tell her to slow down and relax. Clearly, the girl needed a bit more time to wake up and get ready in the mornings. She could only imagine what it must have been like for the girl's mother and servants in her world.

When Gwyn could get ready on her own, Taenya also started pulling on her gear. Even with all the armor, straps, and weapons, she still finished before the girl. Gwyn was struggling to tame her hair. She kept complaining about it and was definitely swearing in another language. She seemed to be on the verge of tears as she kept trying and failing to put her hair up into a simple ponytail. Her dark curly hair was a frizzy mess. It was everywhere, even sticking straight up.

Taenya had been doing her hair since even before Gwyn's age. It was like the girl could barely function in the mornings. She did not know how to even approach the subject with her. Her job as the head guard and just traveling would be much more difficult if she had to take so much time to care for the princess. It was a bit frustrating.

I have no idea how to fill the role of a caregiver, let alone a mother.

Gwyn sniffled.

Taenya sighed. "Gwyn, come here. Let me help you with your hair," she said.

The human moved to stand in front of her while Taenya sat on the bed. Grabbing her brush from the table, she lifted it up, only for Gwyn to jerk away.

"Wait! My mom has a special brush so my curls aren't ruined," the girl said frantically.

Taenya raised an eyebrow. "Gwyn, I'm telv. Most of my people have curly hair just like yours. Our brushes are made to help with that. Plus, you can't ruin those curls much more than they already are. Come here, let me help you. This is a knotted mess," she said, shaking her head.

Gwyn sniffled again before mumbling under her breath, "It's just wild and free…"

Taenya sighed and started brushing Gwyn's unruly hair. *Definitely should have braided it before sleeping. Clearly, she is accustomed to more assistance than I was.*

Gwyn flinched at first but soon relaxed under Taenya's touch. The telv worked the brush through the tangles and knots, trying to be as gentle as possible. She could tell that the simple act of brushing her hair was having a calming effect on the girl. She was no longer sniffling and her breathing had slowed. After a few minutes, Gwyn's hair was finally pulled back and tamed, looking much more presentable. Taenya quickly worked it into a single braid and tied a piece of ribbon around the end.

"There, all done," she said, giving the knot one final tug to ensure it stayed tight. "You have beautiful hair, Gwyn. It's just a bit difficult to manage in the mornings."

Gwyn looked at Taenya with a small smile. "Thank you, Taenya. I really appreciate it." Her smile wavered. "I don't know what I'd do without you."

Taenya's heart softened as she smiled back. "You're welcome. Now, let's finish getting ready for the day ahead. We have to meet the local lord."

Despite her initial frustration, Taenya felt a sense of satisfaction and accomplishment in helping Gwyn with her hair. She realized this journey involved more than her being the head guard; she was also a support system for Gwyn, helping her through the challenges she faced.

When they resumed that journey, Taenya would make sure to be patient and understanding with Gwyn, helping her through the difficulties and being there for her whenever she needed it. And she was grateful for the opportunity to play this role in the young princess's life.

The girl had been through so much. The least Taenya could do was help Gwyn feel safe and comfortable in an entirely new world.

CHAPTER TWELVE

A NOBLE INTRODUCTION

Gwyn and the others were on their way to meet the local lord, and that man was apparently a knight. According to Mister Onas, if a landed knight was given authority over an area, that made him a lord in duty. It didn't make him a lord anywhere else but upon his land. When Gwyn had expressed her confusion, Taenya explained that it was similar to how someone could be a captain of a ship, but not necessarily have the rank of captain in a nation's navy.

It sort of made sense.

At first, the thought of the knight had made Gwyn excited, as she'd never met one before. Meeting an elf knight? That sounded pretty cool. But when she laid eyes on the "castle" that the man lived in, she was pretty bummed.

Hilshen Castle was only such in name. It was basically a tall stone building with a tower and, funnily enough, what looked like a house plopped down on top of it all. It was surrounded by a broad moat with a small bridge leading to the door. Mister Onas called it a keep.

The bottom two floors of the castle and the four-story tower were made of stone. The part that looked like a house was made of wood with a very tall and steep roof that blended into the tower's conical roof. The lake looked peaceful and the moss-covered bridge was pretty, but Gwyn was honestly disappointed.

"It looks like it's going to fall apart," she said to Mister Onas.

He chuckled. "It kind of does, doesn't it?" Onas shook his head as he scrutinized the castle. "There's a reason I don't usually meet with these small local lords. Landed knights in small areas like this aren't usually wealthy. This one put almost all of his money into the inn back in the village. His job is to maintain the area for his liege. He may have one, maybe two men-at-arms who will in turn be responsible for training the local militia."

Gwyn nodded. "At least he's helping the village. That's nice of him."

Onas sighed. "That's what he would want you to believe, but the village's growth gives him more income and power. It's a gamble, and he may not get to see the benefits of it. A knight is not a hereditary position; his son or daughter will have to attain a knighthood and then be granted the position of Lord of Hilshen by the count."

"Who is the count? Is he a nice guy?" Gwyn asked.

"I have actually never met the man. For all that I have traveled through his town many times. Count Varence resides in the town of Galehaven. I also hear he's a bitter old man." Onas chuckled.

The messenger led them to a set of stables that was next to a small wooden barn and other structures whose purpose eluded her. It appeared that the knight actually had his own farm.

Onas leaned over before they hopped down from the wagon. "Remember, we go with Taenya's plan," he whispered. "You're her niece, learning to become a merchant. Not a princess. We'll talk more about my plan after we leave here."

"Got it. My hair is tied in place and not moving. Operation Hidden Ears is a go," she said with a salute.

He gave her a quizzical look before turning and directing her to join Taenya.

She sighed. *People just do not get me.* She followed Taenya as the group approached the keep. Several people were standing and waiting for them.

The knight was a pudgy, old high elf with a balding head and slightly worn clothes. He was neither tall nor short, but every one of Onas's guards stood taller than the man. Raafe towered over him, but the man seemed to be taller than most people she saw. The elf knight had a large smile plastered on his face, displaying the overall dull color and a large gap between his two front teeth. Her mom would probably snap at her if she said it out loud, but she did not get a good vibe from this guy.

"Welcome! Welcome to Hilshen Castle! You must be the merchant of the famous Fenren Trading House," the man said loudly.

"Thank you, Lord Bekker. I am Onas Fenren. I must say, I was surprised to receive your invitation," the merchant stated.

The man slapped his leg as he laughed. Clearly, an act that was exaggerated.

"Of course, of course. My demesne is humble, but I make it a priority to know all that happens within it," he said.

Well, that *isn't weird.* Did the guy have people spying on them in the village? Were people telling him about them?

Mister Onas smiled. Gwyn thought it looked a little forced. "I am pleased to make your acquaintance. Allow me to introduce my employees." One by one, he introduced his guards.

The knight's focus passed over the group as Onas introduced them. Gwyn watched as he slowed and then focused on her when Onas did not introduce her. She tensed up as his mouth opened to speak.

"And who might this be?"

Taenya straightened and dipped her head respectfully. "This is my niece, milord. She is studying to become a merchant. Mister Fenren graciously offered to take her as an apprentice," the telv woman explained.

They had shown Gwyn how to pretend, and since the man was only a knight, he did not get a curtsey or bow. However, since he was a landed knight and they were on his land, he was due some courtesy. Raafe had explained that most nobles were not nice. That didn't mean that there weren't any nice ones. Just that you had to be careful until you were sure they were.

The man's scrutinizing gaze lingered on her and she found herself fidgeting. After what seemed like an eternity, he nodded.

"Please, come in and partake of my hospitality," he said with a wide gesture of his hands.

Gwyn stopped paying attention to the words that were said as she watched the adults around her react. The man said something softly as they walked toward the door, which made Taenya stiffen next to her. Onas seemed… frustrated. Then, as they followed the man into his keep, she caught sight of Raafe clenching and unclenching his fists together.

Instead of turning left and walking up the spiral staircase in the tower, they walked into a room ahead of them. A fireplace and a few tables punctuated the room, and a single chair sat on a little platform like a stage.

The knight introduced them to three men who were all older, but not by much—the men-at-arms Onas had described. Next, he introduced his four sons and his oldest son's wife, who was a young telv woman, not an elf. The second oldest son kept looking at Gwyn, and it made her uncomfortable. When he looked away after Raafe said something, Gwyn quickly checked to make sure her hair had stayed in place, hoping that he hadn't caught sight of her ears or something.

Finally, the knight introduced his wife. This confused Gwyn because at first, she had thought the young woman was his daughter. She looked significantly younger than him, maybe college-aged. Lord Bekker looked old enough to be her mom's dad. Although nonno was much fitter than the knight.

Gwyn looked around the room as they spoke. The room itself felt damp and smelled bad. Like mildew and mold. At least the fireplace had a big fire going enough to keep the room warm. As Gwyn stared into the fire, she felt as if something inside of her called to it. The crackling, the color, the warmth.

Lord Bekker offered them lunch, and even though Mister Onas had tried to politely decline, the old knight would not take no for an answer. Gwyn put a hand over her mouth the moment she felt herself about to sigh. She followed Taenya and sat between her and Raafe at the table. Soon enough, they found themselves eating poorly made pork and some wilted, limp vegetables. Gwyn was severely unimpressed. Keston at least made decent food from what he had to work with. The man had a gift. In fact, he'd even promised to let her help him cook after they left the village.

The adults all spoke of boring things, so her thoughts drifted to everything that had been going on and what she still needed to do. She was surprised at first by how nice a lot of people were, but it seemed that she had just gotten lucky. They were also only passing through a small village. Who knew what was to come. The city that Mister Onas and the others were from would hopefully be a good place to find her mom.

There was still no news about her. Gwyn really hoped she was okay.

Taenya nudged Gwyn and she looked up to see everyone's face looking at hers. She glanced at the telv guard, who gestured with her head toward the knight.

Gwyn squinted her eyes. "Sorry, I didn't hear you. Could you please repeat yourself?"

The man laughed. She found it quite rude.

"Ah, children. I was asking what you thought about our fine little village?" the man asked.

Gwyn pursed her lips in thought. *I can't mess this up. Be nice!*

"I like it. The people are really nice and I enjoy the inn. Everyone was so helpful yesterday. I'm going to remember them for a long time. I heard that you put a lot of time and money into the inn. I think it was a good idea—the people seem happy," she said with a nod.

Lord Bekker smiled and raised his goblet. "Out of the mouth of babes! Hear, hear!"

Everyone joined in. Gwyn smiled at Taenya.

"Now, Mister Fenren. You've had a chance to see our fair village and can obviously see the potential. I believe we could be good together. You mentioned you have children; do you happen to have any daughters?" the man asked.

Gwyn's eyes narrowed. Why would he ask—

"I do, my oldest. I also have two sons," Mister Onas said, his tone somewhat guarded.

The man smiled and gestured to his second oldest son. "Leth here is in need of a wife! Let us solidify a relationship between our two great families. When our little village grows into a town, our family will be elevated into a barony."

Mister Onas looked shocked. As Gwyn glanced around at the others, she realized that they too were frozen.

It took a moment, but the merchant regained his composure. "Lord Bekker, I appreciate the offer. However, my daughter is already pledged to another," Mister Onas said.

What? He told Taenya she wasn't when they were talking about her the other day...

Onas shook his head. "I regret—"

"What about the girl here," the knight said, punctuating his question with a finger pointed at Gwyn.

Wait... huh? "Me? I'm ten."

The knight lowered his hand and tilted his head. "Huh. That is far too young." He gave her a smile. "You look much older, lass. Well, then—"

His second son, Leth, leaned across his brother and whispered to his father. The pudgy elf nodded and then looked up. "Perhaps we can revisit the matter when the girl gets older? A connection between our families would bring us both great wealth. While she is not of your blood, as your apprentice, I could see such a thing being profitable for us in say, four or five years..."

Mister Onas was very clearly grinding his teeth. "Unfortunately, it is not my place to make such agreements. I will pass along your offer to her parents," he said very deliberately.

He's going to tell Mom? What... oooh, he's lying! Way to go, Mister Onas!

The knight nodded and slapped the table. "Good, good! Now, on to other business! I also hear that you have a large shipment of weapons at the moment. I would love to buy those off you." His voice lowered dangerously. "They're arming up over in Larton and my boys and the villagers could use some reassurance with quality arms. What do you say?"

Mister Onas let out a deep sigh. "Regrettably, those weapons are already sold, Lord Bekker. I do have some other items that are available still, and I also have caravans that I can route through your village when I return to Strathmore. Please, let's discuss your needs."

The knight's eyes narrowed, but the two men began to discuss business.

Gwyn glanced up and saw Taenya looking at Raafe and subtly shaking her head. When she turned to the sun elf, she saw the man's fist gripped underneath the table, a knife in his hand. Her eyes widened and darted back to her plate. She hoped the rest of the meal went quickly so they could leave.

Back at the inn later that evening, Raafe and Keston sat in the tavern, in a booth in a little alcove near the bar. They needed privacy, and because they were not readily visible by those at the bar, they spoke of the situation they'd found themselves in.

"I was ready to—"

Keston nodded. "I know, Raafe. I know. Good thing Taenya had us keep her status a secret. Could you imagine the difficulty we'd have if that man had known?"

The sun elf groaned. "I spoke with the boss a bit on the way back. He has a plan. We're heading to Larton, right? Apparently, he's close with the noble there."

He'd asked Onas what his plan was, but the man had been elusive, stating that he didn't have the full details worked out yet. The high elf did promise to speak with them all in the morning before departing, though.

Raafe wasn't sure how well Onas knew the noble in Larton. Hopefully, the man knew what he was doing.

"They've known each other for over a decade, I believe. The two of them have made it big because of their relationship. They're partners, in a sense. Taenya and I have met the guy before. The baron is as straight an arrow as you can get with the nobility. Only the duke is more liked."

Raafe breathed deeply. "I hope so, Keston. That girl deserves more. Onas could barely handle a knight. Let alone a baron or higher. We're in over our heads."

The high elf guard shrugged. "Don't I know it. Lord Iemes, though. He may be only a baron, but he is wealthy. New money. He has a mine and does a lot of trade with the Kingdom of Meris and even into the Duchy of Edimiss, although I hear that's taking a turn for the worse."

That sounded promising. He didn't know much, but Raafe knew that nobles like that either burned out like a shooting star or rose quickly in prestige. If the man was as wealthy as Keston believed, then there was a chance the man could help the princess. Which, if he was a partner with Onas Fenren, he likely would. The Fenren Trading House was one of the largest land-based traders in the duchy. This meant it was one of the largest in the kingdom, as the Tiloral Duchy was on track to become the wealthiest in the kingdom.

Raafe squinted his eyes and looked at his fellow guard. "Wait, we were just in Galehaven. I thought that town was on the main route into Meris. The boss even has a large store there."

"You're not wrong. However, Lord Iemes's investments are what helped build that store. His town and people also build all of the wagons that Onas uses for his company," Keston explained.

The sun elf found himself nodding. It was starting to add up. If the baron was part of the boss's plans, then maybe... maybe they could keep the princess safe. He took a deep breath.

"What is it, Raafe?" the man asked, concern laced in his voice.

Raafe closed his eyes. *I can trust Keston. At least with this. One step at a time.*

"I plan on telling the boss to take me out of the rotation for the caravans. I want to stay with the princess. She needs people she trusts at her side. I can protect her."

Keston glanced around them and his face took on a sad look. "She's a you-know-what, Raafe." He lowered his voice to a whisper. "She needs knights. Not a merchant guard."

Raafe's eyes narrowed. If she needed a knight, then that is what he would become. She needed a protector. He had failed his sister. His family. He wouldn't fail her too. Then maybe she could help him save them in return.

"Then that is what I will become."

The high elf sucked in a breath. "Raafe—"

A familiar voice made them both freeze.

"Oi, is that merchant and his people around?"

Raafe glanced at the high elf. Keston mouthed, "The knight's son?"

Raafe nodded and put a finger to his lips. Both men lifted their hoods and hunched over their drinks. Raafe was glad anyone coming from the bar would see his back first. Sun elves weren't especially common in Avira.

"Nae. They went to their rooms several bells ago, lad. Now, what can I get ye two?" the innkeeper said loudly.

"Good," came the reply.

Raafe's eyes narrowed. *She's warning us? Why?* His fellow guard looked equally confused.

"Get my man here and I a drink," the second son said. Leth.

He heard the woman slam two mugs onto the counter and fill them. She said something about being in the back and to yell if they needed her.

Raafe and Keston waited, not wanting to bring attention to themselves.

The two men stood at the bar and talked about the meeting. The son seemed upset, while the man with him—who sounded like one of the men-at-arms—tried to calm him down.

Keston and Raafe sat quietly listening for some time before the conversation turned worse.

"I say we grab the girl, Enis. Keep her as a hostage from the merchant. Surely, he'll pay Father to reclaim her," Leth said.

Enis, the telv man-at-arms, tsked. "You need to be careful, Leth. There are three guards. You also have to be careful involving the commoners in the polite war."

Raafe had to stop himself from laughing. *They're commoners too! The polite war is the game of high-level nobles... everyone knows that.*

Leth scoffed. "The merchant is wealthy enough to be considered an aristo-crat, Enis. Did you see how he looked down on us? Father offered him a deal of a lifetime, and he just waved it away. Father is the law here. Look, we can grab the others and be back. Get her in her sleep—"

Raafe stopped listening. His face was burning, his vision going red. He barely registered Keston reaching out to him as he stood. Before he knew it, he was walking toward the man. *The scum.*

He grabbed the little snot's shoulder and yanked him around. The boy's surprise was evident. Raafe's fist connected with his chin and the knight's son dropped like a sack of grain. To Raafe's right, Enis's eyes went wide, but the man-at-arms was much quicker on the take. He grabbed his stein and launched his beer at Raafe's face. The sun elf put up his hands to cover his face just as the man threw a punch. Blocking the fist, Raafe leaned forward and threw a hook into the man-at-arms's side.

The two men launched into a series of blows that quickly settled into neither having the upper hand. Behind him, the young man stumbled back to his feet, just in time for Raafe to round on him and get him with a jab to the nose, which cracked with a spray of blood.

Raafe tried to put his hands up as he was jerked back around by Enis but got rewarded for his poor guard with a fist to his cheek. His head snapped to the side with the blow, but the old man's strength was clearly not what it used to be. Raafe replied with a quick blow to the older telv's gut.

The man grunted as his breath left him, but Keston finally stepped in and grabbed the man from behind. With a firm yank, the man was jerked backward, causing him to trip over himself and fall with a cry.

"OI! WHAT DO YE ALL THINK YER DOIN' IN MY INN?" a loud and very angry woman shouted.

Raafe looked over and his mouth dropped open. The dwarf innkeeper stood there. Her apron stained. Her light brown hair had been pulled up into a ponytail.

His eyes focused on the dagger she had in one hand and a frying pan in the other. And she did not look afraid to use either of them. If she hadn't been so angry, and so terrifying, Raafe would have laughed at the sight.

"All of you. If you want to fight, take it outside! There will be none of that in my inn. Do ye hear me?" she stated.

The knight's son scowled at her. "They started this. My father—"

"Yer father trusts me to run this inn as I see fit. And don't you dare try and throw your family name around at me, lad. I won't hear any of it. OUT!"

Leth grumbled but did not argue with the diminutive woman as the man-at-arms pulled on his arm and led him toward the door.

The innkeeper pointed her dagger at Raafe and Keston. "You two. Bed. Now. I don't want to see either of ye until morning, when you check out of my inn. And pay for damages."

Raafe's eyes widened. "There aren't any damages!"

"Ye damaged my mood, and I'm sure I can find scratches on the bar. Now, bed," she said firmly.

The man-at-arms scowled at the two guards and the lord's son pointed at them as they walked away. "This isn't over. My father will hear of this."

After they walked out, the innkeeper rounded on them. "Ye just had to do that, didn't ye?"

"Did you not hear them? They were planning to hold Gwyn hostage!" Raafe complained.

"They were two men complaining over a beer. If they had tried to take the brat, I would have stabbed 'em myself. You forced their father's hand. Expect to see him in the morning, if not tonight. I suggest you inform yer merchant of yer error in judgment. It may just cost him."

Keston pulled at Raafe's shoulder. "Come on, Raafe. Let's go upstairs. Thank you, miss. I am sorry for the trouble."

The woman just shook her head.

As the two men walked upstairs, Raafe looked at his fellow guard. "Sorry. I—I will take the first watch tonight."

Keston scoffed. "After you inform Taenya."

He groaned. Raafe wasn't scared of many things, but that telv scared him. They'd sparred. Many times. No matter how hard he tried, he'd yet to beat her.

Shit. She's going to kick my ass.

CHAPTER THIRTEEN

THE FEELING WITHIN

Taenya woke early. She stretched, yawning. It was early, she could tell—before the morning bell, even. It was exactly how she liked it. As a morning person through and through, she felt that starting the day off properly was vital to being alert and active. It ensured that she could handle whatever came at her.

Out of bed, she quietly lit the oil lamp, twisting the knob until it ensured the light would remain dim. From the pitcher next to the lamp, she poured herself a cup of water.

A light snore behind her forced her to let out an airy chuckle. Unlike Taenya, the princess would not be disturbed by anything as mundane as noise during her sleep. Every new day, it appeared that only an act of the gods would awaken the young human from her slumber. Like a hibernating beast.

Taenya glanced down at the cup in her hand with a hard look. She needed tea. But later. After getting ready.

Stifling a yawn, she began her morning routine. Her small rug sat rolled off to the side, and she cleared an area on the floor. The girl in the room didn't even budge as Taenya lowered herself to her knees on the rug.

She took a deep breath, held it for three seconds, and then let it out as she placed her hands on the rug in front of herself. She arched her back and slowly lifted her body until her arms were straight and her gaze aimed at the ceiling. After a ten count, she shifted her pose until she was sitting on her feet with her head touching the ground and her arms stretched out in front of her. She kept that pose for thirty seconds before shifting to her next position.

Her stretches relaxed her. They allowed her to still her mind and gain insight into herself. Most importantly, they allowed her to ensure her body was in peak condition and healthy. It helped her train longer and harder, and prevent injury. Flexibility in mind and body maintains stability and strength.

With a deep breath, Taenya straightened her legs and lifted her hips as high as possible, keeping her head on the floor and her arms stretched forward. Feeling the stretch in her leg muscles, she counted off before transitioning to another pose.

Her routine followed a sequence of stretches that flowed seamlessly from one to the next, starting on the floor, moving to her feet, and eventually returning to the ground.

The morning bell sounded just as she was finishing, her face damp with sweat. She lifted herself from the ground and rolled up her rug before pouring another cup of water.

A light knock sounded on the door, eliciting a slightly higher-pitched snore from the child in the room. Taenya shook her head.

When she opened the door, she found herself unsurprised to see Raafe. She narrowed her eyes, ignoring the sweaty mess that was her blond hair as she regarded the sun elf.

His bright smile was not what she wanted to see right after the morning bell. His tight braids were perfect, his face clean and shaven. His armor was already on. It meant he had been waiting just for that moment.

"What is it, Raafe? And why didn't you come to me sooner?" she demanded. His look of shock was a small nudge toward making her feel better.

"How did you—"

Her expression shut that down quickly. The tall sun elf rubbed the back of his head. "Well, boss, you see… I didn't want to wake you. However, now that the first bell has gone off… we have an issue."

Taenya gestured for him to start speaking. He told her what had happened the night prior. Her disappointment was immeasurable, and her day was already ruined.

"You did what?" She took a deep breath. "Fuck. Damn it, Raafe. Why didn't you wake me up sooner?"

The dark-skinned sun elf had the sense to look guilty. However, she would not be swayed by those pretty yellow-orange eyes. She'd leave that to weaker women.

"Alright. I messed up. But I think we need to leave sooner than later. Before… uhhh… the lord gets here," he said.

She closed her eyes and counted to three. "Fine," she said, forcing her eyes back open. "But you need to get Keston—"

"He's ready," Raafe said quickly.

She groaned. "Onas?"

A shake of his head.

"Fine. Have Keston wake up Onas. Prep the wagon. I'll rouse the beast," she said drily.

Taenya ignored the man's raised brow. "And I am cleaning up." She groaned again before shutting the door in the man's face.

"Damn it… I got all damn sweaty and gross and…" she mumbled to herself before taking a deep breath. First things first: clean up, then get Gwyn.

She hadn't rushed that fast to wash in a long time. Not since her time working as a mercenary before signing on with Onas.

Those were the times. Fighting for various groups, usually between baronies and the like as they sought to increase their standing or power. It was what had led her away from the Kingdom of Meris and into Avira in the first place.

She'd been young and dumb. Thinking that she'd been good enough to take on anything. Now, that was a hard-learned lesson. Eventually, she realized that to continue that path was to wind up dead.

Now, Taenya was good at what she did, but it had taken her a long time to get to the level she felt she was at. At this point, the only people who really gave her pause in a fair fight were the paladins.

Heh… and I wanted to be one when I was younger. Silly.

At almost thirty, she felt she'd led a good life thus far. Her parents—well, more like her mother—wanted her to find a husband and settle down. To give them grandchildren.

She looked at the girl sleeping and then down at her armored form.

"Gwyn? It's time to wake up. We have to leave soon," she said, gently shaking the princess.

The girl's eyes shot open. "What? I'm late? I'm up!"

Taenya closed her eyes and counted off again as the girl jumped up and rushed around, frantically trying to get ready.

Clearly, the life of a mother had never been a path meant for Taenya.

Gwyn and Taenya slowly made their way downstairs and into the tavern of the inn. Taenya had helped her get dressed in record time before helping tie her hair into a single braid. In fact, Taenya had already been entirely ready to go before Gwyn even managed to get out of bed. For the life of her, she couldn't remember being asked to wake up.

Back home, as soon as her mom got out of bed, she would wake Gwyn up. Then she'd head off to do what she did to start the day. By the time Gwyn finished getting ready and made it to the kitchen, her mom would have breakfast out and her other stuff all set to go. Gwyn didn't know how her mom did it.

Maybe Taenya just doesn't know the trick to wake me up as mom did? I swear

I didn't hear her…

Gwyn really had no idea why mornings were the bane of her existence. She hoped one day she'd figure it out. Just the thought made her roll her eyes. *Yeah right…*

Downstairs, Keston had food ready for them, while Mister Onas and Raafe were outside preparing the wagon to leave. Gwyn quickly sat down and started eating the bowl of something vaguely like oatmeal the innkeeper had provided them.

Gwyn was pretty sure the woman just did not know how to cook. It was okay, though. She was hungry, and as long as what the woman made wasn't disgusting, Gwyn knew she had to eat. Her mom would be so proud.

She glanced up at Keston. "So, Keston. Since we're leaving, does that mean tonight you and I get to cook again?" she asked.

The high elf smiled. "That sounds fantastic! What do you think we should have?"

She thought about it. "Can we get rice? We can make some chicken and rice?" Her eyes lit up. "What about pasta? Chili mac and cheese? Wait a second! Mom made me something called campfire potatoes once! It was potatoes and Parmesan and mozzarella… She cut up and tossed the potatoes in oil and herbs with some salt and pepper. Then wrapped them in foil before putting them on the fire. When they were cooked, she would unwrap them from the foil and put both types of cheeses on them and then put them back on the fire until they were nice and melty. Mmm. Keston, let's have that!"

The man's smile fell slightly. "Gwyn, I don't think we can make that. Not here at least."

Oh. "Oh. Right. You guys don't have foil. Do you have potatoes?" she asked.

Taenya glanced between the two cooks and set down her small cup of tea. "Of course, we have potatoes. Although, I am not sure what types of cheese those are. How about we go to the market together in Strathmore? We can look at the cheeses and you can tell me if you see any that look familiar," she suggested.

That sounded like fun to Gwyn. *Cheese tasting tour with Taenya? Count me in!* They could just walk around the market and try all the street food. *I looove street food! The trip to Seoul with Mom… oh my goodness. The street food alley was so good. That guy that cooked steak… mmm…*

She let out a wistful sigh. "I miss home." Gwyn forced a smile at the telv woman. "I would love that, Taenya. Cheese tasting tour, here we come!"

The blonde chuckled. "Sounds like a plan."

All three of them fell quiet as they went back to their food. Taenya excused herself to go check on things and left Gwyn with Keston.

Gwyn was still hungry when she finished. As she and Keston walked toward the exit, her stomach rumbled. A loud sigh sounded. Gwyn turned and saw the dwarf woman standing there with her hand on her hip. Her light brown hair was pulled into a ponytail instead of the braid Gwyn had seen her with before.

"Lass, come here. Let's get you a snack to take with you on the road," the woman said.

Gwyn nodded and followed her back toward the kitchen, Keston behind her. The dwarf rifled through her supplies until she found several bags of dried fruit and peanuts, which she quickly mixed together into one small sack for Gwyn.

The innkeeper stuck a hand out to Keston, who narrowed his eyes before reaching into a pocket and grabbing a couple of coins for the dwarf. The woman snatched them with a smile and tucked them into a little pouch attached to her waist.

"Well, lass. Stay out of trouble and watch how ye speak to yer elders," she admonished with a waggle of her finger.

"As long as you remember to watch how you speak to your customers!" Gwyn smiled. "Thank you for your help."

The woman shook her head. "Ye won't be getting any affection from me, lass. Go on with ye."

Gwyn rolled her eyes as she turned away. But as she and Keston walked to the door, the innkeeper called out.

"Be safe, little one!"

Gwyn laughed. "Bye!"

When she and Keston stepped outside, the sun was still low, but the clear sky ensured it was bright out. The air of the village and its unpleasant smells assaulted her senses.

A telv villager strolled by holding a big basket of vegetables. The woman smiled and nodded at Keston as the man paused to give way to her. A door opened across the street and a man emerged from his house carrying a basket of wet clothing. He promptly set it down on a narrow table under his window and started hanging up the laundry on some rope to dry.

It was all so peaceful.

Mister Onas's wagon sat ready, the horses hooked up, with their heads in their sacks to eat. The other two horses stood nearby, tied to a post. Keston nudged Gwyn and pointed to the rest of their party. Taenya and Raafe stood on either side of Onas, their arms crossed as the three stared into the distance. Gwyn looked to see what they were focused on and saw a wagon approaching.

Seeing the old knight approach, Taenya instantly regretted her decision to not leave earlier. Lord Bekker rode at the head of his group, which consisted of three other riders and a fabric-covered wagon. She caught sight of his two older sons driving the wagon, which left the lord's three men-at-arms riding on the horses. They all wore gambesons and swords.

The lord said something to his men and they spread out to cover the entirety of the narrow road.

Taenya glanced behind her and saw Keston standing with Gwyn, hand already resting on his hilt. She wanted to tell him to get the princess into the wagon, but that would keep him too far away. She sighed. They needed to leave without any trouble.

That's a long shot. Taenya glanced at Onas, wishing she could will her thoughts into his mind. *Don't mess this up.*

The old high elf stopped his horse at a comfortable distance and observed them for a moment before speaking.

"Seems you are all set to leave. Why the hurry?" Lord Bekker asked.

Onas answered immediately. "We would like to make a good start toward our next destination."

Lord Bekker nodded. "Sensible. However, I came because of two things. First, your guard there assaulted my boy and man. Now, all this just after the hospitality I showed you. Of course, you're welcome to leave, but the sun elf will spend the night in the stocks. As his employer, you're going to pay a fine."

Taenya's eyes narrowed. Raafe stepped forward.

"Did your boy tell—"

"Raafe. Enough," Onas snapped.

The sun elf clenched his fists but nodded.

"My guard told me about the altercation, of course," Onas said. "And I believe that we should let cooler heads prevail. Having my man put into stocks because of hostile comments from your son... Now, that is not acceptable, *Ser* Bekker."

The man tilted his head. "Hostile comments? I think we have different interpretations, Mister Fenren. Now, I am not unfair. I realize that you have a timeline you must stick to. Therefore, I will accept a fine of two large gold coins and your stock of weapons."

Beside her, Onas ground his teeth. She knew the man wouldn't be giving away items meant for the baron of Larton. It was clear that the lord was simply trying to wring every bit he could from them. And Raafe had given him an excuse.

"Lord Bekker, I already informed you that this shipment is accounted for," Onas said, his frustration evident in his tone and stance. "I will pay you three small golds to let the matter drop. And I will dispatch a merchant to your village upon my return to Strathmore. With items you would like to order."

The man sighed. "Three small? I don't think that will be enough, Mister Fenren. Your man injured my boy. I will have justice for the lad. Now, I have a duty to defend my demesne. I have learned that the uppity baron in Larton is arming his lads and looking for a fight. As lord of this land, I simply need to confiscate weapons that are meant to support those who could harm my fair village."

Onas cocked his head to the side and glanced at Taenya, giving her a subtle nod.

She took a deep breath. Decided to take Onas's cue on small insults. "Ser Bekker—"

"It's *milord!*" Leth shouted.

Taenya fought to not roll her eyes. "*Lord* Bekker. Many laws prevent your authority to confiscate lawful merchant goods backed by the guilds. By royal law, it is considered theft for you to take them. Mister Fenren offered a fair settlement for the fact that your son conspired to kidnap and ransom a minor child. I kindly suggest you take the offer," she stated calmly.

She knew he wouldn't go for it. But she had to try.

"You suggest to me, lass?" The lord gestured around. "This is my land. You are on my land. You city folk think you can do whatever you want. The fact is, you are commoners. You broke my laws, and seek to get away with it. The fine has gone up. Four large golds. I suggest you take the offer or all of you will be in stocks. Even if I have to build one for the little lass myself."

Did he just…?

He did.

Taenya sighed and shook her head. "Well, it seems we are at an impasse. We may be commoners, but we will not be intimidated and taken advantage of by some landed country knight in the middle of nowhere."

Onas sucked in a breath and mumbled her name quietly. Taenya shook her head.

Lord Bekker's men yanked their swords out of their sheaths and held them up awkwardly. The two boys jumped to their feet on the wagon bench. The older nearly toppled over before catching himself.

She just shook her head again.

"Don't stand for that, Father!" the younger son yelled out.

Taenya lifted her shield off her back and strapped it to her arm before pulling out her blade. Keston stepped to her side and drew his blade at the same time as Raafe, on the other side of Onas, drew his.

Taenya rolled her shoulders, actually glad she'd done her morning stretches.

"Onas, will you—"

"Would you all just stop?!" Gwyn yelled.

Taenya closed her eyes. *Shit. Not the time, Gwyn.*

Gwyn was so angry. It was as if her anger were rolling around inside her and wanted to erupt. The old creep was being a jerk to Mister Onas and Taenya. Then he wanted to put Raafe in stocks? *What the heck even is that?* She didn't know, but it didn't sound good.

Then she saw how upset Mister Onas was when the fat, bald man tried to make him pay. She didn't know how the money worked here, but clearly, they didn't take euros.

But she could tell when someone wanted to cheat someone else. And this man just wanted to steal from Mister Onas. That wasn't right.

"You should let your betters speak, child," Lord Bekker said condescendingly.

She narrowed her eyes. This man wasn't anything like the innkeeper, who was ornery and just didn't want to be friends with someone who was going to leave. Gwyn could understand that. It was clear the dwarf lady would have been sad if she became friends with Gwyn just to see her leave so soon. As her mom would say when other kids were mean to her: it was a defense mechanism. Whatever that meant.

This guy, though. Nope. He was just a big fat jerk. And it made her mad. Gwyn's mind was racing, and all she could think about was how she just wanted to rage. To blow up and give him a piece of her mind.

She stared at the man before [**Focusing**] her anger on the two sons in the wagon. The one who apparently wanted to kidnap her? *That just... Argh! She* felt a click and let go. Letting her anger blaze. She felt it rush out of her in a burst of energy.

"You are not better! You are just some bad man who thinks he can do whatever he wants! My mom would kick—" She stopped. Smoke was coming from the back of the wagon. And where there was smoke...

The man huffed and yelled at Mister Onas. "Control your child! How dare she—" Lord Bekker stopped as his sons started yelling.

Everyone turned. Suddenly, they heard a loud crackling sound as flames flared from the wagon. Gwyn's eyes widened as she saw the orange and red fire flick up from the wood, quickly reaching the fabric covering the wagon. She watched in horror as the material burst into a blaze and quickly spread.

The two sons cried out as they jumped down from the wagon. With barely any hesitation, Taenya turned to the others. "Run!" she shouted.

Gwyn jerked into motion as Taenya grabbed her hand and rushed back toward the wagon. She didn't even slow as the knight all but tossed her up onto the wagon's bench and jumped up behind her.

"Raafe, Keston! The horses!" Taenya yelled.

Onas rushed forward and climbed onto the bench, squishing Gwyn between him and Taenya. The other two guards jumped on their horses even as the telv woman snapped the reins and urged the hitched horses into a run. Their wagon sped by the burning one amid the screams and yells of Lord Bekker and his men.

"Get them!" Gwyn heard Lord Bekker yell. She could just make out several of the men start running. A loud bang sounded as something heavy hit the wagon and made it suddenly lurch. At least one of the lord's men was charging them on his horse.

Raafe and Keston called out to each other and shouted for Taenya to not slow down. A clash of metal sounded, followed by more yelling. Mister Onas sat quietly, his hand clutching at his tunic.

Soon enough they were out of the village and rushing down the road. Gwyn's heart was pounding in her chest, but as she tried to calm herself, she felt as if her heart wasn't the only thing inside of her making her nerves race. Something was burning inside of her. It didn't hurt; instead, it felt like a rush of energy that wouldn't die down.

She felt a bit of relief when the two guards rode up alongside them. "They fell back. Raafe tagged one of them," Keston called out.

"This is why you use a saber on horseback," Raafe replied.

Taenya exhaled. "Let's take it easy now. Give the horses a chance to breathe."

Mister Onas sighed and stretched his fingers. The man hadn't stopped gripping his shirt since they'd sat down.

As the wagon slowed and the group caught their breath, Gwyn's thoughts were still racing.

Even much later she had managed to get some sleep, she couldn't figure it out.

How did that wagon catch fire? And why is the word **[Pyromancy]** seared into my mind?

CHAPTER FOURTEEN

FOLLOWING LEADS

Sloane and the Knights of Haven's Hope arrived in Tunstead as the sun began to set, casting a warm, orange-red glow across the rolling hills that surrounded the townlet and the large lake just south of it. They had traveled for several days so far and the journey was starting to affect her more than she would care to admit. She could only imagine how she appeared to the others, if she was starting to notice it herself. Decreased energy, tiredness, irritability…

Let's be honest, I feel like shit. She was either not used to the medieval outdoors life, or Sloane was starting to recognize the signs of depression in herself. *Google MD would probably tell me it's a brain tumor.*

Despite her weariness, Sloane tried to not let it affect her ability to converse with others. After all, she needed to learn about the world she'd found herself in. If anything, maintaining a facade of determined strength was helping her cope with everything.

Plus, it's easy to just wave everything away as being tired.

When describing Tunstead, Ernald had explained that the people enjoyed the very communal feel to it, so even if the place had over a thousand people, the inhabitants liked to consider themselves just a large village.

That conversation had turned into a series of discussions about all of the local towns and other locales the knights had visited. Which, to her amusement, spilled into a plethora of other subjects with everyone else. Thus, she had spent the last couple of days during their travels taking turns speaking to Ernald and Maud about their journey, while getting to know the other knights during the evenings. Even the merchant Maud had saved, Raolin, and his guard, Averet, spoke excitedly about all that she could experience.

The group had tried to explain their world as best as they could, each giving little anecdotes about what was best about it.

The more they spoke of it, the more Sloane wished she'd arrived in another kingdom. It made her realize how lucky it was that the knights had found her. Thus far, everyone else she'd met had been relatively nice, but apparently that was mostly just for show, to get her money.

When she'd pressed Maud on the topic, the knight-medic told her that the temples heavily preached the importance of providing assistance to strangers. That mainly meant that people were outwardly nice in public, but would quickly stab you in the back in a dark alley.

However, there were pockets of good everywhere—mainly due to the fact that, for the most part, commoners knew they had to stick together. Raolin and Averet were a perfect example of this: the two were lifelong friends. When the merchant had expressed an interest in traveling, his best friend had dropped everything to join him as his guard. Maud explained that while generally the people were nicer, the nobles were ready to do anything to solidify their power.

It appeared that Sloane had arrived during a somewhat tense period, and kingdoms everywhere were on edge. She could only imagine what effect the Flash would have on such a situation.

As their wagon drove into the village, Sloane was struck by the bustling energy of the place. It was a stark contrast to the anxiety-filled atmosphere exhibited by the people of Valesbeck.

The sounds of horses, carts, and people filled the air, and the smells of cooking food and wood smoke wafted from the homes and small businesses lining the streets.

Sloane sat between Ernald and Maud as the sun elf man navigated the wagon toward the central square, where they hoped to find an inn to rest for the night.

Once everyone got settled, she would start her search for the lead she had been given back in Valesbeck.

Gwyn could be here.

Sloane had to keep her eyes out.

She noticed the market first, a lively hub of activity with vendors shouting out their wares and customers haggling over prices. Farmers sold fresh vegetables and fruits, while craftsmen displayed their wares, from baskets to pottery to finely crafted swords.

The group made its way through the square, where Sloane immediately noticed two inns and three taverns lining the streets leading to and from the square. Gisele guided them toward the closest inn, a modest establishment with a sign hanging outside displaying a crude painting of a horse.

A man in worn clothes stepped forward from where he stood outside the inn and asked Gisele if she needed assistance in tending to the horses. As everyone else began unpacking, Sloane joined Ismeld and led the way inside.

She pushed open the door and was greeted by the warmth of a fire burning in the hearth, and the smells of roasted meat and ale.

The innkeeper, a middle-aged raithe with a balding head and friendly smile, greeted her warmly as she stepped up, likely believing she was the one to talk to over the armored knight.

"Good evening, milady. What can I do for you?"

Yup, thought I was a noble. She smiled. "We're just arriving. Do you have rooms available for seven people?" she asked.

The man looked back at a board that held a few keys. "I have three rooms left. That work?"

Sloane glanced at Ismeld, who nodded.

"Yes. Thank you," she told the man.

"Good! That will be one small silver a night per room. Also, each meal is twenty large copper per person if you pay in advance," he explained.

Ismeld stepped forward and pulled out a pouch, and before long, Sloane held a key. She followed the high elf back outside just in time to see Maud and Gisele saying goodbye to the merchant.

"Thank you again, Ser Maud. If it weren't for you, I would have died," the telv merchant, Raolin, said. "Ser Gisele, thank you kindly for the escort to the town. We will continue our journey from here after I see the Banking Guild."

His friend, the sun elf guardsman, Averet, saw Sloane and waved. She smiled as she lifted her hand. Gisele and Maud joined her and Ismeld.

"We have rooms. Three," Ismeld said.

Gisele nodded. "We'll make it work. Sloane, you and me?"

Sloane glanced at Maud, who was looking at Ismeld with a smile, apparently enjoying the development. Ismeld rolled her eyes.

Sloane looked at the orkun woman and shrugged. "Sure," she said and held out the room key. "Here, I am going to go check out the market before it gets too late."

Gisele squinted. "You can hold on to it. I'll join you."

That surprised Sloane. She hadn't expected Gisele to offer help without prompt. "Are you sure? I'm just curious. This town is much more settled down than the last. I just wanted to explore," she explained.

Gisele smiled. "I'm sure. It'll be nice to stretch my legs after a long journey. Plus, I've always enjoyed exploring new places."

Sloane nodded.

Gisele spoke quickly with Maud and Ismeld, and when the two women had departed, she smiled and gestured for Sloane to lead the way. Together, they walked back into the bustling square and toward the market, weaving through the crowd of people and vendors.

Despite the lively hub of activity, Sloane couldn't shake the somber mood that had settled over her. She was here to find a lead on Gwyn, and the weight of that mission was heavy on her heart.

As they walked through the market, vendors shouted out their wares and customers haggled over prices. The smells of fresh produce, baked goods, and meats filled the air. Sloane kept her eyes peeled for any sign of Gwyn, her heart racing with each passing child as she searched for anyone who resembled her daughter. She knew it was a long shot—Tunstead was a large village and Gwyn could be anywhere. But she had to try.

The market was a labyrinth of stalls and tents, and Sloane struggled to keep her bearings as she weaved through the crowds. Everywhere she looked, there were people laughing, chatting, and enjoying themselves.

Sloane couldn't help but feel a twinge of jealousy. She wished she could be one of those carefree people, able to wander through the market without a care in the world. But she knew that was impossible. Every time she saw someone with dark hair, her heart would skip a beat, but it was never her daughter. Gwyn was out there somewhere, and she had to find her.

Out of the corner of her eye, a sudden movement caught her attention. She turned to see a young girl with dark brown hair darting through the crowds, her tattered dress flapping in the wind.

Sloane's heart leaped in her chest. "Gwyn!" she shouted.

Gisele reached out for her. "Sloane? What—"

Sloane ignored her and hastened forward. The girl was just ahead and darting through the market. Same height. Same curly hair. It's a bit shorter... did she cut off the pink tips? Maybe to blend in?

"Gwyn!" she called out.

Several people turned and stared at her as she rushed through the crowd. More than a few started searching for who she was calling.

Gisele yelled her name, but it did not take long for Sloane to lose the orkun knight in the crowd. On she went, catching glimpses of the girl until suddenly... she disappeared.

Sloane stood in the middle of an intersection and found herself spinning, trying to decide which road to go down. She made a decision and moved. Determined to find her.

As the sun began to set, Sloane's search became more frantic. She walked faster, darting down narrow alleys and squeezing through crowds of people. But no matter where she looked, she couldn't find Gwyn.

Eventually, Sloane started to feel a sense of dread. People were heading home for the night and the streets were too crowded. Gwyn could be anywhere. Sloane slumped down onto a nearby bench, feeling defeated. She glanced around. Where was Gisele?

She turned her head and her eyes widened. *It's her!*

At the end of the street and staring at something off to the side was the girl that looked like Gwyn.

Sloane jumped to her feet. "Gwyn!"

The girl ran.

No!

Sloane burst into a sprint, her traveling dress billowing behind her as she ran. She pushed herself to her limit, ignoring the fabric tugging at her as she raced forward. As she reached where the girl had stood, Sloane found herself in front of an alley.

She caught sight of the girl again moving around a corner. Sloane's heart was pounding in her chest as she dashed forward, her eyes scanning the area.

Suddenly, she felt something collide with her side, and she stumbled, her feet flying out from under her. She fell hard to the ground, her hands instinctively reaching out to break her fall.

"Umph!"

The impact was jarring, and Sloane let out a sharp cry of pain as the rough cobblestone scraped her skin. Her head spun as she tried to get her bearings.

As her vision cleared, she saw a figure looming over her—a tall, muscular man with a snarl on his face. In his hand, he held a wooden club, which he had used to strike her in the side. Sloane's breath caught in her throat as she realized she was in danger.

She scrambled to her feet, her heart pounding with fear and adrenaline. The man advanced toward her, swinging the club menacingly. Sloane backed away, her eyes darting around frantically for an escape route. She knew she was out-matched: the man was bigger and stronger than her, and he seemed to be filled with a savage fury.

"What ya doin' scarin' one of my girls? Eh?" a moon elf man asked.

Sloane blinked. The girl was standing next to him. Her hair was tucked behind a pointed ear. A telv ear.

Sloane sucked in a breath.

"Who sent you?" he demanded.

"No one. It was an accident! Just let me go," she pleaded. She hoped the man would see her as not worth the effort, even as her mind raced, trying to think of a way to defend herself.

"Too late for that," he said icily.

The man rushed forward and swung. Sloane ducked under it as she tried to **[Focus]** on finding a solution. She spotted the lid to a discarded crate nearby and quickly grabbed it, using it as a makeshift shield to fend off the man's attacks.

The man growled in frustration as he swung his club at her again and again. Sloane deflected the blows, her muscles straining with effort as the weapon crashed against her protection. She narrowed her eyes, watching the man's movements, waiting for an opportunity to strike. She deftly dodged his next swing and landed a solid punch to his jaw, feeling the satisfying crack of bone under her knuckles. The man stumbled back, dazed, as Sloane readied herself for the next round.

Just when it seemed as if Sloane might be able to hold her own, the man suddenly lunged forward, his fist replying by connecting with her jaw. A sharp pain shot through her head, and she stumbled backward, her vision blurring. She tried to steady herself, but the man seized the opportunity to strike again, his club smashing into her side once more.

Sloane let out a cry of pain as she felt herself falling backward. She hit the ground hard, her body wracked with agony. She lay there, gasping for breath, the man looming over her, his eyes filled with cruel satisfaction.

Sloane's vision blurred with tears as she looked up at the moon elf thug towering over her. He was imposing, with pointed ears, and silver hair pulled back in a ponytail. But to Sloane, his features were distorted by the rage and pain she felt.

As he lifted his club threateningly, she caught a glimpse of his cold, cruel eyes. They were a piercing blue that seemed to glint with malice in the dim light of the alley. His sharp cheekbones and angular jaw were set in a scowl, and his thin lips twisted into a sneer.

Sloane struggled to get up, but the pain in her ribs made it difficult to breathe. She looked back up at the man, her eyes full of fear and anger. He reached down and grabbed her by the hair, pulling her to her knees.

Through her tears, Sloane could see the intricate tattoos that snaked up his purple-hued neck and across his jawline, which appeared to mark him as a member of some gang.

Sloane knew she had to fight back, but her body was weak and her mind clouded by pain. As the thug raised the club again, she closed her eyes and braced for the impact.

Her head jerked forward as the man was yanked backward with a cry. She opened her eyes and watched as armored gauntlets grabbed him from behind in a tight grip. Sloane recognized Gisele as the woman turned and threw the man against the stone wall of the building next to them.

Before the man even started to fall, the orkun knight-captain of the Knights of Haven's Hope pinned the elf against the wall. The man struggled to break free from Gisele's grasp, but her strong arms held him firmly in place. With a look of intense anger, Gisele began to beat him with her free hand.

Each blow landed with a heavy thud, and the moon elf cried out in pain. The force of Gisele's punches knocked him off balance, and he stumbled to the side, still trying desperately to break free.

But Gisele was relentless, raining down blow after blow on Sloane's attacker.

Her fists were like hammers, striking with incredible force, and the moon elf could do nothing to defend himself. His cries grew weaker and weaker, until finally he fell to the ground, defeated and bloodied. Unconscious.

Gisele stood over him, panting heavily, her eyes blazing with fury. She gave one look at the telv girl in her tattered dress, and that was the only cue the girl needed to flee.

Gisele turned to Sloane, her expression quickly shifting to one of concern. "Are you alright?" she asked, her tone gentle.

Sloane nodded weakly, her body trembling with shock and pain. "She—She looked like Gwyn," she said by way of explanation.

Gisele's expression softened and she glanced at the girl running in the distance. "Come on. Let's get you back to the inn," she said, helping Sloane to her feet.

Ignoring the moon elf, the two women slowly made their way down the street.

Sloane blew softly on the hot soup on her spoon before bringing it to her lips and lightly slurping it down. The warmth of the broth made its way through her body and brought a bit of relief that was almost instantly replaced again by pain.

"Just let me do it," Maud said, beside her.

"No. Let me wallow in my failure," Sloan mumbled. She took another sip of her soup and winced. Suddenly, a new warmth flowed through her, until all of her pain vanished. She turned, seeing the green glow surrounding the healer's hands dissipate.

"Why'd you do that? We don't want anyone to see," she hissed.

The redheaded telv rolled her eyes. "We're away from prying eyes and there isn't really anyone around. Stop fussing."

"Fine." Sloane sighed. "Thank you," she said softly.

Maud nodded. Gisele slid into the booth across from them.

"Better?"

"Did you wait until Maud healed me before deciding to sit down?"

Gisele winked at her. "No. I would never do such a thing."

Sloane rolled her eyes. "Yes, I am better. Anything?"

"I have the others out looking for any signs that we were followed or may have visitors," the orkun said. "I spoke with the guard captain, and he said the man was gone before his people arrived. However, he was apparently aware of him. He's part of a gang that's trying to move into the town."

I knew it. "Do the tattoos identify their affiliation?" Sloane asked.

Gisele tilted her head in confusion. "What? No. Why would they use tattoos to tell that? Wouldn't that just give them away to everyone who saw them?"

"Oh. Right. Of course, that makes sense," she said.

Well, then. Gang tats are not a thing here. Thanks, Hollywood.

Sloane dipped her spoon into her bowl and scooped up the remainder of her soup, relishing the taste as she sipped it. It reminded her of *minestra maritata*, a clear broth filled with greens, tiny orzo-like pasta, and small bits of meat. The soup she was eating now was almost an exact replica. It brought back so many memories.

It was Gwyn's favorite.

"Sloane?"

She glanced up. Maud and Gisele were looking at her. "Hm?"

"Are you sure you are alright?" Maud asked.

Sloane nodded, quickly wiping at her face. "Yes. Just... reminiscing. This soup reminds me of one from back home." Returning the spoon to the bowl, she sat up and looked at Maud. "I think... I think it's time for me to go to bed. Can I squeeze by you?"

The two knights shared a look.

"Alright," Maud said hesitantly. She slid out of the booth and stood.

Sloane gave Maud a half-hearted smile as she got up. "Thank you for the healing. I'll see you tomorrow." She started making her way toward the stairs, then paused as she heard footsteps behind her. Sloane narrowed her eyes when she saw both women following her.

"I can make it upstairs alone, you two."

Gisele stretched and let out an exaggerated yawn. "I feel tired too. Beating up thugs will do that to you."

Sloane rolled her eyes. She looked at Maud. "And you?"

The redhead gave her a lopsided smile. "Why sit down here alone? I may as well go relax before Ismeld comes and cuts off the light and demands I go to sleep."

Sloane sighed. *These two...*

Sloane unlocked the door to her and Gisele's room and pushed it open, gesturing for the orkun woman to follow her in. The room was small and cozy, with two beds, a small desk, and a window that overlooked the street below. Sloane sat on a bed and let out a sigh of relief, grateful for the chance to finally rest after such an exhausting day.

She started removing her boots, slowly unlacing them before pulling them off, letting them fall haphazardly to the floor. She looked up and gave Gisele a tired smile. The woman smiled back and began to undress.

Sloane watched as Gisele struggled to remove her armor, her sweat making it difficult to pull off. She couldn't help but feel a sense of guilt. If it weren't for her, Gisele wouldn't have had to fight so hard.

"Here, let me help you," she said, walking over to the other woman.

Gisele smiled gratefully, and the two of them worked together to remove the armor piece by piece. It was a slow process, but eventually, they managed to get it off. Gisele neatly set it up on the chair and desk.

Next, she poured water into a bowl and dipped a rag into it. She wiped the sweat and grime from her face. Sloane realized she should do the same and took the bowl and rag from Gisele after the woman had finished.

As she cleaned her face, Sloane couldn't help but think about the fight with the moon elf. It had been a close call, and she couldn't shake the feeling of how much she'd messed up. She'd left her sword behind in the wagon before going to the market. Gisele hadn't brought it up, thankfully, but Sloane knew she had to make sure to keep it on her at all times.

Gisele noticed the worried look on Sloane's face and spoke up. "Hey, it's alright. You are fine now. We both got away fine, didn't we?"

Sloane nodded but couldn't shake the feeling of dread in the pit of her stomach. "I just feel bad."

Gisele put a comforting hand on her shoulder. "We all make mistakes. That's why we have others we can rely on. For pulling us out of the fire when we stumble."

Sloane smiled weakly, feeling a bit better. She handed the rag back to Gisele, who huffed a laugh and tossed the dirty cloth on the small table where the water bowl sat.

"Let's get some rest," Gisele said.

The two of them got into their respective beds. Sloane's eyes slowly adjusted to the darkness and she watched across the room as Gisele drifted off to sleep, feeling grateful for her presence.

I need to figure out a way to repay their kindness. They dropped everything to help me.

As she too felt herself falling asleep, memories of Gwyn flooded her mind and pushed the drowsiness away. The two of them sitting at the kitchen table last winter, both bundled up in cozy blankets and eating steaming bowls of soup as the snowflakes fell softly outside. It was a rare occurrence near Milan, so Gwyn was excited as they talked about all they would do when it stopped. The warmth of the soup and the love between her and her daughter made it a moment Sloane would never forget, especially since it led to a day both would remember.

She smiled, recalling the memory. Only a few centimeters of snow had fallen that day. She'd ended up driving with Gwyn over an hour into the mountains to go sledding and to make a snowman. Gwyn was so happy and kept singing about how the cold didn't bother her anyway. The snowman turned into the only hiding spot during their impromptu snowball fight...

That poor snowdude, as Gwyn called him, never had a chance. Sloane smiled to herself even as tears fell, grateful for the precious memories that brought her joy even on the toughest days.

CHAPTER FIFTEEN

TAVERN HOPPING

Although not typically prone to inebriation, Sloane Reinhart had thrown caution to the wind after drinking four ales and nursing a fifth, no longer concerned with the idea of limits. With her weight primarily on one elbow, she swayed slightly as she precariously balanced on the polished wooden bar top. She twirled a strand of her curly brown hair around her index finger in slow, absent-minded movements. Sloane's thoughts continued to spiral with each passing ale as she gazed into the amber liquid of the mug.

She had never been in a fight with another person before. Sure, like every girl on her college fencing team, over ten years ago, she'd dabbled in kickboxing. Fighting the wolves had been instinctual and fierce, yet different. Fighting against a real person was nothing like she thought it would be.

I'm just lucky the guy wasn't trying to actually kill me.

The moment a potential to find Gwyn had shown itself, she had completely lost her mind. There had to be a better way to look for her. There was no way she was going to find her by simply walking around the continent. There was a looming deadline for figuring her shit out.

Coming to grips with the fact that one day the knights would leave was a necessity. She narrowed her eyes. *I've done that. No, what I need to do is figure out how to support myself.*

The thing was, she didn't know how to do that while traveling. Her needs weren't great—just having supplies to continue her search was all she required. But simply finding replacement allies wouldn't be enough. Figuring out how to take advantage of some sort of network would be ideal. The knights had spoken of the Order of Secrets. *Perhaps I can make use of their network?*

The problem of payment arose. What if these spies wanted to restrict her ability to search for Gwyn? What if they used Gwyn or simply knowledge of her as a way to coerce Sloane into working for them?

There were so many horrible things they could do. Sloane wasn't arrogant, but she did represent a repository of knowledge they probably couldn't gain from anywhere else. She was a well-educated woman; she could give them things that could launch them ahead decades or more. Even further if she figured out this whole magic and mana thing.

No, she couldn't let herself be stopped. An organization of spies was not a group she should rely on or trust. That was the height of folly. So, if not the government of a nation that she was quickly learning was corrupt, then who?

At her core, Sloane was a creator. A thinker. A tinkerer. She loved to make things. So, why not find like-minded individuals? She knew business. While she was no CEO, she was quite well-positioned in her career. She knew how to run the operations of a company. Logistics, personnel, organization… she knew all of this.

Yet, applying that knowledge here would be a struggle while she was also on the move. What she needed was to find people she could reasonably trust to partner with. What she needed were merchants. That was even one option for *her*: to be a traveling merchant. It would likely help her cross borders with less scrutiny. But that required capital.

She groaned and banged her head on the bar.

"The ale that bad?" a voice asked drily. "I can make you something a bit better tasting."

Sloane looked up at the bartender, involuntarily shivering as she once more took in the raithe man's appearance.

The bartender was a haunting figure who had immediately drawn her attention when she entered the establishment. His pale complexion appeared almost translucent, and his dark hair was slicked back, revealing elaborate silver cuffs that fit snugly around his short, pointed ears. His eyes were a piercing shade of crimson, and they seemed to flicker with an otherworldly intelligence. He wore a black vest over a white shirt with frilled cuffs, giving him a slightly formal air. His long, thin fingers moved gracefully as he poured drinks and mixed cocktails with expert precision.

Despite his eerie appearance, the vampire-like bartender was a friendly and engaging presence in the tavern. He spoke in a deep, resonant voice that seemed to echo through the room, and he had a dry sense of humor that she felt could put even the most nervous patrons at ease. Although, when he smiled, his rather long canines gave him a decidedly predatory mien.

She glanced down at her mug, which was half full still. "This is fine. Anything better tasting is too good for my mood."

The man huffed a laugh. "Fair enough. So, what brings you to Tunstead?"

"We're just traveling through. Heading to Thirdghyll," Sloane said.

A nod.

"Don't envy you there. I left that city the moment that I could afford to. Any business in particular?" the raithe man asked.

She gave the man a look. Bartenders get a lot of traffic, right?

"I'm looking for someone. Actually, maybe you can help me. We were in Valesbeck not too long ago. I was told that someone who matched the description of who I am searching for was heading in this direction. Any chance you recall any travelers passing through town since the Flash? They would have had a young girl with them," she asked.

Sloane mentally crossed her fingers. *The worst he can say is no.*

The man paused and appeared to give it an appropriate amount of thought. His slender fingers tapped rhythmically against the bar top.

Finally, he shrugged. "There have been travelers, but I can't recall any with a child. That said, I am a bartender. Children don't sit here often. Maybe you could ask around the inns? Or, actually, the Loping Lizard caters more to families. Their bar is small, maybe you can also ask there."

She smiled at the man, it was more than she expected, even if it was less than she hoped. "Thank you. Can you give me a shot of something? I don't care what it is," she said.

The man laughed. "I have just the thing."

His feral grin made her second-guess her decision.

Sloane stumbled through a crowd that was entering as she made her way out of the tavern. Not because she was drunk—she was only starting to feel it—but because people didn't care to be courteous to the woman leaving and clearly at the door first. She sighed.

"Sloane. What are you doing?"

She jumped at hearing her name and turned, seeing Deryk there. The orkun man usually sat around brooding and silent. It was one of the few times she'd seen him without his armor. He wore a simple leather tunic and trousers with sturdy boots that had seen their fair share of wear and tear. A wide leather belt cinched his waist, with a pouch and a sheathed dagger hanging from it. The knight was about Sloane's height, with the kind of muscular build one had from daily physical labor. Like Gisele's, his greenish skin gave him a menacing appearance. His prominent jawline was covered in light stubble.

Deryk focused his sharp, piercing brown eyes on her as she stood outside the tavern. His two tusks, half as large as the knight-captain's, were set in a way that made his disappointed look seem sterner.

Sloane still couldn't believe she was living alongside what was essentially half-orcs and, of course, elves. The others had spoken of dwarves, and she couldn't wait to meet one.

The man narrowed his eyes when she didn't respond immediately.

"Sorry. I'm just out getting a drink. What are you up to?" she asked innocently. The others hadn't been happy about the back alley fighting, and they wanted to make sure she remained safe. She was fine, though. Just out in the central square.

Deryk shook his head. "Why are you out drinking alone?"

Since getting to know him, Sloane knew he chose his words carefully. He was usually silent, but when he did speak, he did so with a deep, resonant tone and quiet confidence that commanded attention.

"We're going to the next tavern, getting a drink, and asking questions. Then we'll finish up at the Loping Lizard. I'm information gathering," she said seriously. *Don't tell him you were originally trying to drown away your sorrows.*

The man grunted and joined her as she started walking. He sighed. "Sloane. That way," he said with a gesture.

She nodded and spun on her heel dramatically, pointing where he indicated. "Onward, my faithful knight!"

Deryk's lip turned up at the corner and he kept step with her as she redirected them to the second in her bar hop. It was a modest building with a thatched roof and a wooden sign hanging over the door. The sign depicted a mug of ale, and the name "The Thirsty Wench" was painted in faded letters beneath it.

They found themselves in a cozy, dimly lit space with a low ceiling and a fire burning in the hearth. The tavern was packed with patrons, with barely enough space to move around. The wooden tables and stools were closely arranged, leaving little room for privacy, and the noise level was high with laughter, chatter, and the clinking of glasses. Despite the lack of space, the atmosphere was friendly and convivial, with people from all walks of life gathering to share a drink and a story.

Deryk and Sloane had to squeeze through the crowded tavern to make it to the bar. They carefully navigated their way through the throngs of people, sidestepping chairs and bumping into patrons along the way. It was a slow and arduous journey that really made her realize she probably shouldn't have had that shot, but they finally made it to the bar and were greeted by the friendly bartender.

The bartender at The Thirsty Wench was a striking moon elf woman. She had shimmering silver hair that cascaded down her back in loose waves, framing her delicate features. Her piercing blue eyes sparkled with an inner light that seemed to reflect the tavern's warm and welcoming atmosphere.

I don't think the wench was the only thirsty one. I'm sure many of these guys are here just for her, thought Sloane.

"Good evening! Don't see many orkun through these parts. How's it goin', hon? What can I get for you?"

Sloane frowned at being slighted. *I'm right here!* The orkun next to her, however, smiled. "A Ghyll Spruce, please. My companion here will have your best local ale."

The woman did a double take as if just realizing Sloane was there. "Oh. Certainly."

She turned back to Deryk and spoke to him so quietly that Sloane could barely hear over the commotion in the room. "A Ghyll Spruce? A bit fancy for these parts, but I believe we have a few in the cellar." She seemed to ponder for a moment, tapping a finger to her lip. Her eyes lit up as she thought of something. "You know, I think they may be on one of the shelves. Any chance you could help me reach it?"

Thirsty Wench indeed. Sloane had to cover her mouth as she watched the look of realization settle on Deryk's face.

He glanced at Sloane. The moon elf did as well.

"If it helps, hon. She's welcome to… assist," the bartender stated a bit too confidently before leaning closer and whispering to Deryk.

Sloane's eyes widened as she heard the bartender's uncouth comments. She felt her throat constrict as she struggled to swallow, causing her to choke on her own spit. She quickly composed herself, trying to avoid any further awkwardness in the already uncomfortable situation.

Deryk, for his part, also seemed ill at ease. "My apologies, but as a knight, I would not feel right doing that to my friend, here," he replied.

The moon elf gave him a searching look before smiling. "Oh! She's just your friend. Wonderful. I will be right back with your drinks."

Sloane narrowed her eyes. *That was too easy.*

The woman quickly returned with a bottle of ale that had a cork in the top and a mug filled with another. She set the two drinks down in front of them and focused on Deryk.

"Feel free to come back after your friend goes to sleep tonight, ser," she said with a wink. She gave Sloane a positively feral smirk before making her way to the other side of the bar to help other patrons.

Deryk just shook his head before uncorking the cloudy glass bottle. Sloane looked down at her heady and thick ale.

"Does that look like spit to you?" she asked the orkun. He glanced over, but before he could respond, she shrugged.

"Aw, fuck it." She took a big swig, only to realize it was much stronger than she had anticipated. She tried to swallow, but her throat constricted, and for the second time, she began choking. Her face turned red as she coughed and sputtered, hoping no one other than Deryk was witness to her embarrassing moment.

Deryk looked amused. "Are you alright?"

She recovered, nodding.

A laugh on her left made her turn her head. Next to her, a raithe man was looking at her with an amused glint in his green eyes. He leaned close. "First time drinking the Tunstead Special?" he asked.

She raised a brow as she wiped at her face. "Was it that obvious?"

The man laughed again.

Sloane narrowed her eyes. "What's so funny?"

His boisterous sound tapered off and he took a few deep breaths to settle himself. "Ah, sorry. It was just your reaction. So, what brings you two to Tunstead?" he asked.

Sloane glanced at Deryk, who gave her a subtle nod. The orkun man had settled back into his quiet demeanor and wasn't going to speak.

"We're traveling through. Are you from here?"

The man nodded. "Sure am! Born and raised," he said with a lift of his mug.

Sloane smiled. "It's nice to meet you." Taking a much smaller sip, she nodded with a smile. "Better."

The man raised his mug and took a sip of his beer too.

Sloane suddenly had a brilliant idea, since the bartender likely wouldn't be of any assistance to anyone but Deryk. "Hey, actually… you haven't seen any travelers recently, have you?"

She had expected a shake of the head, a no, but instead, the man nodded immediately.

"I do remember some! Let's see, there was that group of merchants. A family. Two telv couples that were heading toward Thirdghyll. Let's see, oh there was that man and woman. The woman almost looked like a telv but with the skin tone of a sun elf. Strange lass that." He paused. "Although, now that I consider it, both she and the man had unnatural ears as well. Like a dwarf's."

Sloane's eyes widened. Humans? Her hair covered her ears, so the man wouldn't be able to tell she wasn't telv either. She briefly considered pushing but decided she didn't want that attention.

Wait. Family?

"You said a family? With kids? Did they all look similar?"

The man shrugged. "Well, I think it was a family. A husband and wife, along with a man who may have been the grandfather. They had four kids with 'em. Um, actually one of the kids wasn't blond like the others. She had brown hair. Actually—"

He glanced at Sloane's hair and lowered his voice. "Her hair looked awfully like yours." His eyes narrowed into slits, and his face reddened slightly as his countenance darkened with anger. "They didn't take your child, did they miss?"

She sucked in a breath. "I don't know who they are. I am just looking for someone. Are they still in town?"

The man's eyes somehow narrowed further. "I saw them getting food at the Loping Lizard not two days ago." His demeanor seemed to soften as if a wave had washed over him. He glanced at Deryk, then added, "The bartender there is much nicer, and won't try to steal your friend away for a night to add another notch in her bed. She's all about the conquests, that one."

Deryk coughed. "Thank you for your information. We appreciate it." He passed a few small silver coins to the man. "For your next few rounds. On us."

The man smiled big. "Thank you! I'll put this to good use."

The orkun knight gestured with his head to leave as he put more coins on the bar next to their mugs. They stood up, but the raithe man grabbed Sloane's arm and pulled her close to whisper in her ear. "I hope you find them. Don't give up," he said.

She smiled weakly and felt a surge of emotions fill her. "Thank you…"

The man nodded and let go of her arm.

As Sloane and Deryk walked out of the tavern, they were greeted by the cool night air and the muffled sound of patrons coming from behind them. The few remaining townspeople out and about seemed to be either heading to the various taverns, or back to their homes, and outside of the businesses dedicated to the nightlife, Tunstead was quiet.

Deryk led Sloane through the quiet streets of the townlet, the sound of their footsteps echoing in the night.

"So, why did you come out to join me and not one of the others?" she asked him as they walked.

He shrugged. "Gisele was… busy at the wagon and asked Cristole to help her. Ernald, Ismeld, and Maud were drinking. I noticed you were gone, so I decided to find you and make sure you were alright."

That was nice. She could appreciate the gesture.

"Thanks for joining me. One last place, then we can head back?"

The orkun nodded. "I'll follow your lead."

She smiled as they continued to the last of the three taverns. The Loping Lizard was a large wooden building with a sloping roof and a sign hanging above the door depicting a green lizard mid-stride with a lopsided grin. The sound of lively music and chatter spilled out into the street, and the smell of roasting meat and ale filled the air.

They entered a spacious main room with several large tables intended for groups of patrons, but about half were empty because it was late. A pair of moon elves sang a jaunty tune, playing instruments similar to lutes. The tables nearest the two entertainers were filled with patrons singing along. Various hunting trophies and trinkets likely from far-off lands adorned the walls.

Sloane and Deryk made their way to the bar at back of the tavern, which was smaller, with only six stools. They sat at the last two spots available, prompting the bartender to immediately walk up. The older woman behind the bar was striking with her black and silver hair. She had crow's feet etched around her light-red eyes, evidence of a life filled with laughter and long hours of work.

Sloane had no doubt the woman was the source of all the decor. She could only imagine the stories the old raithe could tell her.

"Welcome, you two! What can I get ya?" the wizened woman asked.

"We'll take two ales—and some information," Sloane said with what she hoped was a disarming smile.

The raithe woman chuckled at Sloane's request for information. "Well, I've got plenty of ale, and some information too, if you're willing to pay for it," she said, her voice low and gravelly.

She poured the two ales and slid them over to Sloane and Deryk. "So, what do you want to know?" she asked, leaning against the bar.

Sloane smiled as she grabbed the proffered ale and took a drink, the taste much more palatable than the swill supplied at The Thirsty Wench.

"I was told a traveling family came through here a couple of days ago. Three adults and four children. Are they still around?"

The woman glanced between the two of them and held up three fingers. Sloane looked at Deryk, and the man rolled his eyes. He dug into a pouch at his waist and passed three small silver coins to the woman, who smiled as she made the coins vanish.

"They left a day ago. Hitched a ride with a merchant heading to Vilstaf," she said.

Sloane nodded. "They had a girl with them, looked a bit different?"

The woman shrugged. "There were two girls, but I think I know which one you mean… Yeah, the woman's niece, I believe they said. The older gentleman, the grandfather, was watching her most of the time. She was quiet. Barely spoke, that one. Those piercing blue eyes, though… she'll have to fight boys off with a stick one day," she said with a chuckle. Her eyes narrowed. "Didn't quite like my food. Kept talking about spices and herbs…"

Sloane's eyes went wide and she stared at the raithe woman open-mouthed.

"Thank you, miss. We appreciate the drinks and the help," Deryk said, sliding more coins to the woman.

The woman smiled. The second offering of coins also vanished quickly. "Thank you, kindly. I'll leave you two to it."

Sloane jerked her head to yell at Deryk, but the man cut her off with a gesture. When the woman was out of earshot, he said under his breath, "Not here. We are leaving tomorrow. Let's finish our ales and get back."

Nodding slowly, Sloane took a deep breath and turned back to her ale.

She wanted to jump up and run. To rush to the inn and get everyone to leave immediately. She knew that was unrealistic. Traveling during the night was dangerous—who knew if there were other monsters out there like the wolves? Leaving in the morning was sensible.

She tried to not give anything away, but internally she was screaming. There were signs in the woman's explanation. Her blue eyes and talk of higher-quality food...

Could it be her?

CHAPTER SIXTEEN

BURGEONING REALITY

Sloane walked outside and was greeted by the sight of not one, but two wagons. The presence of the telv merchant Raolin—the man who had been injured on the road and saved by Maud—was a surprise. But there he stood, with his sun elf friend, speaking with Gisele and Cristole.

Ismeld stood off to the side with her arms crossed and a frown set on her face.

"What's wrong?" Sloane asked, coming to stand beside the knight.

Ismeld flung her hand forward to indicate the scene before them. "This. It will slow our trip dramatically."

Sloane couldn't really see how, but she figured she'd humor the blond high elf. "Why are they coming with us?"

Ismeld sighed. "They offered to pay us to escort them to Vilstaf."

"That's good, right?"

Ismeld nodded. "It is, but I would prefer to not stay on the road overlong. The region is dangerous, as we have already seen. I am worried about us spreading too thin," she said.

Sloane gave her a sympathetic look. "I can understand that, but there's only two of them, and Averet is a guard, so it's not as if they're completely helpless."

Ismeld seemed to consider this for a moment before conceding. "I suppose you are correct. We will just have to make sure to keep a steady pace and not let them slow us down too much."

"Exactly. We can handle this," Sloane said, smiling.

The high elf gave her an amused look. "We?"

Sloane chuckled. "Of course! You saw how well I did with the wolves. I will admit my performance with the thug was subpar, but I got this," she said, flexing her arm.

Ismeld shook her head and laughed. "You are something else. Thank you. I appreciate the gesture," she said. She gave Sloane one more nod before turning and walking away.

I was being serious!

Averet noticed Sloane approach and perked up as he raised his hand in a wave. "Lady Reinhart! It is good to see you," the sun elf guard greeted her.

"Nice to see you, too, Averet," Sloane said, smiling for the man's benefit.

My, he's got quite the… sunny demeanor.

She smiled at her own joke, wishing Gwyn was around to nudge. Her daughter loved her "mom jokes," as Gwyn liked to call them—after all, it was just the two of them. It was tough at times, but they both got through it. Sloane's family had helped a lot after…

Sloane froze as a pang of sadness washed over her. Not only was she missing her daughter, but also both of them had been forcibly ripped away from all they knew.

The two of them were good about keeping up with family. Sloane had talked to her sister every day for hours at a time. She also called her mamma every couple of days, and her father whenever he wasn't working. But that didn't allay the feelings of guilt that had burrowed into her heart, forcing her to recall the last times she saw her family in person.

She and Gwyn were alone and might never see their family again.

Or each other.

Sloane didn't even realize she had started hyperventilating or fallen to her knees until Maud was sitting next to her, holding her. Looking up through her tears, she noticed Ismeld and Deryk standing protectively nearby. Gisele stood behind Maud.

Sloane took a few deep breaths, trying to calm herself as she felt Maud's comforting presence beside her. She leaned into the healer's embrace, grounding herself with the warmth of her body and the softness of her touch as the woman gently caressed her hair.

"I'm sorry," Sloane murmured, her voice shaky. "I don't know what came over me."

"It's okay," Maud said soothingly. "You don't have to apologize. We all have our moments."

Sloane nodded, feeling embarrassed but also grateful. She wiped away her tears and took another deep breath.

"I just miss my daughter so much," she admitted. "And I'm scared that I might never see her again."

"Would you like to rest in the wagon? We can speak privately if you wish," the knight-medic offered.

Sloane shook her head. "No need, I'm fine," she said. She couldn't help but laugh ruefully at the circumstances. "Look at me. This is so embarrassing. One errant thought and I'm on the ground losing myself." She stood and glanced around, realizing that the others appeared ready to leave. Sloane took a deep breath. *Shit, I'm delaying us leaving. We need to get to that village where Gwyn could be.*

"Are we all set?" she asked, trying to sound confident.

The telv redhead nodded, giving her a look of concern. "We are."

Sloane sucked in another breath. "Alright. Sorry, let's go."

Maud put her arm around Sloane and guided her toward the wagon while the others prepared to leave.

Later, as she lay down on the cot in the wagon, her thoughts ran through everything that had gone wrong with the fight against the thug. She really needed to figure out a better way to fight.

Sloane's eyes fluttered open as she was jolted awake by the sound of horses snorting and neighing. She felt disoriented and confused for a moment, her mind still foggy with sleep. She noticed that the wagon had come to a stop and she was the only one inside. She sat up, rubbing her eyes and trying to gather her bearings.

Getting up, she cracked open the door to peer outside and saw that they were in the middle of a dense forest. Tall trees loomed overhead, casting a shadow over everything. She couldn't see anyone else around, but she could hear the sound of a stream nearby. Sloane wondered where the rest of the group had gone and why they had stopped in the middle of nowhere.

She pushed the door fully open and stepped out of the wagon. The cool air hit her face, and she took a deep breath, feeling more awake and alert. She looked around, trying to spot any sign of the knights, but other than the horses tied to the wagons, everything was quiet and still. She walked a few steps away from the wagon, careful not to stray too far, and tried to listen for any sounds that might indicate where the others were.

Someone laughed and Sloane released a breath she didn't realize she'd been holding. She heard footsteps approaching and turned to see Ernald walking toward her, carrying a cup and a wooden bowl filled with steaming stew. The spoon sticking out of the bowl made her stomach growl, reminding her that she hadn't eaten in a while.

"Sloane, you are awake!" Ernald said. He lifted the bowl up. "I brought you food. We figured you would be hungry."

Relieved to see a friendly face, Sloane smiled and greeted him back. "Yes, I am. Thank you for bringing this. I'm starving."

Ernald chuckled, handing her the cup and bowl. "I thought you might be. I made this stew only an hour ago, and it's been simmering ever since. It's not the fanciest, but it should be filling."

"Thank you, Ernald," Sloane said, accepting the food and drink. "How long was I asleep?"

"Only a few hours," the knight replied. "We had to stop for a bit to give the horses a rest, and the merchant asked to eat, but we should be moving again soon."

Sloane scanned her surroundings, hoping to spot the group. Ernald pointed behind him. "Everyone is over there, in a small clearing. The road is narrow and the trees are too thick to move the wagons through, so we had to stop here. Deryk is keeping an eye out, so you were not left unguarded. In fact—"

Before Ernald could finish his sentence, the sound of approaching footsteps made Sloane turn around. The orkun knight emerged from the nearby brush. He looked around cautiously before nodding at Sloane and Ernald.

"Good to see you're up and about, Sloane," he said in his deep voice.

She glanced down at the food just as her stomach rumbled, eliciting a laugh from the sun elf. "Do you want to eat here, or join the group?" Ernald asked.

"Let's join the group," she said.

Deryk returned to his patrol and the sun elf nodded and motioned for her to follow him. Sloane followed Ernald as he walked along a narrow dirt path through the trees and into the clearing he had mentioned. The group sat on stone seating circling a fire; it was clearly a well-used camping spot for travelers. She couldn't help but wonder how many others had passed through this place before them.

As she approached, the group greeted her warmly. Maud patted the space next to her, inviting Sloane to sit.

The merchant, Raolin, smiled as she sat. "Greetings, Lady Reinhart. I trust you are feeling better. I cannot imagine what it is like to have to travel for so long while your child is at home, let alone as a mother," the man said.

Maud leaned closer to her and whispered, "We told him that you left Gwyn at home while you traveled the continent on diplomatic business. You aren't from this region of Ikios."

"Shit, Maud! Deryk and I got a lead on Gwyn last night. She might be in Vilstaf! What do we do when they find out we lied?"

Maud shrugged. "You'll have Gwyn, so what does it matter? They're not a bad pair. I'm sure they'd understand."

Sloane slowly nodded before looking at the merchant, who was quietly observing her and Maud with an expectant gaze.

She took a deep breath. "It is tough, but I am lucky to have the knights with me. I apologize for not greeting you sooner. I heard you are traveling to... Vilstaf? Is that right?"

The man smiled. "Yes. With the loss of most of my goods, I am unable to continue my route," he said, before turning toward the sun elf guard and putting a hand on his shoulder. "Luckily, Averet had convinced me to put almost all of our funds into the Banking Guild before leaving the port of Moonlock. We managed to purchase enough items so that we can start a small stall in Vilstaf."

Sloane nodded. "Isn't Vilstaf a village?"

The man chuckled. "It is! But it is on a popular trade route. All traffic from the capital and from Moonlock travel through there to Thirdghyll, and then on to the Sovereign Cities."

She had no idea what any of that meant, but she knew she could pester Ernald into telling her later. For now, she simply nodded along and paused to take bites of her food as the man spoke.

As everyone finished up and put things away, Sloane joined Gisele as she spoke with the merchant.

"Thank you for letting us stop for lunch, Ser Gisele," the man was saying. "We will be good until we stop for the night."

Gisele winced slightly. "Indeed. We will stop at a good place to camp for the evening, then make it to Vilstaf before lunch," the orkun knight explained.

The man nodded. "Sounds good! I will make sure my wagon is ready."

"Perfect. We are just about ready and will wait for you. Ser Cristole will be riding alongside you, so let him know if you have any issues."

As the merchant walked away, Gisele turned and looked at Sloane with a strained expression. "We could have made it to Vilstaf by nightfall."

Sloane winced. That meant she could have been looking for Gwyn before the day was up. She mentally cursed the merchant.

Gisele must have noticed her struggling with her thoughts, for she placed a hand on her shoulder. "Deryk told me what you learned after I had already made a deal with the merchant. Had I known—"

Sloane gave her a weak smile. "It's fine. I understand. We'll just have a busy day tomorrow! Will… will you join me as I look?"

Gisele smiled. "Of course. Now, come on, let's not dawdle. We need to go," she said.

Sloane nodded. She completely agreed. Time to get a move on.

As they exited the woods, the trees thinned out and gave way to a wide-open space. The wagon bounced and jolted as it traveled over the uneven terrain, but Sloane and Ernald held on tight. The rolling plains stretched out before them, the horizon dotted with distant hills and small clusters of trees.

Sloane breathed in the fresh air and took in the vast expanse of greenery before them, happy to leave the woods and its scent of pine behind.

As the two wagons and mounted knights continued their journey across the rolling plains, Ernald began to tell her more about his homeland, which, she noted, was a pleasant distraction, and tugged at her love of fantasy settings. He explained that the island kingdom of Blightwych consisted of three main islands with a lot of smaller ones, most of those not even populated. Each island had its own unique culture and customs, but they were all united under the rule of the king.

Ernald told Sloane about his own hometown, the city of Brievé. He described it as a bustling port city, where ships from all over the world came to trade goods and share news. He told her about the tall, elegant buildings made of white stone, and the narrow streets that wound their way through the city like a maze. He also told her about the famous Brievéan market, where one could find everything from exotic spices to rare books.

Sloane listened intently to Ernald's stories, fascinated by this new world that she was discovering. She asked him questions about the kingdom and its people, eager to learn more. Ernald was happy to share his knowledge with her, and they continued to chat as the wagon rolled on.

Sloan told him about the curious similarities between the cultures of this world and her own. As they discussed it, she realized that there were some differences, mainly due to having at least seven different races of people. The one that surprised her the most, however, was that other than the dwarves, all of the various races mixed together and made up national cultures, rather than species-based ones.

When pressed on that fact, the knight-scholar explained that it was mainly due to the dwarves building their cities and kingdoms in and under mountains. Which was one of the few tropes fantasy on Earth got right.

She appreciated that fact, although she was laughed at when she asked if female dwarves had beards.

"What? Why would they have beards? Do women in your world have beards? That's so strange!" he said, but then his eyes widened. "Wait, can you grow a beard?"

"No!" she laughed at the thought. "Sorry, just a silly question," she said sheepishly.

The sun elf laughed as she shook her head.

As they crested a small hill, Ernald suddenly sat up straighter and pointed ahead of them. "Look," he said, "do you see that smoke rising in the distance?"

Sloane strained her eyes, and sure enough, she could see a thin column of smoke rising up into the clear blue sky.

"What do you think it could be?" she asked, a note of concern in her voice.

Ernald's expression darkened. "I'm not sure, but it could be trouble."

She glanced up. Gisele was making her way back to the wagons. At her approach, the other knights rode to the front of the two-wagon caravan, while the merchant and his guard stayed back.

Sloane's heart raced with worry, which wasn't calmed at all when Gisele confirmed to the rest of the group that she had indeed seen the smoke rising in the distance.

Maud, who had been taking a few moments to rest inside one of the wagons, peered out of the door, her curious expression betraying her confusion at why they had suddenly come to a stop. "What's happening?" she asked, squinting in the direction of the smoke.

Gisele offered her a calm and reassuring smile. "It's alright, Maud. We just need to check something out," she said, her voice steady.

Despite Gisele's attempt at reassurance, Maud still appeared uncertain. "Should I come out and assist? Was there anyone hurt?" she asked, her hand hovering near the door handle.

Gisele shook her head. "I don't know, but for now, just stay inside and keep yourself safe. We'll call out if there are any issues." She turned back to the group.

Ismeld rode up, looking thoughtful as she considered the source of the smoke. "Do you think it could be a cooking fire?" she asked, her voice laced with uncertainty.

Gisele turned, her face etched with concern. "I doubt it," she said firmly. "The smoke is too thick and dark for it to be just a cooking fire."

Ernald and the other knights exchanged worried glances at Gisele's words. If it wasn't a cooking fire, then what was causing the smoke? The uncertainty only heightened their sense of unease.

"Well, we cannot simply ignore it," Cristole said.

Gisele shook her head. "No, we cannot. Especially since it is already coming from somewhere near the road, it will be impossible to ignore."

Deryk shrugged. "Then our choice is decided. We will investigate," the orkun man stated simply.

Sloane nodded, feeling a mixture of excitement and apprehension. She knew that this could be the beginning of something dangerous, but she also knew she had to make sure it wasn't the group she was searching for that had left Tunstead and headed for Vilstaf. While the timeline did not add up, it was better to be safe than sorry.

The group urged their horses forward, moving toward the source of the smoke, their hearts pounding with anticipation and fear.

Or at least just mine is. With a deep breath, Sloane instinctively went for her sword, her grip tight around the hilt. She knew they couldn't afford to be caught off guard, especially with the ominous smoke ahead. Despite the uncertainty, she was determined to be prepared for whatever might come their way.

The two wagons, creaking and groaning under the weight of their cargo and the urgency of their movement, were escorted by the mounted knights, who kept a watchful eye on their surroundings. Next to Sloane, Ernald, the sun elf scholar—but no less capable in a fight—urged the wagon's horses to speed along faster, his eyes scanning the landscape for signs of danger.

Meanwhile, Gisele and Cristole rode ahead of the wagons with their swords at the ready, their alertness heightened by the thick smoke in the distance. Sloane fixed her eyes on her watch while her hand still rested on her sword.

She knew that time was of the essence and any delay could prove fatal. As her watch continued its constant scan of any signs of mana use, Sloane couldn't help but feel a sense of unease. She was just a normal woman from a modern society. She wasn't a knight, let alone a soldier back home. She had never been in a situation like this before, and the gravity of the situation was not lost on her.

Behind the small caravan, Ismeld and Deryk rode closely behind the merchant's wagon, their heads on swivels as they watched for ambushes from behind.

The smoke was growing thicker now, casting an eerie glow over the surrounding landscape. Sloane couldn't shake the feeling that they were walking into a trap.

As the group approached the source of the smoke, their worst fears were realized. Three merchant wagons lay smoldering by the side of the road. Some bits of debris were still on fire.

"Let's dismount and search the area," Gisele ordered. "Look for survivors or bodies."

The knights fanned out to investigate the area, their eyes peeled for any signs of the attackers. Sloane's heart was pounding in her chest as she too started walking around the area, her eyes glancing at her watch screen for any trace of mana use, her fingers trembling slightly as she gripped the hilt of her sword.

It was clear that the wagons had been deliberately set on fire, but with no bodies or signs of struggle, all it did was leave them more questions than answers. The only sounds Sloane could hear over the sound of her own breathing were the crackling of the flames and the occasional whinny of a frightened horse. It was eerily apocalyptic in her mind.

Gisele glanced at Sloane and gave her a questioning look.

"My watch doesn't sense any mana use," she said quietly, her voice tense with apprehension.

Gisele nodded, her jaw clenched in determination. "We need to search the area and see if we can find any clues as to who did this and why," she said, her eyes narrowing as she surveyed the scene.

She watched as the knights circled the wagons, examining the damage and looking for any signs of who might have been responsible.

After several minutes of searching, one of the knights called out to the group. "Over here! I've found something!"

The group hurried over to Ismeld, who pointed. In the distance, they could see a figure running away from them, disappearing into the trees. "It looks like we have a suspect," Gisele said. "We need to catch them before they get away."

Sloane watched an unspoken command pass among the knights. Gisele, Deryk, and Ismeld took off in a sprint toward the figure rushing away.

Sloane moved to catch up, but Cristole grabbed her shoulder.

"Stay here. We will watch the wagons in case whoever that is, is simply trying to lead us away," he explained.

Cristole spoke with authority, his voice cutting through the tense atmosphere.

"Ernald, please get Maud and the merchant guard. Sloane, join them. Keep your sword on you and ready. Set up close to the wagons," he instructed firmly. "I will patrol the perimeter, making sure there are no surprises waiting for us."

His words were met with nods of agreement from them. While Ernald quickly moved to gather Maud and the guard, Cristole set off on his patrol.

For her part, Sloane stayed close to the wagons, keeping watchful eyes on the surrounding area. She couldn't help but feel uneasy, knowing that danger could be lurking in the shadows.

I am completely out of my element. Is this my reality now? Monsters, bandits, and magic?

Well… that would require me to have magic.

CHAPTER SEVENTEEN

NEW NORMS

Sloane knew that she should have expected something to happen. It was only logical that something would transpire while the other knights were away. It had been too quiet. The absence of the usual rustling and chirping of the natural world should have raised a red flag. It was as if all the creatures had retreated, leaving a hollow, silent void in their wake.

When the strangeness of it all finally settled into her thoughts, the silence was shattered by a shout from Cristole. He came running back toward the wagon, his sword drawn and his face etched with urgency.

"Attack! We're under attack!" he yelled, his voice ringing out across the open land. Sloane's heart skipped a beat as she saw him spin and bring his shield up just in time to catch an arrow on it.

Without a second thought, she drew her sword and turned toward the source of the attack, her eyes scanning the area for any sign of the enemy.

As she looked around, an arrow whizzed past her ear and struck Averet. The man had tried to dodge out of the way but was not fast enough. The arrow sliced through the side of his neck. He fell to the ground, clutching at the wound as blood began to seep through his fingers. Maud was already sprinting toward him, her hands glowing as she drew mana and prepared to heal him.

The knight tossed Sloane her shield as she passed. "Cover us!" Maud ordered.

Sloane nodded and rushed after her, holding on to the round shield protectively as Maud knelt beside the merchant guard. Sloane's eyes widened, and she jerked her head down, screaming as an arrow slammed into the shield.

"Fuck!"

"Just give me a bit more time, Sloane! You're doing great!" Maud yelled.

Sloane glanced around the shield and saw the first bandits make it to the wagon and immediately launch into a fight with Cristole and Ernald. The two knights fought with a skill and precision that Sloane could only dream of. Their swords flashed in the sunlight as they parried and thrust, their movements graceful and deadly.

A raithe man broke away from the fight with the knights and rushed toward her.

Sloane gritted her teeth and charged forward, shield raised to deflect any incoming blows. She felt a sharp pain in her left shoulder as the man's sword glanced off the edge of her shield and sliced through the cloth of her shirt. She hissed in pain but did not falter, swinging her sword in a wide arc and managing to connect with his arm.

He cried out in pain and backed away. Sloane shifted her stance and kept the shield in front of her, trying to use what knowledge she had of fencing to help her. It was probably making her situation worse.

Sloane felt a jolt of pain shoot through her arm as the bandit's sword collided with her shield repeatedly. She gritted her teeth and tightened her grip, trying to maintain her balance under the onslaught. The man was relentless, and Sloane was struggling to keep up with his attacks. She knew she couldn't keep this up for much longer, and her thoughts turned to Maud and Averet. She had to watch over them, but she couldn't leave Cristole and Ernald alone to fight the bandits.

He pulled his sword back and slammed his shoulder into her, trying to shove her off balance, but Sloane used the force of the shove to spin around. She struck out again, managing to slice through the man's side.

The man grunted in pain and held his sword up weakly as he backed away. Sloane didn't pursue him. She was breathing heavily and her heart was pounding in her chest. She didn't want to stray too far from Maud, whom she stole a quick glance at and saw was finishing up healing the wounded guard. Sloane let out a sigh of relief knowing that Averet was in good hands.

The guard's wound was still pink, but he rolled his neck and nodded at the redhead. Sloane took a deep breath and turned back to the battle. Cristole and Ernald were still fighting the other bandits, but they seemed to be holding their own. Sloane knew she needed to join them if they were going to have any chance of winning this fight.

She sprinted toward the closest bandit, her sword at the ready. The man saw her coming and lunged forward with his own sword. Sloane parried the blow and counterattacked, but the man was quick and managed to dodge out of the way. They exchanged several blows, each one trying to gain the upper hand, and each hit sent a surge of pain through her wrist.

Sloane was getting tired, but she refused to let it show. She knew her strength was waning and her movements were slowing down. It was a matter of time before the bandit would land a fatal blow. She had to think of a way to end this quickly.

The man saw an opening and lunged at her again. This time, Sloane sidestepped and kicked out, hitting him in the hip with her foot. He stumbled backward, surprised by her move. She took advantage of the moment and lunged forward, disarming him with a swift movement of her sword.

The man recoiled in fear, his hands jerking up shakily into a fighting pose. His eyes widened as he saw something, and then a bolt struck him in the chest, sending him to the ground.

Sloane gasped. She turned and saw Averet reloading a crossbow. She let out a breath of relief as she watched Averet join the fight. She knew she couldn't keep going much longer, and she was grateful for the backup. Maud was running toward her, and the healer's worried expression made her heart clench.

"Sloane! Are you hurt?" Maud asked, checking her over quickly for any wounds.

"I'm fine, just a scratch," Sloane replied, wincing as Maud prodded at her injured shoulder.

The healer nodded. "I'll heal it after. Get back to the wagons," she said, but Sloane shook her head.

"I can't leave them," she said, nodding toward the other knights who were still fighting.

Maud hesitated, then nodded. "Okay, let's go, but be careful."

Sloane nodded and turned back to the battle. She offered Maud her shield, but the woman waved her off. "You need it more than me. Let's go. Stay close."

Together, Sloane and Maud made their way toward the other knights. She saw that Cristole and Ernald had managed to take down two more of the bandits, but there were still three left.

As she and Maud approached, the bandits hesitated. Suddenly, there was a loud whistle, and the bandits turned to look.

Sloane took advantage of the distraction and rushed forward. She swung her sword, managing to disarm one of them. Maud used the moment and struck out, her mace bashing the bandit in the chest.

"Retreat!" the bandit leader shouted, and the remaining two quickly backed away before turning and running away as fast as they could.

As the man Maud had hit slowly slumped to his knees, Sloane watched the others go, her heart pounding. She had survived her first real battle, but it had been a close call. She turned to see Cristole and Ernald making their way to her, both of them battered but alive.

The knights stood panting, their weapons at the ready, waiting for any more attackers. But none came. The area was quiet, except for the sound of their heavy breathing.

"Thanks for the backup," Cristole said, turning to Sloane and Maud.

Sloane smiled despite her weariness, feeling a sense of camaraderie with the knights.

"We need to get you two looked at," Maud said, looking at their injuries.

Cristole sighed and looked down at a particularly deep gash. "Yes, that will probably be best."

Sloane nodded, feeling the adrenaline wearing off and the pain starting to set in. She followed Maud back to the wagons as the redhead spoke with Cristole.

As they walked, Sloane couldn't help but think about how close she had come to being killed. She realized she had a lot to learn and needed to improve her skills if she wanted to survive in this world. She made a mental note to train harder and to learn from the experienced knights around her.

Maud quickly tended to Cristole's wound using her healing magic to close the gash. Sloane watched as the healer worked, impressed by her ability. As the healer finished up, Cristole stood and thanked Maud before returning to Ernald. The telv woman turned to Sloane.

"Let me take a look at that shoulder now," she said, motioning for Sloane to sit down.

Sloane winced as Maud prodded at the wound, but she knew it was necessary. After a few minutes, the healer had finished, and Sloane felt the pain start to subside. She thanked Maud and went to join the other knights.

Cristole and Ernald were talking quietly, looking serious. "That was close," Cristole said, looking up at Sloane. "We need to check on the others. Ernald and I will grab the horses and ride out. I think things will be fine here until we return."

Sloane nodded. She looked around at all of the bodies and suddenly felt a wave of nausea hit her. Her stomach churned and she stumbled backward, nearly falling to the ground. She held up a hand to signal to the others before rushing away and bending over, retching.

Maud rushed over, concerned. "Sloane, are you alright?" she asked, putting a hand on Sloane's back.

Sloane shook her head, still heaving. She didn't know what was happening to her, but she couldn't stop the vomiting. After she relieved her stomach of what felt like a week's worth of food, she started to feel a little better. She wiped her mouth on her sleeve.

"I'm sorry," she muttered, embarrassed.

Maud looked at her with concern. "It's alright. It's just a physical reaction to the stress and adrenaline. It happens to many people after a battle. Let's get you some water, and then you should rest," she said, leading Sloane back to the wagons.

"What about the others?"

Maud gave her a small smile. "They'll be fine. Cristole and Ernald are already heading that way."

Sloane felt a little better after drinking water and lying down for a while. She still felt shaky and weak, but the nausea had passed. She realized that she had a lot to learn about herself and how she reacted to stressful situations like this. She made a mental note to talk to Maud about it later and to work on building her resilience.

Sloane stepped out of the wagon a few hours later, noticing they were in a different location. A campfire was going, and all of the knights were sitting around it. The merchant, Raolin, and his guard, Averet, sat together off to the side. She narrowed her eyes. *I didn't even feel us moving.*

Sloane walked toward the group, realizing she was hungry. Her stomach grumbled. She sat down next to Cristole, who handed her a bowl of soup and a piece of bread.

"Thanks," Sloane said, taking the bowl gratefully. She ate the soup hungrily, feeling the warmth spread through her body. After a few moments, she felt a little better and let out a contented sigh.

"Nice to see you up and about," Cristole said. "How are you feeling?"

Sloane gave a shrug and rotated her arm, feeling the ache in her shoulder. "I'm okay, just a little sore."

Ernald chuckled at her response. "You took quite the beating out there. That first bandit you fought really liked bashing on your shield."

Sloane felt a sense of pride in her accomplishments. "I think I did pretty well," she said, a small smile tugging at the corners of her lips. "I managed to land a few hits on one of the bandits and even disarmed another."

Deryk gave her a nod of approval. "That's good to hear."

Maud chimed in, "And you kept us safe while I was helping Averet."

Sloane glanced at the guard, who gave her a silent nod of thanks.

"Yeah, I wasn't ready to block an arrow. I got lucky," Sloane admitted, her pride quickly dissipating as she remembered her scream.

Maud shook her head. "Still, you were brave enough to rush in and help. That's a good quality to have."

Sloane's smile faltered slightly. "It felt good for a moment... until I threw up."

Everyone fell silent, unsure of how to respond. After a few moments, Ismeld spoke up. "It happens to the best of us," she said. "I remember vomiting after my first battle."

Deryk nodded in agreement. "It's the adrenaline, it can make you sick to your stomach. Especially when you see people lose their lives. It's not easy."

Cristole and Ernald shared a look. The high elf let out a sigh and spoke in a respectful tone. "Sloane, I must say, the bandits were terribly inept at fighting,"

Cristole said. "It was your first time, and you did well. But we must focus on training you more."

Sloane's face fell as she winced in acknowledgment. "I guess I still have a lot to learn," she said, feeling a tinge of embarrassment creeping up on her.

Gisele's concern was palpable as she spoke. "Don't worry, Sloane. We'll teach you," she said, her gaze unwavering. But a small smudge of food on her cheek stole Sloane's attention, and she couldn't help but let out a soft chuckle.

"Thanks, Gisele. You have a little something…" Sloane pointed to her own cheek to signal where the stray morsel was.

Gisele's eyes widened in surprise and she hastily wiped the smudge of food from her cheek, grinning sheepishly. "Thanks."

Ernald snickered. "You know, Gisele, for a captain, you seem to miss a lot of things," he teased with a grin.

Gisele pointed a spoon at him. "Let's not talk about how unobservant you are."

Ernald grinned. "I'm not unobservant, Gisele. I just prefer to let the details reveal themselves to me in due time."

Deryk took a sip of water, his face lighting up with a bit of mirth. "Reminds me of the time Gisele mistook a tree for a person during a night watch. Woke everyone up thinking we were under attack," he said with a small smirk, before disappearing behind his cup again.

Gisele scowled at the other orkun, her tone becoming darker. "Shut up, Deryk. At least I didn't get us ambushed."

Deryk raised his hands in mock surrender. "I probably could have told you both that would happen," he confessed.

Gisele narrowed her eyes. "Then why didn't you?"

"You're the captain," Deryk said, before taking another bite of food.

An awkward silence fell over the group, and Sloane could feel the tension in the air. It seemed to be centered on the three that had sprinted away when the bandits had attacked.

"So," Sloane started, breaking the silence. "What happened with you after you ran after that guy?"

Deryk cleared his throat and began to speak, his tone serious. "We caught up to the man, but he had friends with him. We were outnumbered, but we managed to hold our own."

Ismeld snorted, clearly frustrated. "We got ambushed. That's what happens when you don't have a plan."

Sloane raised an eyebrow in surprise. "You guys just ran off without a plan?" she asked, a hint of disbelief in her voice.

"Ismeld alerted the man that we saw him," Gisele said. "So I had to wing it. But still, we handled it."

The blonde turned and narrowed her eyes at Gisele, who stared back.

Sloane nodded. "That's really impressive."

Gisele turned back to Sloane and smirked. "We're knights, Sloane. We know how to fight."

Sloane chuckled. "Right, of course."

An uncomfortable silence fell over the group once again, and Sloane could feel the tension building. She couldn't help but feel there was more to the story than what they were telling her.

"So, what happened after that?" she asked, trying to keep the conversation going.

"Maud had to heal me when we returned," Ismeld said drily. "It itches."

"Don't be a baby, Issy. It was a tiny cut," Gisele retorted.

Ismeld put down her bowl and gestured with her arm. "My arm almost got sliced off because you went left when I said to go right!"

The orkun knight also set her bowl aside, her frustration palpable. "You gestured left! And said right!" she exclaimed, her hands flailing to emphasize her point. "There was a guy to the left! What was I supposed to do?"

The high elf's ear twitched and her eyes narrowed, ready to argue. But before she could speak, Maud intervened in a calm voice.

"Ismeld, let it go. You're fine. I healed you."

Ismeld let out a strangled cry of frustration before getting up. "You're right. Thank you, Maud. Your magic is indeed a blessing, and luckily, I didn't lose my arm to infection. I'm going to my tent." All eyes followed her as she stormed off, leaving the group in silence.

After a moment, Gisele let out a sigh and slowly pushed herself up, brushing off her leggings as she stood. "I'll go talk to her," she said, her voice carrying a sense of determination as she walked after the high elf knight.

Sloane watched as Gisele disappeared into the darkness, her footsteps crunching on the dirt path. The fire flickered, casting long shadows across the faces of the remaining knights. Ernald cleared his throat, breaking the silence.

"Well, that was certainly interesting," he said, his tone light but with an underlying sense of concern.

"I hope everything's okay between them," Sloane said, turning to face the group.

Ernald huffed a laugh. "They argue all the time. It's mostly entertaining."

Deryk raised an eyebrow. "Ismeld is... She's always been a little... hot-headed."

Maud smiled. "Yes, but that's what makes her such a great knight. She's fiercely loyal and won't back down from a fight."

Sloane chuckled. "So, what do Ismeld and Gisele argue about?"

Maud answered before anyone else could. "Oh, all sorts of things. Tactics, strategy, who has the better weapon..."

"And who has the better aim," Ernald added, smirking. "Who can drink more."

"That's enough, Ernald," Cristole said.

The knight-scholar's eyes widened. "Sorry, Cristole. I was just—"

"Now isn't the time," the elf replied.

Maud let out a groan.

"Is everything okay with her, though? She seemed pretty upset when she left," Sloane said. She looked at Maud questioningly, but it was Cristole who spoke.

"Don't worry about it," he said. "This is just the way Ismeld gets sometimes. She's not used to being the one to make a mistake. She works harder than the rest of us…" The knight trailed off.

"Because she constantly strives to prove that she belongs," Deryk finished for him.

Sloane nodded and looked over at the tent where Ismeld and Gisele had gone.

"It's not always easy, our travels," Cristole said softly. "We all have our own struggles and reasons for continuing. But in the end, we have each other's backs. Ismeld and Gisele more than anyone. They're the reason we're all here."

Maud looked over at the knight and gave a small shake of her head. With a resigned sigh, Cristole stood up and circled around to collect the empty bowls. After a brief pause, Maud followed suit.

Sloane turned to Deryk. The stoic orkun man sat quietly. "Deryk," she began, "did you all learn anything about the bandits?"

He nodded. "Yes."

Her gaze sharpened when he remained silent. With a deep sigh, he finally relented. "They weren't just bandits."

Sloane's eyebrows furrowed. "What were they, then?"

"Slavers," he said, before he got up and walked away.

Her eyes widened. Slavers?

Ernald gave her a smile that almost seemed apologetic before he too jumped up and raced after Deryk.

"Well. That was certainly something," Raolin said with an awkward chuckle.

Sloane turned and looked at the two men everyone seemed to have forgotten about. She huffed out a breathy laugh.

"They completely forgot you two were there, didn't they?" she asked.

Averet nodded. "Yeah, I think so."

Raolin smiled weakly. "It's alright. We're just glad that the knights were here for protection. Especially after seeing those other wagons…"

Sloane tilted her head. "Do you know anything about these slavers?"

Averet shook his head. "Not much. They tend to operate in the shadows, keeping to themselves. Slavery is legal in some places, but not anywhere this far west. So, it's strange to even see them."

"It's horrible that it is legal at all," Sloane said.

Raolin nodded. "I agree. Slavery is abhorrent. The only two nations that allow it in the region are Zhaoloka, an island nation southeast of the continent, and the Turest Order."

"Where is the Turest Order?" Sloane asked.

"They're north of the Kingdom of Avira. Quite far," he explained.

Sloane furrowed her eyebrows. "Why are these slavers operating here, then?"

Averet scratched his chin. "Maybe they were hired by someone in the area who wanted to keep their activities hidden."

Raolin's expression turned grave. "That's a chilling thought."

Sloane nodded in agreement. "We should be even more vigilant from now on."

The group fell into a heavy silence as they pondered the implications of the slavers' presence. The thought of innocent people being sold into slavery was sickening, and Sloane couldn't help but wonder how many others had fallen victim to their cruel trade.

Averet spoke up. "We're living in dangerous times. The world is shifting, especially after the Flash, and we have to adapt to survive."

Raolin nodded. "There is much opportunity for those who would take it. But now, more than ever, it is important to find trustworthy people and band together. Monsters, bandits, slavers… magic. All these things make up this new normal for us. I can see all this change causing great turmoil in our civilization."

The group's conversation turned to the current state of the world. Sloane listened as they discussed the increasing frequency of bandit attacks and the growing tensions between nations. It seemed that war was on the horizon, and everyone was bracing themselves for the inevitable conflict.

Eventually, Sloane bid the two good night and joined Maud in her tent to sleep. Maud was already fast asleep, her armor still on and her mace at her side. Sloane sighed softly, feeling a sense of sadness wash over her.

How bad do things have to be for this to be normal?

Sloane shook her head and climbed into her own bedroll. She couldn't help but feel worry for Maud and the others on this journey. The revelation that the bandits were actually slavers had shaken her to her core, and she knew they couldn't let their guard down for even a moment.

What if they had Gwyn?

She closed her eyes and tried to push away her fears, reminding herself that they had a lead in Vilstaf. She just hoped the people they were following had made it through the area and weren't attacked. But even as she drifted off to sleep, Sloane couldn't shake the feeling that something dangerous was lurking just around the corner.

CHAPTER EIGHTEEN

ROAD TO LARTON

Even after mana reverberated throughout the world, it took some time before the denizens of Eona realized all that it could accomplish. The discovery of the First Mage created widespread political scrambling over the new status quo and potential. Their origin and heritage was only marginally contested, mainly because all wished to bring the mage into their sphere. It is believed that the nobility at the time simply wanted any reason to solidify their own standing within society. Acknowledging the status of the mage was wholly self-serving, even if the benefits it would later provide the First One were profound.

A History of Mana. 184 SA

Raafe sat beside Taenya by the fire, watching Gwyn and Keston work together to prepare their meal. Gwyn was animatedly describing the different cooking methods she had learned from a cook her mother had hired to help them when she got busy with work. Raafe couldn't help but smile as he watched her talk with such enthusiasm. Despite the danger they faced, Gwyn's spirit remained unbroken.

Turning to Taenya, Raafe spoke quietly. "I hope I can help her in any way I can. She reminds me of my younger sister. If something happened to her, I don't know what I would do." His voice was tinged with worry and sadness.

Taenya placed a hand on his shoulder, giving it a reassuring squeeze. "We'll protect her, Raafe. No matter what happens, we'll keep her safe."

Raafe nodded, grateful for Taenya's support. He knew that they would all have to work together to ensure Gwyn's safety. He couldn't bear the thought of losing her or failing in his duty to protect her.

"I will admit that I also hope that by helping her, I can help my family," Raafe continued hesitantly. He knew Taenya was a good woman, and he felt it was time to tell someone. They could have been killed by Ser Bekker's men, and then no one would know about what his family was going through.

Taenya watched him, letting him gather his thoughts.

"My family's debt was bought by a lord and they were moved to the capital," he said quietly. "And now they work for him without any hope of paying off their debt. My father has been ill, and I can't stand the thought of them living in servitude like that." Raafe's voice was filled with emotion, and he looked down at his hands, feeling ashamed for burdening Taenya with his troubles.

Taenya placed a hand on Raafe's arm, giving it a gentle squeeze. "You don't have to face this alone, Raafe. We're a team, and we'll help each other. We'll find a way to help your family and Gwyn."

Raafe looked up at Taenya, feeling a glimmer of hope. He had been carrying this burden alone for so long, and it felt good to share it with someone who understood. "Thank you, Taenya. I don't know what I would do without you and the others."

Taenya smiled, her eyes full of warmth and kindness. "We're in this together, Raafe. We'll help each other, no matter what."

He nodded. "You're right. I need to become a knight and protect Gwyn that way. She needs nobility on her side, and all I see within the nobility are those who will take advantage of her."

"Onas has an idea to approach a friend of his, a baron in Larton," Taenya explained. Noticing his confusion, she continued, "You haven't met Lord Iemes. He and Onas are good friends, and I have to admit, he's a good man. Likely because he was a commoner first; he wasn't born into the peerage."

Raafe listened carefully as Taenya explained Onas's plan. He was relieved knowing they had someone who could potentially help them.

"Lord Iemes, huh? I hope he's as good as you say he is. The princess could use someone like him on her side."

Taenya nodded. "I have faith in Onas's judgment. He wouldn't lead us astray. Besides, we have something that might convince the baron to help us."

"What's that?" Raafe asked, his curiosity piqued.

Taenya smiled mischievously. "Gwyn, of course. She's a princess, and one from another world at that. If we can prove her identity, it might convince the baron to help us."

Raafe considered it, his attention settling back on Keston and Gwyn. As they seasoned the meal with the scant amount of salt they had and a generous helping of herbs, Gwyn continued to share memories of her world, from the bustling town markets in the mornings to the lively streets filled with laughter and music at night. She spoke of how she and her mother would wander through the market, hand in hand, selecting the freshest produce and learning about the origins of the various ingredients they used in their culinary creations.

What I would give for a queen here to live a life so in tune with her people.

Raafe, thoroughly engaged in Gwyn's stories, couldn't help but feel a connection with the young princess. Her passion for cooking, as well as her appreciation for the simple pleasures in life, resonated deeply with him. As the two cooks finished preparing the meal, the aroma of their labor filled the air, and they joined Raafe and the others who had already gathered around the fire. Taenya patted Raafe's shoulder as she got up to join the princess.

Gwyn sat on one side of the fire, quickly diving into an animated discussion with Taenya and Onas, while Keston took a seat next to Raafe on the other side. The conversation between the women and the merchant was light-hearted, with occasional bursts of laughter as they shared jokes and stories. Meanwhile, Keston and Raafe talked quietly, their voices low enough not to disturb the others.

"Good job during the rush out of the village, Keston," Raafe told the other guard.

Keston smiled. "Thanks. You were pretty good yourself. That was quite the fight we had back there."

Raafe chuckled. "Yeah, I don't think Bekker will forget us anytime soon."

Keston glanced at Gwyn and laughed. "Imagine if Gwyn ever reached a point where she could send one of us to lord over him."

The sun elf choked on his food as he laughed. "Oh, the look on his face would be priceless. I'd love to see it."

"You should have heard her talk about us. She's given us roles, you know?" Keston said quietly. "It makes me hopeful. I don't know how serious she is, or if she's just lonely and trying to make friends, but I think we're doing a good job."

They both fell quiet for a moment, lost in their own thoughts. Raafe couldn't help but think about what Taenya had told him about approaching Lord Iemes for help. It seemed like their best bet, but he couldn't shake the feeling that things were going to get even more complicated from here on out.

As they ate, Raafe listened to Gwyn talk about her experiences in Italy, marveling at how different her life had been from his own. He found himself feeling a mixture of envy and admiration for the princess, who seemed to have lived a life full of adventure and excitement. He couldn't imagine what it would be like to travel the world. His life had been contained to one small area of the continent.

Raafe cleared his throat, drawing the attention of the group as they finished their meal. "Princess Gwyn, you've shared so many fascinating stories about your life in Italy and the delicious food you and your mother cooked. Would you be willing to share another story from your world? We'd love to hear more."

Gwyn smiled at Raafe, pleased to have been asked. "Of course, Raafe. Let me think for a moment." She closed her eyes, concentrating for a few moments before opening them again. "Oh, I have one! This year my mom and I got to go to the Carnevale di Venezia. Do you guys have carnivals or anything like that here?"

Raafe and Keston shook their heads, intrigued.

Gwyn continued, "It's a festival held in my world, in the city of Venice—or Venezia, in Italian. People from all over the world come to participate in the festivities, which last for about two weeks. There are gorgeous costumes and masks, music and dancing, and, of course, yummy food. It's like a time to not think about anything that makes you sad or scared, and just have fun and be happy!"

Taenya leaned forward, her interest piqued. "That sounds incredible. What kind of costumes and masks do people wear?"

Gwyn's eyes sparkled as she described the elaborate costumes and masks, from the simple to the ornate. She explained how each mask had a different meaning and how people would use them to express themselves in ways they couldn't normally.

Raafe had never heard of anything like this in his own world, and it fascinated him to hear about the traditions and customs of another place. He could see the excitement in the eyes of the others as they listened to Gwyn's story, and he felt grateful for the chance to share in such a unique experience.

When she finally finished, a few moments of silence hung in the air as everyone absorbed the enchanting tale.

Raafe, still captivated by the thought of such a colorful and lively event, suddenly recalled his earlier curiosity about whether Gwyn's world had any knowledge of sword fighting that could be of help to them. Trying to gently steer the conversation in that direction, he asked, "By the way, Gwyn, did you mention anything about using swords in your world?"

Gwyn shook her head and smiled. "Nope, no swords in my world. That's ancient history. But my mom used to do something called 'fencing' in college. It's a sport where you use special swords to hit each other, but not for real. It's a sport, just for fun and exercise."

Raafe nodded, feeling a bit disappointed. But he understood that her world was different, and they would have to rely on their own skills and training.

Just then, an idea struck him. "Gwyn, would you like to learn how to use a sword? It could be helpful on our journey, and I'd be happy to teach you."

Gwyn's eyes sparkled with excitement. "Yes! That sounds amazing! I've always wanted to try sword fighting, even if it's just for fun!"

Raafe glanced at Onas, who had been listening to their conversation with interest. The merchant grinned and said, "Well, it just so happens I have a training sword that would be perfect for a beginner like the young princess here. I'd be happy to gift it to you."

Gwyn's eyes went wide with anticipation, and she could hardly contain her excitement. "Oh, thank you so much, Mister Onas! I can't wait to start learning!"

Taenya, who had been watching the exchange with amusement, laughed and said, "Alright, let's not get too carried away. We can begin your training tomorrow, Gwyn. For now, let's focus on getting a good night's rest. We have a long journey ahead of us."

Gwyn nodded, still beaming with excitement, and the group finished their meal.

As the night wore on, they made their way to their beds. Raafe and Keston took the first watch. Raafe thought about the challenges that lay ahead of them, but he had hope knowing they had each other and the possibility of Lord Iemes's help. And for the first time in a long while, he felt a sense of purpose, knowing that he was fighting for something greater than himself.

Taenya had seen nobility, of course, but she'd had the opportunity to meet and speak with a noble only once. Onas had brought her along to meet a local lord; the man was barely a baron. He had recently been elevated to the peerage based on services rendered to the kingdom and wanted to establish a more stable trade route within his domain. Onas had managed to come out of that meeting with a much more profitable route than he had expected. One that catapulted the Fenren Trading House to the status of one of the larger houses in the region.

Onas established a branch of his merchant house within Larton and set up routes for other merchants under his employ. That Onas still performed a route himself while his wife maintained his primary storefront was admirable. Keen on maintaining connections with village and town heads, local knights, and even nobility, he made the most of the circuit he did once a year. These connections had brought him and the lower nobles he had relations with incredible wealth. His friendship with Lord Iemes had been a foregone conclusion; both men were charismatic to a fault and hit it off almost immediately when the baron had invited Onas into his small castle hall to discuss a joint venture. Which was why they were heading to Larton now.

Taenya's gaze shifted to Gwyn. Raafe sat on the driver's bench of the wagon, with the young princess perched beside him. Keston was riding the sun elf's horse along the other side of the wagon, while Onas remained inside, poring over his books in preparation for their arrival in Larton.

Taenya knew she should be concentrating on her surroundings, but she couldn't help being captivated by the presence of a real princess in their midst. Gwyn seemed so... ordinary, far from the haughty, unreachable figure she had imagined. Taenya found herself daydreaming about what it would be like to be in such a position, secretly delighted by Gwyn's down-to-earth demeanor. She wondered if this was simply how princesses were in Gwyn's world, or if Gwyn was a rare exception.

The head guard listened in after she heard Raafe and Princess Gwyn laugh. "Mister Raafe! That's not nice! Mister Keston is really kind. You shouldn't make fun of him like that."

"But Your Highness! If I do not keep Keston on the ground, I fear all the compliments you give him will make him float away!" Raafe teased.

Gwyn giggled. "That's not how it works, silly!" She was quiet for a few moments. Then, "Do you think we'll find my mom in Larton?"

Raafe patted the girl's shoulder. "I don't know, milady. If not, I'm sure we can find more information when we arrive back at Strathmore. The city has all sorts of people that should be able to help! Mister Onas has plenty of connections, and I have no doubt he'll be able to come up with a plan to locate your mother. At the very least, I believe we can get a lead."

Gwyn nodded, "I hope so. I really miss her. You think she's okay, right?"

Raafe wrapped his arm around the girl. "I'm sure of it. From what you've told me, your mother is a strong woman. She will be looking for you while we look for her. If we're lucky, we'll meet somewhere in the middle."

Taenya was completely surprised by the level of familiarity they were showing after only a little over a week. The trip was only minimally delayed from its original timeline. She had thought she, herself, was good with children, but the level of empathy and understanding Raafe showed genuinely impressed her.

Keston sped up to pull alongside the two. "Princess, is Raafe talking about me again?" he asked with a smile on his face.

The girl looked between the two. "Oh no. Nuh-uh. You two won't get me in the middle of this. I'm Switzerland."

Raafe laughed.

Keston chuckled. "While I don't know what 'Switzerland means,' I can guess." Looking to Raafe, he feigned hurt. "I'm disappointed, Raafe, you turned my best cooking friend against me," he said playfully.

"I would never! Her Highness has determined that you are the royal chef, while I am the captain of the royal guard," he replied, laughing. "Plus, we know she loves to show us more about food than anything about martial prowess." Looking at the royal in question, he said, "Don't worry, Your Highness, I'll make a swordswoman of you yet!"

Gwyn's eyes sparkled with excitement. "You promise? I can't wait to kick your butt with a sword."

"I promise!" Raafe managed to respond through his laughter.

Taeyna chuckled to herself, admiring the determination and surety that poured forth from the girl. She looked up at the sky, trying to ascertain how much longer they had until needing to set up camp. She looked around, then at the others.

"Keston, let's find a place to make camp. We'll continue in the morning, and reach Larton by nightfall. Perhaps Raafe and Her Highness can practice their swordsmanship."

The wagon had come to a stop, and the group had begun setting up camp for the night. Taenya had peeked inside the wagon to inform Onas that they would take care of everything, allowing him to focus on his work. Seizing the opportunity, Onas had dedicated his time to updating his ledgers meticulously.

When he finally emerged from the wagon, he found that the tents were already set up and neatly arranged. Taenya and Keston worked together, skillfully starting a campfire that crackled and flickered, casting warm, inviting light on their surroundings. Meanwhile, Raafe was off to the side with Princess Gwyn, showing her how to stand properly with her sword. Onas had provided the young girl with a beautifully crafted training blade from his stock. He always kept a few on hand to sell to the children of knights or nobility.

The sword was perfectly balanced and designed for beginners, making it an ideal choice for Gwyn. Intricate engravings of vines and leaves adorned the hilt, giving it an elegant appearance. The blade itself was blunt, ensuring that Gwyn could practice her swordsmanship with little risk of serious injury.

He walked over, intent on greeting the princess. Onas thought back to the conversation when she had brought up being a princess. He had, of course, asked more questions just to ensure the child wasn't playing a game. Every young girl pretends to be a princess. But no, he was thoroughly convinced. Especially after she described the size of her home and how her mother was constantly in meetings with important clients and telling them what to do. She spoke of the gated school that she attended. How she had private tutors and people to clean her home and cook for her. All of the little details that spoke to someone of influence.

One thing that stood out, however, was Gwyn's hesitation when he had asked about her father. Onas assumed it was because she had been with her mother when they were brought to Ikios and might be upset over the possibility of never seeing her father again.

Princess Gwyn turned as he walked up. "Hi, Mister Onas! Are you done with your work?"

He gave her a small bow, as one should to a foreign noble. They were no longer trying to avoid scrutiny from anyone in Hilshen, so decorum was again important. He'd have to remind his guards.

"I am at a stopping point, Your Highness. I wanted to come and see if you needed anything."

She shook her head. "Nope! I'm good. Raafe is teaching me how to fight with a sword. It's really cool!"

"Her Highness takes to the sword quite well, Master Onas. She is a very tenacious young lady."

Princess Gwyn smiled as she took in the compliment. Onas smiled too—Raafe was more than earning his keep with how he had taken a role in looking after the royal child.

"As one would expect of such a prodigious child." Looking at the girl, he added, "Your Highness, when we arrive in Larton tomorrow, we will meet with Lord Iemes. He is a trusted acquaintance that I have worked with for many years now."

"I will help, Mister Onas, but I'm unsure what you want me to do," the girl replied hesitantly.

"Fret not, Lord Iemes is the perfect choice for you to meet the true nobility of Avira. He will help us determine what will be needed to establish your status. He is a very nice man, and he has two children around your age, Lady Ryia, who is ten, and Lady Arlette, who is eight." Onas still couldn't believe the princess was only ten; based on her height and speech, he would have guessed twelve, at least.

He looked at Raafe. "I think it may be time to get ready for dinner, Raafe. Her Highness must be hungry."

Gwyn perked up. "I am! Oh, and tonight I get to help Mister Keston cook again! Thank you, Raafe, for helping me learn how to use a sword." She reached out to hand Raafe her sword and made to take off her scabbard.

Raafe crossed his arms. "Your Highness, it's your blade now. Please, wear it with pride. It's a beautiful training sword." Onas agreed; he had made sure that she had received the best-looking of the selection.

Gwyn looked sheepish. "Sorry! It's my first sword, I will remember. Thank you!" She placed the sword in its scabbard at her hip and started toward the campfire where Taenya was.

Raafe stepped next to Onas as they watched the girl walk away. "That girl is going to bring a lot of trouble, boss. Are you sure you can handle it? I mean no disrespect, but you're not exactly a big name."

Onas rubbed his hand through his hair. "You're not wrong, Raafe. However, this has the potential to add a lot of clout to the company. We'll have a firmer idea after we meet with the baron."

Raafe nodded. "I hope so boss, but one thing's for sure. That girl knows exactly what she's doing. I'll make sure she stays safe until we can figure something out or until we find her mother." He scoffed, shaking his head before continuing, "Or until her mother finds us. If the ten-year-old daughter can mobilize the four of us to help her, I wonder just who her mother has levied to her side."

Onas thought for a second. "I wonder, indeed."

Under a sky dotted with cottony clouds, Raafe rode his chestnut horse slightly ahead of Taenya as she rode alongside the wagon. The sun cast a warm golden hue on the forest, painting the verdant leaves and the path with streaks of light.

Birds sang in the trees, their melodies intertwining with the gentle rustling of leaves as a soft breeze danced through the branches. Keston was back at the reins, driving the wagon, with Onas beside him, keeping a watchful eye on the road ahead.

Inside the wagon, Princess Gwyn was likely still asleep, recovering from a night spent regaling Raafe and the others with tales of her world. Her stories had become an almost nightly occurrence, and last night's in particular had been so enchanting that they had stayed up far too late, listening with rapt attention. Raafe couldn't deny that the young princess had charmed them all, and her presence seemed to have a profound effect on the group.

As they traveled along the dirt road bordered by a dense forest on either side, Raafe scanned their surroundings. The lush greenery provided a sense of peace and tranquility, but he knew that dangers could lurk just beyond his line of sight. He contemplated the future, wondering how he could best serve and protect the princess in the days to come. Even if it wasn't reasonable to simply go out and search for the girl's mother, she would need people near her just within Strathmore.

It was proper for nobles to have a personal guard. Maybe he could request to fill this role for her; he didn't think Onas would mind. He would likely want to protect the girl himself, not just out of being the good man he was, but to protect the investment the princess would inevitably become. Even with the best interests in mind, Onas would have to justify having the princess around.

Nobles would happily swoop in to try and take the girl away, just so they could marry her to some heir somewhere only to have the prestige of their house having a princess attached to it. It disgusted Raafe how the nobility treated their own blood as something to be bartered and traded away.

They continued toward Larton at a reasonable pace, thinking they would arrive by that evening. Taenya was back in her ever stoic persona. Having the girl around seemed to soften her a bit. Not that he was complaining—it was definitely a positive development. He liked Taenya and Keston, they were good people, and he was keen on anything that improved his work environment.

The journey since the village of Hilshen had, thus far, been uneventful, but as Raafe rounded a bend in the road, he spotted a fallen tree blocking their path. The tree's massive trunk and gnarled branches sprawled across the road, making passage impossible. The leaves were still green, indicating that it had fallen recently. Raafe halted his horse, a sense of caution rising within him.

He waited for the others to catch up, the sound of the wagon's wooden wheels crunching on the gravelly path as it drew nearer. When they were close enough, he called out to Taenya. "There's an obstruction ahead. A tree fell across the road."

CHAPTER NINETEEN

RESPECT THE FIRE WITHIN

The moment Taenya heard Raafe call out about the fallen tree, her senses sharpened. The sun was still low in the sky, casting long shadows across the dirt road. The scent of damp earth and pine filled the air.

"Potential trouble ahead," she said to Keston and Onas. "Stay alert and ready for action. Onas, take over driving the wagon. Keston, hang on to the side and keep an eye out. Watch for archers. Shout if you spot anything."

Keston handed the reins to Onas and leaped to comply. "Understood," he replied. He grabbed a railing and stepped onto a small platform that stood over the wheel and positioned his shield at the ready as he searched the surrounding area.

Taenya turned her horse toward Raafe, grabbed her shield from its place on the saddle, and drew her sword. Fighting on horseback would be more effective, but she wasn't sure if there would be enough room for it. The terrain was challenging—a ditch to their left and trees to their right—an ideal ambush location. Birds chirped nervously in the treetops, almost as if they too sensed the tension below.

Reaching Raafe, she said, "Draw your sword. Do you see anything?"

"Nothing. You think the tree was deliberate?" he responded. Slowly, he drew his saber.

She nodded. "I do. Stay close to the wagon; don't get separated. We'll likely be outnumbered, so we need to stay together. If things go south, I need you to get the princess out of here. No hesitation. Understood?"

"I understand. I'll keep her safe," Raafe confirmed.

"Good. Don't dismount yet. Slowly move around and scan the ditch. I'll check the trees."

As Taenya approached the tree line, Keston called out, "Boss! We have trouble." She turned to see four men emerging from the trees behind the wagon. Three telv and an orkun armed with crude short swords and wearing gambesons. Realizing this was likely a diversion, she kept an eye on both the rear and the downed tree.

Raafe called out, "Taenya, there's a second group. Should we collapse to the wagon?"

"Yes, but don't turn your back on them. Fall back, and I'll address them," she responded as she evaluated the second group.

The orkun at the center appeared to be the leader of the bandits. He wore a leather cuirass and wielded a longsword. A raithe and another telv flanked him, while a high elf stood at the side, holding an axe and a javelin, with a bundle of more on his back. They stood confidently, smirks on their faces as they relished the prospect of an easy victory.

Ignoring the leader, she addressed the group. "Good morning, gentlemen. We're just passing through, and it's fortunate you're here as well, since we've come upon a fallen tree. Perhaps you could help us clear it from the road so we can all safely go about our day? In fact, we're willing to pay you a fee for the trouble."

The orkun laughed. "That's good. Sure, we'll help you, but I'm sure you understand if we want more than a simple fee. Let's say, you give us everything you own, and maybe a little attention, then we'll help you move it."

Taenya sneered in disgust. "This won't end the way you think it will. Just let us pass, and we'll not tell anyone we saw you."

The bandit leader laughed once more. "That's not going to work for us. Either your men drop their weapons and start unloading everything from your wagon while you come and talk to me privately, or we will simply go through you. You won't like that option. It ends with everyone on your side dead. Trust me, even if you do kill us, our first act will be to kill your horses, so you'll lose the wagon and everything in it anyway. Make the wise choice here."

Taenya weighed their chances. While Onas might be able to hold his own against one bandit, victory wasn't guaranteed. That still left the others facing at least two bandits each. She winced, realizing the odds were not in their favor. With a sigh, she raised her sword and shield, steeling herself for the fight.

"Yeah, we're going to have to decline. Run along now, and you might live."

The leader's smirk confirmed her suspicion as she spurred her horse into motion. She charged directly at the telv on the orkun's left, aiming to reduce the number her group had to fight. The bandit leader and raithe leaped away, but the telv wasn't fast enough. As she rode past him, she slashed her sword, catching him across the shoulder. Though not a clean hit, her blade sliced through flesh and bone. He screamed, collapsing to the ground and effectively out of the fight.

She whirled around just in time to see the high elf hurl a javelin at her horse. Desperate to avoid the missile, she yanked the reins, causing her steed to rear. But just as its front hooves left the ground, the javelin struck its shoulder. Screaming in pain, the horse toppled to the side. Taenya leaped clear, but the impact knocked her sword and shield from her grasp, leaving her breathless.

As she looked up, she saw the remaining four bandits charging the wagon.

The situation became even more dire as a second javelin flew through the air, this time targeting Raafe's horse. Raafe, seeing the incoming missile, desperately tried to pull his horse away, but the javelin found its mark, striking the animal's flank. The horse reared in pain, bucking wildly and throwing Raafe off. He hit the ground hard, rolling to avoid being trampled by the panicked animal. His sword clattered to the ground nearby as he struggled to regain his footing.

Raafe scrambled to retrieve his weapon, his eyes darting between the bandits and his injured horse. The poor creature continued to thrash about, clearly in agony. Raafe moved to put himself next to the wagon's entrance at the rear. Keston had moved to the opposite side of Onas, placing the merchant between him and Raafe.

Taenya's heart raced as she searched for her sword and spotted it lying on the ground far out of reach. Cursing her luck, she abandoned her shield and rushed toward her blade, hoping to grab it before the bandits reached her. But as she ran, she heard the whistle of a javelin flying through the air. Instinctively, she dove to the side, narrowly avoiding the projectile as it whizzed past her ear.

Her heart pounding, Taenya scrambled to her feet, her eyes locked on the high elf charging toward her, brandishing his axe. She barely had time to react before he swung the weapon at her. Instinct took over as Taenya dodged the attack, grabbing the high elf's arm and using his momentum to twist him around. With a fierce kick to his back, she sent him sprawling to the ground. Before he could recover, Taenya picked up his axe and plunged it into his chest.

Taking a deep breath, she hurriedly scanned the area for any more threats, her eyes locking on her sword lying on the ground nearby. With a quick sprint, she reached for her sword and held it tightly, quickly spinning around as the last two men of the group charged her.

She swung at the oncoming raithe to force him back, then immediately raised her sword to block a downward strike from the bandit leader.

With a quick thrust toward him, she forced him to back off. A follow-up with a reverse cut toward the raithe almost worked, but the man managed to catch the attack on his blade. Taenya pulled back and immediately kicked out at the him, catching him in the knee. Immediately, she blocked a diagonal slice from the orkun, stepping back toward the wagon.

The orkun continued to attack her with hard overhead strikes, while the raithe tried to keep her off balance and unable to press any opening she could take advantage of. The battle continued on, with Taenya holding her own against the two bandits. She was slowly being pushed back, but she remained determined to keep the bandits away from the wagon and her companions.

As she fought, she suddenly heard a yell from behind the wagon. The voice was young, and it was clear someone was in trouble. With fierce determination, Taenya redoubled her efforts, hoping to end the fight quickly so she could see what was happening at the wagon.

Raafe was being pressed hard, barely managing to stay ahead of the two bandits attacking him. Keston was busy with one of the telv, while Onas was acquitting himself well against another. Of the two he fought, the telv was not much of an issue, but the real problem in front of Raafe right now was the other orkun. He was doubtlessly the second in command of this group, which made sense—orkun were well-known for their natural martial ability. This one wasn't great, but it was enough that Raafe wasn't able to push them back while fighting both at the same time. He needed help.

Looking over at Keston, he yelled, "Hey! Need a little help over here!"

Keston responded, "I'm trying! Just hang on."

The orkun in front of Raafe laughed. "You won't last long enough, whelp. You're tiring out. Give up now, and I'll give you a merciful death."

Raafe replied with his sword, catching the telv's arm in a superficial cut and immediately flipping and swinging his blade back toward the other man. The bandit managed to block, but he backed off, clearly not expecting the move.

The orkun quickly yanked a dagger from his belt and threw it at Raafe. The sun elf easily dodged it but heard it thud loudly into the wagon behind him. A faint scream sounded from inside.

Oh no. Raafe was about to press forward when he heard the wagon's rear door opening. *Don't come out!* A little head emerged, eyes widening as she took in the sight in front of her.

"Raafe? What's happening?" Her brows furrowed as she took in the two bandits with swords. "Stop! Go away! You're going to hurt him!"

With the orkun pressing him, Raafe couldn't do much else, but he called out to her. "Gwyn! Go back inside, and lock the door! Now!"

Before the princess could retreat, the telv turned away from Raafe and tried to get to her. "Come here, you!" he snarled.

Gwyn screamed, her face filled with sudden terror, but still, she pulled out the training sword, her hand shaking as the man ran toward her.

Raafe panicked, his heart pounding as he swung his sword hard at the orkun bandit. Although his blow was blocked, it managed to push his opponent back far enough that Raafe was able to pivot and lunge at the telv. With a swift movement, he caught the man in the back, plunging his blade deep into the bandit's flesh. He quickly pulled it out and turned back to the orkun, ready to finish him off.

But just as he got his sword in place, he felt a sudden, sharp pain in his stomach. He looked down to see the orkun's sword protruding from his gut, and his mind reeled in shock and disbelief. How had he let this happen? In a flash, Raafe realized that he had underestimated the orkun's skill, and his overconfidence had cost him dearly.

"No! Raafe! Get away from him!" Gwyn screamed.

The orkun laughed. "Put away that sword, little girl. It's a toy."

"Gwyn, get back inside," Raafe choked out.

"No, I won't!"

She snarled something in anger, a look of concentration on her face as she stared at her hands.

Raafe gritted his teeth, forcing himself to fight, and faced the bandit. He stumbled backward, trying to dislodge the orkun's sword from his body. But the bandit had a firm grip on his weapon and wasn't letting go. Raafe felt his strength ebbing away, and he knew that he had to act fast if he wanted to survive.

With a last burst of determination, Raafe aimed his sword and lunged at the orkun's throat, ignoring the pain of the blade digging deeper into his own body. The bandit evaded the strike with ease, but Raafe countered with a swift thrust to the chest. Thrown off balance, the orkun staggered back, giving Raafe the chance to yank the blade from himself.

The bandit, for his part, was clearly impressed by Raafe's determination. He smiled cruelly, reaching down to grab the telv's blade, and charged forward, sword raised high. Raafe met him head-on, parrying the orkun's blows with his own sword. The two fighters clashed again and again, trading blow for blow in a fierce battle of skill and will.

Despite his injuries, Raafe fought with all his might, determined to protect Princess Gwyn and his companions from the bandits' wrath. He put her screams of anger aside as he focused on the bandit in front of him. He swung his sword with all his might, but the orkun was too fast for Raafe's injured state. The bandit parried Raafe's blow and countered with a swift strike of his own, which Raafe barely managed to dodge.

The pain was excruciating, but Raafe refused to give up. He raised his sword and prepared to face the orkun once more. His vision was blurry, and his movements were slow and unsteady, but he managed to parry the orkun's next attack. He tried to counter with a strike of his own, but his sword felt heavy and unwieldy in his hand. The orkun saw his weakness and took advantage, striking hard at Raafe's left side. The blow landed with a sickening thud, and Raafe felt a sharp pain shoot through his body. He staggered backward, his knees buckling under him, but he refused to fall.

"I told you that you wouldn't last, whelp," the orkun sneered, raising his blade. The bandit swung at him, and Raafe managed to get his blade up in time, but the force of the blow wrenched his sword from his hand. It clattered to the ground, leaving him defenseless against the orkun's onslaught.

But Raafe was not one to give up easily. Summoning all his remaining strength, he launched himself forward, surprising and punching the orkun in the face with all his might. The bandit reeled back, blood spilling from his nose as he stumbled backward.

Raafe stood there for a moment, breathing heavily, his body wracked with pain. He felt weak and dizzy, and his wounds were too much for him to bear any longer. With a final effort, he knelt down, clumsily reaching for his sword while clutching the wound in his stomach.

Emotions washed over him, thoughts about all of the things he wanted to do. Everything he had promised himself. Protecting Gwyn. Freeing his sister and family. He had failed.

"Raafe? Get up, Raafe. Come on," Gwyn begged in between sobs.

Raafe Sarkas looked at the young girl one last time, and with tears in his eyes, he forced himself to speak. "I'm sorry, Your Highness. I—" He coughed. "I failed you."

As he focused back on the bandit, the orkun lifted his sword and stepped forward toward him. Raafe stared the man in the eyes, intent on meeting his death with his head held high.

A shrill scream split the air. "Nooo! *Ti ammazzo!*"

Before he could react, a ball of fire shot past him and exploded against the orkun's face. The flash was blinding, and as his vision cleared, he saw the bandit dead on the ground, his face partially melted.

Gwyn rushed over to Raafe, getting in front of him to try and hold him up. He smiled at her as his eyes closed and he slumped forward onto her shoulder. The last thing he heard was the princess screaming his name.

Taenya's ears perked up at the sound of Princess Gwyn's sharp cry calling out Raafe's name. Surprised, she and the two bandits she had been fighting turned toward the source. There, she saw Raafe lying on the ground with two bandits lying next to him, and her heart sank.

Before she could react, the bandit leader barked orders to his man. "Get that girl! I'll deal with this bitch."

Taenya's eyes widened in alarm as the raithe ran toward Gwyn. As the orkun's sword came down, she dropped her sword and ducked under his blade, getting closer to him. The orkun was caught off guard by her sudden move, and she hit him as hard as she could with a palm strike aimed just under his chin, followed by a swift elbow to his jaw. Should have aimed for the nose. Damn it.

As the orkun fell backward, she turned toward the raithe, pulling out her knife and throwing it. The blade sailed through the air, and Taenya realized too late that she had missed her intended target. The knife embedded itself into the spine just below the bandit's neck, causing him to scream in agony. In that moment of distraction, the bandit leader struck her head from behind, and Taenya fell to the ground, her head spinning.

She rolled onto her back. She quickly pulled out her dagger from the sheath at her lower back and looked up at the orkun standing above her, glaring down with a snarl. "You're going to pay for all you've done," he spat. "When I'm done, we're going to take that little girl too. I bet she'll make us plenty of money when we sell her off."

She readied herself to fight the orkun off, but then she heard a wail of pure terror, followed by a scream.

"Get away from her!"

Taenya turned her gaze toward Princess Gwyn, who was standing protectively over Raafe. Suddenly, the girl threw a ball of fire that was as big as her head from her bare hand. The flame shot toward the bandit leader, who had no chance to dodge it. He tried to cover his face with his hands, but the fire caught him right in the throat. His eyes went wide with shock and pain as the flames washed over him. He pressed his hands to the wound, trying to hold together his melted throat, gurgling as he swayed. Taenya saw him start to sag, and he fell with one last glazed-over look down at her.

The chaos around them suddenly came to a halt. All fighting, talking, and even breathing seemed to stop as everyone's attention turned to the little girl. Princess Gwyn stood with her hand raised off to her side at chest level, holding a ball of fire floating above it. Her face was etched with pure fury, daring anyone to try and hurt someone she cared for. It was a look that commanded respect and demanded that everyone around her recognize her power.

Taenya got up and stood tall, looking at the remaining bandits who were slowly backing away from the group.

"Drop your weapons. Now," she commanded, her voice cold and firm. The two bandits hesitated for a moment, but then quickly complied, dropping their swords to the ground. They slowly backed away from the scene, and finally turned and sprinted away.

As Taenya watched the fleeing bandits, she felt a mix of relief and anger. Her attention was quickly diverted as Princess Gwyn called out to her urgently.

"Taenya! Raafe needs help! Hurry! He's hurt really bad!"

Onas watched helplessly as Taenya rushed over to tend to Raafe's injuries. He had seen Raafe get run through by the sword but he had been unable to do anything to prevent it. They had to act fast.

"Help her with Raafe," he said to Keston. "I'll get the princess and the wagon. We need to get to Larton as quickly as possible."

Keston nodded and went to assist Taenya. Onas assessed the fallen tree blocking their path. It didn't look large, and he was confident he could move it. But their need to hurry was urgent.

Onas turned to Gwyn. "Princess, I may need your help, and your... fire. We have to move this tree to get the wagon moving toward the town. The quicker we can get there, the quicker we can help Raafe. Do you understand?" he asked.

Gwyn nodded, her face set with determination. "Okay. We have to hurry. He's bleeding a lot. We have to save my friend," she said resolutely.

As they rushed along the road toward Larton, Onas's mind was in a whirlwind. Princess Gwyn quietly sobbed next to him, occasionally muttering to herself in that other language, interspersed with desperate pleas for him to go faster. He recognized the surrounding area and knew they would soon reach the fields that encircled the town.

Just as the farms came into view, he heard Taenya call out from the back, "Onas! We need to hurry! Now!"

Onas yelled back, "We're almost there! Keep him stable and alert!"

After ten long minutes of frantic shouting and dodging pedestrians, Onas and Princess Gwyn finally caught sight of the town gate. A group of guards on horseback rushed out to meet them. As they drew closer, the lead rider urged his horse to keep pace and called out, "What's the emergency? How can we help?"

Onas was grateful for their quick thinking. He shouted back, "Bandits! My guard has been stabbed in the stomach! He needs a surgeon!"

The guard nodded and yelled back, "Follow us to the guard barracks! We have a surgeon on call!" With that, they took the lead and urged their horses forward, clearing the way for the wagon.

They arrived at the barracks without further incident and a team of guards swiftly came to their aid with a stretcher. They carefully placed Raafe on it and quickly rushed him inside, with Keston running alongside them.

Taenya joined Onas, covered in blood, shaking her head. With tear-filled eyes, she looked at him. "Onas, I'm not sure—"

"Wait. Let the surgeons work. He's a fighter," he interrupted, glancing at the princess, who stood next to him.

Gwyn's words tumbled out in a jumbled stream as she desperately tried to reassure herself. "He's going to be okay. He promised. He has to teach me to be the greatest sword fighter ever. He's going to be my knight."

Taenya and Onas exchanged a worried glance, their hearts heavy as they heard the girl's words. Unsure of how to comfort her, Taenya simply pulled Gwyn into a tight embrace. The princess cried for the man who had been in her life for only a short time, but whom she already considered a friend.

The image of the girl summoning flames from the Father to vanquish the bandits was etched deep in Onas's mind. They were ruthless fiends who sought only to plunder and kill, but the girl had shown them what it meant to face true power.

As he stole a quick glance at Taenya and the princess, a sudden mixture of fear and awe coursed through him. Gwyn was lost in thought, nestled in the embrace of the telv, her irises burning and flaming like the red sun. Only the eclipses that were her pupils interrupted the flames in her eyes.

It was a look that demanded both respect and fear from anyone who might consider harming those she cared for.

CHAPTER TWENTY

FAKE IT TILL YOU MAKE IT

Taenya gazed up at the guard captain who was addressing her, struggling to recall his name. The high elf had been interrogating her about the incident, but she was finding it difficult to concentrate. The captain sighed and perched on the edge of the desk, his hands clasped in his lap, and she discerned a look of understanding on his countenance—one that was all too familiar to her. He was a man who had also experienced loss.

"Miss Taenya, please," he implored. "I understand your situation, but could you please recount how the attack took place?"

Although Taenya was disinclined to remain there, she knew that it was her duty to do so. As Onas's head guard, it was her responsibility to deal with the guards, particularly since it was their territory. Furthermore, the high elf merchant would submit his report to the Guild later.

I had just left his room…

"Captain, could we do this later?" she interjected.

"Miss Taenya," the guard captain interrupted gently. "No one has informed me of what occurred yet. Please understand, I won't take up much of your time, but I do need to know. I dislike this just as much as you do. You can keep it brief, but provide me with some details."

Taenya assented and drew in a deep breath. "It all began when we stumbled upon a fallen tree that obstructed the entire road. It was too large for our wagon to simply pass over, and given the trees flanking the road, we couldn't circumvent it. After we stopped, eight men ambushed us. The leader was a massive orkun—I didn't manage to catch his name. Accompanying him were a raithe, four telv, a high elf, and another orkun. I tried to dissuade him from attacking us and even offered payment, considering we only had three guards, but he wasn't receptive. We engaged in combat and were able to kill six of them."

The guard captain raised his eyebrows in surprise. "An orkun leader, a raithe, and another orkun? That sounds like Winton the Reaver's group. We've been hunting them for several seasons. You truly killed him? How?"

Taenya hesitated, acutely aware that she could not reveal Gwyn's use of magic to the elf guard captain. *Absolutely not. I won't betray her.* She contemplated her options, feeling as though she had no choice but to lie. Her eyes scanned the office, searching for inspiration. They eventually alighted on a lamp positioned on a nearby table. As she gazed at the flickering flame, memories of the fight began to resurface. The fire within the lamp appeared tranquil and serene when compared to the miniature blazing suns that Gwyn had created out of thin air. Taenya recalled the fear etched on the young girl's visage, which swiftly transformed into an expression of fury and rage, as if she were the embodiment of Alos himself.

I was so close to being taken or dying...

"Miss Taenya?"

Taenya was startled by the sound of the guard captain's voice, and as she turned to face him, she saw nothing but genuine concern in his expression. She closed her eyes and took a deep breath, attempting to compose herself. He sat patiently, waiting for her response.

I know what I have to say.

"Raafe, one of my guards, was injured during the fight and used an oil lamp to defend himself against the orkun who attacked him. After he had managed to dispatch the orkun, Raafe grabbed another lamp just as I approached them. At that moment, the girl who was accompanying us began to scream, which served as a distraction. We used the opportunity to strike Winton in the neck with the second lamp, and he perished shortly afterward."

The high elf's eyes widened in astonishment. "You mean to say that you and your guard used oil lamps to kill two of their men?"

Taenya shrugged nonchalantly. "We made do with whatever we had at hand. The orkun leader had spoken of selling the girl, and I couldn't permit that to occur."

The guard captain gave Taenya a sympathetic nod. "For what it's worth, I am sorry for what you had to endure, Miss Taenya. Thank you for relaying the details to me. I will file the report accordingly. We can discuss this matter further at a later time."

Taenya nodded in response, not desiring to prolong the conversation any further. She rose from her seat and departed, cognizant of the fact that she needed to locate Keston and talk with him. She intended to discuss the situation with Onas as well, particularly since he might inform the baron about what had transpired.

Taenya was apprehensive, realizing that she needed to clear everything up before either of them spoke to anyone else. She trusted that Keston wouldn't divulge anything if she requested him not to, but Onas was a different story. She cursed inwardly at the predicament.

He's going to tell the baron.

Taenya sat on the ground, leaning against the wall of an alley behind the inn that Onas had arranged. Keston was sitting beside her. She had told him about the lie she had given the guard captain, and he had agreed that it was best to keep some things to themselves.

Taenya could sense Keston's pain, which hung in the air between them like a heavy cloud. They both sat in silence, absorbed in their thoughts. She knew he was consumed with regret about losing Raafe just an hour ago. *He's blaming himself for not getting there on time*, she thought. Poor Keston. I know how much he cared for Raafe.

She noticed how Keston had pushed his sorrow down, as was expected in their line of work. *But bottling up these emotions won't do him any good in the long run*, she thought.

Breaking the silence, she said softly, "Keston, we need to talk." Her voice barely rose above the noise of the town. "I . . . I don't know how to break the news to her."

Keston turned to look at her. She saw the pain in his eyes, but he was studying her, trying to read her expression. *Does he think I have the answers?* she asked herself. She was no stranger to loss, but this was a different matter altogether.

Keston let out a heavy sigh. "I'm at a loss too, Taenya. Raafe. . ." He seemed to struggle with the words. "Raafe was my friend, and I saw how much that little girl meant to him. She ignited a passion in him, gave him a sense of purpose. He was ready to leave the company and go with her to find her mother, wherever that might be."

Taenya had to fight back a sob. She looked down at the sheathed sword leaning against the wall next to her. "He truly was, wasn't he?" Her voice was choked.

"What do we do now?" Keston asked. "You've been through this before, haven't you? I mean, you've experienced loss in your duties, but I haven't. I don't know how to move on." His eyes were pleading with her, hoping she could give him some guidance.

"You're right. I have experienced loss before," Taenya replied, her voice strained. "But it's never easy. And none of those times involved a child, which makes this situation so much harder. In the past, the company guards who died on a route didn't leave any children behind. This . . . this is different." She couldn't help feeling a heavy weight on her shoulders, a burden that was too big for her to carry alone.

"It really is."

Taenya sat in silence with Keston, each absorbed in their own thoughts. The sorrow and contemplation seemed to consume the space around them. *How much time has passed?* Taenya wondered. She noticed Keston looking increasingly anxious, as if he had just remembered something.

"Taenya?" he said, turning to face her.

"Mm?" she responded, her thoughts still miles away.

"Perhaps we should talk about the other things that happened today," he suggested. Taenya inhaled deeply, and Keston turned to face her more directly. "We both saw what she did," he added, a note of concern evident in his voice.

That's right, Gwyn . . . and the fire, Taenya closed her eyes briefly, collecting her thoughts. "Yes," she finally said, her voice heavy with concern. "That little girl conjured up fire and used it to kill two grown men. Right in front of us."

"But she also saved our lives," Keston said.

"She did."

"What does it mean?" he asked, his voice filled with uncertainty.

The two of them sat there for a long time, lost in their thoughts. *What does it mean?* Taenya repeated the question to herself. She finally broke the silence, asking, "What do you think it means, Keston?" She shook her head, but continued, "It's clear that the girl possesses magical abilities. Onas was terrified of her, and I had to talk to him about it. But you're right, she saved us." Taenya sat there, her thoughts swirling as she tried to grapple with the implications of what they had witnessed.

Keston leaned back against the wall, and she knew that both of their minds had drifted back to the fight and the way the fire had exploded against the two bandits. *I saw it too, that second bandit being consumed by fire. And how that orkun died just before he could attack me.* The image was seared into her memory.

Gwyn had saved her life.

"I felt something too. And I still feel it," Taenya said suddenly, her voice heavy with concern.

Keston looked at her, his eyebrows furrowed. "What do you mean?"

"When I killed the bandits, I felt a rush. I felt almost . . . refreshed." Taenya looked down at her hand and curled it into a fist, as if trying to hold on to the sensation. "I feel different, Keston. Stronger. It's not much, but I am not the same person I was yesterday or even this morning."

"Maybe the thing that brought that little girl to us did much more than we thought," she said, her voice filled with wonder and speculation. "Was it the gods? I don't know. I'm not a huge believer, but I know what I saw, and that was a little girl using magic." Taenya's tone was tinged with uncertainty and fear as she realized the gravity of what they had witnessed. *What have we gotten ourselves into?*

Keston nodded. "And Taenya, we can't let anyone know," he said, reminding her of Raafe's dying request to protect the girl.

Taenya sighed. "Onas is going to talk to the baron about it. Of this I'm sure. Their friendship is too close for him not to."

Keston shook his head. "Do you think the baron will tell anyone?"

Taenya shrugged. "I don't know. Despite how often Onas has met with him, I've only spoken with him once. Other times, I simply saw him from a distance or hadn't joined Onas."

I hope Onas knows what he's doing.

"Taenya, this is going to change so much. I—I don't see a future that isn't filled with trouble for that girl," Keston said, his voice heavy with worry.

"I know." Taenya took a deep breath. *Trust me, I know.* "That girl, she's going to go far, though, Keston. And I believe her magic is going to be a key part of it. But it's not just that. She's genuinely an amazing young girl, one who naturally draws people in. That's a trait many search for and many fight for."

"What do you think we should do?" Keston asked.

"I think..." Taenya paused and looked up at the sky. *What should we do?* she thought, her mind racing. Keston waited patiently, not interrupting her thoughts. She felt the emotions build up inside of her, and tears welled up in her eyes. *I have to do this. I have to be strong.* Finally, she nodded, coming to a decision.

She wiped at her eyes and faced him. "I think I want to finish what Raafe started. He wanted to help her, to protect her. I feel like something in me changed, and I think that girl is the key to figuring it out. The world is going to change, Keston. I don't know how—"

"But you can feel it," he said, shaking his head in disbelief. "A girl used magic. This is a turning point. I don't know what a world with magic looks like, but I agree with you: Gwyn is the key to all of this. We need to understand what she's capable of and how she fits into all of this."

Taenya nodded slowly.

"And the princess may be the key to changing our lives as well," he said, his tone determined. He absently patted his leg as he considered his future. "We need to make sure she finds her mother safely and protect her at all costs."

"Is that what you want to do, Keston?" Taenya asked. "Or is it because you feel obligated?"

He shrugged. "The least I can do for Raafe . . . is continue what he started. I am going to stay with her. We'll see what the future holds, and maybe that leads me somewhere else. For now, she needs us."

Taenya nodded in agreement and stood up, causing Keston to look at her quizzically. She reached out to help him up and he grabbed her hand, letting her pull him to his feet. She looked directly into his eyes.

"I understand, I do," she said. "That girl is going to need a lot of help." Taenya placed a hand on his shoulder and leaned in close, speaking in a whisper, "She's going to be a target. Are you prepared for that? Because once it gets out, people will come for her, and not just because she's a princess," she asked him.

Keston shook his head slowly. "Honestly? No, I'm not prepared for it. But someone has to be, Taenya. We can't just leave her to fend for herself. She has no one else," he said, his voice firm with resolve. "It's not going to be easy. We'll face challenges and dangers that make the little spat with Lord Bekker seem like child's play. But we made a promise to Raafe, and we have to keep it. We have to protect her, no matter what."

Taenya nodded slowly. "You're right," she said. "Onas will be okay without us. Gwyn, on the other hand, is going to need help. Let's be honest: Onas is not going to be able to keep her hidden, and he doesn't have the clout to go against any nobles."

Keston narrowed his eyes. "We don't either, Taenya."

Taenya let out a sigh. "Yeah… That's the challenge."

He put a reassuring hand on her shoulder. "You'll figure it out, just like you always do, boss. I'll be right there to help."

A small wave of relief washed over Taenya, and her shoulders relaxed slightly. She nodded again. "Thanks, Keston." She paused, knowing what she had to do next. "I need to go tell her now, don't I?"

Keston nodded. "Yeah. I'll get things ready so we can go see him."

Taenya sighed softly, the weight of her responsibility heavy on her mind. *It's all on my shoulders now,* she thought. She turned and walked away from Keston, leaving him with his own thoughts.

As Taenya made her way to where Gwyn was waiting, she couldn't help but reflect on how much had changed.Gwyn was the key to understanding and adapting to this new world. It's not just her magic that made Taenya want to help her. It wasn't even the fact that she was a princess from another world, because that doesn't matter. What mattered was her pure heart and her need for her mother. She recalled how Raafe had spoken so often of helping the child he barely knew, and how his last moments were spent trying to help her.

Taenya couldn't help but feel a sense of duty and responsibility to carry on Raafe's legacy. *Helping Gwyn find her mother is the right thing to do, even if it means putting myself and Keston in danger,* she thought. *I have to honor Raafe's memory and ensure that Gwyn is safe. Honor. Raafe, you died more a knight than many can claim.*

She knew it wasn't going to be easy, but she was determined to be strong for Gwyn. The girl had already been through so much, and Taenya didn't want to add to her pain. She'd fake it for her if she had to. With a resolute nod, she continued walking toward where the little girl waited.

She would be there to help a little girl grieve in her own way. It was the least she could do.

She was going to make a difference in this new world, and she was going to do it for the people around her and for Gwyn, but most importantly, for herself.

Raafe was dying. Taenya, Keston, and Mister Onas all knew it. She was sure that even Raafe knew it… if he was awake. Gwyn knew it, she really did. However, that did not stop her from hoping and praying to anyone listening that he would be okay. The world had an entire pantheon of gods—surely one would hear her. Right?

Taenya, Keston, and Mister Onas were all really kind and so willing to help, but Raafe had been different. He was her friend. He hadn't treated her like a child, but rather as a person with her own thoughts and wants. Even though Gwyn knew she was still just a child, she felt seen and respected when he was around. Since arriving on Eona, and after the fight, she felt like more.

She had used actual, real-life magic. For real this time. It was both terrifying and amazing. But it meant that the knight's wagon catching on fire was because of her. With the bandits, though, she had done it deliberately. She had created the spell and used it to save everyone—well, not everyone.

The thought made her sad again. If only she had not made Raafe need to save her. If only she had called to the magic sooner.

The first cast had been difficult; she'd had to think really hard. It's why it took so long to help Raafe. The magic sang, and she listened. It was tricky at first, like quietly listening to the TV on the weekends when Mom was still asleep. The more she tried, the easier it got to hear it. She realized it was like listening to different types of music at once, but then one of them sang a little louder.

Finally, Gwyn told it what she wanted, and then the magic had listened to her.

The second time she threw the fire was much easier. It was like she knew what it was, just like in all of the fantasy shows she and her mom watched. A real [**Fireball**].

Everything seemed to get a little clearer after that. It took a while for her to realize exactly what she had done, and she didn't mean with the magic—she had hurt them. Killed them. *I wanted to. I was so… angry. They hurt him, stabbed him. And I just wanted them to burn.*

Gwyn sniffled. She knew she should talk to someone, but who? Onas was kind, but he didn't understand. He was too old. Taenya and Keston had been kind to her, but she didn't want to burden them with her problems. She needed someone who understood her situation, someone who could help her understand her magic. Someone to just listen.

She longed for her mom. She felt so alone and scared. Mom always knew how to make things better and say the right things. Gwyn missed her so much.

Gwyn realized she had messed up really badly. She didn't think Onas and Taenya would believe her when she joked about being a princess. Back home, everyone pretended to be a princess at some point. But then everyone started acting so serious around her, like they would get in trouble if they said anything wrong. Even though they acted like they would help her even more, she couldn't shake off the guilt. Raafe had even said he would be her knight and protect her. Gwyn had laughed because she thought he was just joking. But he wasn't. He did protect her, until he couldn't do anything else.

As tears streamed down her face, she couldn't shake the feeling that everything was wrong. Gwyn felt like an imposter, like she didn't belong in this strange world without humans. What if she was the only one of her kind? What if her mom really wasn't here? The thought of being alone forever terrified her. Why did everything feel so uncertain and scary? And why did these people want to help her so much?

It didn't make sense to Gwyn that these people were going out of their way to help her find her mother. Back home, most kids who were lost or without parents ended up in orphanages, forgotten and alone. She couldn't believe that normal people would go to such lengths for a stranger like her. Gwyn couldn't help feeling like she didn't deserve it, especially after what happened to Raafe.

After all, it was her fault that he got hurt.

But the people she had met were so nice, and it felt good.

There was something Mom would always tell her Aunt Katie: fake it till you make it. And Gwyn knew she would need to... a lot. She just had to keep faking it until they helped find Mom.

Gwyn could do that. She could be strong. Gwyn had magic, and it listened to her.

She was still crying when Taenya came to talk.

Gwyn knew what she was going to say.

I really hoped someone up there would listen.

CHAPTER TWENTY-ONE

HONOR AND SACRIFICE

Taenya gently guided Gwyn toward the room where Raafe's body lay. The wooden door, adorned with simple decorative carvings, stood solemnly before them. Taenya held Gwyn back, crouching down to speak to her.

"Gwyn, you don't have to see him like this, but if you want to say your good-byes, now is the time. I'll be right here with you. If you want to leave, just tug on my hand. You don't even need to say anything. Alright?"

"Okay," Gwyn whispered, her voice barely audible.

Taenya took a deep breath to steady herself for Gwyn's sake and slowly pushed the door open. Hand in hand, they entered the room. The oil lamps ensconced on the walls cast flickering shadows that danced around them. Keston stood off to the side, a solemn figure bathed in the warm glow of the room.

Gwyn approached the bed, her eyes locking on to Raafe's motionless figure. Taenya watched her carefully, noting the exact moment when the girl's face crumpled and she couldn't hold back her sobs any longer.

Gwyn hurried to Raafe's side, her small hand trembling as she hesitated before reaching out to touch the edge of the bed. The silence in the room was palpable as she stared at him, seemingly willing him to open his eyes and greet her with his smile. The town surgeon had carefully cleaned Raafe's body, making him look as presentable as possible given the circumstances, and it was clear that they had done their best to make him comfortable in his final resting place.

Taenya placed a comforting hand on Gwyn's shoulder, her eyes lingering on the fallen guard who had given his life to protect a child he had barely known. Raafe's expression was peaceful in death, just as it had been in his final moments. He had told them he didn't regret his actions—the girl was worth it, he had said.

Someone special. Raafe had even made Onas swear to never let anyone take Gwyn away.

Gwyn's soft whimpers soon gave way to unrestrained weeping, her small frame shaking with sorrow. The room seemed to absorb her cries, the flickering oil lamps casting elongated shadows on the wooden walls, elevating the somber atmosphere of the last viewing.

Keston stood near a tall, narrow window that offered a view of the streets of Larton, where life continued at its usual pace, seemingly unaware of the young princess's grief. When Gwyn tugged on Taenya's hand, Taenya led her out of the room, and he followed.

Once the door was closed, Keston spoke in a gentle voice, the faint echo of their footsteps still resonating in the hallway. "Princess Gwyn, I know this is tough for you, but Raafe wanted us to give you something after you'd said goodbye."

Gwyn turned to look up at him, her eyes brimming with tears. The lamps illuminated her tear-streaked face, revealing both her vulnerability and her determination to persevere.

"He did?"

Taenya nodded, her tone warm and comforting. "Yeah, he wanted to pass on something special to you—a family heirloom he thought you'd cherish and take care of."

Gwyn nodded, her determination shining through her tears. "I will. What is it?"

Keston knelt down, carefully unwrapping Raafe's saber before presenting it to Gwyn. Gathering himself for a moment, he spoke with reverence.

"Princess Gwyneth, I give you Raafe's Legacy. This cavalry saber was given to his grandfather by the Duke of Tiloral as a token of gratitude for his service. Raafe was truly honored to teach you how to wield a sword. Your dedication and eagerness to learn during his lessons made him incredibly proud."

Gwyn's eyes widened as she gazed at the saber, the torchlight glinting off its polished surface, reflecting the history and pride woven into its craftsmanship. She nodded again, fresh tears welling up in her eyes as she beheld the saber, a tangible symbol of Raafe's legacy. With a trembling hand, she reached out to grasp the hilt, her other hand instinctively cradling the blade just beneath it.

Sniffling, Gwyn managed a small smile. "It's so beautiful. Raafe was really skilled with it. But it's still too big for me." She turned her tearful gaze to Taenya and asked, "Could you help me keep it safe? I can't use it yet, but I want to take good care of it."

Taenya gently placed a hand on the girl's shoulder, her expression warm and reassuring. "Of course, Gwyn. I'd be honored to teach you how to care for a blade, especially one as exquisite and significant as this. And when you're ready, we'll make sure you learn to wield it, just as Raafe intended."

* * *

Three days later, Onas had finished coordinating with the necessary people to arrange for Raafe's transportation to his family. Although he wasn't entirely sure where most of the man's relatives resided, he knew that Raafe had at least one family member in Strathmore. He vaguely recalled Raafe mentioning something about the capital, but with so little information, it was difficult to know where to begin. At the very least, the family member in Strathmore could make decisions regarding Raafe's final arrangements, ensuring that his family could lay him to rest according to their wishes. Onas considered delegating this task to Taenya, but her emotional state following Raafe's death made him reconsider.

Raafe wasn't the first guard Onas had lost during his journeys, and he and Taenya had established a process for providing support to the families left behind. He would send them the earnings Raafe would have received from the trip, along with an additional sum as his personal contribution. The night before, Onas had penned a heartfelt letter and gathered Raafe's personal belongings. He vowed to personally deliver everything to the family member in Strathmore upon his return to the city.

Onas planned to depart in a day or two, but first, he needed to meet with Lord Iemes. After giving them the customary time to address their affairs in the wake of Raafe's passing, the baron had extended an invitation for dinner. Consequently, Onas and Princess Gwyn found themselves riding in a carriage toward the baron's castle. Taenya accompanied them, seated with the driver, as her role involved coordinating with the baron's men and making the necessary preparations.

The old castle of the baron rose up before them as they approached, its functional structure and strategic location speaking to its importance in the area. The ancient stones that made up its imposing facade had seen countless meetings and gatherings throughout its history, giving it a sense of weight and gravitas. Despite its lack of grandeur, the castle held a certain charm in its simplicity and practicality. As the day began to fade into night, the stronghold took on an air of mystery, the fading light casting long shadows across its walls.

House Iemes was just one in a long line of custodians of the proud Castle Larton. It was a place of history and tradition, a symbol of strength and stability that had stood the test of time. Lord Iemes and his small retinue of knights were already assembled in the castle's courtyard when Onas and his party arrived. The carriage halted at a respectful distance, and Onas watched through the window as Taenya climbed down from her seat and strode over to confer with the head knight.

The head knight of House Iemes was a striking sun elf, his rich, dark brown complexion and vibrant yellow eyes perfectly complementing the burgundy and gold colors of the baron's house. His regal appearance was further enhanced by the ornate five-loop earrings adorning his pointed ears and the intricately engraved breastplate he wore over his fine clothes. A curved blade hung from his hip, completing his formidable yet elegant look.

As Taenya approached him, the sun elf knight stood tall and proud, exuding an air of authority and confidence. He briefly scanned the carriage, taking note of its occupants, before returning his attention to Taenya. After a short bow from the telv woman, they exchanged a few words, their expressions conveying a mutual understanding and respect for one another's positions.

In the background, the baron's other knights stood at attention, their polished armor gleaming in the waning light. They were an impressive sight, a testament to the baron's power and influence in the region. Together, they presented a united front, ready to serve and protect their lord and his esteemed guests.

One of the knights, a younger high elf with black hair, stood at attention, carefully scanning the area. She appeared to be slightly apart from the other knights, as if in charge of watching the surroundings for potential threats. Her gaze was sharp, and it was clear that she was taking her duty seriously. Her armor was polished to a shine, and she held herself with an air of confidence and authority. She was no doubt a skilled warrior, and not someone to be underestimated.

The head knight's gaze snapped toward the carriage, and he quickly turned to walk toward his lord. Onas observed as the baron spoke with the knight, who then gestured for Taenya to join them.

Onas glanced at Gwyn, a small smile playing on his lips. "It seems they're trying to figure out the proper protocol for greeting and hosting you, Princess."

Gwyn eagerly scooted to the edge of her seat to get a better view through the window. "Are those the knights you told me about? Why aren't they wearing traditional knight armor? There are only five. I thought there would be more."

Onas chuckled. "They are just wearing the armor that is more comfortable to use around their hold. They have other armor as well."

Gwyn considered. "That makes sense, I suppose. Other armor would be heavy—I wouldn't like wearing it all the time. Why are there only five—oh, and there are two girl knights! That's so cool."

Onas smiled as he gazed out the window, observing the castle grounds. "Lord Iemes commands a force of around eleven knights, Your Highness. The others you don't see are likely attending to their other duties. Nobles of higher standing may have even more knights sworn to them. Beyond that, most nobles also employ a larger force of men-at-arms in their service. While knights hold a more social rank and are considered the lowest form of nobility, men- and women-at-arms fulfill more martial roles, whether they are of noble birth or not."

Gwyn's curiosity was piqued. "What's the difference between a knight and a guard?"

Onas considered the question. "Knighthood can be defined by two distinctions. First, knights may be part of an order, in which case they are sworn to a higher calling or role and work for the benefit of their cause or nation as a whole. Secondly, knights can be sworn to a lord. These knights are usually granted land and serve as the elite fighters and advisors to their lord. They may even shoulder some of the responsibilities of governance across the lord's domain. As members of the lord's house, they are seen as extensions of the lord himself."

Gwyn listened intently, her eyes wide with curiosity as she tried to take in every detail of the scene unfolding before her. This glimpse into the world of nobility and its intricacies was a learning experience for the young princess, one that would serve her well in the years to come.

"Men-at-arms, on the other hand, are professional soldiers who form the core of a lord's garrison," Onas continued. "They aren't all knights, but all knights will, by default, be considered men- or women-at-arms. These soldiers are the backbone of any competent army, being far better equipped and trained than a simple militia.

"To answer your question, guards serve a more focused protective role. They can be part of a lord's house guard, tasked with safeguarding the lord's domicile or specific holdings, or they can be town guards, who protect towns from external threats and maintain law and order. Lastly, there are private guards, like Taenya, Raafe, and Keston, who are hired by individuals like me to protect either us or our belongings. Does that help?"

Gwyn nodded, attempting to absorb the information. He suspected they would need to explain it again when necessary based on her slightly bemused expression. "Thank you," she said. She paused for a moment, her voice growing softer. "Raafe was going to be my knight..." Her words trailed off, a touch of sadness in her tone.

Onas remained silent, allowing Gwyn to process her thoughts. Taenya concluded her conversation with the baron and then began walking toward the carriage, the baron and his knights following her. Taenya waited by the door as the knights positioned themselves two to a side. The lead knight stood by the baron.

Nodding, Taenya opened the door and leaned her head in, addressing Onas and Gwyn. "They wish to greet Her Highness with the appropriate formalities. Onas, you will exit first, and Gwyn, after counting to five, you will follow. Onas and I will accompany you as you approach the baron. Walk in a straight line, centered between the knights, and don't pause. Simply nod your head; the baron will speak first. Remember our practice, alright?"

Gwyn smoothed out the dress that Onas had provided her. He had sent Taenya with a coin purse to find the finest dress she could for the young princess. The dress was a deep, rich blue with buttons running down the entire front. Made of a heavier material, it was designed to be worn over a lighter dress.

The high collar and long sleeves that flared out allowed for easy movement and accommodated Gwyn's magic. Delicate silver flames were embroidered along the bottom edge and up the centerline, adding an elegant touch. Underneath the blue dress, Gwyn wore a thinner, black dress that ended at her neckline, creating a sophisticated layering effect. Her feet were clad in high-quality leather traveler's boots, fit for a noble, with three silver buttons for closure.

The ensemble had cost a considerable sum, but Onas recognized it as a worthy investment. Demonstrating that his house could support the lifestyle expected of royalty would prove challenging, especially once word of Gwyn's existence spread.

Gwyn slowly nodded, mentally rehearsing the instructions. "Okay, got it. I can do this," she affirmed, determination glinting in her eyes as she prepared to face the awaiting baron and his knights.

Onas nodded and stepped out of the carriage, giving Gwyn space to prepare herself. The young princess took a deep breath, counting slowly before stepping out with as much grace as she could muster.

Taenya turned and addressed the baron as Gwyn descended the carriage's stairs. "Presenting Her Royal Highness, Princess Gwyneth Reinhart of Italy and America."

At the announcement, Onas noticed the girl's face take on a strange expression. Perhaps she was nervous, he thought. He watched as she took a deep breath to calm herself and stepped to the ground with Taenya's assistance. He and Taenya flanked her, offering their support as they guided her toward the awaiting baron and his knights.

The air was filled with a sense of anticipation as Gwyn walked between the knights. The courtyard, adorned with banners and statues, seemed to come alive with the colors of House Iemes, lending an air of grandeur to the occasion. Gwyn appeared to be focused on maintaining her composure. Using the etiquette lessons Taenya had given her, she approached the nobleman who was standing there patiently with a small smile on his face.

Onas could tell she struggled to not look at the knights as she passed, but she undoubtedly gave the lead knight a once-over before facing the baron. Onas and Taenya stopped a few steps behind her, allowing her to greet the noble.

With a slight nod, Gwyn greeted the Lord of Larton while Taenya and Onas bowed as they had practiced.

"Greetings, Lord Iemes. Thank you for the courtesy of your invitation and for allowing Mister Onas the time to handle the affairs of his brave guard, who gave his life protecting my own."

She had forgotten to let the baron speak first, but Onas still smiled, proud of her effort. Gwyn had recited the rest of the practiced greeting flawlessly. He and Taenya stepped forward as the high elf baron smiled in return.

Lord Iemes was impeccably groomed, with short blond hair, a goatee, and a mustache all trimmed and styled to perfection. He wore a long tunic with intricate golden embroidery, and the burgundy fabric appeared vibrant and fresh, with no signs of fading. A short ceremonial blade hung from his right hip, and he rested his hand upon it, exuding confidence and grace.

Lord Iemes clasped his hands in front of himself and addressed the princess. "Your Highness, I regret that I was not made aware of your arrival earlier. However, given the circumstances surrounding the day you were due to arrive, it is completely understandable. I must say that I am appalled that bandits would prey on travelers so close to our humble town. As soon as I heard, I tasked Ser Grisom here with dispatching teams of our town guard to scour my lands for any sign of them. As the lord of this fief, you have my promise that not a single bandit will draw breath much longer.

"That said, I humbly welcome you to my home. I hope our quaint abode meets your expectations, Your Highness. We shall bring out our finest for dinner. Perhaps we can discuss more of your travels and those of my good friend, Onas."

Gwyn nodded slowly, almost forcibly, as she reached the extent of what they had practiced. Onas realized she would have to start improvising soon.

"Thank you, Lord Iemes. Your castle is amazing; no one builds castles anymore where I live. They're all really old and worn down," Gwyn explained.

The baron looked a bit surprised but maintained his composure well, glancing at Onas, who gave a small nod to his friend.

Lord Iemes smiled and looked at the merchant. "Onas, my old friend! How are you? I am terribly sorry about your guard. We will send something with you for the man's family. This happened on my lands, and I am incensed by the matter."

Onas smiled back. "I am well, my lord. I'm just happy we are finally here in Larton. The trip here was a tense affair. My people and the princess herself handled themselves admirably."

The baron's knight, Ser Grisom, chose that moment to speak up. "I have heard the report," he said, looking at Taenya. "To face that many bandits as just three guards and win, despite the regrettable loss, is beyond commendable. It would be an honor to have any of you within our ranks."

Taenya gave a curt nod. "I am honored, Ser Grisom. Thank you. I will say that the princess herself was the reason we survived. Her actions were definitive in the resolution to the combat—but perhaps that is something we can all speak on later."

Lord Iemes raised his eyebrows, clearly intrigued by Taenya's statement. "Indeed, it seems we have much to discuss over dinner, then. I look forward to hearing more about the bravery and resourcefulness of Her Highness and her protectors."

Gwyn blushed slightly at the praise, and Onas smiled proudly at her. Ser Grisom nodded in agreement as he gave the princess an appraising once-over.

"Shall we proceed to the dining hall, then?" Lord Iemes suggested, gesturing for them to follow him. "I would be delighted to introduce you to my family over a meal. I trust our cooks have prepared a meal befitting a princess and her esteemed companions."

As they walked through the castle, Gwyn marveled at the elaborate tapestries and well-polished suits of armor adorning the walls. The castle was well-maintained and spoke to the baron's attention to detail and pride in his home. She was nervous, and everything was moving so fast, but Onas had told her it was important to get Lord Iemes's help. She was determined to do her part. A quick glance at the merchant as she followed the baron helped her nerves when Onas immediately gave her a reassuring smile.

Upon reaching the dining hall, they were greeted by an impressive feast laid out on a long, elegant table. The aroma of roasted meats, fresh-baked bread, and a variety of delectable side dishes filled the room. Ornate candelabras cast a warm glow over the table, and a fire crackled merrily in the large hearth. A woman and two girls who were shorter than her stood patiently just inside the hall.

As Gwyn entered the hall, Lord Iemes took a moment to introduce his family before they all took their seats.

"Allow me to introduce my lovely wife, Lady Cella," he said, gesturing to the elegant woman standing beside him. Her golden hair was arranged in an intricate updo, and her emerald green eyes sparkled with warmth and intelligence. She wore a finely tailored gown of deep burgundy adorned with golden embroidery that complemented her husband's attire.

"And these are our daughters," he continued, smiling fondly at the two girls who stood nearby. "Our eldest, Ryia, is ten years old." *Oh! She's my age.*

The girl had definitely inherited her mother's golden hair and father's smile. She wore a simple yet elegant dress in a shade of burgundy that matched both their house colors and her curious hazel eyes.

The baron introduced the final member of his family with a gesture. "And our younger daughter, Arlette, is eight." Arlette had the same emerald eyes as her mother, and her auburn hair was braided neatly down her back. She wore a dress similar to her sister's but in a shade of soft green that highlighted her eyes.

"It is a pleasure to meet you all," Gwyn said, her eyes wide with admiration as she regarded the baron's family.

"The pleasure is ours, Your Highness," Lady Cella replied graciously, giving Gwyn a warm smile.

With the introductions made, they all took their seats at the table. The baron led Gwyn to her seat at the head of the table, while Onas and Taenya took their places a few chairs down from her. Lady Cella sat beside her husband, and the two girls eagerly seated themselves next to Gwyn, and she heard them whisper to each other how exciting it was to be seated by a real princess. *Oh no*, she thought.

Onas and the baron spoke of many topics, including the recent events and the political climate of the kingdom. Gwyn sat quietly as Onas and Taenya shared the details of their harrowing encounter with the bandits, which apparently earned further admiration and respect from their hosts. The atmosphere was warm and friendly, and Gwyn was happy that the baron's family was so welcoming. *I just can't let the truth slip.*

As the plates from the previous course were being cleared, Lady Cella turned to Gwyn with a warm smile. "Princess Gwyn, it has been a pleasure getting to know you this evening. I was wondering if you would like to join Ryia, Arlette and me for some tea in the drawing room after dinner? Miss Taenya could attend, of course. It would be a lovely opportunity for us to get to know each other better, and I'm sure the girls would be thrilled to spend more time with you."

Gwyn's eyes lit up at the invitation, and she glanced at Onas, who gave her an encouraging nod.

"I would be delighted to join you, Lady Cella. Thank you for the invitation."

"Excellent!" Lady Cella beamed, clearly pleased with Gwyn's acceptance. "I will have the servants prepare the drawing room for us, and we can retire there once we've finished our dessert."

As they enjoyed the final course of the meal, it seemed all of the tension and anxiety she had been feeling had melted away. The more they spoke, the more Gwyn couldn't help but feel excited about the prospect of spending more time with the baron's family, particularly the two young girls, who seemed so eager to befriend her. It was a welcome change from the challenges and dangers she had faced on her journey thus far, and she looked forward to a pleasant evening of conversation and socializing.

I'll get through this for you, Raafe.

CHAPTER TWENTY-TWO

HOUSE IEMES

Gwyn followed Lady Cella into the drawing room, with Ryia and Arlette excitedly skipping beside her, their eyes wide with curiosity and admiration. Taenya trailed behind them, quietly following along, looking a bit awkward.

The room itself was beautifully furnished, with warm tones and elegant decorations that made it feel both grand and inviting. Large windows allowed moonlight to filter in, casting a gentle glow upon the plush seating arranged around a low table. A fire crackled softly in the ornate fireplace, providing additional warmth and comfort.

Lady Cella gestured for everyone to take a seat, and they all settled into the comfortable chairs. A maid entered the room and carefully poured tea into delicate china cups, which she offered to each of them. The aroma of the tea was soothing and fragrant, and Gwyn couldn't help but smile as she took a sip. It was piping hot, and Taenya's eyes widened slightly in surprise when Gwyn didn't react to the temperature.

The heat never bothered me anyway. She stifled a laugh.

"So, Princess Gwyn," Lady Cella began, ignoring the fact that Gwyn was the only one already drinking her tea, her tone both gracious and inquisitive. "Tell us more about yourself. We are all eager to learn about your life and experiences."

Gwyn hesitated for a moment, unsure of where to begin, but then launched into her story since arriving. She spoke of all of the things they'd had to do, and how it was so different from what she was used to. She tried to relate everything she explained to how it was different back home, and that seemed to draw the three nobles in even more. Taenya seemed to loosen up as Gwyn recalled the moment she'd taken a bath for the first time, interjecting little tidbits into the conversation.

Ryia and Arlette listened with rapt attention, their eyes wide with wonder and fascination.

"Your home had water that flowed inside?" Ryia asked, completely astounded.

Gwyn chuckled softly into her hand as Taenya had taught her. "Yup! And let me tell you about showers." She found herself releasing more and more tension as the conversation progressed. Their cups were filled several times. Lady Cella and her daughters were completely refreshing, and oh so different from Lord Bekker.

I wish Raafe could have met them, Gwyn thought.

Lady Cella took a sip of her tea and turned to Gwyn, her expression thoughtful. "I can't imagine what it would be like to be whisked away to an entirely different culture, let alone a new land," she said with a slow shake of her head. "While I think Onas Fenren is quite capable, he has not navigated the noble society. I am sure you have all sorts of questions about what to expect. I almost wish you had arrived in, say, the Queendom of Lehelia. Their nobility is much kinder if you're a young lady. What questions do you have for me, darling? You must have so many."

Gwyn smiled. The lady seemed really nice and she couldn't help but feel comfortable with her. "Can you tell me a bit more about your… house?" she asked, trying to remember the term Onas had explained before.

The noblewoman nodded as she took another sip of tea, and even Taenya leaned forward in a way that betrayed her interest in the subject.

"Our family's history is quite unique, and our peerage was actually bestowed upon us due to my husband's successful business endeavors, particularly the silver mine he owns and operates. The friendship and relationship he built with Onas was particularly beneficial to the both of them, with the Fenren Trading House helping us expand our dealings with the whole region."

Ryia and Arlette listened intently as their mother spoke, clearly proud of their family's accomplishments. Lady Cella went on, "My husband's peerage was a great honor, of course, but it is also a responsibility we do not take lightly. The mine has provided many jobs and resources for the people of Larton, and we strive to maintain our good standing in the community. But our peerage is not hereditary, which means it will not pass on to our daughters. Still, we believe that in teaching them the value of hard work and dedication, they will forge their own paths and create a legacy of their own.

"While our position as newcomers has been met with some resistance among our peers, it has also given us a unique opportunity to catch the eye of the duke himself. Our dedication to our work, the prosperity we've brought to Larton, and our willingness to contribute to the betterment of the region have garnered his attention and support.

"In fact," she added with a touch of pride, "the duke established a relationship with our house by offering the services of a well-respected knight who served him personally. The man joined our house and provides valuable advice to our barony. He now serves as our majordomo and resides in Strathmore, the ducal capital, representing our house's interests and maintaining our connections with the duke and other influential figures. His presence and support have been invaluable to us, and we are honored to have him as part of our family."

Gwyn nodded, fascinated by the story of House Iemes. "That's really impressive, Lady Cella. And I'm sure Ryia and Arlette will achieve great things, just like their parents."

Ryia beamed at the compliment. Arlette blushed and hid her face behind her tea cup. The conversation shifted to Gwyn, who spoke more about her own life and her dreams for the future, her eyes shining with determination and hope. She kept everything about her mom private, and it seemed that the noblewoman picked up on that—though she glanced at Taenya a few times, she never pressed.

As they continued to share stories, Lady Cella encouraged Taenya to open up about her own background.

Taenya sipped her tea and began, "I come from a family of modest means in the Kingdom of Meris. We were farmers, and while we were never wealthy, we were happy. But I always felt there was something more out there for me, so when I came of age, I decided to leave my family's farm and join the Guards Guild. That led to me taking a job for which I traveled to Strathmore, where I decided to stay in search of better opportunities."

Gwyn and the others listened attentively as Taenya continued. "It wasn't easy at first, but I worked hard and eventually found myself in the employ of Onas as his head guard. He's been a good employer and a loyal friend, and I'm grateful for the life I've built with him and our team. I remember the first time I met Lord Iemes, with Onas. I was so shocked and scared when Onas treated him like an old friend. I thought we were going to get yelled at, but then Lord Iemes just laughed and hugged Onas. I think they both took way too much joy in my reaction."

Lady Cella laughed lightly. "That sounds like my husband. For all that we are now nobility, he has always felt most comfortable around people like Onas— merchants and other business people."

Taenya nodded. "I've come to realize that. It's refreshing. I hope Princess Gwyn is able to meet more families and houses such as yours. She could use all the support she can get."

Gwyn nodded as the two talked. She had constant butterflies in her stomach as she expected that any minute, her lie would be found out. Still, she had to play the part. Keep up the act, and hope that things would work out.

She *did* need support and help. But not really for herself. Gwyn had the people she needed, but Onas and Taenya said that they needed to grow in order to keep other nobles away, which she guessed was understandable, but it made her feel worse. Everyone knew that the more people you had to lie to, the greater the chances that the lie could be found out.

No, what Gwyn really needed help with was finding her mom.

But if I have to take help for being a princess, I won't say no. I just have to be extra careful.

And maybe rely on Taenya more.

Lady Cella smiled gently at Taenya. "What you've done to help acclimate the young princess here is to be commended, Miss Taenya. Your journey has been an inspiring one, and I am sure your family back in Meris would be proud of your accomplishments."

Taenya seemed touched by the kind words. "Thank you, Lady Cella. I do hope to make them proud, and I am grateful for the opportunities that have come my way. I just hope to continue my support of Princess Gwyn as she learns to navigate the kingdom's politics."

As the evening progressed, the conversation flowed effortlessly, weaving in and out of personal stories, shared experiences, and lighthearted moments of laughter. The drawing room, bathed in the soft glow of the firelight and the delicate scent of the tea, became a haven of friendship and understanding.

Gwyn watched as Ryia's eyes sparkled with excitement while everyone shared their stories. The young girl seemed eager to share more of her world with Gwyn. Ryia gently placed her teacup on the small table next to her and leaned forward, a hopeful expression on her face.

"Mother," she began, her voice almost a whisper. "Could we show Princess Gwyn around the manor? I think she would enjoy seeing the gardens and the library. And maybe we could introduce her to our horses as well?"

Gwyn observed Lady Cella as she smiled warmly at her daughter's enthusiasm, giving her an apologetic glance as she considered the request. Gwyn could see that Ryia and Arlette were excited to spend time with her, and she also thought it would be a wonderful opportunity for her to experience more of their way of life.

"That sounds like a lovely idea, Ryia. However, why don't we do it tomorrow, when the sun is up," Lady Cella suggested. She turned her attention to Gwyn. "If you'd like, Princess, we would be delighted to give you a tour of our home. I believe you might find it quite interesting, and it would be a wonderful chance for you to get to know us better."

Gwyn smiled as she took note of Ryia's and Arlette's hopeful expressions. "I would be happy to see more of your home," she replied, eliciting more excitement from the two girls.

"Excellent!" Lady Cella exclaimed, clapping her hands together gently. She rose from her seat, smoothing the fabric of her elegant gown. "Then you must return tomorrow. We will show you everything we can. Taenya, you are welcome to join us, of course."

As they left to join Onas to depart for the night, Gwyn couldn't help but feel both hopeful and worried. Raafe's warnings about nobility sat at the back of her mind, and while the idea of exploring her new surroundings was fun and interesting, she couldn't shake away her thoughts of her mom and the worry over where she could be.

Still, with Taenya also looking hopeful, she decided to embrace the opportunity to learn more about the people who were offering their support.

Onas sat in a comfortable chair in the well-lit parlor, sharing a drink with the baron from the noble's personal collection. Elsewhere in the castle, Taenya and Gwyn were enjoying tea with the baron's wife, Lady Cella. The discussion of the princess's origins had been going on for some time, and the baron was gradually coming to terms with the extraordinary revelations Onas had shared with him.

Lord Varciel Iemes placed his glass on the polished wooden side table, leaning back into the plush armrests of his chair. He interlaced his fingers, his eyes narrowing in contemplation. Looking intently at Onas over his steepled hands, he asked for clarification.

"So, let me make sure I understand. The princess hails from another world and arrived simultaneously with the blue flash that seemingly occurred everywhere. Additionally, she possesses magical abilities, having killed two bandits by launching balls of fire created from thin air. We'll revisit this topic shortly. Is there any other pertinent information I should be aware of?"

Onas pondered for a moment before responding, "She's convinced that her mother is here, somewhere. They were together when she was transported to our world, but they didn't arrive at the same location. I'm afraid I have no idea where her mother might be."

The nobleman nodded. "Onas, are you absolutely certain she's a princess? Our actions will be closely examined, and although we can mitigate some scrutiny, she will eventually interact with high-ranking nobles. The level of investment required for her support is considerable..."

"I'm quite certain," Onas affirmed. "She described her home and daily life in great detail, and everything points to a life of privilege. Her mother has servants and commands the respect of others, and she mentioned how her mother traveled the world, meeting with people from different nations who sought her counsel."

Onas paused for a moment before continuing, "The princess has private tutors who help her learn languages and attend to her education. She goes to a prestigious academy handpicked by her mother. She mentioned meeting with tutors who specifically instructed her on proper speech and etiquette. Just by observing her interactions and the way she speaks, it's evident that she's had extensive training in these areas.

"I even tested her knowledge with questions that most commoner children wouldn't know, and she answered them all. Her education in mathematics is highly advanced, surpassing even that of nobles much older than her. This knowledge could be applied to economics, logistics, architecture, and potentially even warfare and siegecraft. It's clear she's from a different culture, but based on her mathematical prowess alone, I'd say she was being groomed for a leadership role. Additionally, she has an appreciation for the arts and told me she's been learning several musical instruments, although they are ones I'm not familiar with."

Several moments of silence passed as the baron absorbed the information, his brow furrowed in thought. Eventually, he sighed. "So, there's a queen out there searching for her daughter, potentially possessing unknown abilities. Onas, we must keep Princess Gwyn's magical abilities a secret from other nobles. They'll try to forcibly marry her into their families after the initial shock of magic's existence fades. Taenya's report to the guard cleverly avoids mentioning Gwyn's abilities. Although her magic is a game-changer, she lacks proof of her lineage. We'll need to collaborate to ensure her well-being. I assume you've shared this with me because you seek my assistance?"

Onas nodded, taking a sip of his drink. "Indeed. I believe there's much to gain from helping her. She's remarkably intelligent for her age, and the knowledge she possesses is invaluable. Imagine the potential rewards of meeting her mother after caring for and protecting her daughter."

The baron tilted his head. "Let's return to the topic of magic. Historically, magic and miracles have been associated with the gods. Are you suggesting…"

Onas shook his head. "No, I witnessed her conjure fire. Varciel, she did it. The princess can wield magic at will. I'm confident that she's not an emissary of the gods."

"How can you be so sure?" Varciel inquired, his tone reflecting curiosity rather than skepticism.

"She's not even from our world, my friend. I've never been devout, but this is something entirely different. I can't quite put it into words, but everything feels changed since the Flash. Have you felt it too?"

Varciel set his drink down on the table beside him. "I'm not sure, Onas. I can't tell if something has genuinely changed, if I'm merely anxious, or if it's just heartburn." He chuckled. "What I do know is that this knowledge must be handled with great care."

Onas considered the baron's words, then drained the rest of his drink. "I agree, but we need to be at the front of this," he suggested with rising confidence. "Just like our business in the past. When have we ever shirked away from risk? Never. This is something new and exciting. The princess presents us with opportunities. If we can benefit just from assisting a young girl, should we not?"

Varciel nodded in agreement, his expression reflecting a thoughtful determination. "You make a valid point, Onas. The stakes are high for both of us in this endeavor, and it is imperative that we handle it with utmost care. Gwyn must appear legitimate in every way. While your financial resources are substantial, I am willing to contribute as well," the nobleman offered.

He paused as he collected his thoughts. "Additionally, I will release two of my knights here to ensure her protection and service. As a baron, there are limitations on the number of knights my house may hold. This does have the benefit of allowing my house to fill the vacancies with fresh knights, which will benefit this partnership. Admittedly, it may not be a significant number, but perhaps you can utilize them to hire auxiliary staff and guards who will be under their authority. As the princess's retinue grows, we can gradually expand her support network. Your household in Strathmore might not be sufficient, but she can utilize mine and its staff as a starting point. While I am loath to lose Siveril's advice, truth be told, I rarely visit him. Not to mention, that estate is expensive to maintain. It would be more practical to acquire something more modest for my house's future business purposes."

Onas nodded. He'd met Ser Siveril only a few times, but the man seemed quite shrewd. The high elf knight had a long career of ducal service that had turned into helping guide a young barony. After five years of valuable advice, Varciel was probably safe in continuing without the man's guidance.

The baron nodded thoughtfully as he retrieved and swirled his drink, musing quietly to himself. "Taenya, I think..." He looked up and smiled at his realization. "Yes, the service Taenya provided to my land by fighting those bandits certainly merits a knighthood. She can learn from the two knights I'll send with Her Highness. However, that will require you to release Taenya to serve in the princess's retinue. A knight cannot be beholden to a commoner. No offense," he said with a wince.

Onas waved off the man's concern, unaffected by simple facts.

"For the time being, it might be best if you remain in Strathmore, my friend," Varciel added. "Concentrate on expanding your business."

Onas rubbed a hand through his hair. He enjoyed the ability to travel, but he couldn't deny that this new venture would be... time-consuming.

"Perhaps you're right," he said slowly, his mind still weighing the need against his desires. "With all that we'll need to accomplish, I suppose it is a wiser decision to remain where I can better oversee everything. While it will be unfortunate to lose Taenya, having her gain a knighthood and take on the protection of the princess would benefit us all. This will allow me to reassign Keston to Her Highness as well. I know how much Raafe's death affected him."

Varciel raised his glass. "To your guard. May Relena give him the peace he deserves."

"Relena guide him," Onas replied, raising his own empty glass.

They sat in silence for a moment before the baron said, "You may need to adopt the role of managing Her Highness's merchant assets and trade interests. I know you've always been hesitant to tie your company and family to a noble house, but as you pointed out earlier, the potential benefits may well outweigh the risks."

Onas considered Varciel's words and agreed. "You are correct, of course. The girl is young. I believe we will be well-positioned to ensure our own interests are not threatened while we expand hers. As her influence grows, ours will as well. Also, Varciel, your standing is widely known in the duchy. While you are indeed quite wealthy for your peerage, you're still just a baron, and I, a merchant. We need to figure out a way to secure something better. And we will need an ally of higher standing."

Varciel gestured in agreement, his brow furrowed. "You are right, of course. She is ten years old, isn't she?"

"Yes," Onas replied. "She mentioned her eleventh birthday would be coming in the next couple of months. However, after some initial confusion, we learned that, of course, her people use a different calendar. Upon further discussion, I learned she meant by the end of this season."

A smile crossed Varciel's face as an idea struck him. He snapped his fingers. "I've got it. The Royal Academy in the capital! A student must be twelve to attend. While our sponsorship alone isn't enough for her to gain attendance, her status all but guarantees her at least an opportunity to be considered. We can pool our resources to purchase a suitable abode in the capital. I'll also reach out to my contacts in Meris. They might be more inclined to offer support to a foreign royal navigating Aviran politics. Perhaps there will be an opportunity for her to secure a friendship to support her within the school."

Onas nodded. "That plan could work. I can arrange transportation and provide funds to Taenya for securing additional personnel. If I am to be a sworn agent of the princess, I'll need to register with the duchy and ensure proper payouts to her, as that will be audited. I will work with Siveril to ensure she is well taken care of."

Varciel took a deep breath and looked at Onas with resolve. "Once the princess's house is officially acknowledged, I too will need to formally join my house to hers. It's a necessary step to strengthen her position and ensure our influence and mutual protection."

Onas nodded thoughtfully, understanding the implications of their mutual decision. "It's a wise move, Varciel. It will certainly help solidify her standing among the nobility and give her a more robust support network." He furrowed his brow, then, and raised a concern that had been nagging at him. "Varciel, what about Gwyn's mother? I have no idea where to start with finding her. The princess believes she's here somewhere, but this world is vast and the task feels daunting."

Varciel considered the challenge before them. "You're right, it won't be easy. However, we can't ignore the possibility that her mother may be in a similar situation, seeking allies and support. We should keep our ears to the ground and make discreet inquiries among the nobility and those we trust. Remember, information is power, and if we can find Gwyn's mother, it will strengthen not only the princess's position but also our own."

As the two fell into silent contemplation, Onas's mind raced as he mulled over the enormity of the task before them. He considered the deceptively simple details of their plan to assist the princess while simultaneously furthering their own interests. From his perspective, the air in the room was charged with a mix of excitement and apprehension as he weighed the risks and rewards of their involvement. As thoughts and strategies filled his mind, he knew they were on the cusp of something extraordinary, a venture that could change their lives forever. He glanced over at Varciel, noticing the same intensity in his friend's eyes, and felt a surge of confidence in this shared endeavor.

Finally, Lord Iemes finished his drink, stood up, and extended a hand to his friend. "Come, Onas, we have much work to do. But we stand to gain far more from this endeavor than we initially imagined."

Onas grasped the baron's hand, allowing him to help pull him to his feet. "That we do… That we do, my friend."

CHAPTER TWENTY~THREE

ADVANCING STATIONS

Ser Sabina Dominis, a knight pledged to House Iemes, strolled through the manor's ornate hallways with her fellow knight, Ser Theran Rhodan. Soft sunlight streamed through the windows, casting a warm and natural glow that illuminated the exquisite tapestries adorning the walls. Engrossed in their relaxed conversation, they delved into diverse topics, including the recent bandit assault on the princess and the baron's merchant acquaintance, as well as their respective responsibilities within the barony.

Sabina's attention, however, was drawn away by a group emerging from the gardens visible through a nearby window: Lady Cella accompanied by her daughters, the princess, and the blond telv guard who worked for the merchant. Sabina remembered seeing the princess when she first arrived the day prior, and she recalled the baron's earlier warning that the girl was from another world. This concept didn't fully register with Sabina until she saw the princess in person. She couldn't help but be intrigued by the foreign girl, and wondered what kind of life she had led.

As Theran continued to speak animatedly about preparing for an excursion into the Larn Forest with Ser Grisom, Sabina's thoughts were elsewhere. She absently brushed a stray strand of hair behind her ear as she listened.

"And that's when I told him, 'You can't possibly expect me to wear that old armor just because mine is with the smith. It's falling apart at the seams!'" Theran recounted, laughing at his own story.

Sabina chuckled politely in response, but her focus remained on the group in the garden. "Do you see that, Theran?" she asked, pointing discreetly. "Lady Iemes is with her daughters and the princess everyone's talking about. I'm quite curious to meet her."

Theran followed her gaze and nodded, his eyes widening with interest. "Ah, yes, the... what was it... hue-man?... the princess," he recalled as he scratched at his neatly trimmed beard. "She's been spending the evening with the baron's family. You should go introduce yourself, Sabina. I'm sure she would appreciate meeting another of the knights sworn to House Iemes. She only got to meet Grumpy Grisom."

Sabina huffed in response, crossing her arms defensively. "Don't call him that. He'll make you train longer."

Theran shrugged, grinning mischievously. "I wouldn't complain. Maybe you should be joining me as I train more."

"I train quite often, Theran," she replied, rolling her eyes. "You know how busy the lady keeps me. She's constantly traveling the barony and going to various markets, and she loves when we host fairs—a bit too much."

Sabina couldn't help but feel envious of the blond telv's travels. While she was sympathetic to the woman having lost a fellow guard, Sabina had long hoped to make a difference too. She'd never been attacked by bandits or the like. Her role as a knight had been to protect someone who was already safe from most harm. That said, she did understand the prudence of maintaining vigilance; she wasn't an imbecile. Sabina simply desired that sense of fulfillment that came with following your path in life.

"That is true," Theran conceded with a nod. "If I'm not at the mines or in the forest, I spend most of my time around the manor. I would love to go to Strathmore to work with Ser Siveril. The city would be much more exciting."

"I would love to leave the barony," Sabina said with a wistful sigh, her gaze lingering on the group in the garden. "I've never left it."

He chuckled, placing a reassuring hand on her shoulder. "Go meet the princess, Sabina. Who knows? Maybe she has stories to share that could inspire your own adventures."

Just as Sabina was about to step forward and approach the group, Grisom appeared, his face serious and focused. "Ser Theran, Ser Sabina," he called out, catching their attention.

Sabina glanced between the group in the garden and Grisom, her curiosity about the princess momentarily pushed aside by the urgency in Grisom's voice. With a nod to Theran, she turned to face the older knight. "Yes, Ser Grisom?"

Theran, having also picked up on the seriousness of Grisom's tone, stood at attention beside Sabina, ready to listen to whatever news or concerns their fellow knight had to share.

"The baron would like for you both to meet with him," he informed them, his gaze steady and resolute. "It is a matter of some urgency, and he has requested your presence immediately."

Sabina exchanged a quick glance with Theran, and they both nodded in acknowledgment of the summons. Although she felt a pang of disappointment at having to postpone her introduction to the princess, she knew that the baron's request took precedence. After all, duty was paramount for the knights of House Iemes.

As they followed Grisom through the manor's corridors, Sabina couldn't help but wonder what the urgent matter might be. Was it related to the princess, or something else entirely? In her mind, she rehearsed the proper etiquette for addressing the baron, determined to maintain her composure regardless of the topic at hand. As lower ranking knights, it wasn't often their lord addressed them personally. They were not one of the landed knights who had the baron's ear and helped him govern his lands. They were the elite protectors of the family and able combatants of the house.

Theran, too, seemed to be deep in thought as they walked, his usual light-hearted demeanor replaced by a solemn expression. It was clear that both knights understood the gravity of the situation, and they steeled themselves for the discussion that lay ahead.

As they entered the baron's study, Sabina and Theran bowed respectfully before their liege. Lord Iemes stood with his back to them, gazing out of the window at the setting sun. The room was steeped in a warm, golden light, casting a serene ambiance that belied the urgency of their meeting. Turning to face them, the baron gestured for them to rise.

"Ser Sabina, Ser Theran, thank you for coming so quickly," he began, his voice firm yet measured. "I have a matter of great importance to discuss with you, and I will need your utmost discretion and loyalty in the days to come."

Taenya felt a knot of nervousness in her stomach. Lunch, once more, was an extravagant event, as the baron had spared no effort to impress Gwyn. The conversation progressed smoothly, with Gwyn and Lord Iemes engaging in a lively discussion about her homeland in her own world.

The atmosphere became charged with excitement when the princess showcased her magical abilities, levitating a ball of fire above one hand. However, both Onas and Taenya couldn't hold back their gasps of surprise when Gwyn proceeded to freeze the water inside a nearby pitcher, demonstrating a progression of her magic they hadn't been aware of.

When Taenya quietly pressed the girl later, she simply said that magic sang and she listened. She was excited about something, but even when Taenya asked, Gwyn wouldn't tell her, saying it was a surprise.

The head guard's mind race with possibilities.

Before lunch, Gwyn and Onas had met privately with the baron, leaving Taenya with Keston, who had joined them this time. As they waited, Taenya had shared with Keston what she had learned about House Iemes the previous night. She had also expressed her suspicions about Onas and the baron's secretive behavior, feeling frustrated that her merchant friend hadn't confided in her. Keston offered sympathy and suggested that perhaps Onas was waiting for the right time to share the information. He encouraged Taenya to be patient and trust in their friendship.

The meal had concluded with the baron inviting everyone to gather in the main hall, leading Taenya to her current, confusing situation.

The main hall of the baron's manor was awash with sunlight streaming through the tall, arched windows, casting vibrant patterns across the stone walls adorned with the banners and coat of arms of House Iemes. The polished wooden floors gleamed underfoot, and a tall, arched ceiling loomed above. The room, although bustling with activity as they arrived after lunch, was now silent with anticipation.

She glanced up the stairs where Lord Iemes sat on his modest, high-backed chair on a dais. Gwyn stood to his right, a beaming smile on her face as she looked at Taenya, while Onas took his place behind and to her right. To the baron's left stood two of his knights, both high elves: a woman with black hair and a man with blond hair. They appeared to be around the same age as Taenya and wore their full armor, minus the helmets. Along the walls stood the guardsmen and women of House Iemes.

Taenya jumped slightly as the baron addressed her.

"Taenya, loyal head guard of my friend Onas," the baron began, his deep voice resonating throughout the hall as he gestured to the merchant standing nearby. "You have provided him years of service and protection. You have also done my land a great service in ending the predations of a large group of bandits upon my roads. Further, you have done all you could to ensure the safety and comfort of the princess."

The weight of his words hung in the air, and Taenya could feel the eyes of everyone present on her. "That brings us to this: a small token of my house to honor both you and Her Highness. Taenya, kneel."

Taenya's heart pounded in her chest as she knelt on one knee and clasped her hands together. Lords did not tell you to kneel without reason, and there were only two possibilities that came to mind. Her thoughts raced, wondering what she could possibly have done to deserve what she hoped—nay, what she *knew*— was coming. One such as her, a woman from a family of farmers, was not honored in such a way. But before she could dwell on it further, the baron continued.

"By the power granted to my house by the Duchy of Tiloral," Lord Iemes intoned solemnly, drawing his gleaming sword from its scabbard. The sunlight caught the steel, casting shimmering reflections on the surrounding walls. He placed the flat of the blade gently on Taenya's shoulder. "I charge you with protecting Her Highness and joining in Her service. Though I pass your fealty to

Princess Gwyneth, your person and honor shall always uphold the virtues of the barony of Larton, for your actions reflect upon my name."

As he moved the sword to her other shoulder, the gravity of the moment seemed to envelop the room, creating an atmosphere of reverence and solemnity. "Speak your oath to your liege."

Taenya took a deep breath, steadying herself against the weight of the responsibility she was about to undertake. She looked Princess Gwyn directly in the eyes, her voice unwavering as she spoke her heartfelt oath. "I promise on my faith that I will in the future be faithful to Her Highness, never cause her harm, and will observe my homage to her completely against all persons in good faith and without deceit."

As Lord Iemes removed the sword from Taenya's shoulder, the room seemed to hold its breath, anticipating the momentous occasion unfolding before them. "I dub thee Ser Taenya Alea Shavyre," he proclaimed with a mixture of pride and solemnity. With a nod, he stepped aside, allowing Princess Gwyn to move in front of Taenya.

The young princess, her eyes filled with determination and sincerity, placed her small hand gently on Taenya's cheek. Speaking softly, yet with a level of seriousness that belied her tender years, she said, "You're a true knight now... I wish Raafe could be here to become one as well, but I'm grateful that I have you by my side. We'll protect each other, Ser Taenya, and we'll find my mother. Together. Rise, my knight."

With a heartfelt smile and tears shimmering in her eyes, Ser Taenya Shavyre, Knight of House Reinhart, rose to her feet, bowing her head in respect to her princess. "I am honored to stand by your side, Your Highness. Together, we will find your mother."

As Princess Gwyn nodded in affirmation, Taenya took her place at the young royal's side, standing half a step behind her, ready to fulfill her oath and protect her liege with unwavering loyalty. The room, a witness to this poignant scene, remained hushed, as if honoring the unbreakable bond that had just been forged between the princess and her newly appointed knight.

Lord Iemes beamed with pride. "Princess Gwyneth, please allow me to introduce Ser Sabina Dominis and Ser Theran Rhodan. I release their service from my house, and with their consent, I pass their fealty to House Reinhart."

Taenya watched in astonishment as both knights saluted and then knelt before the princess.

Sabina spoke, her voice filled with determination. "Your Highness, it would be our greatest honor to serve under the command of your knight-captain. We pledge ourselves to protect you and your interests, and to accompany you on your quest to find your mother and establish your house in this new world."

As Taenya listened to the words of Sabina and Theran, the weight of her new title as knight-captain truly sank in. She realized that she would be responsible for not only her own actions but also those of others under her command. The authority and responsibility that came with her position were immense, but she felt ready and determined to embrace them fully. She knew that as the knight-captain, she would have the opportunity to work with the knights who now swore their allegiance to Princess Gwyneth, and while she had much to learn, Taenya was eager to take on this challenge in service to the princess.

Princess Gwyn surveyed the two knights and offered them a warm smile. "I am truly grateful for your willingness to join us. Thank you. Taenya, would you please assist them?"

Taenya caught the subtle hint in Gwyn's gaze, silently conveying a plea of *Please handle this for me, we didn't practice this.* She felt a surge of pride in the young princess, who had managed to handle herself with grace and poise. She stepped forward and addressed the two knights. "Welcome to House Reinhart. I eagerly anticipate working alongside you and learning from your expertise." She extended her hand to Sabina, who took it and rose. Taenya then turned to Theran and did the same.

Her eyes briefly scanned their armor as they stood at attention. Both sets were well-crafted and polished, bearing the burgundy fabric and accents of House Iemes. She couldn't help but feel a sense of anticipation as she imagined herself donning similar armor, tailored to House Reinhart's colors and insignia—which they would now need to create—and standing proudly beside her newfound comrades. With a light chuckle, she added, "It appears I will need to obtain some new armor to reflect my new role."

Lord Iemes joined in the laughter. "Indeed, Ser Taenya, providing a newly appointed knight with proper armor is a lord's responsibility. Rest assured, we will outfit you and your new fellows in the distinguished colors of your new house."

Two days later, Gwyn found herself seated in a luxurious carriage, a thoughtful gift from Lord Iemes to her—or, well, to House Reinhart, as he called it. Mister Onas followed closely behind them, driving his merchant wagon. The carriage's fancy interior made Gwyn feel like a true princess. Taenya sat opposite her, animatedly discussing their upcoming plans. Gwyn's two new knights and the freshly hired guards rode alongside them, while Keston shared the driver's bench of the carriage with a skilled coachman Taenya had employed.

As Taenya finished speaking, Gwyn realized she hadn't been paying attention. "Taenya, I'm sorry. I didn't hear anything you said."

Taenya exhaled, a hint of frustration in her voice. "Gwyn, this is important. We have a lot to go over."

Gwyn let her head fall back against the plush seat cushion, feeling overwhelmed.

"You sound just like my mom. I know I have to listen, but it's all so much right now. Can you just tell me again? I promise I'll pay attention this time."

"Fine," Taenya acquiesced, taking a deep breath before beginning anew. "Once we reach Strathmore, we'll work on establishing House Reinhart more formally. This will help spread the word about your house and allow us to signal to your mother that she can access its assets. The baron and Onas have generously provided enough funds for us to start, albeit modestly. It should be sufficient to get you settled."

As the carriage rolled gently along the dirt road, Gwyn listened attentively, her eyes fixed on Taenya.

"Lord Iemes will sponsor your entry into the Royal Academy, which will not only help you establish yourself and your house more securely, but also give us access to the most knowledgeable scholars within the kingdom. They may be able to shed light on the Flash that brought you here, and help us locate your mother."

Gwyn nodded, her fingers absentmindedly twirling a strand of her hair. "I'm going to need help learning all the fancy noble etiquette for this world. I had such a hard time with the baron."

Taenya gave a reassuring smile. "Don't worry, Gwyn. We'll find someone in Strathmore who can tutor you in the necessary customs and manners. They'll help prepare you for your journey to the capital and beyond."

A sense of reassurance washed over Gwyn as she contemplated the support she now had. Ever since arriving in this world, she had grown stronger and her thoughts had become clearer. After the recent fight, it was as if something within her had awakened, unlocking newfound abilities she couldn't quite comprehend. And she wasn't just talking about the magic, which seemed to be growing more too.

While she had always been considered one of the smarter students in her class, certain subjects used to require effort. Now, she could do things in her head quickly, stuff like math, and figuring out what to say or do. Her improved memory would undoubtedly be useful as she familiarized herself with the way the nobles lived and acted.

Gwyn found solace in knowing she now had additional help, and that three knights would be by her side. She couldn't help but miss Raafe, and wished he had been able to become an actual knight. In her heart, though, he would always be her first knight. She glanced at Raafe's Legacy, resting on the shelf above Taenya's head, a constant reminder that she would never forget him.

After their discussion, Taenya's focus had shifted to a small book that Grisom had given her about the responsibilities of a knight. She had been reading it intently, her face etched with determination and resolve. It made Gwyn proud that she was able to give something back to the woman who had helped her so much since she had arrived.

Gwyn's eyes drifted out the window, reflecting on the recent events. Despite the challenges and misfortunes she had faced, she couldn't help but feel that things might finally be moving in the right direction.

At the baron's, the princess had astonished Taenya and Onas when she had demonstrated her ability to create ice. She had been practicing extensively every chance she got since that fateful day, finding that magic came naturally to her. All it required was a bit of concentration on her desired outcome, and once it clicked in her mind, everything seemed to fall into place with ease.

The magic was both something amazing and, if she were honest, scary. She resolved to practice as much as possible because she didn't want to hurt anyone by accident, and after the fight… she wasn't sure when she may need to use it to protect people again.

It was as if she had a sixth sense, an ability to perceive the magic all around them. To her senses, it was a dance of colors, and the red came to her so easily. It was fierce and strong like fire, while the blue magic that had come to her in the past few nights was calm and collected, inspiring her thoughts. As Gwyn listened to the enchanting music of the magic, she found that when she reached out to it, it swirled within her, empowering her to perform remarkable feats.

She wasn't sure how much more she should or could learn, but she wanted to find out. When she called out to it, it surged into her and danced in a ball inside of her chest before spreading throughout her body. It made her feel so strong, and she wanted more of it. With a smirk, she called to it, letting it form per her desire.

A small orb of fire circled above her hand in a tight, mesmerizing orbit. Guided by a magical melody, she focused her efforts to keep the flaming sphere in a stable rotation. She attempted to deepen her concentration and summon an icy orb, but it appeared that the blue magic refused to extend beyond a mere flicker within her chest while the red magic remained active and obedient.

But that didn't deter her. She kept practicing, trying to force the magic little by little, and it was slowly but surely responding. It was a delicate balance, requiring Gwyn to simultaneously embrace the fiery strength of the red magic and the soothing tranquility of the blue magic. As she focused on the harmonious song of the magic within her, she felt a profound connection to the world around her, as if she were tapping into its very essence. While it was beyond her at that moment, it wasn't something that would hold her back for long.

Taenya's unwavering gaze remained fixed on the swirling magic, her eyes never faltering as the orb traced a perilous celestial path. The young princess, however, was determined to master her abilities and use them to find her mother.

"We're going to find her, Taenya," Gwyn declared, her determination unwavering. "I don't care what I have to do, or how much magic I need to learn. No one will keep us from finding my mom."

CHAPTER TWENTY-FOUR

BUSIER THAN EXPECTED

Under a rare dark sky, brought on by both moons in their new moon phase, the group settled around the campfire, its comforting glow a stark contrast against the surrounding darkness. The fire crackled and popped, casting a warm, reassuring light that reached out into the dark, fighting against the moonless obscurity.

The chill in the evening air brought a sharp clarity to Sloane's senses.

When asked, Gisele had explained that having both Sisters, as she called them, in a new moon phase had an important meaning within their religion. A night to spend among others by a bonfire as a way to stave off the creatures of the night.

All it did was increase Sloane's anxiety. It reminded her of her vulnerability, making her skin prickle and heightening her awareness of the wilderness just beyond their circle of light. Sounds of nocturnal creatures echoed in the distance, stirring the silence and tugging at the edges of Sloane's consciousness. Each rustle of foliage and strange hoot of the night animals seemed magnified, a stark reminder of their encounter with the dire wolves. Despite the jumpy feelings they stirred, these sounds also provided a rhythmic backdrop for their gathering around the fire.

The campfire served as a beacon of solace amid the unfamiliar sounds and the darkness. Around its warm light, the knights' laughter and shared tales created an impenetrable barrier, a stark contrast to the uncertainty that lurked in the unlit expanses beyond. Slowly, in that pool of firelight and camaraderie, Sloane started to feel a comfort that made the darkness seem less ominous.

Ernald's laughter caught her attention, and she looked over to see his eyes sparkling mischievously in the firelight as he broke into a wide grin. "Ismeld, remember that chap in Moonlock? You know—"

Ismeld, who always seemed to wear a scowl like a shield, halted his recollections with a strict voice. "Ernald, if you wish to keep your tongue, do not mention that... unmentionable being again." Her words, while stern, bore the undercurrent of a long-standing familiarity between the two.

Seizing the moment, Cristole chimed in with a bright smile, further prodding the scowling blond high elf. "Ismeld, you really must tell us. Why didn't you rip that man in two?"

"Truly, Issy, your penchant for tearing men apart is something of legend. Between your wrath and their heartbreak, we've certainly left a trail of unfortunate fellows in our path," Ernald quipped, quickly ducking to avoid retribution.

Sloane couldn't contain her laughter as Ismeld landed a smack on Ernald's arm and reached for his head for another strike.

"I swear to Relena, Ernald, I swear I'll make you a eunuch," Ismeld retorted, her threat laced with mock seriousness.

Unable to contain his cheeky demeanor, Ernald leaped up, a wide grin stretched across his face. "Sounds like your kind of date!" he called out, and he ran off into the night.

Gisele, visibly amused by their antics, chimed in. "Ismeld, if you don't go after him, I'll do it for you." Her laughter punctuated her words.

Ismeld gave chase, disappearing after Ernald. Her laughter trailed behind her, filling the air and mingling with the sounds of the night.

Gisele's gaze settled on Deryk. "Are we prepared for tomorrow, Deryk?"

His reply was brief, in line with his stoic nature. "We are. We'll reach Vilstaf by mid-afternoon."

Gisele nodded, her relief evident. "Excellent. We'll rest there for a few days. A breather before our final trek to Thirdghyll." A sigh slipped through her lips. "At last, we'll be somewhere we can rest. The constant travel has been exhausting."

Maud echoed Gisele's sentiment with a nod. "A chance to relax, without the need to immediately set off for the next location, sounds heavenly. How long do we plan on staying in Thirdghyll before we head to Swanbrook? I could use a nice bath."

Cristole scratched his cheek, weighing in. "And I could use a change from inn and tavern fare. A decent wine for once."

Gisele considered their comments. Her eyes swept over Sloane briefly before she responded. "We can afford to stay two or three weeks at least. It'll provide time for us to search for signs of Gwyn, and for Sloane to get some quality equipment. Plus, it will allow her to become familiar with the higher echelons of society." A smirk graced her lips as she caught Sloane's eye. "I assure you, there's more to Westaren than just the countryside you've seen so far."

Cristole raised a hand in protest. "Gisele, did you just suggest that Thirdghyll is an upgrade? You know well that the central district is the only respectable area. The rest of the city can be… rough."

Maud shook her head. "It's not that awful. The last time I was there, when that lord contracted the order for escort, they were making efforts to improve the conditions in the outskirts. Although I will admit, the outer city leaves much to be desired."

"As knights, we'll be granted accommodation within the central district. We'll be fine." Gisele's words held reassurance, but her expression tightened slightly as she turned to Sloane. "Just make sure to keep a firm hold on your coin purse until we reach that point."

Sloane nodded in understanding. "The next time we come across a market, I'd like to explore. There are quite a few things I'd like to try crafting. Being in a city for a few weeks will provide the perfect opportunity to experiment and dive into my work."

"As long as we do not have an incident like the last market… that's fine," Gisele said with a raised brow that made Sloane wince. She thought back to the thug that had attacked her in the alley… *Maybe she's not wrong.*

"But we can also introduce you to the banking guild once we reach Thirdghyll," Gisele added.

"I can assist with that," Cristole said. "I have some dealings with them myself."

"Thank you, I appreciate that."

Sloane's gaze drifted over to Deryk, who sat alone, staring off into the darkness. She couldn't help but call him out. "Deryk, buddy. You know the silent brooding type is a bit cliché. Come on, you know you can talk too."

Deryk's eyes narrowed slightly. "I have nothing to say."

Cristole chuckled. "Don't mind him, Sloane. This is just who he is."

"Absolutely, we still love him!" said Maud. "It just makes everything he does say that much more impactful."

Sloane smirked. After he'd joined her in her bar hop, she knew how he could be. He was a softy inside.

The conversation eventually faded and Sloane leaned back, listening to the soft murmurs of Maud and Cristole as they engaged in a private conversation. Gisele was engrossed in her notebook, her expression one of deep contemplation.

Sloane's curiosity was piqued by Gisele's hand moving deftly across the page with a piece of charcoal. Careful not to intrude on the knight's concentration, she drew nearer, watching the sketch take form. It was Cristole and Maud, captured in the midst of their conversation. Gisele was taking great care in getting Cristole's hair just right. The detail was astounding, their expressions captured perfectly, with an almost life-like realism. Gisele had captured a quiet moment between friends with incredible skill and accuracy.

"Wow, Gisele, this is truly amazing," Sloane praised, her voice quiet but filled with admiration.

Gisele glanced up, startled by her voice. Sloane winced as she realized Gisele hadn't noticed her moving closer. Gisele met Sloane's admiring gaze, and a brief flicker of embarrassment swept across her face, an unusual blush tingeing her cheeks. It was a rare moment of vulnerability for the typically confident leader.

She recovered quickly, though, a warm smile gracing her lips. She nodded in appreciation of Sloane's compliment. "Thank you."

She went back to her sketch. It was clear that she took great joy in her artistic pursuits, a side of her that Sloane was grateful to have discovered.

After a while, Sloane decided it was time to call it a night and stood up, capturing the attention of the others as she did. "Good night, everyone," she said.

The others wished her good night and she moved away from the fire's comforting glow and headed for the grouping of tents.

As she approached, her attention was drawn to the silhouette of a person quietly sitting alone on the steps to the wagon. It was Ismeld, her eyes reflecting the dancing flames of the campfire.

"Where's Ernald?" Sloane asked, breaking the silence between them. Ismeld shrugged nonchalantly, her attention not leaving the fire.

"He went to relieve himself, said he was going to sleep after," she replied, her voice somewhat distant.

"Are you... are you alright?"

"I am fine," Ismeld lied, but her tone made it clear she did not wish to speak of it further.

Sloane nodded, and as she turned to leave, she caught a glimpse of longing in Ismeld's eyes, a desire for something just out of reach. Intrigued but mindful of boundaries, Sloane decided to not pry further.

She retreated to the sanctuary of her tent, leaving the others to their night under the twin new moons. The soft murmurs and quietude of the others drifted behind her, as she prepared herself to sleep.

Lost in introspection, Sloane rested in the wagon's dim interior, the occasional shuddering of the wooden panels beneath her the only interruption to her thoughts. They were drawing closer to the city of Thirdghyll, a journey that had stretched out over a week more than their initial estimations. The delay, however, had served a purpose; it was a chance to gather snippets of information about Gwyn or any other human presence, though the yield thus far had been disappointingly meager.

Each pit stop at the multitude of villages and towns that speckled their route had afforded Sloane precious time to decipher the mana around them as well as try and form her own magic. The magic within her, she felt, was on the brink of blooming—a raw, untamed force seeking form and function. Yet, as she probed deeper, she couldn't shake the feeling that maybe she had been looking at things wrong.

Sloane believed that Maud had definitely used something related to life, yet that interpretation didn't seem to encompass the full spectrum of mana completely. Her mind had begun to map mana types to their respective color expressions. Red, blue, green—each hue a distinct signature that her watch had captured.

She kept trying to apply elements to each color of mana, but it seemed more and more that instead of elements, that mana was based on a concept or something deeper. It was certainly something she needed to explore more. She could sense that there was mana all around them, but even then, some of the mana seemed to be of a type that was not one of the other hues. This type was a bit different.

Sloane's current goal was to tap into the colorless, or white, mana. Her hypothesis was simple: the core of a person dictated the accessible affinity of their mana. And by starting with this neutral, colorless mana, she might identify her core's natural affinity.

That, or simply figure out how to get her MagiWatch—name pending, she thought with a chuckle—to interact with something other than active mana use. This way she could simply scan cores within people.

As she sat in the back of the wagon, Sloane tried concentrating on her core. The sensation of mana swirling within her was undeniable, yet she couldn't muster so much as a spark let alone a fireball. It was like reaching for a word on the tip of her tongue, maddeningly elusive. After another fruitless half-hour, she resigned for the day. Her futile attempts had yielded nothing but growing frustration.

Groaning, she arose and meandered toward the wagon door. With a tentative push, she cracked it open, a gust of wind brushing past her as she surveyed the surrounding scenery, a welcome distraction from her internal struggles.

Sloane leaned precariously out the wagon door. Cristole's horse carried him effortlessly as it trotted beside the wagon. "Cristole, just how much farther is it?" she hollered, her voice competing with the rumble of wheels on rough dirt. The promise of an inn's comfort was all she desired at the moment.

"Just a couple hours more, Sloane. We'll soon reach Vilstaf," the knight responded, his words carried on the wind. "How are your experiments with magic going?"

She let out a guttural groan that echoed off the wagon's wooden walls. "I can sense my core. I can feel the mana seeping into me. But to channel it, to use it... I'm at a loss."

A sympathetic shrug rippled through Cristole. "I'm sorry. I wish I could help, but admittedly, I have even less of an idea about how it works than you."

"I know, sorry, just feeling frustrated," Sloane assured him.

She turned her attention to the front of the wagon, aiming her voice around the wall. "Ernald! Maud! Do either of you want to swap?"

Ernald popped his head around the corner, his face brightening with relief. "By the gods, yes! I swear my arse has forgotten the concept of feeling!"

Sloane laughed, the momentary escape from her frustrations a welcome respite.

A few hours later, their journey was punctuated by the warm, earthy scent of tilled soil and the bucolic sights of farmland, a clear sign of their proximity to civilization. Vilstaf lay nestled amid these swathes of green, the comings and goings of carts and wagons punctuating the activity of the town. Seated beside Maud at the wagon's helm, Sloane reveled in the final stretches of the road. After all, Vilstaf and one more village would serve as their last waystations before reaching an actual city.

"Seems Vilstaf has grown a bit," Maud remarked, sounding disgruntled. "Should have known Moonlock wouldn't have the latest news. And our map clearly needs an update."

"What's the deal with Vilstaf?" Sloane asked, curious. "Each village we've passed so far seems to revolve around some peculiar specialty." She frowned. "Kind of odd, really, when you say it out loud."

Maud took a moment, her gaze shifting from the road to meet Sloane's curious eyes. "Well, every settlement has something that sets it apart, doesn't it? Here, it's gemstones. There's a mine nearby that unearths a bounty of the stuff. So the people, they either work the market, peddling these precious stones and all things related, or they're involved directly in the mining.

"Now that I think about it, it's pretty obvious that Vilstaf has grown. It's set at a key point where three main roads converge. All traffic from the port of Moonlock, and the capital of Westaren, and the towns and cities along the eastern border travel through here on the way to Thirdghyll and the central plains of the Sovereign Cities."

As she spoke, the fringes of the town came into view. The myriad stalls that lined the streets all the way to what seemed to be a central plaza, even at this distance, appeared bustling with traders and buyers, their vibrant hues punctuating the monotone of the stone and wood buildings. Vilstaf, it seemed, was a hub of trade and commerce, its humble roots as a village forgotten amid its burgeoning growth.

"As for your other question, the Kingdom of Westaren was once part of the Sovereign Cities, continued Maud. "Eventually, a king established himself in the port city of Olineva and conquered the main cities that now make up the kingdom. The Sovereign Cities traditionally have villages within their demesne that provide specific functions to the city they belong to. Westaren took this concept and applied it to the entire kingdom."

"Seems oddly practical, that a town should be known for one specialty. But tell me," Sloane said, her gaze trailed over the approaching expanse of Vilstaf, "how do the Sovereign Cities manage to hold on to their independence? From the map I saw, they're ringed by kingdoms and even an empire."

"The Cities do find themselves at war with each other quite often, each striving to gain some advantage over the others. But when threatened by an external power, they unite. Their unity was even more firmly entrenched with the formation of Westaren. Similarly, if any one city tried to establish a new kingdom by conquering its neighbors, the others would be quick to put a stop to it."

"That's fascinating," Sloane mused. "I can't think of a direct parallel in my world. I can come up with a few similar situations, but nothing quite like this." She paused, and then asked, "So, why is it named Thirdghyll? Was there a first and second?" She grinned playfully at Maud.

Maud chuckled "Indeed, there was! Originally, it was simply Ghyll. But when the city fell during the formation of Westaren, it had to be rebuilt, and the locals cheekily renamed it Secondghyll. Then, almost a hundred years later, a fire razed two-thirds of the city, leading to its current name. It's become a bit of a running joke, with bets on whether another disaster will strike the city."

Sloane blinked in surprise. "People actually wager on something like that?"

Maud nodded, a smile playing on her lips. "The people of Ghyll pride themselves on their resilience. They claim they can bounce back from any disaster. Funnily enough, we're nearing the hundred-year mark since the fire."

Sloane frowned, a sense of unease settling in. "Oh, great. So we're headed to a city that's due for a disaster? I'd rather the city not fall apart around me, Maud."

Laughing, Maud reassured her. "Easy now, we'll be fine. It's all in good humor. Nothing's actually going to happen."

As the wagon trundled into the heart of Vilstaf, Sloane's eyes were immediately drawn to the bustling central market. Nearby inns were a hive of activity with caravans loading and unloading goods. The thrum of life and commerce was palpable, a stark contrast to the relatively small size of the town. It seemed inconceivable that such a burgeoning trade hub remained so quaint. This town, she mused, was ready to blossom further.

As they pulled to a halt, waiting for Gisele to secure their lodgings within the inn, Sloane turned to Maud. "How long has this town been around?"

"About a year, I reckon." Maud responded, sounding unsure. "Maybe a bit longer."

Ah, so I was right. This town is on the precipice of further expansion.

"I could do with earning some money," Sloane mused out loud. "Those gem-stones and the rest of the goods you talked about are tempting. I want to start crafting things."

Maud smiled at her enthusiasm. "You demonstrated your knowledge when you helped create my mace. We'd be glad to fund your crafting endeavors—within reason, of course. It'd be even better if you could resell your creations."

"So, I could potentially pay back some of the investment and also earn a bit for myself?" Sloane concluded, the wheels in her mind already spinning.

"Just so," Maud affirmed.

Sloane grinned. "Thank you. There's a wealth of opportunity here to be explored. Especially if I can craft items that might be of use to the group."

"That would be fantastic, Sloane."

Gisele emerged from the inn at that moment, waving them over. "We're all set! You can park the wagon at the back. Ismeld and I are going to meet with the town guard about our… incidents on the way here."

"Hang on," Maud said to Sloane, before rapping on the wagon wall.

After a beat, Ernald popped his head out, looking a bit bleary. "What is it, Maud?" he called out.

Maud turned and looked around the corner at him. "Get off your arse. Need you to put the wagon in the back. We're going inside," Maud instructed the tired sun elf.

Sloane couldn't help but chuckle at Ernald's groan of protest as she dis-mounted from the wagon. The prospect of exploring the market was thrilling and she could hardly wait.

While Gisele and Ismeld contacted the guards, the rest of the knights settled in at The Restful Crossroads, indulging in their earned rest and drink, leaving Sloane the freedom to investigate the bustling market. Before she'd left, Deryk had handed her a small pouch filled with various denominations of coins to spend as she saw fit, and walked away without a word.

The market was a spectacle of meticulous organization; the expansive plaza was systematically divided into sections, each devoted to a specific type of goods or wares. Traveling merchants had their own distinct section, with their colorful wagons and carts serving as impromptu shops, eagerly peddling their goods to both town folk and fellow travelers.

As she meandered through the labyrinth of stalls, she carefully scanned the crowd. An eclectic mix of elves, telv, and raithe milled about, their various hues and textures creating a riot of colors. But her eyes were trained for a specific form, a specific face. She was looking for humans, specifically for any who resembled Gwyn. She was resolute not to repeat her previous mistake, not to impulsively run off again without thoroughly thinking through her actions.

Hawkers' calls echoed in her ears as she passed the vibrant booths. "Milady!

Come try our exquisite linens!" one vendor cried. Another merchant crooned, "Madame, with your impeccable skin, you simply must see our extensive range of beauty products!"

At the mention of beauty products, Sloane almost faltered. Not due to an interest in buying any, but out of pure curiosity. Were they made with lead, as some of Earth's old cosmetics were? Should she step forward to educate the merchant about the long-term damaging effects of the metal? She pondered for a moment but then shrugged. She held no credible standing at the moment and her warnings were likely to fall on deaf ears. Instead, she continued her quest, her eyes unwavering in their search.

Sloane halted upon noticing two dwarves managing a booth stationed outside a quaint shop. The booth was an unexpected treasure trove filled with materials she imagined would prove indispensable for her magical endeavors. It was almost too good to be true. A bit cliché of the first dwarves she met to be selling ore and gems... *Though*... she looked a bit closer... *the wood is different.*

She studied the dwarven pair, a man and woman. They were near-identical to her expectations drawn from various fantasy settings. She felt a hint of disappointment when she observed that the woman lacked the characteristic beard found in some of the versions. The dwarves were stout, with long, wavy brunette hair. The man sported a striking walnut-brown beard, skillfully braided and tied together with an intricate cap of gold and silver. On the other hand, the woman had a long, neatly woven braid, adorned with a matching metal clamp. They both possessed mesmerizing turquoise eyes, and the woman's face was punctuated by a sprinkling of cute freckles.

They weren't quite as short as she had envisioned, standing roughly the same height as her daughter's one hundred fifty centimeters. Their facial features were remarkably similar, leading her to assume they were siblings.

Noticing Sloane's keen stare, the male dwarf beckoned. "Ay lass, come on over and take a look at what we have ta offer."

Sloane approached them with a warm smile, apologizing for her blatant curiosity. "Hi, there! I'm sorry for staring! What do you have here?"

Laughing heartily, the woman assured her, "It's quite alright, dear! Not see many dwarves where yer from?"

Sloane shook her head, as she looked at the various metals and wood on one side and then delicately crafted decorative objects on the other. "No, you're the first two I've met," she admitted, extending a hand toward the woman in greeting. "I'm Sloane, it's a pleasure to meet you."

The stocky woman shook Sloane's hand with an unexpectedly delicate touch and smiled. "Nice to meet ya. Folks call me Reanny." She released Sloane's hand and jerked her thumb toward the man standing beside her. "This obstinate lout is my brother, Murinn."

A chuckle bubbled from Sloane's lips. "A pleasure, indeed, Murinn the Lout."

Attempting to feign an offended expression, the man couldn't quite suppress a grin. "Milady! You've chosen to side with this wretched sister of mine barely a moment after meeting? That stings, it truly does."

Amid her laughter, Sloane took a moment to appraise their goods, and deciding she liked the pair of dwarves, she had some fun. "You have a wide assortment of materials: raw ore, wood, gems, and crystals. You even have various things you've made from them. I can't help but feel this is fate. It's too perfect. Tell me, who told you I was coming?"

Reanny's broad smile never faded. "Why, but a wee birdie, of course. I had my brother go and mine the ore and strip the forest while I slaved away crafting my humble wares, all while awaiting your kind coin—I mean, person!—to finally make your way to our simple shop."

Murinn blinked in confusion. "Wait, what? I just procured the ore from Brende and the gems from Igglann this week. You were there!"

Laughter echoed around the stall once again. Reanny shook her head at Sloane. "My brother, he has a head for numbers and goods to buy or sell. Absolute zero social sense. Thank Erbium that I'm here, aye?"

Sloane nodded in amusement. "It's okay, Mister Murinn, I apologize. Your sister is just too much fun. But on a more serious note, you two may actually have some of what I'm looking for. Provided we can reach a good deal, mind you."

Reanny nodded. "Of course... Of course, only the best for my new friend."

After a quick appraisal of their goods, Sloane paused. "Alright, so. I need materials and tools. Just a moment." Sloane dug into her satchel, extracting the notebook Maud had handed her. Flipping to the page containing her meticulous notes, she took a moment to review her requirements.

Magical Crafting Items
~~Gem polishing supplies~~
Iron bracelet?
Leather bracer
Tools! Jewelcrafting, smithing, woodcarving, All the tools!
Goggles or stuff to make some, with magnification!
Gems and crystals of various types
Glass?
~~A burger~~
Rings of various types
Scrap metal
A weapon of some type
A Hammer
A magical all-purpose tool! Come on!

Glass beakers? bottles? vials? ~~A whole damn lab~~
~~Sanity?~~
~~Magic~~
~~Fireballs~~
Few ounces of silver
A small foundry crucible
~~Tongs~~ Smithing tools

Cross-referencing the items on the table with her list, Sloane finally made up her mind. "Alright, so... I need..."

Her ensuing discussion with the dwarves yielded an assortment of gems, which were astonishingly more affordable and plentiful than their Earth counterparts. She also managed to secure variously sized ingots of iron, a collection of crystals, pieces of wood, six rings of diverse materials, a bracelet, a bracer, and an iron rod.

"Hey, Reanny, do you know anyone who can sell me tools?" Sloane asked. "I need to be able to work with all of this stuff."

"Why, we've got everything you need right in the shop. I work on the stuff too, dear," Reanny replied with a chuckle.

Sloane gave the crafted items another cursory glance, realization dawning. "Of course. That makes sense. Well, let's get those as well, then." She checked over the assembled items she'd chosen, ensuring she'd covered everything on her list.

Looking up from the haul, she found herself meeting Reanny's wide, predatory grin. "So, what do you say, Sloane? Once we've sealed the deal, how about we celebrate over an ale? We can share a few more jests at the expense of men and brothers."

"You know, Reanny, if I didn't know any better, I'd think you were trying to sweeten me up before relieving me of all my coin."

Reanny's laugh filled the air. "Well, now comes the fun part, dear."

"Remember, I won't hesitate to return all these items if the price isn't right. So, why don't you tell me what you think I should pay..." Sloane teased, her eyes twinkling with playful defiance.

CHAPTER TWENTY-FIVE

A STEP TOWARD REVOLUTION

After what seemed like an exorbitant amount of time later, they had finalized their sale and moved to a tavern to have an ale together—because, of course, that was what dwarves did.

Unfortunately, the bartering and negotiations that had occurred were literally nothing like the stories and movies that Sloane had read. She'd been merch-slapped. Hard. At least, according to her observations of Ernald and the other knights' haggling abilities. Reanny was clearly a professional, and Sloane would not have been surprised to find out the dwarf woman really did have merchant mana that gave her overpowered negotiation magic. Yup, that was the headcanon that Sloane had settled on. There was no other way she'd have less than an eighth of the money the knights had given her.

Sighing, Sloane wrapped a hand around her fourth mug, which she was nursing. She looked across the table at Reanny. The dwarf had brought them to a tavern away from the plaza, which meant it was only slightly less busy, and more tailored to the locals than the traveling merchants.

They had been there a few hours at that point, but thankfully, Reanny had paid for the drinks. Sloane doubted she could have afforded it.

Okay, maybe she could. But to be fair, it had been a long time since her disposable income was so little compared to her total available funds. It was messing with her. She really needed to make some money.

Reanny seemed to recognize her self-pity and reached over to pat her hand gently. "Oh dear, don't sweat it. It happens to everyone the first time. If it's any consolation, you only paid a fifteen percent markup from our cost. All things considered, you did quite well! That essentially covers our overhead and ensures we stay in business. A fair deal in my book!"

"I was successful back where I come from, Reanny. I was a team leader and earned quite a good living. However..." Sloane attempted a smile. "I'm just worried about my ability to support myself here. I don't like being dependent on others. Hopefully, with the materials I just bought, I'll be able to start contributing!"

Raising her mug high, the hearty dwarf woman called out, "Now there's the spirit! With Dylenia's favor and a touch of Erbium's guidance, you'll be crafting masterpieces and earning your keep in no time! Here's to wealth and the delightful trinkets it can procure!"

Sloane chuckled and raised her own mug. Their glasses collided with a resonating clink, after which they tossed back their ales in unison. Setting her mug back on the table, Sloane wiped at the beer still on her lips and paused as she noticed Reanny's puzzled look. The dwarf seemed to be focused on something ... behind her?

No. On the side of her head.

Realization dawned and her hands darted up to her ears, which were meant to be hidden beneath her hood. Sloane hastily pulled the hood back over her head, casting a wary glance at the dwarf for any reaction.

Reanny leaned forward on an elbow, her voice dropping to a hush. "Eh? Wait a moment, are you one of those terrans? Why didn't you mention that before?"

Sloane's brow furrowed in confusion. "A terran?" She'd never heard the term. It instantly sparked both curiosity and caution within her.

"We had some visitors about a fortnight ago—two men and a woman—who called themselves terrans. They were part of a caravan headed toward the twin undercities of Dheg Malduhr and Von Ladholm."

"Is it... problematic that I'm a... terran?" Sloane asked, trepidation lacing her voice.

"No, no. At least, I don't think so. There has been a lot of interest in your people, though. Where you come from, what you want. A few other travelers mentioned having met some. Word's just spreading, you know, that sort of thing. I figured you wanted your privacy," Reanny explained.

Sloane straightened in her chair, her mind buzzing. "Has there been anyone with a child? A young girl? She's slightly shorter than you, with brown hair that has pink tips. She's a bit thin and is all legs. Blue eyes. Skin tone similar to mine... actually, no, she's paler. She was wearing some black boots, black pants, and a gray jacket... Uhm... Shit... Oh, her shirt underneath was blue." Her breath began to quicken, her heart pounding in her chest.

Noticing Sloane's distress, Reanny's expression turned to one of concern. "Woah, slow down, Sloane. No need to panic. There were no children with the terrans. Just breathe."

Nodding, Sloane tried to regain her composure. Apparently, all it took was the news of other humans passing through this area to rattle her.

"I'm sorry," Sloane murmured, looking away. She flapped her hand in front of her face in a futile attempt to hide the rising emotions.

"Is it your daughter who's missing?" Reanny queried, her voice gentle, her eyes filled with understanding.

Nodding, Sloane expanded on the situation. "Yes. When we were brought here, we didn't arrive together. I've been trying to find her since. The knights with me have been helping as well." She wiped at the tears threatening to spill from her eyes.

Reanny's hand found Sloane's, offering a comforting touch. "I can't even begin to fathom what you must be going through, lass. Tell me, what are your plans for all the items you bought from us?"

Sloane took a moment to compose herself. "I need to craft items that will aid the knights. You're aware of the blue flash?"

Reanny nodded. "Aye, who isn't? It's the talk of every town."

"It's what transported my people here from our own world," Sloane began, holding up a hand as Reanny started to interject. "Please, let me finish. Not only did it bring us here, but I believe it also brought mana to your world. Mana is what makes magic possible. My plan is to craft a variety of tools and even weapons that utilize this mana. We've already produced one such item, and I intend to create more. I've gathered that gems, crystals, and different metals interact with mana in diverse ways. I have numerous ideas that I want to test out. I just need to start trying."

Throughout Sloane's explanation, Reanny's eyes grew progressively wider. She attempted to interrupt several times, but Sloane continued on undeterred. After Sloane finished, Reanny remained silent, mouth slightly agape, before she finally gathered her thoughts.

"Magic... another world? You mean to say you can harness this... mana... to create magical items?" Reanny asked, her voice a mixture of disbelief and awe.

Sloane paused, looking down at the remnants of her drink, her thoughts swirling. "My ultimate goal is to make something that might aid me in finding Gwyn, my daughter. If that isn't feasible, at the very least, I need to create items that will provide me protection as I continue my search."

Reanny's brows knitted together in concern, her lively demeanor dimming momentarily. She nodded, understanding the gravity of Sloane's situation. "Not to add to your worries, lass," she began gently. "But the longer your search goes on, the more coin it will demand. You'll need a reliable way to sustain your income to fund everything you need."

"Yes, you're right. I know it can be done based on the two magical items we have, so I want to make more. I need to make more, and I need to harness my own magic. I need to find a way to use all of this to both make money and find my daughter."

Seeing the determination in Sloane's eyes, Reanny abruptly slapped the table and finished off her ale with one swift gulp. "Come on," she urged, pushing away from the table and standing up. She reached out and took Sloane's hand, pulling her along as she headed for the door.

The jovial merchant who had been sipping ale and trading jests was now all business. "Other worlds? Terrans journeying between realms? Mana?" She looked up at Sloane, a spark of excitement igniting in her eyes. "Lass, you should've led with the part about making money! Come on, we've got coin to make and a daughter to find!"

They stepped out into the cool embrace of the night. Darkness had fallen, blanketing the city with an unexpected quiet. Even the busy streets had settled down, with only a few occasional sounds of laughter or distant footsteps disturbing the peace.

Seeing the stars twinkling high above, Reanny let out an audible sigh of disappointment. "Well, shit," she muttered, glancing up at the moons with a crestfallen expression. She turned back to Sloane, her excitement from moments ago dampened by the reality of the late hour. "I didn't realize we'd been chatting for that long. Got all fired up for nothing, didn't I?"

Sloane, for her part, also felt the sting of disappointment. She had been eager to start, her mind already swirling with ideas and plans. But she also knew the importance of patience, particularly when dealing with the unknown.

With a determined smile, Reanny shook off her deflation. "Fine, tomorrow it is, then!" she announced, pointing a stout finger at Sloane. "Meet me at first light. I'll hold on to your goods till then, and don't worry, they'll be safe. My word on it. We've got a lot to do and no time to waste. Let's make the most of it, lass. Now, off to get some rest!"

The warmth of the inn washed over Sloane as she pushed the heavy door open and stepped inside. The typical evening din of laughter, soft murmurs, and clinking glasses filled the air. Scanning the room, she found Ismeld sitting alone at a table, her golden eyes staring thoughtfully into the glowing fireplace. Sloane made her way over, her heart throbbing with anticipation of sharing the events of her day.

"Mind if I join you?" she asked, pulling out the chair across from Ismeld.

The high elf looked up, a hint of surprise crossing her features before a small frown spread across her face. "Sloane," she greeted curtly. A moment later she sighed and gestured for Sloane to sit down. "How was your day at the market? You were out late."

Sloane smiled, a combination of relief and excitement filling her as she began to share her experiences. She spoke of the bustling marketplace, the myriad of wares on offer, and her encounter with Reanny, the jovial dwarf merchant. She talked about the items she had acquired, her plan to create useful and possibly magical objects, and how it might assist the knights and aid in her ongoing search for her daughter.

As she listened, Ismeld nodded thoughtfully, her eyes revealing a deep understanding. "Gisele and I have also been making our way around the town," she shared, her voice hushed. "We've heard rumors of other humans in town. We did not find any leads yet about the family or girl with Gwyn's description, though." She leaned back in her chair, running a hand through her hair. "It's proving to be a difficult endeavor, finding your daughter. While I am sure the others will agree in continuing to search as we go, I am starting to fear your journey will continue after we must depart. However, with luck, Thirdghyll will have at least some answers you seek."

She paused, her eyes meeting Sloane's. "Your plan to work with this merchant tomorrow—it's a good one. Keeping yourself focused and productive will help you in the long run. If we cannot find Gwyn immediately, you need to secure your position here. Your skill in craft might be your ticket."

Sloane sighed, frustration building inside her. The knight wasn't wrong; in fact, she had only reiterated what she had come to acknowledge herself. She wasn't sure why it stung more when one of the knights said it.

"Why are you sitting here alone, Ismeld?" Sloane asked.

Ismeld was silent for a long moment, her gaze turning back toward the fire. The flickering flames reflected in her eyes, revealing a hidden depth of sadness. "There are... things that I've desired," she finally said, her voice soft. "Things I've realized may never come to pass." She offered a small, sad smile. "Things I should have realized many winters ago, but it seems it took my aging to really... hammer it home. But that's a story for another day. Let's drop it, alright?"

Sloane wanted to probe further, to offer a comforting ear, but the look in Ismeld's eyes stopped her. It was the look of someone carrying a burden they weren't ready to share.

Nodding, Sloane decided to respect her wish and instead asked another question that had been bothering her. "Why were you guys heading to Thirdghyll, anyway?"

A heavy silence enveloped them, broken only by the occasional pops of the burning logs in the fireplace as Ismeld seemed to ponder the question.

"I know Maud told you some of our story, about what happened to us," Ismeld began, her voice low and contemplative. "I will not delve into that further, for that is a story for Gisele to tell." There was a profound weight in her words, and Sloane wasn't quite sure what to make of it.

"After we... left our homeland, we felt we had to make amends, to do something more to attempt to regain our lost honor. So, we began journeying, traversing the lengths and breadths of this world, lending our aid wherever it was needed."

She listed the places they'd been—the Queendom of Lehelia, the southern coast of the Sovereign Cities, the Kingdom of Rosale, and now the Kingdom of Westaren. "At each place, we tried to make a difference, to be a beacon of hope amid despair. To find those with the greatest need, and provide succor. A life of errantry."

When they'd arrived in Westaren, she explained, they'd heard rumors through the temple in Moonlock. "The rumors spoke of great need in Thirdghyll. They suggested we would be best served there. That's why we were on our way.

"But now..." Ismeld's gaze returned to Sloane, a newfound determination simmering within her gilded irises. "We have another purpose as well: to help you find your daughter, Gwyn, or if not, give you enough stability and guidance that you may continue the quest alone without fear. Money is no concern, Sloane. No matter what worries Ernald or Maud hold. Establish yourself, and create a path forward without worrying about us."

Her narrow eyes shifted back to the fire, her brows scrunched together in pained contemplation. "We deserve the life we have been dealt."

With the promise of a new day, Sloane found herself filled with resolute determination. After bidding Gisele and Ismeld a good morning, she made her way through the awakening town, the first rays of sunlight painting the cobblestone streets in hues of gold. The air was fresh, carrying with it the scent of the dew that had settled on the surrounding foliage.

At the dwarven siblings' shop, Mulinn gestured to follow him behind the counter and past several shelves filled with an array of items into a small, well-lit back room.

This was Reanny's workshop. It was a cozy space, packed with a plethora of tools and equipment. At a large sturdy workbench covered with blueprints and unfinished projects, the dwarven woman was already hard at work, cleaning up. On a table to the side sat all of Sloane's supplies that she had purchased the day before.

As Sloane walked into the workshop, Reanny turned around, her beaming smile revealing the excitement she felt about their impending work. "Ah, there y'are, lass!" she greeted warmly. "Ready for a day of crafting?"

Sloane chuckled at the shorter woman's infectious enthusiasm. "I sure am."

"So, what do you wish to create first?" Reanny asked, her eyes shining with curiosity.

Sloane took a moment to ponder. "I believe a ring would be the most suitable starting point. One designed to enhance the ability to use or connect to the mana around us. I believe it should be the simplest item for a beginner. I do have other concepts in mind, but they might require more complex procedures, like metal shaping and incorporating different types of mana cores."

Turning her attention to the supplies spread out before her, Sloane picked up an iron ring and carefully examined it. She put it back, seeing another ring, with a groove running along the center of the band. Nodding in approval, she stated, "I think this one will work well for a trial."

Reanny scrutinized Sloane's selection. "Sounds like a plan, lass. How about I handle this one and show you my process? You can attempt the next one."

"Works for me. Let's get started."

Taking a seat on a nearby stool, Sloane positioned herself in an ideal spot to observe and write down Reanny's work process. Once the dwarf was fully equipped, she initiated her work on the band. She began by inserting a prefabricated silver wire into the groove of the ring. With precise alignment, she carefully hammered it in place around the circumference.

While Reanny was focused on her work, Sloane's attention was drawn to her Watch Series M. A smirk tugged at her lips—yet another name that didn't seem to fit quite right. On the display, she noticed a small swirl of blue, seemingly pointing in Reanny's direction.

A gasp escaped Sloane's lips, her gaze darting back to the dwarf who remained oblivious to her sudden interest, absorbed in completing the inlay.

"We'll add a prong setting to this. It will allow us to incorporate the gem you've chosen," Reanny explained as she positioned the setting on the band. She reached for her soldering tools.

But Sloane noticed that the setting and ring began to heat up even before Reanny could redirect her attention to them. "Reanny, hold on. Look at the setting. What are you doing?" she asked.

Caught off guard, Reanny looked down, her eyes widening in surprise. "Oh! I don't... What—" She gasped as the setting abruptly stopped merging with the ring, her gaze fixed on the seemingly altered jewelry.

Visibly shaken, the dwarf turned to Sloane. "What just happened?"

Her excitement barely contained, Sloane looked back at her watch, which had now returned to its normal display. "You used mana, Reanny! Blue mana!" she exclaimed.

Stammering in confusion, Reanny retorted, "B-but I... I don't know how to use magic!"

"Take hold of the ring and the setting, then concentrate. Your aim is to attach the setting to the ring. Search for the rush within you, then grab ahold and push it into the ring," Sloane explained, reciting the instructions Maud had given her about healing.

Hesitantly, Reanny picked up the ring—which still had the setting barely attached—and looked intently at it. Sloane looked down at the Manasense (*that was good!*) function of the watch and observed the blue mana mist return. It converged on the side toward the woman, or blue alterer, as Sloane figured she could be called.

The setting slowly melded with the ring, creating a solid connection and point where a gem could be placed. Once the task was complete, Reanny turned to Sloane, a glint of triumph in her eyes. "I did it! This is incredible, Sloane! Thank you."

Sloane couldn't help but smile at the elated dwarf. "Absolutely! It's truly fascinating. You're using your mana in a way I hadn't anticipated…"

Reanny realized Sloane had drifted into her thoughts and gave her time. Sloane mentally reached inside, feeling her core out. Trying to figure out why she hadn't been able to use her magic. The core was there, churning with mana, she knew it, but why couldn't she use it? What did Reanny do differently?

Wait, she used her mana to combine metals—she altered the metal.

Suddenly, the understanding dawned on her, and she felt a sense of profound realization wash over her. "Holy shit, there are different types of magic. Maud's magic protects and heals. You alter materials. Mana takes on different colors, which suggests that it likely has distinct functions within each type. Do you understand what this means, Reanny?"

Reanny appeared utterly perplexed. "Er… can't say I do."

Brimming with excitement about her newfound understanding, Sloane brushed past Reanny's confusion. "I need my journal. Gather every different type of gem you have. We're going to run some experiments. This is just what I've been waiting for!"

"Lass, your journal is right in your hand," Reanny pointed out helpfully, amusement twinkling in her eyes.

"Right, of course…" Sloane chuckled, slightly embarrassed. "Okay, just a moment." She quickly flipped to a blank page in her journal. "Alright, I'm ready! Do you have the gems?"

"Sloane, take a breath. Slow down. Give me a moment." Reanny chuckled, rising to collect the requested gemstones. Each was about the same size and cut into a round shape. She arrayed them neatly in a line. "Okay, what do you want me to do next?"

"Wait just a moment while I write these down. You have a—" Sloane glanced over the array of gems, able to identify only a couple of the stones. "Can you just tell me what each of these are, please?" She ended with a laugh at her own expense.

Reanny let out a mild sigh. "Alright, I'll point to each one and tell you its name." She proceeded down the line of gemstones, tapping the table in front of each one as she named it. "Diamond, black diamond, amethyst, sapphire, opal, emerald, ruby, topaz, and lastly, onyx."

Sloane diligently wrote down each name. "Alright. Now we need to figure out what each gem does. But first, let me disassemble my watch so we can use it as a reference."

Reanny observed with interest as Sloane meticulously took her watch apart. Once the magic device lay in pieces, Sloane began explaining its function as she understood it. "I think this crystal here is providing power, or at least supplementing it. I don't feel like the watch is drawing power from me, but I can't be sure. Its complexity is beyond anything we could manufacture at this point."

Indicating the gems, Reanny asked, "So, these gems here are responsible for the functionality you described earlier? They allow it to sense mana being utilized?"

"Right," Sloane acknowledged, nodding her head. "I don't know what each gem does, either. This larger gem here is where the processor—the brain of the device—goes.

Reanny leaned closer, scrutinizing the gems. To assist Sloane, she began identifying them, "The large one is onyx. There are four diamonds." Pointing to each in turn, she continued, "And here we have two sapphires and two topazes. Interestingly, there's one of each type of gem we had previously set aside. It appears we're on the right track in terms of selection... though..."

She picked up a magnifying loupe and examined a small pink gem set apart from the others. "This here is a pink sapphire, which we didn't include in our original lineup. Unfortunately, I don't have one to spare. While it's not exactly rare—you could certainly find one in Thirdghyll—our stock here isn't fully established yet."

Sloane nodded in understanding. "So, we just need to experiment with the ring you prepared. Should we start with the obvious and insert an onyx?"

Reanny pondered for a moment before nodding to herself. "Either an onyx or a sapphire would be a good choice. If you examine the silver pathways," she said, pointing at Sloane's exposed watch, "you'll see there are five connecting to the onyx and another five leading to the leftmost sapphire. The diamonds are situated at what appear to be key junctures, each linked to at least two other gems.

"So with that in mind, let's see what the onyx does first. We can always remove it later and try a sapphire. Or, better yet, we can create two separate pieces and see what happens," she concluded with a chuckle.

"Okay, let's proceed. I'll reassemble my watch while you work on the first piece. What will you need me to do afterward?" Sloane asked.

Reanny smiled. "For the first few, just stand there and look pretty, lass. Once you're comfortable, you can try your hand at creating a couple."

I can't believe I'm going to make magical items. Sloane couldn't help the smile that grew on her face. It felt good to be back doing things she loved. Crafting gadgets, except this time... with magic.

This is going to be revolutionary.

CHAPTER TWENTY-SIX

PROFITING IN A NEW REALITY

Sloane refastened her watch to her wrist, looking up just in time to see Reanny finish her examination of the newly modified ring.

"I think it's ready, lass," the dwarf announced.

Sloane accepted the ring, took a deep breath, and slid it onto her finger. She waited for a moment, expecting some kind of sensation or change, but nothing happened. Seeing Sloane's puzzled expression, Reanny asked, "Nothing?"

"Nope. I don't feel anything. Maybe you should try?" She removed the ring and passed it to Reanny, who slipped it on.

"Nay, I don't feel anything either." Reanny shrugged as she removed the ring. "Next?"

"Let's try the sapphire next," Sloane suggested.

"Give me a moment," Reanny responded as she set to work. Using her magic to manipulate the metal setting, she managed to remove the onyx and replace it with the sapphire in no time. "My turn this time?" she asked.

"Go for it," Sloane replied, smiling as Reanny dramatically inhaled and exhaled three times, holding her breath on the last inhale. She then slid the ring onto her finger and paused, blinking a few times before letting out her breath.

"Nay, nothing here either. Your turn?" Reanny asked, a slight note of disappointment coloring her voice.

"No, that's alright! We have to keep testing. We know something will work. My watch works, after all. We've got all day! Don't be discouraged. This is part of the process." Sloane reassured her, trying to uplift Reanny's spirits.

"You're right. Now, pay close attention, and you can do the next one. I'll use the standard method this time," Reanny said, collecting her tools.

Sloane observed as Reanny carefully pried back the prongs and extracted the gem, then prepared the setting to accommodate another gem of identical size.

As Reanny worked, she walked Sloane through the process. "So, we're going to carefully insert the gem into the setting and check the fit. You want to ensure the gem is aligned properly. It should fit snugly within the prongs. There shouldn't be any rocking. The gem should be positioned at the right depth so that we can carefully secure the prongs over the top."

Once Reanny finished, she passed the ring, now set with a ruby, back to Sloane. Keeping her expectations in check, Sloane slid the ring onto her finger. As soon as she did, she experienced a vague sensation. The room felt a bit stuffier, somehow. Reaching inside herself, she found her connection to her mana core was slightly stronger. It wasn't a significant change, but it was enough to give her hope they were heading in the right direction.

Sloane removed the ring and returned it to Reanny. "Give it a try. I think I felt something. It was peculiar, almost like the humidity suddenly increased."

Reanny slid the ring onto her finger and concentrated. "Aye, I think I feel it too. Wait a moment..."

She took several bits of metal into her hands. Her eyes were focused, intensely studying the fragments as they started to slowly gravitate toward the center of her open palm, merging together into a single cluster. Reanny's hand trembled slightly from the strain. A bead of sweat trickled down her temple. The clump of metal vibrated, and, with eyes wide, Sloane observed as it gradually combined into a spherical form under the woman's magic.

With a relieving exhale, Reanny gently placed the newly formed metallic orb on the workbench. She leaned over it, catching her breath. "Whew, lass," she managed to get out between deep breaths. "That took a bit outta me. But I reckon I was able to control my magic, or mana, I should say, a bit better." Reanny held out the orb for Sloane. "What do ye think?"

Sloane carefully picked up the ball, rolling it between her fingers. The orb wasn't perfect, bearing marks of their fledgling experiments, but it was undeniably a step forward. Reanny had successfully fused the bits of metal into a cohesive whole. "This is impressive, Reanny," Sloane praised, sincerely acknowledging the remarkable progress made in such a short span.

Nodding to herself, Sloane handed the orb back to Reanny. "You know, I think I have an idea before we start on the next one. Can you hold this?"

Reanny looked at her curiously, but accepted the orb. "Sure, lass. What do you want me to do?"

"Can you channel your mana into it? Describe to me what you experience," Sloane suggested, her eyes gleaming with anticipation.

Reanny's intense concentration radiated across the room as she furrowed a brow and slightly bit her bottom lip while Sloane keenly observed the manifestation of her mana through the watch. Before Reanny could report back, Sloane sensed the shift in the woman's mana use, signaling the end of her examination.

With a curious glint in her eyes, Reanny shared her experience. "It feels like I can discern how to utilize the metal most efficiently to extract its maximum potential."

"That's perfect! Exactly what I was hoping for," Sloane responded with a beaming smile. She nudged the array of gems toward Reanny. "Now, I'd like you to do the same with each type of gem. Focus your mana on each and try to feel what it can be used for. Its purpose with mana."

Reanny turned her attention to the gemstones spread before her. "Sure, figure out the intent of a gem, as if it's the simplest task in the world," she said dryly. Nevertheless, she reached out and picked up the onyx gem, directing her focus toward it.

As Reanny engaged with the onyx, Sloane glanced at her watch, noting the fluctuations in mana usage.

It wasn't long before Reanny surfaced from her concentration. "Interesting," she mused, an intrigued smile crossing her face. "That was actually simpler than I'd imagined. I get this sensation of... being able to divine my surroundings more distinctly."

Sloane noticed that Reanny's dialect thickened when she shared her spontaneous thoughts. She quickly processed this information. "Divine your surroundings... that could indicate sensory augmentation. My watch probably uses it to detect mana use." As she mulled over these ideas, she diligently jotted down Reanny's findings. The puzzle was beginning to take shape.

Gripping the next gem, a topaz, in her palm, Reanny honed her focus once more. "This one's a bit odd," she noted, furrowing her brows in thought. "It's as if... it desires to... relay what it sees—or knows?"

At Reanny's seemingly perplexed explanation, Sloane's eyebrows shot up in a moment of insight. "Oh! I think it wants to display or project information, similar to a screen. It's like a GPU in my world!"

Reanny tilted her head in confusion. "Gee pee you?"

Sloane chuckled at the dwarf's puzzled expression. "Sorry, it's a term from my world. Basically, the topaz might take in mana and allow it to be visualized in some manner."

"Like creating an illusion?" Reanny inquired.

"Yeah, that's probably the magical way of putting it. Good thought," Sloane affirmed, smiling at Reanny's understanding.

When they reached the sapphire, Reanny seemed to hit a roadblock. "I can't quite grasp this one... It feels as though it wants to communicate with the... mind, perhaps, of the surrounding mana? I'm really unsure, Sloane." The dwarf struggled to articulate her baffling sensations.

"Okay, let me think." Attempting to decode Reanny's cryptic explanation, Sloane pondered aloud, "So, you're saying it desires to interact with mana in some way?"

"So, it's different from the ruby we tried. This sapphire seems to want to converse with mana. Not merely manipulate it." Reanny endeavored to clarify.

"What? Wait… does that mean mana has a governing intelligence? No, that can't be it. Perhaps mana carries instructions or information that govern its use, like a… mana system?" Sloane proposed, her thoughts cascading into increasingly fantastical theories.

Reanny continued to study the sapphire. "It feels as though it's seeking intent."

Sloane's eyes lit up with sudden comprehension. "That might just be it. Maybe mana possesses an inherent intent that interacts with cores to enable magic. So, the sapphire is essentially deciphering this intent to instruct the mana. Interesting… mana is starting to seem more and more like the backend structure of an operating system."

With that, they went through each gemstone. Sloane took notes of everything, and she realized that each had a specific function, which made sense to her. One gem couldn't do everything, just like one chip in a device couldn't. It needed others to work together and create a coherent whole to provide the functionality desired.

She suspected the gems worked with the magic types in some way. Perhaps, the types—no, there had to be a better way to classify the magic—dictated what the gems provided. Each represented each… school? No, that name didn't work either.

Turning to Reanny, Sloane shared her thoughts. "I think the gems work in tandem with magic, and that there are different types of magic. However, this classification doesn't quite capture the essence of their function. They seem intertwined, sharing a higher level of correlation. What do you think?"

"So you're suggesting that magic has different ways of being used? You mentioned it also has different forms. It reminds me of our gods, each assuming a unique form and ruling a particular domain."

Sloane's eyes brightened at Reanny's comparison. "Yes! That's brilliant. Your magical core might be… attuned… to a specific color of mana, possibly more, and you can manipulate magic within distinct domains. This could also be influenced by your core. We need to explore more." Excitement bubbled up inside her as she hastily scribbled notes in her journal.

"Let's identify the domains associated with the gems based on their functionalities. They likely correspond to the type of magic a person can manifest," Sloane proposed excitedly.

Reanny seemed to catch on quickly. "Aye, like the sapphire. It revolves around knowledge and its application. My initial thought was Crafting, but it feels too limited."

Suddenly, a flash of inspiration struck Sloane. Drawing on her fantasy knowledge—chuckling at the connection—she burst out, "I got it. We'll call the domain Artifice."

Reanny's grin matched Sloane's enthusiasm. "The name certainly resonates with you, and I can't argue against that. Artifice it is, then."

They continued to dissect each gem's potential domain, engaging in lively debates about the most appropriate terms. Although they examined only a limited set of gems, Sloane felt confident that they had uncovered some fundamental aspects of magic. Considering that the gemstones chosen by Reanny were among the most common, their findings likely held general applicability.

Once they finished their analysis, Sloane scanned the list of domains neatly inscribed in her journal.

Diamond: Connects to and amplifies mana use – **Evocation**
Black Diamond: Allows for spell storage/use – **Conjuration**
Amethyst: Allows spell targeting/shaping – **Alteration**
Ruby: Allows mana manipulation – **Alteration**
Sapphire: Connects to and exchanges mana intent – **Artifice**
Opal: Connects to user – **Mind**
Emerald: Connects to user's core (mana biology?) – **Abjuration**
Topaz: Projects mana information – **Illusion**
Onyx: Allows sensing (Manasense?) – **Divination**

They had narrowed their findings down to what they surmised were eight domains: Evocation, Conjuration, Alteration, Artifice, Mind, Abjuration, Illusion, and Divination. Sloane conjectured that each person's core could only facilitate casting spells within any particular domain. This theory helped explain her inability to cast spells like Maud—their cores were different. Maud's core, she figured, might be linked to either Evocation or Abjuration, considering her spell's healing nature and its direct connection to the biology of the target. As for her own domain, she was yet uncertain, but at least now she knew where to begin.

"Reanny, I think I have a plan," Sloane declared as she finished going through her notes.

The dwarf tilted her head. "What is it, lass? Is it related to the ring you want to create?"

"Yes, and with your magic, this task will be much simpler." Sloane paused for a moment before explaining her thoughts more in-depth. "I suspect we'll need to use multiple gems. I'm not sure what differentiates cores when channeling magic, but I suspect the process is similar, albeit possibly less efficient.

"My idea is to have small gems, each providing the necessary function, embedded into the ring. I suggest setting them into the band's underside so they'll be hidden against the wearer's skin, yet could establish a closer connection to the user. For the first ring, I think we will need a sapphire, opal, and ruby on the inside. The opal should be slightly larger, flanked by the sapphire and ruby. Additionally, a diamond should be set on top. It should be the largest gem, as it's likely to bear the brunt of the work.

"As for the runic language of mana, I haven't fully grasped it yet, but I'm confident I can figure it out after studying my watch more. For now, the opal should enable the ring to interpret my core's mana intent as I attempt to cast magic."

Reanny was already sketching a design.

"What do you think?" Sloane asked her. "Can we do it?"

Reanny nodded. "Aye, I don't often set gems flush, especially on the inside of a ring, but I can manage. Let's get started!"

Sloane watched as Reanny rummaged through her shop's stock to find a solid silver band and the required gemstones. "I'll make you a deal, lass. If this ring works as you believe—and for helping me understand my own magic—you can keep it."

"I appreciate that, Reanny."

The alterer, as Sloane began to think of her, began working on the ring while Sloane observed her mana flare at key moments. She went closer and observed intently as Reanny used a hand drill to start a hole for the flush sets. After getting the hole started, Reanny paused, seemingly coming up with a plan. She put the drill down and grabbed the ring. Sloane's eyes widened as Reanny used her magic to manipulate the silver into opening up just enough for the gems.

"That's amazingly useful," Reanny commented, surprised by her own success. "You've just saved us a lot of coin, Sloane. I'll talk to Murinn, but we owe you for this."

Reanny kept working at the ring, and finally, with the setting of the large round-cut diamond set flush into the band, the ring was complete. It was elegant in its simplicity, and Sloane found herself growing nervous about its potential functionality.

Seeing Sloane's anticipation, Reanny chuckled, "Heh, you ready to give it a shot?"

"Very much so! May I?" she asked, reaching for the ring.

"Of course, lass. Good luck!" Reanny said, handing the ring to Sloane with an encouraging smile.

Taking a deep breath and closing her eyes, Sloane slid the ring onto her middle finger.

Immediately, she felt an immense surge of energy coursing from her core into the ring, and then expanding outward in a powerful ripple. The energy then settled back into her, as if establishing a new equilibrium, and it felt as though she didn't even need to consciously channel through the ring to wield her magic.

She felt at the mana in her core, as she had done for weeks now, and instantly detected a marked difference. It was as though her proficiency in channeling mana had amplified exponentially. She understood instantly where she had previously erred. Her newfound connection to mana illuminated everything with stark clarity.

She was correct in one way at least; her magic was Evocation, but her way of trying to use it was wrong, but the magic she had been trying to use instead was Abjuration. She laughed. She hadn't even been trying to use magic like an Evoker, she'd been trying to cast like someone who wanted to protect or shield people.

Sloane knew she wasn't an Abjurer. That much she was certain of. But she was equally certain that Maud was one. This realization led to another: domains weren't directly tied to one's core, but to the individual themselves, their very being. Sloane felt a kinship with the domain of Artifice. She resonated with Alteration.

She felt further and... *Ah, there it is. I do have Evocation, but it's just a bit weaker.*

Her affinity—yes, that was the right term—with the Evocation domain was lesser. Sloane would need to learn if it was possible to strengthen her connection with a domain, as she suspected Evocation would be quite important in the future. Especially if she found herself in combat again.

That said, she knew exactly how to manipulate the mana to do what she wanted in an object.

It had all happened within a span of moments, although it felt like much longer. She opened her eyes, meeting Reanny's keen gaze. Sloane couldn't help but smile before sharing her revelation. "This works. It works exceptionally well. I now understand my previous mistake—I was using my mana incorrectly. This ring seems to amplify the amount of mana I can access. And I also know my domains."

Reanny's eyebrow arched. "Domains?" she repeated, stressing the plural.

"Yes," Sloane explained. "I was mistaken in my earlier assumption that the domains were tied to the core, or that we could connect with only one. They're linked to something more intrinsic to us. For instance, I resonate with the Artifice, Alteration, and to a lesser degree, Evocation domains. With that in mind, I'd like to attempt crafting another ring, if that's alright."

"Absolutely!" Reanny responded, gesturing toward the materials laid out. "You observed me making the first one, so here's everything you'll need. Is there anything else you want?"

Sloane paused, contemplating. "Could I have an amethyst too? I believe it might prove useful."

"Aye, go ahead." Reanny procured an amethyst and placed it beside the gems already arranged for the next ring. She moved so she could observe Sloane's process from an optimal angle.

Sloane picked up the silver ring and tentatively pushed her mana into it. To her satisfaction, she found she could indeed influence it. This connection seemed to heighten her understanding of the ring—its flaws, its resilience, and the optimal placements for the gems. She even thought she had an idea of how to make it magically stronger, but figured that would need runes she didn't know yet.

She probed the ring with mana until she discerned the perfect spot to embed the opal. Positioning the gem against the inside of the ring, she channeled her mana into the metal, coaxing it to expand ever so slightly. This subtle alteration created an impeccable hole for the gem. Carefully, Sloane set the gem into its new home, and then gently molded the metal to secure the opal snugly in place.

Sloane followed the same procedure four more times. The final arrangement had an amethyst and ruby on either side of the diamond that occupied the central position on top. She set the remaining sapphire, ruby and amethyst on the inner side of the ring, next to the opal, to maintain contact with her skin and act like a sensor.

A bell sounded in the distance, signaling an hour of intense concentration and manipulation before Sloane finally nodded in satisfaction. The lack of physical tools had made the process significantly smoother, yet she was acutely aware of the fatigue seeping into her. She hadn't anticipated that using mana would be so draining.

She handed the ring over to Reanny, who turned it over in her fingers, scrutinizing the craftsmanship. Raising an eyebrow, Reanny offered an approving smirk. "This is incredible. If I hadn't seen you use magic to craft this, I'd swear you were a master jeweler. Shall we swap? I'm quite eager to try it myself."

"Thank you, Reanny. Absolutely, this one is yours." Sloane slipped off the ring she was wearing and handed it to Reanny, instantly feeling the previous surge of power ebb away. In its wake, her fatigue seemed to intensify.

These are absolutely augmenting my magic, and the mana I'm capable of working with seems to affect how I feel.

Slipping her newly crafted ring onto her finger, she felt the familiar rush of power return, but this time it felt slightly stronger. *Almost as if my core recognizes that I made this ring.*

Simultaneously, Reanny slid on the ring she'd crafted herself, impressing Sloane by using a touch of her magic to improve the fit.

Sloane watched her closely. "Well?"

Reanny grinned broadly. "Lass? So. Much. Coin."

Sloane burst into laughter, carried away by the infectious optimism of the merchant.

* * *

The two dwarf siblings sat across from Sloane at the kitchen table in their snug apartment above the shop. The rings sat in front of them.

Mulinn picked one up, scrutinized it, and then set it back down. He locked eyes with Sloane, who promptly fixed her full attention on him.

"So, both of ye have succeeded," he said with a nod of satisfaction. "These rings will be a lucrative venture, indeed. What is your asking price for the rights to sell them? Now, before you answer, bear in mind that my sister provided all the materials and lent her expertise. This is your design, lass. However, I believe it's only fair that she should have some stake in the claim for the design."

Before Sloane could reply, Reanny chimed in, "What my brother is trying to convey, lass, is that we're more than happy to compensate you for your design." She shot her brother a meaningful look. "The technique you taught me will substantially increase our profits. Now, what do you think?"

"Well, I do need funds. So, how about—" Sloane stopped, her eyes widening as an idea dawned on her.

"What's the matter, lass?" Reanny queried.

Sloane's mind was racing. The siblings were ideally positioned in a rapidly growing town, located along a bustling route. If Maud's predictions were accurate, the town was poised to grow as large as a city. With their prime location, the siblings were certain to make a fortune.

Especially if they were potentially the first people in the world to sell magical items. If Sloane quickly supplied them with designs for more possible products, they would owe her a great deal. Not that she intended to exploit them, but this was a golden opportunity to secure funding for the foreseeable future.

Wearing a smile, Sloane glanced back and forth between Mulinn and Reanny. She could barely contain her excitement; she forced herself not to rub her hands together. "I have an idea, one that I believe will be mutually beneficial for all of us. I have numerous ideas for different items that could be made using gems and their connection to mana. These would be magical items, the designs for which I'm willing to offer you to create and sell. Instead of a flat fee, we could establish a profit-sharing arrangement."

Reanny and Mulinn Farum both broke into wide grins. Sloane surmised that their enthusiasm likely stemmed from different reasons, yet they shared a common goal: wealth.

Reanny, contrary to Sloane, did rub her hands together. *That's such a fantasy merchant thing to do.*

Looking Sloane straight in the eye, the dwarven woman declared, "Lass, I think we're going to be friends for a long time. Let's strike a deal."

CHAPTER TWENTY~SEVEN

WHAT'S IN A NAME?

Four town bells later, the sun was setting, and Sloane was walking back to the inn. She had six more rings of various types in her satchel and they were made according to what Sloane felt would fit the knights. She believed she had selected ones that would work well with each person, but if not, well, she could easily swap around gems.

She, Mulinn, and Reanny had talked for a solid two hours, or bells, about the future, just sitting at a table, discussing designs.

In the end, she walked away with a contract. One that would give Sloane fifteen percent of any sales the siblings would make in the future and a stake in their business. They also gave Sloane an advance on what Mulinn expected to make from the new magic-focused business plan.

After mentioning that the knights would introduce her to the Banking Guild, Mulinn huffed. The dwarf gave her a brief overview of the Banking and Merchant Guilds, telling her that she would need to open an account with them once she arrived in Thirdghyll. There was a small branch for both in the market but, apparently, it was only available to current members.

Which would allow the siblings to directly transfer her portion of the profits into her account.

Upon entering the inn, Sloane immediately spotted the group of knights congregating around a central table. Seeing her, Maud waved energetically, drawing the attention of the others as she called out, "Sloane! Come join us! We have so much to tell you!"

Sloane returned her smile, brimming with news of her own to share. Progress was being made, and she now possessed a means of searching for Gwyn without being entirely dependent on others. Nevertheless, that wouldn't deter her from attempting to persuade the knights into joining her more permanently.

Responding to Maud's call, she jovially shouted as she approached the group, "I'm comin'! Ernald, you better have gotten me some food! I'm starving."

Sloane chuckled as the sun elf's eyes widened in surprise, prompting him to dash toward the barmaid.

The remaining knights greeted her warmly as she took her seat among them. "So! What do you all have to tell me?" she asked.

Gisele responded with a slight smile. "Maud seems to be overdramatizing a bit. We merely have some minor news from Thirdghyll."

Maud's expression fluctuated between surprise, betrayal, and indignation before she retorted, "Knight-Captain! That's just rude!"

She turned toward Sloane to clarify. "Since Gisele wishes to downplay it… a member from Count Sylvain Kayser's court in Thirdghyll happened to be passing through and, after a discussion with Gisele, extended an invitation to us to attend a ball in a few weeks. Evidently, the count wishes to introduce members of a new people who have arrived in Westaren."

Sloane's eyes widened in astonishment. "All of you received an invitation to this ball? And there are going to be other humans present?"

As Ernald placed a plate of food and a cup of water in front of her, he chuckled. "That's not the entire story. Ser Gisele might have slightly misrepresented our group to secure the invitation."

This time it was Gisele's turn to feign offense. "Ser Ernald, I merely presented certain facts in a manner that would appeal to the sensibilities of Western Ikios high society."

She glanced at Sloane, explaining further, "Sloane, by her own admission, qualifies as a landed baroness, according to our standards. To introduce her as a republican aristocrat would be disadvantageous during any visits to the kingdoms here."

Taken aback, Sloane turned to Gisele to articulate her thoughts, only to find herself speechless.

Ismeld brushed her blond hair from her eyes and, while pointing a chunk of bread at Sloane, added, "She's right. In your quest to find Gwyn, acquiring more access and potentially more connections than a mere commoner is critical. You need an advantage. This provides it."

Ismeld straightened, looking at Sloane with an unwavering gaze. "From now on, you will be recognized as Baroness of Blightwych," she declared, her tone leaving no room for argument. At Sloane's wide-eyed expression and subsequent puzzled question about the plausibility of such a status, Gisele turned an expectant gaze toward Ismeld.

Unperturbed, the blond knight raised her hands and shrugged nonchalantly.

"Don't fret over the details. You're a baroness now. Congratulations. Woo." The word "woo" was delivered with a twirl of her raised finger and a dry sense of humor that did nothing to diminish the seriousness of the situation.

Sloane looked at Cristole, who subtly nodded before taking another sip of his ale.

Slowly, she nodded, weighing the implications. "Alright, your points are valid. However, I'm unsure about how to conduct myself as a noble here. While I have a vague idea of what it might involve in my world, the etiquette classes my parents enrolled me in as a child never covered interactions with nobility from the Middle Ages."

Both Ernald and Ismeld simultaneously facepalmed, and the high elf woman muttered, "Of course, you would have attended etiquette classes…"

Ernald clarified, "Here, Sloane, only nobility attend etiquette classes."

Deryk, who had remained silent, as was his custom, chose that moment to interject. "I'll have you know I'm merely twenty-six. I'm not middle-aged."

Sloane huffed a breathy laugh, trying hard not to facepalm as well. "First thing I've heard you say since we arrived in town and it's a dad joke? Very well," Sloane acknowledged, conceding to the situation with amusement. "I will be this… Lady Reinhart. Are there any specifics I should know? How does it work?"

The gaze of the group shifted toward Gisele and Ismeld, seeking their input. Ismeld bore a playful smirk on her face before turning her eyes to Gisele. The orkun woman let out a sigh, shaking her head lightly before addressing Sloane's query.

"We'll guide you as we move forward. As for now, nothing in particular comes to mind. Just continue to be yourself. We'll arrange for a seal to be made for you that represents your house and status. That's about it," Gisele explained, dismissing any immediate concerns.

Sloane sighed, realizing that they may not be the best teachers when it came to the subject; there was definitely some type of history there. "Is there any other news I should be aware of, or is it my turn?" she asked.

Gisele nodded. "Yes, and this news isn't as great. We got word about rumblings of escalating tensions between the Vlaredia Empire and the Sovereign Cities. Specifically, the city of Constanden. The Vlaredians are concocting a pretext to intimidate the city and have assembled an army along their borders, claiming the protection of their 'sovereignty.' A clear provocation aimed at the Sovereign Cities. While no action has been taken yet, we must remain vigilant as we journey through Goosebourne and onward to Swanbrook.

"The Vlaredia Empire is over two hundred and fifty kilometers from here, beyond the Dheg Laseig Mountains. They'd have to venture nearly three hundred kilometers south from their border, and then traverse approximately two hundred and forty more through the southern pass to even reach Goosebourne.

"Despite its size, Westaren boasts a formidable navy. The Vlaredian navy would not be granted passage through their waters to strike the coastal cities, compelling them to sail farther out to circumvent the kingdom.

"With all that said, I believe we'll be safe. Nevertheless, the Sovereigns become particularly wary of outsiders when facing external threats, especially those hailing from Westaren. Your status as a baroness and our presence as a knightly order in your service should alleviate any suspicions."

The knights stirred in their seats as Gisele concluded, exchanging uneasy glances. Their reactions did little to instill confidence in Sloane.

"You all don't seem convinced," Sloane observed.

Ismeld's eyes flicked to Deryk, who exhaled a resigned sigh. "If war does break out, the Sovereign Cities won't be easy opponents. Their internal disputes don't hinder their capacity to unite against common threats. You could describe them as a loose federation. They're in constant conflict with one another, perpetually seeking opportunities for subterfuge." With that, the orkun leaned back, signaling the end of his contribution.

Ernald took it upon himself to conclude Deryk's thought. The scholar suddenly appeared wearied, his earlier jovial demeanor giving way to more somber reflections. "Such internal strife only sharpens their defenses when their sovereignty is under threat. They don't call themselves the Sovereigns lightly, they take it very seriously. In times of war, they tend to flex their might to ensure all know better than to interfere with their particular brand of organized chaos.

"And their chaotic mess of a political situation compels individual cities to puff up their feathered arses—"

"Their fashion often features large feathers from the ostriches that inhabit the plains along the central corridor," Maud interjected quietly, in an attempt to clarify Ernald's metaphor.

"And consequently, they tend to lash out at the nearest outsiders," Ernald finished.

"So, we just need to be mindful of one another and avoid inciting these feather-admiring individuals with inflated egos. Could this conflict affect my ability to gain passage into Swanbrook?" Sloane inquired, attempting to keep her growing concern at bay.

Gisele shook her head. "No, it shouldn't. Especially if their attention is distracted more than we suspect by the imperials. However, nothing concrete has happened. We must not dwell excessively on factors beyond our control. We'll take the necessary precautions and prepare you adequately before our arrival in Swanbrook."

The orkun woman lightly slapped the table to draw everyone's attention. "Now, let's change the subject. What did you have to share with us?"

Sloane's eyes narrowed in confusion. "What do I ha— Oh! Right! So, I've been busy. Like, extremely busy. First, I will need to set up an account at the Banking Guild in Thirdghyll."

Ernald's eyes widened. "Oh, really? I was planning to help you do that, but we hadn't discussed that yet."

Cristole huffed a laugh. "Sorry, Ernald. I already promised the baroness that I would take her."

Sloane's smile faltered, but she didn't let the casual slip of a title deter her. "Yup! So, I have a contract with a pair of sibling merchants here."

Her announcement sparked surprise among all present, and she seized this moment to retrieve the contract from her satchel and pass it around. As the others perused it, she detailed the profit-sharing agreement based on her designs. Gisele and Ernald appeared particularly intrigued, but everyone chimed in with queries.

Having scrutinized the contract, Ernald raised his gaze to Sloane. "This is an excellent contract, enforceable by both the Banking and Merchant Guilds, and featuring mutually beneficial terms. Your designs must have greatly benefited them. Could you elaborate on these designs a bit more? Are they inspired by something from your world?"

Sloane responded with a shake of her head and a smile. "Nope! They're all from your world." Reaching into her satchel, she produced a leather roll that contained the rings.

As she began to untie the leather cord, Maud reached out, capturing Sloane's hand. "What is this ring?! It's gorgeous! How have I not noticed this before? You've been hiding it!"

Sloane laughed. "No! That's what all this is about, just wait!" She unrolled the leather to reveal the six rings. "This... this is what I've been crafting all day with Reanny. I've made one for each of you." She paused, glancing around the semi-populated inn. "However, I think we should continue this somewhere a bit more private."

In the secluded rear courtyard of the inn, night was settling in, the murmur of patrons from inside creating a soft backdrop to the gathering outside. A lamp hanging on a wall nearby cast its warm glow over the cobblestones and onto the faces of the gathered knights. The group huddled around the wagon stationed near the stables, the knights radiating a collective sense of anticipatory energy.

Sloane couldn't exactly pinpoint when they began linking her with all things magical, but now, as they gazed expectantly at her, she realized she had to deliver. Stationed at the rear of the wagon with its doors flung open, she placed the rings neatly along its edge.

"Alright, I've already given you the basics about the contract and all. Now, let's delve into the interesting part. Reanny and I made some significant discoveries.

Specifically, we've found what we believe to be eight to ten main gem types. Each of these gems has a distinct role when interacting with mana.

"Mana itself possesses what we call 'Intent'—a grand design or purpose. We didn't delve deeply into this aspect, but the key point is that the magic derived from mana aligns with different domains. I suspect that each of us manifests our magic based on the mana within our cores. Each of us has a domain associated with our being, and our cores are attuned to a mana color."

Maud shuffled, seemingly uncomfortable. Spotting her slight hand raise, Sloane gave her a nod to proceed.

"So," the redheaded telv began. "I have a green mana core like those wolves. That's why your watch displays green when I use magic. So, what would my domain be, as you term it?"

"I believe your affinity is with Abjuration," Sloane explained. "It's about using mana to protect, block, or dispel. You use it to cast restorative spells on people. It's likely that you'll be able to learn spells that enhance the physical abilities of the others here.

"Now, let's delve into the domains and their functions. You just heard about Abjuration. There are seven others." Sloane went on to enlighten the knights about the various domains and their fundamental characteristics. There were a few inquiries, but mostly they all listened attentively.

Finally, Gisele voiced the question that was on everyone's mind. "These rings you have, they're supposed to assist us with our mana, right? Does that mean you know our mana and domains?"

Sloane contemplated her response, not wanting to mislead them. After a moment, she confidently replied, "I think I know what domains you are. Based on my observations of you since our time together, I'm confident in my assessment. It aligns with your personalities and dispositions, as we've seen with Maud, Reanny, and me. If I've gotten it wrong for anyone, it's alright! We won't know for sure about your mana until you've used it. Now, I'm not sure how mana interacts with us physically, only when you use it to cast a spell. I know the wolves were using some kind of green mana magic, but I still don't know exactly what they did. But learning should be easy. For me, it was almost instinctual, as if it clicked in my mind, once I understood how to do it."

"I'm not so confident in your observations making a reliable determination. I shall reserve judgment," Ismeld stated, her words dripping with skepticism.

Sloane just rolled her eyes.

"So, domains." She directed her finger at the orkun woman and identified her magical focus. "Gisele, I think you're an Abjurer."

"Because... why? I do not fight with a shield if I can help it," Gisele responded, visibly perplexed.

"Perhaps not, but you constantly use yourself to protect and shield others.

You utilize your physique and your enormous sword—that's clearly compensating for something—to accomplish this. You just need to apply that protective mentality to your magic."

"Take it easy, Sloane, Gisele is self-conscious about the size of her sword," Ernald teased.

The woman looked offended. "I'm not self-conscious, I simply handle a large sword better than a small one."

Maud choked, and Ernald and Cristole burst into laughter. Ismeld pinched the bridge of her nose as she chimed in, "Gisele... seriously?"

Gisele surveyed the group before grimacing. "Fair enough."

With restrained laughter, Sloane continued. "So, keeping that in mind, please accept these tokens of my gratitude. Let's see if we can unlock magic in you! We'll start with Gisele and then proceed around the group."

Sloane distributed the rings to the knights, who exchanged bemused glances while examining their new gifts.

Gisele straightened her posture. "I express my sincere thanks, Lady Sloane. You have certainly demonstrated a willingness to contribute significantly to our group."

The knight-captain's smile broadened, her short tusks showing just a bit more, as she glanced around the group. "I will admit that this is a bit exciting." She slid the ring on her left middle finger.

Sloane observed Gisele, who seemed to have slipped into a trance-like state. Her eyes were slightly unfocused as if seeing something beyond their immediate surroundings. Each person present held their breath, waiting to see what would transpire next. But as the moment stretched out, Maud appeared ready to administer some restoration magic to her captain.

Cristole gently placed a hand on Gisele's shoulder. "Gisele, are you alright?"

Gisele twitched slightly and Sloane watched as she took a moment to regain her composure. Ignoring Cristole, she addressed Sloane.

"Sloane, this... this is incredible. I can sense it. You were absolutely correct. It's as if the ring stimulated something within me and unlocked a hidden potential."

Maud moved closer, examining Gisele with a clinical eye. "Gisele, please look at me."

Gisele turned to Maud. "I'm perfectly fine, Maud. In fact, I feel better than fine. I... I want to attempt something. Similar to your experience. You mentioned you feel for your magic and push it towards your object of protection."

Her gaze scanned the group before settling on Cristole, who had stepped back to allow Maud room. Gisele closed her eyes and lifted her left hand in his direction. Her mouth scrunched up in intense concentration.

Her focused expression is pretty cute. Sloane watched the Manameter—she cringed, why are names so hard?—as red swirls moved around on the glass, pointing at Gisele.

Nothing seemed to be happening visually as Cristole stood, a look of confusion crossing his face while the woman pointed her hand at him.

"Give her a moment, it takes longer the first time around," said Sloane. "You have to walk before you can run."

Just then, Gisele emitted a sound Sloane never would have anticipated from the muscular orkun woman.

She squeaked.

Instantly, a small arch of red energy rose from the ground in front of Cristole until it reached a height level with his chin.

But the shimmering shield was unstable. It flickered like a candle fighting the wind, its outline wavering as it struggled to maintain form. Moments after it had appeared, the shield fizzled out, leaving an empty space where it had stood.

Undeterred, Gisele regrouped, squaring her shoulders and closing her eyes as she refocused her energies. She breathed deeply, each exhalation a picture of determination. As seconds ticked by, a change began to take place within Gisele. A renewed concentration settled on her features, her expression morphing from determination to surprise, then elation. Her eyes snapped open and widened with an almost childlike wonder, as if a significant realization had just dawned on her.

Gisele stretched her hand forward once again, this time with an air of confidence enveloping her. As if propelled by an unseen force, a burst of red energy surged forth, expanding rapidly from its origin. In the blink of an eye, it coalesced into a larger shield—a curved barrier about two and a half meters across at its base and reaching a height of approximately two meters.

Unlike before, the shield didn't flicker or waver. It remained solid and stable, its ethereal, glowing surface illuminating the surrounding space with a warm, ruddy light. The shield was like a translucent wall, shimmering with an inner light and radiating a powerful aura of defense and protection.

Everyone gasped in unison, their eyes wide and their breaths held in collective astonishment. There was a moment of profound silence as they admired the beautiful spectacle, before they were interrupted by the second strangest noise of the evening.

Gisele giggled.

Her laughter was entirely unexpected, an incongruous melody that echoed in the quiet evening air. The group stared at her in open-mouthed shock. Ernald articulated the thoughts running through everyone's minds.

"Who *are* you?"

Sloane decided to experiment. She took out her sword, walked straight up to the shield, and swung at it, causing more shocked expressions and noises from the group of knights.

When the sword made contact, red energy, or mana, sparked from the strike. Despite Sloane having put a decent amount of strength into the swing, the magic shield managed to stop the sword solidly.

Without hesitation, Sloane pulled back her sword, placed her left hand over the hilt for additional force, and launched a thrust at the shield. The sword tip barely managed to breach the field, causing a web of cracks to spider out from the point of penetration. Nodding in satisfaction, she withdrew her weapon and returned it to its sheath.

Turning her attention back to the shield, Sloane probed it with her hand, noting its peculiar feel. It possessed a tangible solidity that seemed to hum subtly beneath her touch. Convinced that her test was successful, she turned to face the knights. Their expressions were of stunned disbelief, jaws slack and eyes wide. Even Deryk, typically unflappable, was visibly taken aback by her demonstration.

A sly smirk played on Sloane's lips as she nonchalantly shrugged at their astonishment. "What? We needed to see how much abuse it could hold up against. Now, we just need to subject it to some stress tests—you know, whack it a few times, shoot arrows at it… all the things."

Gisele, who had been watching intently, raised her hand toward the shield and closed it, which caused the shield to dissipate.

Sloane thought that was a neat trick and decided to try and show off her third domain's magic. As she reached inward, the unfamiliar sensation of tapping directly into her mana core was disconcerting, akin to standing at the precipice of a vast chasm of power within herself. This daunting abyss was a reservoir of latent energy waiting to be harnessed. The raw potency of her own mana was slightly overwhelming, and she had to wrestle to keep her focus honed and the flow of energy under control.

The process was like threading a needle in the dark; she had to rely purely on her innate sense of her own mana and the mental image she held of the destructive orb she sought to create. Beads of sweat dotting her forehead as the intense concentration and mental exertion required to handle the effort almost overwhelmed her.

The mana's reluctant obedience, too, was a challenge. It surged and flickered like a wild animal being tamed for the first time, resisting her efforts to mold it into a specific form. With each wave of resistance, she knew that what she was doing was dangerous and she had to maintain proper control or risk injuring the others.

Yet, amid these hurdles, Sloane began to see progress. The energy began to stir, responding to her unwavering will. It crackled to life, forming a swirling mass of purple and blue light that shimmered and flickered in front of her. This nucleus of energy was unstable at first, pulsating irregularly as it cycled between states of form and formlessness.

As the orb started settling into its final shape, Sloane could feel her mental strength wavering, strained by the effort of maintaining control over the manifestation of her raw mana. The arcane orb reached what she thought was the maximum size she could sustain and control.

Summoning one final surge of mana, she pivoted swiftly and hurled the **[Mana Bolt]** at a nearby cobblestone wall. Upon collision, the orb detonated, discharging a potent wave of energy that shook the wall violently, dislodging stones in a chaotic spray of rubble.

Still buzzing with adrenaline, Sloane twirled back to face the group, a self-satisfied smirk gracing her face. Her laughter filled the air, echoing in the stunned silence of the knights who could only stare in awe. "Well?" she said, breaking the silence. "Does anyone want to volunteer to go next?"

Ismeld's mouth opened and closed a couple of times before she regained control enough to speak. "What the f—"

"How did you do that?!" Maud blurted.

With a shrug, Sloane decided to reveal her secret. "Evocation is my third domain. Artifice and Alteration are my first two. That was my first time trying that. These rings really help with our capabilities."

Gisele just shook her head. "Three domains? I got the impression you could only have one? Ugh. It's too much for right now. I think that may be enough for tonight." She glanced at the demolished wall, rubbing her temples. "Did you really have to destroy that wall?"

Ernald, looking between Sloane, Gisele, and the wall, shook his head and mused, "Sloane, what in the world did that wall ever do to you?"

Before anyone else could respond, Cristole voiced the general consensus. "We should probably, uh, leave. Like now. We can focus on magic another time, where we won't get accidentally spotted. Let's get back inside the inn."

Despite her protestations, Sloane watched as the knights ambled away from the scene of the crime. However, her shock was multiplied when Deryk slapped her on the back as he passed, declaring, "You get to buy the round, milady."

His casual remark left Sloane momentarily stunned. Maud's laughter rang in her ears as she was tugged onward. "Come on! Don't stop now, you have to buy me a drink!"

Defeated, Sloane sputtered, but then just dropped her head and allowed Maud to drag her along.

CHAPTER TWENTY-EIGHT

A COMMON TONGUE

Taenya subtly shifted in her saddle, trying to portray the image of confidence and strength she felt the knight-captain of House Reinhart should have. *Which is impossible with how much my arse hurts.* They were on the final leg of their journey to Strathmore, and she was already yearning for the respite that awaited them.

Well... or at least to gather my things to move to my new home. Taenya still couldn't believe the sequence of events that had culminated with the formation of House Reinhart and her as a knight.

She nudged her horse forward, shaking her head, thinking back on the frenzied pace of the past weeks. Between the myriad of villages they had traversed, she had spent countless evenings discussing plans for House Reinhart with Theran and Sabina. Their insights had proved invaluable in determining what they would need to accomplish once in the city.

She glanced over at Sabina, who was riding her horse with far more poise than Taenya. *I bet her arse hurts. She just hides it better.*

Sabina, perceptive as always, caught Taenya's gaze and waved. "Everything alright, Ser Taenya?"

Realizing she had been caught, Taenya chose to play along. "Of course, and please, just Taenya. I've reminded you of that before, Sabina."

Sabina responded with a gentle sigh. "Ser Taenya, it's not proper. You are the captain."

Taenya rolled her eyes. "We're practically in private. In public, you can maintain the protocol, but out here? Loosen up a bit."

With a nod and a trace of a grimace, Sabina conceded. "I will... try."

Observing the high elf woman as she resumed her vigil, Taenya admired her striking features. Sabina's raven hair cascaded just below her shoulder blades, punctuated by a single, intricate braid. Her face was adorned with paint—a dark blue line that arched elegantly from her temple, across her bright, almond-shaped blue eye, and ending at her jawline. The scar that ran diagonally from her cheekbone through her lips to her chin gave her an aura of experience.

From their talks, Taenya got the impression the woman would be a pleasure to work with, and could already tell she was a great knight.

Although she was slightly shorter than Taenya, her skill in combat did not seem to be affected whatsoever. They had sparred a few times, and each bout only reaffirmed Sabina's exceptional ability. Granted, Taenya had won every one, but still, she was impressed.

Theran was also no exception. The other knight who had joined her in House Reinhart was an expert swordsman. Taenya actually had difficulty when she fought him. Luckily, she was able to keep up just from her… unorthodox fighting style.

Sometimes you gotta fight dirty.

Given his prowess, she had already determined that he would be responsible for overseeing the weapons training within the house. The seasoned knight was positioned at the front of their formation, vigilantly scanning the road ahead for potential threats. The six guards that Onas had hired back in Larton were dispersed among their convoy, their primary focus being the protection of Onas's wagon and the rear flank. They were competent, she supposed. At least they listened to her orders.

Taenya felt a little bad. She had barely acquainted herself with the guards, knowing they had been hired solely for the journey to the city. Their tendency to keep to themselves and avoid interacting with the knights didn't facilitate any bonding either.

Her gaze roamed the sky, taking in the waning light. "Sabina, we should start looking for a suitable place to set up camp for tonight," Taenya proposed. "Please inform Theran to begin the search. I'll tell Her Highness and coordinate with Onas's guards."

"Of course, Captain." Sabina promptly nodded before urging her horse forward to relay the message to Theran.

Taenya slowed her pace, moving alongside the carriage. "Keston, how are you holding up? We're about to start our search for a good place to settle for the night."

"I'm fine, Taenya," Keston responded, his tone bearing a hint of relief. "Though, I could certainly use a rest. Gwyn's been inside practicing her magic again," he added with a good-natured eye roll.

Before she could reply, the small sliding window behind Keston opened and a small head popped out next to him. "I'm not practicing fire this time. Don't worry! Are we going to stop soon, Taenya?"

Her amusement surfacing in the form of a small smirk, Taenya shook her head at Gwyn's perceptiveness. *I could have just been coming to talk*, she thought. "Yes, Gwyn," she confirmed, restraining the impulse to tease the girl—she'd leave that for Keston. Although, that had waned since Raafe...

She forced a smile on her face. "Ser Theran is currently scouting for a suitable place to make camp."

As if on cue, Keston let out a soft sigh. "I'll begin prepping for dinner once we've halted for the day. We really need to recruit more help, Taenya."

Gwyn, ever enthusiastic, bobbed her head in agreement. "Yeah, we do. Poor Keston. Sabina is super nice, and Theran is pretty cool, but..." she trailed off.

"They're more accustomed to combat than performing support tasks for a house," Taenya finished for her, reading the young girl's hesitation.

"They're trying, at least," Keston conceded. "They know how to set up camp and do basic field tasks, but they are clearly not comfortable yet in the roles that are needed for Gwyn. On the bright side, they've never regarded me as lesser, as some knights might."

With a sudden burst of energy, Gwyn thrust her small fist through the open window, shaking it in a playful threat. "They better not! I'll beat them up."

Suppressing a laugh, Taenya retorted, "They wouldn't dare. They're well aware of your stance on such matters, Princess."

Her words, however, drew a scowl from Gwyn. "Taenya..."

Keston smirked. "Yeah, Taenya, I saw you earlier when Sabina refused to address you informally."

Feeling a touch of sheepishness, Taenya sighed in concession. "You're right, I suppose. My apologies, Gwyn. This is all quite different for us, isn't it?"

Emulating Taenya, Gwyn exhaled deeply. "Yeah... I'm gonna—I'm going to practice some more magic," she said, shifting her gaze to Keston. "Please tell me when you're about to cook, Keston. I want to help."

Keston adjusted his seating to face Gwyn fully. "Of course, Gwyn. We wouldn't dare disrupt a good routine, now would we?"

Friedrich pulled his horse to a halt outside of one of the small inns within Innsbruck and handed it to one of the stable boys. As the boy was walking away, he stopped and dropped the horse's reins.

"He! Boy!" Friedrich called out. He moved to grab his horse and scold the boy, but then he noticed everyone nearby had their gaze turned upward. He stopped and looked up.

The sky was a swirling river of greenish-blue. As quickly as it came, it changed. A mixture of yellows and reds joined the other colors. It was beautiful—a tapestry of colors that moved and danced to no pattern he could discern. Friedrich's eyes went wide as the colors grew even more vivid.

Suddenly, a loud burst sounded. Deafening and powerful, like he imagined of a volcano. Screams filled the air as those around him cowered in fear. His mind went to his wife, who would be busy at their home in Hall. I wonder if Ka—

His vision turned white as the sky flashed. He instinctively jerked just as a sudden rush of air blew into him. Friedrich's head started spinning. Unable to keep his balance, he felt himself reaching out as he started to fall.

The ground rushed up at him and he cried out as he crashed into it. The impact forced all of the breath out of his chest. He gasped for air and tried looking around but his blurred vision failed him.

Friedrich panicked.

Katherine—

His vision went black.

Jerking awake from his fitful sleep, Sir Friedrich von Boden snapped into alertness, the eerie symphony of the forest night causing his heart to pound in his chest. The growls that woke him were low, throaty, and resonating in a manner that suggested monstrous size and strength. From within the confines of his makeshift lean-to, woven from the fern-like branches of the strange trees and blanketed with vibrant moss, he held his breath, listening for signs of movement.

That damn dream of what brought me here again.

His thoughts sobered. *Oh Katherine… I miss you.*

The foreign world he had found himself in was fraught with beasts and monsters, creatures far removed from the quiet confines of Innsbruck. His hand instinctively gripped the hilt of the stolen sword, the cool steel beneath his palm providing a semblance of comfort amid the tumultuous uncertainty.

It brought back memories, his mind unwillingly spiraling back to the day he had finally come across a road after so long lost in what had seemed an endless forest, only to immediately cross paths with bandits. The memory was still fresh, a glaring contrast against the strangeness that had since become his reality. They were humanoid, but utterly alien—skin the color of fresh leaves, sharp tusks protruding from their mouths, and eyes that held a hint of demonic delight. Among them, the individuals who looked eerily like the fae from the old legends his grandmother used to tell.

The encounter had been a violent dance of steel and blood, a test of survival. They were clearly untrained, and his experience had saved his life after he had relieved one of the fae of their sword, quickly shifting the odds in his favor as he fended off their relentless attack. The memory of their surprised expressions as he fought back and won still brought a grim satisfaction.

He'd taken off with one of their packs, luckily filled with a blanket and rations, in his escape into yet another forest, the group hot on his trail. They had pursued for the better part of two days, but he had evaded them. Even in this alien world, his ability to navigate the wilderness had proved fruitful.

Suddenly, a chorus of chilling howls cut through the night, the sounds echoing through the dense woodland. The howls sounded terrifyingly close.

I need to move. *Sofort!*

With immediate resolve, Friedrich surged off the ground, swung his pack onto his back, and bolted. Each primal instinct screamed at him to escape, a call he readily heeded. His leather boots drummed against the forest floor and his sword was clutched firmly in his grasp. Twisted branches reached out like skeletal arms, tearing at his clothes and scratching his face as he sprinted. The growls behind him grew louder, and the underbrush rustled ominously, heralding the approach of his pursuers. His lungs burned, and his legs felt like lead, but he pushed onward, driven by the urge to survive.

Bathed in sporadic moonlight filtering through the overhead canopy, casting eerie shadows in his path, he ran, his sole hope to breach the forest's edge before the nocturnal creatures could close the distance.

After what felt like an eternity of sprinting through the foreign forest, Friedrich spotted a flicker of light in the distance. The telltale sign of a campfire, a tiny beacon amid the gloom, was like a promise of safety. It was distant but growing closer with each pounding stride.

Around him, the wolves continued their circling game, their growls and snarls echoing ominously, punctuated by the occasional howl. They hadn't yet launched an attack, perhaps hesitating because of the memory of their brethren lying dead by his sword the previous night.

Despite the threat of imminent danger, Friedrich felt a strange sense of respect for these creatures. They were, after all, survivors in this harsh realm, just like him. With renewed resolve, he charged toward the campfire, a glimmer of hope guiding his path through the impending darkness.

With luck, they would be human. If they didn't speak German, he'd figure it out. Any common tongue would do, it was just unfortunate his English was so poor.

All he needed to figure out was a way back home to Katherine. He'd do whatever it took. Follow any noble-hearted person if it bought him a chance.

Ich hoffe, dass sie Deutsch sprechen können.

Sabina sat at a distance from Taenya and Theran. Their conversation, revolving around the details and nuances of establishing their house upon reaching Strathmore, floated through the quiet air as the night wore on. Sabina had resolved to join the discussion later, but for now, she sought a moment of solitude, content to enjoy the meal that Keston and the young princess had prepared for the group.

The camp was bathed in the warm glow of the fire, with the comforting crackle of burning wood punctuating the otherwise quiet evening. Silhouettes danced and shifted around the site as the flames flickered, casting an enchanting play of light and shadow across the surrounding trees and tents. Overhead, the canopy of the night sky spread wide, revealing an infinite blanket of twinkling stars.

Sabina admired the dedication the princess demonstrated, taking on common tasks like cooking. It was a testament to her character and the level of rapport she had established with her people. Such humility, combined with her royal stature, intrigued Sabina. The princess's actions served as a heartening reminder that despite the differences in their stations, at the end of the day, they were all part of the same house, working toward the same goals.

Keston and Princess Gwyneth sat engrossed in a game, a charming blend of playfulness and learning that the young royal was teaching the guard. Despite his repeated losses, Keston's face bore a good-natured grin, which only widened at the sound of the princess's infectious giggles. "*Allora… basta*. Keston! Like this!" Gwyneth's voice chimed as she demonstrated the proper sequence of sayings and hand gestures required for the children's game. Her quick victory, which followed, had her gleefully celebrating once again.

A soft smile played on Sabina's lips as she watched the delightful exchange. The bond between the guard, the captain, and the princess warmed her heart. Princess Gwyn would need all the help she could get in the days to come.

Sabina chuckled as Keston messed up again, causing Gwyn to throw up her hands and exclaim animatedly in that language of hers—"Italiano," she called it.

Sabina was intrigued by the lyrical ebb and flow of the language, which seemed to have a musicality quite distinct from the common tongue. The girl would go on tangents speaking very fast, leaving everyone else speechless. Princess Gwyneth had explained it was from her home. That was *in another world*. Sabina shook her head. It was so much. At least no one would understand the language—a reason for members of the house to share it. A secret language they would all have to learn from the young girl, who was, fortunately, a very enthusiastic teacher.

Having finished her meal, Sabina rose to attend to nature's call. On her way out, she gave a nod to the merchant guards scattered around another fire. The merchant Onas was working on his ledger in his wagon, having mentioned when they stopped that he was preparing everything needed to tie his company to the princess's house.

Everyone in House Iemes had known about the close relationship that Onas and the baron had shared. So, it didn't surprise her that the rich baron—whose fortune was tied to the merchant—had so readily accepted everything Onas had told him concerning the girl.

As Sabina ventured into the nearby woods to relieve herself, her thoughts drifted back to the circumstances that led her to become involved in the new house.

When Lord Iemes had approached her about the young princess, she saw no hesitation from him in wanting to assist in establishing a new royal house. He had even provided everything they would need so Princess Gwyneth wouldn't be overly scrutinized by the nobles of Strathmore.

Despite their hopes of backing a rising star, both the baron and Onas proved to be honorable men, each in their own way.

That the head of a large regional merchant company was still traveling like a simple route merchant spoke to his willingness to maintain the relationships that helped get him where he was. The Fenren Trading House, under Onas's patronage, had grown into a trading powerhouse within the duchy, the Kingdom of Meris, and even beyond. Sabina marveled at the profound connections that were unfolding, setting a strong foundation for the house they were all committed to building.

Sabina concluded her business in the woods, and was securing her belt when a chilling sound pierced the tranquility of the evening air. A chorus of ominous howls and guttural growling echoed through the forest, seeming to close in from a distance. Her hand instinctively moved to the hilt of her sword, the sharp sounds injecting a surge of adrenaline into her system.

Sabina glanced back at the camp, lifted her fingers to her lips, and blew a sharp, piercing whistle.

The knight unsheathed her sword, her gaze darting through the shadowy surroundings as she caught the alarmed shouts of the guards echoing behind her. Sabina slowly backed toward the camp, but the sound of rustling and cracking twigs caught her attention. She snapped her head toward the sounds, squinting into the darkness. Moonlight glinted off a loosely held piece of steel, revealing a figure leaning against a tree.

She stepped forward, the crunch of a twig underfoot resonating through the quiet forest. The sudden noise jerked the figure alert. He swung his head in her direction, raising a hand. Sabina moved toward him, threading her way among the trees, ready to use them as a shield against whatever lurked in the darkness, howling.

As she approached, the figure resolved into a man who bore the signs of a recent struggle. A bloody gash marred his cheek, and his shirt, ripped and blood-stained, hung loosely from his frame.

Sabina raised a hand and called out, "Do you need help, friend?"

The man stumbled, replying in a language she wasn't familiar with, though she believed she understood the sentiment—he needed help. Sabina turned back to see the guards heading toward the tree line, their weapons drawn and faces alert. Such a slow response.

Meanwhile, the other members of House Reinhart would be busy ensuring the princess's safety— at least, that was the plan. "In here!" she directed the guards, raising her voice. "We have an injured man!"

As she approached the man again, the guards finally reached her. "Milady knight! We're here. What do you need from us?"

A sudden shout of, "Wolves! To arms!" cut through the air. Sabina's head snapped around to the sight of a pack of wolves rushing out from the underbrush, a wall of snarling teeth and gleaming eyes hurtling toward them.

Sabina gripped her sword tighter, her eyes locked on the snarling wolves charging toward them. Her heart pounded in her chest, but her expression remained stern. She was a warrior ready to face the oncoming threat.

"Ser Sabina!" one of the guards cried out, pointing to the left.

A couple of wolves were veering off, aiming to flank them. "Form a circle!" she commanded, her voice cutting through the chill night air. She could hear the guards scramble to follow her order. She hoped their formation would dissuade the wolves from getting behind them.

The first wolf leaped, teeth bared, and Sabina was ready. She swung her sword in a wide arc, connecting with the animal mid-jump. The impact sent it sprawling sideways, yelping in surprise and pain.

Without wasting a moment, Sabina turned to face the next attacker, a larger wolf with a scar running down its snout. The beast lunged, but Sabina was quicker. She darted to the side, then thrust her sword forward. The blade met fur and flesh, and the wolf howled, skittering back.

Out of the corner of her eye, she saw a guard fending off another wolf, his ax swinging with wild desperation. She turned and sprinted toward him, her sword cleaving through the air to meet the wolf attacking him. Its yelp of surprise was cut off abruptly as it fell, lifeless, to the ground.

Two down. Sabina turned back to the wolf with the scar. It was growling, but there was uncertainty in its eyes now. Sabina raised her sword, prepared to strike, but the wolf, perhaps sensing its imminent defeat, turned tail and fled into the forest, followed by the two others still capable of running.

Sabina let out a breath she hadn't realized she'd been holding, her grip relaxing around the hilt of her sword. The threat was over, for now. She turned to the guards, her face grave. "Everyone alright?" she called out, her eyes scanning them for signs of injury.

As it turned out, the guards had weathered the attack unscathed. With that immediate concern assuaged, Sabina's attention swiftly returned to the injured man still propped against the tree. Turning to the guards, she pointed at the man, her voice firm as she issued a new directive. "He's going to need assistance. You have someone trained in aid, yes?"

"Of course, ser," a telv guard said as he moved toward the man.

"I am Ser Sabina," she told the man, not knowing if he understood her. "These are some guards for our small caravan. We can help you."

The injured man looked visibly disoriented and began to sag. One of the guards quickly caught the man and helped him walk toward the camp.

Emerging from the woods and nearing the camp, Sabina noticed Onas and Taenya standing alongside the remaining guard, their gazes fixed in her direction.

Taenya approached, a look of concern etched on her face. "What happened?" she asked.

"Wolves," Sabina succinctly explained. "I found him in the woods. I think they attacked him first, before us. He doesn't seem to understand Common, as he's speaking another language."

She turned to the guard holding up the stranger. "Take him near the fire and place him on a cot. Get some water."

The guard nodded in acknowledgment. "Of course, Ser Sabina. We'll handle it from here."

Taenya watched the injured man, a shocked expression suddenly taking over her features.

"Ser?" Sabina questioned, her thoughts filling with concern.

"Sabina, his ears," the knight-captain pointed out, her voice thick with surprise.

His ears were short and rounded. Just like the princess's.

Taenya cast a quick look back at their section of the camp. "Can you fetch the princess? We may need her. "

"Understood," Sabina responded immediately, swiftly turning on her heel to fetch their young liege.

Gwyn found herself standing alongside Keston and Theran. The guards were scanning their surroundings for danger, swords in their hands. Taenya had run off to see what was wrong with Sabina and hadn't returned since they had heard all of the shouting and howling.

She looked up at Keston, curiosity brimming. "What's going on?"

Keston merely shook his head, a tinge of uncertainty creeping into his voice. "I don't—"

"It appears they've found someone," Theran interjected, his gaze locked on the commotion around Mister Onas's campfire. "An injured individual, I believe. Sabina's making her way back to us now."

"Your Highness!" Sabina called out. "There's one of your people! Can you see if you can talk to him? He speaks a different language."

Gwyn perked up. A human? "Okay! I'm coming!" She glanced up at Keston and Theran, who shared a quick, uncertain look.

Accompanied by Theran, Gwyn hurried over to Sabina. "Is he okay?'

Sabina gave a reassuring nod. "Yes. He's been hurt, but it isn't critical. Some rest and water should suffice, I believe."

Relieved, Gwyn followed Sabina to Onas's part of the camp. There, she saw a man lying on a blanket, propped against a log. His ears were indeed just like hers.

The man was sipping water offered by the guards. He had light brown hair and a funny mustache. It looked like it was coming down a bit on both sides of his mouth and then was twirled out. His gaze, blue and scrutinizing, met hers as she approached.

After a moment's hesitation, Gwyn simply waved and offered a simple greeting. "Hi. I'm Gwyn."

The man started to speak… in something, but not English.

She listened, thinking. "Uh, is that German?" she asked the man.

She glanced back at Taenya and Sabina. "I don't speak German."

Taenya gave a small shrug, looking as clueless as Gwyn felt. "I have no idea what that is. Maybe you should try the other language you know?"

Gwyn's face lit up. Of course! Turning her attention back to the stranger, she offered, *"Ciao! Parli italiano? Come ti senti?"*

CHAPTER TWENTY NINE

HOME AWAY FROM HOME

Taenya observed as Gwyn spoke to the man in the beautiful and melodic language from her world. The man seemed to ponder her words, perking up as he replied in a dialect bearing similarities to Gwyn's speech.

Out of the corner of her eye, Taenya noticed Sabina leaning in closer.

"This was a good idea. I quite enjoy her language," Sabina remarked.

"Agreed. Keep an eye on him—"

"Any sudden moves, and I'll whisk her away," Sabina interjected, echoing Taenya's thoughts.

Good, she's on the same page.

Gwyn and the stranger continued their exchange, a few words stumbling in the linguistic gap between them. As Gwyn spoke, her hands danced through the air, a ballet of gestures that seemed to amuse the man. Taenya mused that the gesturing and slight language discrepancies could be indicative of regional dialects or even slang.

The conversation paused and Gwyn turned, while the man's gaze landed on Taenya and Sabina. "*Allora.* So, he can speak Italian. But it's not perfect. His name is Friedrich. He's a knight too! Uh. Which is actually weird. His clothes are also weird," Gwyn reported.

Suddenly, Gwyn went still, her eyes widening. She began rapid-firing questions at Friedrich, who appeared taken aback. He made a motion and said something, presumably to request that Gwyn slow down. The princess took a deep breath before resuming her questioning at a more tempered pace.

As the confusion on both their faces grew more apparent, Taenya decided to step in. "Your Highness, what is going on?"

Gwyn continued, seemingly oblivious to Taenya's interruption.

"Princess Gwyneth," Taenya repeated.

Caught off guard, Gwyn swiveled her head toward Taenya. "*Cosa?* I mean… what? Sorry."

Undeterred, Taenya pressed again, "What's happening? Is everything alright?"

Before Taenya even finished, Gwyn began shaking her head vehemently. "No! Everything is not okay." She gestured emphatically at the man. "He's not from home. He knows nothing about it. He keeps mentioning a place called Tirol, the Holy Roman Empire, and something about Hapsburg lands. I have no clue what he's talking about. Hold on."

Gwyn resumed her dialogue with the man, her growing frustration evident in the way her questions bore down on him. His bewildered expressions suggested he was as lost as she was.

"Should we, uh, step in again?" Sabina questioned uncertainly.

Taenya raised a hand. "Wait a moment."

The man launched a series of questions of his own, leaving Gwyn equally puzzled. His final question provoked a look from Gwyn as if he'd sprouted another head.

"What was his question?" Taenya asked.

"What the year is," Gwyn replied, utterly perplexed. "How could he not know the year?"

"Please, answer him."

With a roll of her eyes, Gwyn responded to the man's query. "Duemila ventiquattro."

Taenya knew from prior conversations that Gwyn believed the year was 2024, according to her world's calendar.

The man's eyes widened in shock, and he frantically surveyed his surroundings. As he started to ask another question, his gaze fell on Sabina, and he froze. Taenya looked at Sabina and then back at the man, realizing he had finally noticed her long, sharp ears.

Finally, he turned his gaze between Gwyn and Taenya and in heavily accented Common, asked, "Is… they… friend?"

Taenya and Sabina shared a look, and Taenya knew what she had to do. She slowly knelt in front of the man. She couldn't imagine what he had experienced since arriving, and she felt the need to assuage his fears. She placed a hand over her heart and gave him a sympathetic smile. "Yes. I am a friend."

The man nodded slowly, his eyes settling on her own pointed ears. She nodded and stood, patting the man's shoulder before stepping back so that Gwyn could continue to talk with him.

Friedrich asked Gwyn a question, gesturing with his head at Sabina and Taenya, then up at the Sister Moons.

Gwyn's eyes widened in surprise before she began explaining in their common tongue. As she spoke, the man's face contorted in anguish, and by the time she finished, he was quietly sobbing.

Taenya reached forward, placing a comforting hand on Gwyn's shoulders. "Princess, let's give him some space."

Sabina addressed the guards standing nearby. "He's like the princess, though they're not exactly from the same place. His understanding of Common is limited. Please speak slowly, and use gestures to clarify your intentions. He's just lost everything he knows. Be understanding, but remember, he's a knight, so also respectful."

The guard that Taenya recognized as the leader nodded. "Understood, ser. We'll take care of him."

"If you need anything, don't hesitate to reach out to us," Taenya added.

"Taenya, we've got this, I'll make sure he's comfortable," Onas chimed in, having been observing the spectacle from a distance.

Taenya nodded appreciatively at her friend. "Thank you, Onas. We'll discuss this further later. For now, let me escort the princess back to our camp so she can rest."

"I'll be here," he assured her with a somber smile.

Sabina and Taenya accompanied Gwyn back to their camp. The princess headed straight for the fire and sank down onto her cot. Drawing her knees to her chest, she gazed up at the two women. "He's not from home. It's as if he stepped out of a storybook." She began to sniffle. "We're going to find my mom, right? She's here, isn't she?"

Taenya seated herself beside Gwyn and draped an arm around her, pulling her close. The princess started crying softly into Taenya's shoulder. In a show of solidarity, Sabina knelt on the other side of the princess.

"We're going to find her, Gwyn," Taenya reassured her, rubbing the girl's arm soothingly.

She looked up to see Sabina gently patting Gwyn's back. "Don't worry... Gwyn. Theran and I will assist in any way that's needed."

A steely determination had taken hold in Sabina's eyes, hinting at a history that Taenya decided was best left unexplored, at least for now.

As the group made their way closer to the city, Taenya and the company traveled through the quaint villages and pockets of civilization that constituted the surrounding lands of Strathmore. They passed through bustling marketplaces, by fields of bountiful crops and modest homes, all revealing the vibrant life beyond the city's borders.

When they finally reached the outskirts of Strathmore, Taenya was stationed alongside the carriage, keeping pace with Keston, who was at the reins. Gwyn was in the wagon while the remainder of the group steeled themselves for the formality their arrival might entail.

Leading their convoy, Theran guided the carriage and wagon toward the eastern noble gatehouse, a strategic choice, given its smaller size compared to the main gate. The gate itself held a more elaborate appearance, and it promised a quicker entry into the city and a more direct path to the noble district.

Upon reaching the gatehouse, the group was halted by four guards. Another four were stationed around the gate. "Halt! This gate is for nobles only. State your business," one of the guards commanded.

Theran was quick to respond. "We wish entrance into the city. I am Ser Theran, Knight of House Reinhart. I have Her Highness, Princess Gwyneth, and her retinue arriving to take ownership of her manor within the city."

To head off potential problems, Taenya stepped forward. "Ser Theran, is there an issue?" she queried, eyeing the guards.

Theran inclined his head at the city guardsman, who turned toward another guardsman. The older, presumably higher-ranked guardsman sighed before he stepped forward, offering a slight bow.

"Sers, please allow me to retrieve the lieutenant. We will expedite your entry into the city. My apologies."

A short while later, the guardsman returned, accompanied by a tall, dark-haired high elf with striking hazel eyes. His demeanor suggested minor nobility, perhaps a lesser son of a smaller family who had joined the guard for prestige.

With a salute, the elf introduced himself. "Sers, I am Lieutenant Kieran Valro of the Strathmore Guard. I apologize for the delay and the request, but could you please provide your liege's house patents?"

Deferring to Theran, Taenya prompted, "Please provide Her Highness's Royal Patent, Ser Theran."

Upon Taenya's instruction, Theran produced the document case from his satchel and handed it over to Lieutenant Valro. Taenya observed as the lieutenant scrutinized the documents Lord Iemes had prepared.

Once his examination concluded, he said, "Everything seems in order. However, I am obliged to inform His Grace, the Duke of Tiloral, of your arrival. I believe he will likely wish to meet Her Royal Highness at her earliest convenience."

Theran accepted this gracefully. "As expected. Please inform His Grace that Princess Gwyneth is still a child of ten. Our intention is to establish her house before she enrolls in the Royal Academy next year, a task that will undoubtedly keep her occupied."

Understanding their predicament, Lieutenant Valro nodded. "I understand. I will convey this. Please extend my apologies to Her Highness for the delay." Turning to the other guards, he commanded, "Let them through!"

* * *

The group arrived at the future seat of House Reinhart around midday. They were greeted by an imposing manor, a magnificent structure that spoke of power and influence. It was a bastion of stone and timber, grand and commanding, with tall, fortress-like walls enveloped by modest gardens. Twin towers flanked the manor's entrance, an impressive sight that was magnified by the large court-yard within. It was a symbol of grandeur, the likes of which were only matched by the nobility of the highest orders.

Taenya had visited the Iemes house only once before. Its opulence had been downplayed by the baron, but in reality, it was far from modest. Keston too seemed taken aback by the grandeur of the estate, his impressed whistle echoing in the distance. "This isn't bad at all. It has its own wall and a nice courtyard. This is the house of a count, not a baron."

Sabina, ever knowledgeable, chimed in. "Lord Iemes has done very well for himself with Mister Fenren and their trade with the Kingdom of Meris and the Duchy of Tiloral."

Taenya turned at the sound of a chuckle behind her, and spotted Onas.

"We've done alright," he said. "I remember when Varciel—I mean Lord Iemes—purchased this. It was actually a marquess that owned it previously."

Theran affirmed Onas's claim. "I recall that. I was back in Larton at the time, but it was the talk of the castle for weeks." He walked up to the gate, engaging the guard stationed there in conversation.

"And now it's fit for royalty," Sabina said, smiling. She turned to Onas. "Will you be joining us?"

Declining politely, Onas shook his head. "Not this evening. You should all get settled in and meet the servants and staff." He produced a scroll from his bag, extending it toward Taenya. "Here, give this to the majordomo, Ser Siveril Norric. It will explain to him the transfer of personnel from House Iemes to House Reinhart. If he accepts—which I don't doubt he will—then he will handle everything."

Taenya accepted the scroll graciously. "Thanks, Onas. We'll see you soon?"

Onas responded with a warm smile. "Of course! We have to introduce Gwyn to my family! Speaking of…"

As Gwyn emerged from the carriage, she asked Onas, "You're going home, Mister Onas?" The girl's voice was tinged with uncertainty.

"I am. I have been away from my family for some time, but don't worry! We will see each other again soon. For now, you'll have these four."

"What about Sir Friedrich?" Gwyn asked.

"He's going to come with us. You want to help him?" Taenya asked, trying to sus out the girl's thoughts on the matter.

"Yes! We should help him. He lost his home. Even if it's a different home than mine," Gwyn stated with resolve.

"Then Keston will help get him settled, and tomorrow after we have everything in hand, we can invite him to meet with you and you can translate for us. We'll also get him a teacher so he can learn Common," Taenya suggested.

Keston reinforced the promise. "I'll look after him, Princess. Don't you worry."

"I won't if it's you, Keston! Thank you."

"Of course, Your Highness."

Theran turned back to the group. "The guard is going to get the majordomo. He should be here soon."

Taenya observed attentively as a guard engaged in conversation with an older Loreni, presumably the majordomo, Siveril. The majordomo exchanged a few words with a servant who then rushed back inside.

As the two figures moved toward them, Onas announced his departure. He leaned over to Gwyn. "Princess, we'll see each other again soon. We'll be working together quite significantly. Alright?"

"Okay, Mister Onas. See you soon," she replied, and started to walk toward Taenya. abruptly, she stopped, spun around, then ran at Onas, slamming into him and giving him a tight squeeze. "Thank you, Mister Onas. For everything. I can't wait until you meet my mom."

"I can't either, my dear," he replied softly. He bid the princess farewell and proceeded toward his wagon.

Taenya, usually attentive to Onas's departure, shifted her focus toward the impending meeting with the majordomo. She nodded to Sabina and positioned herself next to Theran at the gate, ensuring Sabina was left to accompany the princess.

As the gate opened, Majordomo Siveril greeted them warmly. "Welcome to House Iemes. I am told you are here to speak—" On noticing Taenya, his formal tone eased. "Oh, Taenya! Was that Master Onas leaving as well? What can I do for you?"

Respecting his position, Taenya addressed him formally. "Majordomo Siveril Norric, Ser." Seeing his acknowledgment, she continued, "I am Ser Taenya Shavyre… knight-captain of House Reinhart. With me are Ser Theran and Ser Sabina. We are here escorting Her Royal Highness, Princess Gwyneth of House Reinhart. I have a sealed scroll from Lord Iemes that will inform you as to our purpose. After you have read it, we can discuss it further."

Taenya extended the scroll to the majordomo, a document penned by Iemes and bearing his seal. Accepting the parchment, Siveril carefully broke the seal and unrolled it, the shock of its contents causing his fingers to subtly tremble. As he digested the words, Taenya's gaze swept over her group. Her eyes fell upon Keston, who stood alongside the likely human knight behind the carriage, and then shifted to Princess Gwyn. A shared smile and a quick thumbs-up from the princess brought a pleasing warmth to Taenya.

Turning her attention back to Siveril, she noted the transformation of his expression, shock gradually giving way to a firm resolve and unmistakable determination. He straightened, mumbling a soft, "I see," under his breath. Taking decisive strides forward, Taenya moved aside, allowing him direct access to Princess Gwyn.

Siveril, maintaining his immaculate posture, offered an elegant bow to the princess. "Your Highness, allow me the honor of welcoming you to your new home, House Reinhart, and Strathmore. As majordomo, I am Siveril Norric, entrusted with managing all domestic affairs for the house in the city. It would be my privilege to assist you in establishing your house here and in the kingdom.

"Undoubtedly, the journey from Larton was a long and tiring one. Allow me to guide you inside, while your driver moves the carriage into the courtyard and your belongings are brought in. Once inside, I can introduce you to your new staff, give you a brief tour of your new residence, and show you to your rooms, where you can rest. When you awaken, we can formulate a plan of action. With your approval of course."

Gwyn gave a respectful nod. "Thank you, Ser Siveril. I look forward to working with you, and I would be grateful to get some rest. Sleeping in a carriage is quite uncomfortable." She giggled softly into her hand, as practiced. "Please, do show me around our beautiful home. I can't wait to meet all the wonderful people who help run it."

Watching the young princess handle the situation with such grace, Taenya found her heart swelling with pride.

She is good.

After a lengthy tour of the manor and numerous introductions to staff members, Princess Gwyneth was finally able to retire for a well-deserved rest. Taenya was sure most of the information she had been presented with had overwhelmed her, blurring into a fog of names and faces.

Seated in a comfortable parlor with Majordomo Siveril, Sabina, and Theran, Taenya embarked on a discussion concerning the challenging task before them— establishing a new house. The furniture in the room was sturdy yet luxurious, a reflection of the manor's former owner's opulence, adding an imposing atmosphere to their conversation.

"The princess is resting now, but we mustn't," Siveril began, his tone calm despite the urgency in his message. He stood and walked to a map of the duchy framed on the wall and examined it. "Our task is monumental, and time is an elusive ally. We must move swiftly yet precisely."

Taenya turned to Siveril. "Lord Iemes mentioned he has noble contacts within the Kingdom of Meris," she began, observing Siveril's face for any reaction. "He suggested they might be willing to support Gwyn."

Siveril, completely composed, did not miss a beat. "That could be more detrimental than beneficial," he said, clasping his hands behind him. "While establishing foreign ties can have its advantages, it's crucial to remember that Gwyn is an outsider. Anything she does will be closely scrutinized and dissected by the other houses. If she aligns with more foreign interests, it could be seen as too threatening or alienating."

He stepped toward a grand portrait that hung on the wall, his gaze lingering on it. "What Gwyn needs at this time are allies and vassals from within our own borders. Other houses that pledge fealty to her. Trading houses, like the Fenrens', that can help elevate House Reinhart's wealth and influence. Only then can we gradually incorporate foreign relations into our strategy. It's all about balance, Knight-Captain."

Taenya leaned forward in her chair, her fingers drumming against the mahogany table. "Then what's our first step, Ser Siveril? I will admit that this is all a bit beyond my expertise."

Sabina and Theran seemed to share a similar sense of uncertainty, their expressions a mirror of her own.

Siveril straightened, his back echoing the spine of the books that lined the room's shelves. "As a royal, the princess cannot be seen as weak or without influence. First, we must establish alliances. I have three houses in mind that would make suitable allies, if only because of how expedient it would be. We must press them to tie their houses to Princess Gwyneth's. We already have the support of Fenren Trading House and House Iemes. That will help persuade the three. After, I will request a meeting with the Banking Guild. Their support will be invaluable for the economic stability of House Reinhart. Along with establishing the house's account."

The room fell into silence as his words sank in. Three houses and the Banking Guild; it was an intimidating challenge, yet the determination shared between them was palpable.

Taenya nodded, her resolve solidifying. "When do we start?"

Siveril tilted his head. "Now. First, let us go into the particulars."

Until the following bell, they dove into their strategy, preparing themselves for the whirlwind of diplomacy and politics that lay ahead. They were soldiers on a new battlefield, and their fight was just beginning.

The afternoon sun glistened off the cobblestones as Taenya stepped out of the carriage. She stood tall in an array of gleaming armor and royal blue fabric that the baron had supplied her with. Majordomo Siveril, attired in modest yet dignified clothing, accompanied her as they approached a manor less grand than their own but certainly boasting a sense of refined elegance.

"The viscountess is an astute woman. Let's hope we can sway her," Siveril murmured as they climbed the stone steps to the manor's entrance. Their arrival was quickly noticed, and they were ushered into a warmly lit sitting room adorned with art pieces reflective of a cultured aesthetic.

Moments later, Viscountess Sanna Olacyne joined them, her presence as commanding as the opulent gems adorning her neck. She greeted Siveril with a warm familiarity, a testament to their longstanding professional relationship.

"Siveril, always a pleasure," she began, before her gaze landed on Taenya.

"Lady Olacyne, may I present to you Knight-Captain Taenya Shavyre of House Reinhart," Siveril introduced, his tone hinting at the gravity of the situation. He paused, allowing the words to sink in before adding, "A house to which I have now pledged my services."

The surprise that flashed across the viscountess's face was unmistakable, her well-practiced decorum momentarily slipping. "House Reinhart?" she echoed, her brow furrowing. "What of Lord Iemes?"

"House Iemes and Fenren Trading House have pledged themselves to House Reinhart," Siveril explained, the declaration further deepening the viscountess's surprise.

"I've never heard of House Reinhart," she admitted, her gaze shifting to Taenya with a renewed curiosity.

Taenya met her gaze evenly. "House Reinhart is the house of Princess Gwyneth Reinhart, a terran who has chosen to establish her home in this world following her arrival with the Flash."

The silence that followed was pregnant with intrigue, the viscountess's sharp eyes betraying her interest. It was clear she grasped the implications of Siveril's proposal. "You desire to tie my house to this princess's," she stated, the corners of her mouth quirking upward. "If I consent to this, we will be square, Siveril. You know my situation, so I cannot deny my interest, but I trust this alliance will prove profitable, given that Lord Iemes and Onas Fenren are backing it."

Siveril smiled, his response carrying an undercurrent of certainty. "A new royal house brings opportunities and influence we've never dared to dream about, milady. We're standing at the precipice of a new era, a true faction in the making. One that you can tie yourself with. I believe your daughter, Aleanora, would be a fine addition to Her Highness's closest retinue—a confidante."

Taenya could tell from that suggestion that the woman was sold. She didn't know the circumstances of House Olacyne, but any viscount would be interested in improving their influence at the tail of a royal. It promised great things if that royal survived.

Taenya and Siveril left the manor, a newfound alliance tucked neatly under their belt. It had been only a few bells and everything was off to a promising start.

Taenya and Siveril spent the rest of the day moving in a blur, a whirlwind of negotiations, presentations, and diplomatic conversations. The second meeting

was with Lord Camus, baron of House Trenlore, a notoriously obtuse character. His tactics were confusing, bordering on frustrating. Taenya found herself
clenching her fist on more than one occasion as he danced around their proposal
with irritatingly dense political deflection. Yet, Siveril handled it all with calm,
unyielding patience, managing to secure their commitment with a gracious smile
and well-chosen words.

Their final meeting was with Lord Hagen, baron of House Urileth. A shrewd
and wealthy man, he showed immediate interest in the opportunity that came
with aligning with a royal house, especially one with a terran princess at its helm.
Apparently, his house had very little influence of its own due to the baron having
married into it. His wife's unexpected passing a year prior and had been the start
of his troubles.

As the day drew to a close, Siveril and Taenya returned to their own manor,
weary but satisfied. Their mission had been successful. The heads of all three
houses—Olacyne, Trenlore, and Urileth—had agreed to pledge themselves to
House Reinhart. Moreover, they agreed to meet Princess Gwyneth over breakfast
the following day, alongside the House Reinhart esquire and the guildmistress of
the Banking Guild of Strathmore.

As the moons rose over the bustling city, a new sense of resolve filled the air
within the manor's walls. Taenya had to admit, Siveril moved quickly, and the
future of House Reinhart was beginning to gleam brighter for it.

CHAPTER THIRTY

HOUSE REINHART

After the Reverberation of Mana, many houses were created and dissolved. A surprising number of these were created by the newly arrived terrans and their benefactors with hidden agendas. These houses were unique in that they brought fresh ideas from their origins that potentially had widespread impacts. The older, more established factions clamored to take advantage of these houses and draw them within their respective spheres of influence. In many, success or failure depended solely on where they were formed or the connections they developed.

A History of Mana. 184 SA

Gwyn awoke to a soft light peeking through the curtains that adorned the room she was in. Her room. She reached above her head, stretching her arms and legs out, yawning exaggeratedly. She sat up, looked around in the dimly lit room, and flopped back down on her bed. The oh so soft bed. Gwyn really didn't want to leave the comfy place of sleepy safety. She'd actually had good dreams sleeping here. Clearly, she should never have to leave it.

There was a gentle knock at the door, which was way too far away. Gwyn just raised a hand and grunted loudly. Which caused the door to open and produce the harbinger of all that was evil—the person who would make her get out of bed.

Through a single squinted eye, she identified her visitor: an elf—no, a *high...* elf... Loreni? Gwyn really needed to remember that. *What if calling them only an elf upsets them because they think it's bad or something? Ugh, it's just the short name, like man for human. Yeah, that's it.*

"Your Highness? Are you awake?" the woman inquired in a whisper, her voice trembling with what Gwyn detected as nervousness. An odd reaction, she thought, considering she was just a kid.

What was her name? Elaine? Vivi? Bob? Kiki? Do you love me? Gwyn giggled, then froze. She had given herself away to the enemy.

Upon hearing Gwyn's amusement, the high elf relaxed. "I see you are indeed awake, Your Highness. May I assist you in preparing for the day?"

Gwyn blinked in surprise as she emerged from the blanket and sat up. "You'll help me get ready? My mom usually makes me do it myself. Except my hair, I'm really bad at that."

Her visitor smiled warmly. "Of course, Your Highness. I would be honored to assist you in any way that you need."

Despite the gentle reassurance, Gwyn could only groan in response, pretending to be a dead fish as she was released to the will of gravity. "It's Gwyyyn," she corrected.

"As you wish, Your Highness," the woman said, and chuckled, her eyes twinkling with humor. "Now, let's prepare for the day. We have chosen some clothing for you to wear for the time being. Majordomo Siveril and Ser Taenya mentioned you will be going shopping soon."

Gwyn grabbed a pillow and put it over her head, groaning into it. She felt the blanket get pulled back, exposing her. She grabbed the pillow and dramatically flung it to the other side of the bed. "Fiiine, I'll get up."

She reluctantly sat up for the third time, eyeing the woman who patiently held up a dress. *A dress.* Gwyn sighed. "Miss..." she trailed off a bit, not remembering the woman's name. "Do we have something other than a dress? I wore a dress here that Mr. Onas got me and I just... I don't like them."

The woman's smile was gentle. "My name is Emma, Your Highness. It's okay that you didn't remember, you were quite tired when we were introduced. Regarding your clothing, it would be most fitting for your position to wear a dress."

Returning Emma's kind gesture with a bashful smile, Gwyn offered an apologetic, "Sorry..."

With a dismissive wave, Emma quickly assuaged Gwyn's guilt. "No, no. Please, Your Highness, don't apologize. I am here to assist you as your handmaiden. Whatever you require, do not hesitate to ask. I will ensure your needs are met, either personally or by delegating to another member of the house staff."

She returned to the subject at hand, her tone carefully informative. "Regarding attire, it is customary for one of your status to wear a dress, Your Highness."

Gwyn dragged her hand over her face and left it there, resting over her mouth and chin, a finger aside her nose. "Fine, I'll wear the dress," she mumbled into her hand.

Seizing on her agreement, Emma brightened. "Wonderful! Let's proceed with getting you ready for the day, Your Highness. Afterward, I'll guide you to your dining area for breakfast."

Guided by Emma, Gwyn entered the grand dining room, her eyes immediately drawn to the massive table occupying its center. It was large enough to seat at least twenty people with ease, its proportions appearing far more imposing than her memories of the previous night's tour suggested.

Her gaze darted to the stern-faced guards positioned strategically around the room before settling on the seven individuals already seated at the table. At the table's head was a conspicuously empty chair—one that was quite fancy—toward which Emma was leading her. As they approached the vacant seat, those at the table rose, prompting a curious raise of Gwyn's eyebrow. *Were they waiting for me?*

"Your Highness, good morning!" Siveril greeted her. "Please, your seat is prepared." He gestured toward the fancy chair.

Nodding in response, Gwyn moved toward the chair, which Emma held out for her. Observing that the others remained standing, Gwyn hesitated briefly before shrugging off her uncertainty and seating herself. She gratefully accepted Emma's assistance in pushing in the large chair; it was much too big for her to try and scoot.

She scanned the room, her eyes catching Taenya's supportive smile on her left and Siveril's stern countenance to her right. With Sabina and Theran conspicuously absent, five unfamiliar faces filled the remaining seats. There was a man with ears like Taenya, a telv, seated next to her knight. His brown hair was styled to perfection, as if he'd just gone to the salon. There was an older woman next to the majordomo, who sort of looked like a young grandma, but one that still worked a lot. And she had really long ears. Even longer than Keston's, and those were pretty long. She had two piercings that had earrings connected by a chain that hung down a little bit from her ears. They were pretty.

The remaining three seats were filled by two men and a woman, each appearing to be around the same age as Siveril.

Definitely not used to this.

The realization dawned on Gwyn that the entire group was waiting on her to start. Unaccustomed to this level of attention, she took a moment before speaking up. "Uhm, good morning everyone."

A bright smile spread across Taenya's face, no doubt because Gwyn figured out what they were waiting on. *She acts more and more like a mom every day.*

The knight-captain signaled a servant. "Please bring Her Highness her breakfast."

"At once, ser," the man dutifully responded and promptly exited through a side door.

Turning her attention back to Gwyn, Taenya continued, "While we wait for your food to arrive, Majordomo Siveril would like to introduce everyone."

With a slight bow as he sat, Siveril addressed her. "Yes, Your Highness, allow me to introduce the esteemed individuals who will assist us in fully establishing your house."

He gestured to the woman seated to his right. "This is Lady Maeva Batteux, head of the Banking Guild within the entire Duchy of Tiloral."

With a gracious dip of her head, Lady Batteux acknowledged Gwyn. "Your Highness, I eagerly look forward to what the Guild can do for you."

Siveril nodded in approval before proceeding to the next introduction. "Next, we have Niles Balfiel. He serves as the House Reinhart esquire."

The man next to Taenya bowed his head solemnly, pausing before straightening up. "It's a pleasure, Your Highness."

Siveril proceeded to introduce the remaining attendees. "Lastly, we have three distinguished individuals seeking to establish early ties with your house. Viscountess Sanna of House Olacyne, Lord Camus of House Trenlore, and Lord Hagen of House Urileth are here to petition their daughters' inclusion in your house as your ladies-in-waiting."

Each of the nobles offered gracious greetings and said nice things, but Gwyn could see through their words. Especially those of Lord Camus, who seemed almost as if he were not really paying attention, as if his being there were something she should be thankful for. *They clearly just want to use me. Like Raafe had warned.*

However, she wouldn't become someone to be easily exploited. It was fine; Gwyn would just use them more. If she was to find her mom, she needed all the information she could get, and surrounding herself with people who could provide it would be useful. Taenya wouldn't let them take advantage of her. *I won't either. I'll burn them if they try.*

She cast her gaze over each individual, carefully committing their names and faces to memory—a skill she had markedly improved upon since learning magic.

"Thank you, everyone, for the kind greetings. I look forward to finishing anything that needs to be done so House Reinhart can be started. I also hope to meet your daughters and get to know them first," she said, the formality of her speech grating against her usual candid demeanor.

While they waited for breakfast to arrive, Lord Hagen and Viscountess Olacyne filled the room with light-hearted banter and formal pleasantries. They punctuated their interactions with polite questions directed at Gwyn and Siveril, showing an interest in House Reinhart and its young royal.

"Your Highness, I hope you find our world to your liking," began Lord Hagen, his tone warm yet formal. "I imagine our politics can be quite the culture shock for one from an entirely different world."

You could say that… Uhm, a fancy way to reply… Oh! Just channel Mom!

"I'm adjusting," Gwyn replied with a small, appreciative smile. "There's definitely a lot to take in, but it's all very fascinating."

"I can only imagine, Your Highness," Viscountess Olacyne said. "I assure you, however, that you'll find us quite welcoming. We value resilience, which you seem to possess in abundance."

Siveril, in his usual charismatic demeanor, engaged with the two, reciprocating their interest in House Reinhart, occasionally sharing tidbits of their ambitious plans for growth and stability. .

Meanwhile, Lord Camus stayed detached from the amiable exchanges. His gaze was distant, almost indifferent, as he simply observed the others. The silence he maintained was punctuated only by an occasional nod in response to direct acknowledgments, which really made Gwyn dislike him.

I hope his daughter is different, Gwyn thought.

Feeling the tempo of the meeting winding down, Viscountess Olacyne and Lord Hagen both rose from their seats. "We must take our leave, Your Highness," the viscountess began, her gaze steady on Gwyn.

"Indeed, duties beckon us," Lord Hagen said. "However, this meeting has been most enlightening and pleasant."

The majordomo smiled. "I'm sure Her Highness appreciates your presence here today. I will coordinate with you after breakfast on a proper time for your daughters to arrive and meet Her Highness. House Reinhart looks forward to a mutually beneficial relationship with your houses."

While the barons and viscountess prepared to leave, Lord Hagen paused, directing a cordial smile at Gwyn. "Your Highness, I must commend you on the atmosphere of this fine home. House Reinhart already has a distinct aura about it."

Channel Mom. Channel Mom. Gwyn offered a small smile in return. "Thank you, Lord Hagen. I hope our houses can build a strong relationship."

The older man nodded, turning his attention to Siveril. "Ser Siveril, it was a pleasure seeing you again. Our last meeting seems like ages ago. Your reputation for efficiency is well-deserved."

Siveril reciprocated the nod. "The pleasure is mutual. Time indeed flies, but it is our duty to keep pace with it. I look forward to our next meeting."

Viscountess Olacyne stepped forward with a warm smile. "Your Highness, it's refreshing to see such youthful vigor in the realm. House Olacyne extends its fullest support toward House Reinhart's future endeavors. And thank you, Ser Siveril—always a pleasure. House Olacyne looks forward to a lasting and productive relationship. I will ensure Aleanora is available upon request." She turned and curtseyed to Gwyn. "Your Highness, thank you for your time."

Lord Camus finally broke his silence. "While House Trenlore is known for its historic lineage and powerful connections, we recognize the... potential value your house brings," he began, his voice coated with a condescending sweetness. "It is my belief that aligning ourselves with House Reinhart will not only benefit you but also add a fresh perspective to our endeavors. Thus, I consider it a wise decision to offer you our support, which should indeed be counted as a significant asset to you." His tone suggested he was doing Gwyn a considerable favor. "In line with this, I have decided to have my daughter, Ilyana, serve as your lady-in-waiting. I trust her expertise will prove invaluable in the growth of your house." His words rang through the room, he gave a slight nod before turning and striding from the room amid the stunned looks of everyone present.

The viscountess turned to Siveril, her gaze sharp. "Dealing with that one may prove challenging, Siveril. I wonder if allying with House Trenlore is worth the trouble."

Siveril met her gaze with a strained smile, the muscles in his neck betraying his frustration. "My decision wasn't influenced solely by Lord Camus, but the diamond in the rough," he responded diplomatically. "Regrettably, his behavior was as expected. Regardless, Lady Olacyne, I appreciate your presence today."

With their goodbyes said, the nobles gracefully exited the room, the guards opening the door with a synchronized ease that caught Gwyn's attention.

Once the doors closed behind them, Gwyn voiced her confusion. "Why didn't they stay for breakfast?" she asked, genuinely perplexed. *Not that I'm complaining—that one guy was a jerk.*

Siveril looked slightly taken aback by the question. Taenya chuckled softly. She laid a hand next to Gwyn's, turning her attention. "Their purpose was simply an introductory meeting, Gwyn. Our breakfast will only include us five. For now, Guildmistress Batteux and Niles are far more important to our house, and our discussions with them will require more time, often conducted over meals. We can attend to the remaining details after breakfast."

"The influence of Guildmistress Batteux, as head of the Banking Guild, is far more substantial than that of many other individuals who could've joined us for breakfast," added Siveril.

Lady Batteux received the compliment with a gracious smile. "Thank you, Ser Siveril. Though, if you were to invite the duke, that might be a different story. Although, given your relationship with the man, I have no doubt that such a meeting is in the future."

Siveril responded with a good-natured grunt, his eyes twinkling with amusement. "Indeed, it might be."

The guildmistress let out a lighthearted laugh. "That said, Your Highness," she said to Gwyn, "I wouldn't presume to have more importance than your own subordinates. It's just that our work this morning will have more immediate consequences."

"Indeed," Niles chimed in, nodding in agreement. "My duty is to ensure the legal protection of your house and its growth. I'll be present at most major transactions you make, Your Highness."

"Niles will be with you at nearly every large deal or transaction you accomplish, Your Highness. As an esquire, he may also be empowered to act in your name, if you deem it necessary. Which will be beneficial for many aspects, due to your age," Siveril elaborated.

Gwyn nodded thoughtfully. Adults never took kids seriously. *Having an adult who can get whatever I want will be perfect.*

The sound of a bell chiming drew her attention, and servers began to file into the room with trays of food. She examined the spread, taking in the familiar sight of bread, cheese, and fruit. *A little disappointing—a fancy house should have a better breakfast. Where are the milk, brioches, pastries, and eggs?* She sighed softly.

Taenya noticed her discomfort and leaned toward her. "Princess, later, you and I can discuss your preferences with the head chef. We'll ensure that your meals include foods that remind you of your home. Would that be alright?"

Gwyn returned her smile and whispered back, "That's perfect. Thank you, Taenya."

She snuck a glance at Siveril, noting the hint of a smirk and a playful twinkle in his eye. Catching her gaze, he winked at her before turning to Lady Batteux. "Lady Batteux, we intend to establish an account for House Reinhart with the Guild. We have ample funds at our disposal. I believe..." He paused, exchanging a quick look with Taenya, who nodded in confirmation. "I believe Onas Fenren of the Fenren Trading House will also be registering House Reinhart's controlling interest."

This seemed to shock Lady Batteux, who sputtered in surprise. "Onas Fenren is offering his company and his house to join House Reinhart?"

Taenya smoothly stepped in. "Indeed, that's correct. This is a sealed affidavit affirming the arrangement." Gwyn recognized Mr. Onas's wax seal securing the scroll.

While the guildmistress was occupied with examining the document, Niles found the opportunity to speak.

"House Reinhart would also like to extend full access to Her Highness's mother for the house account. Her Highness requests that any use of this access be duly recorded, and the Guild will inform the house immediately with the relevant documentation. As Her Highness's mother is currently far from Strathmore and, consequently, the house, Her Highness wishes to maintain thorough documentation to ensure funds are always available."

Gwyn was merely picking at her food, not truly in the mood for eating. She took another sip of water and nibbled on her bread. But when Lady Batteux responded, Gwyn found herself freezing mid-motion.

The guildmistress had paused her reading, a note of surprise coloring her voice. "Her mother... a queen."

Gwyn's eyes widened in shock. *Oh... that's bad. Mom is going to be so mad.*

Niles looked at Taenya, who quickly picked up the conversation. "Yes, Her Royal Majesty Sloane the First."

Gwyn's heart pounded in her chest. *Oh... s-sh...SHIT. I'm dead. So dead.* Her breathing quickened, and she tried to regain her composure. *Keep calm. Breathe. They can't know.* Taking a deep breath, Gwyn steadied herself, keeping to the lie.

There's no going back now.

Taenya's gaze briefly flickered to Gwyn, who had finally managed to regain control after her short burst of panic. *Probably just worried about her mother again.* Taenya felt a wave of pride wash over her. The young girl's ability to keep her composure under these circumstances was truly remarkable. She made a mental note to have a talk with Gwyn later, perhaps over some comforting sweets and tea.

"Of course, we will make certain to annotate the House Reinhart's accounts appropriately and maintain the required records. Might I inquire as to where we should send the notifications?" the guildmistress asked, her eyes curious.

Taenya could sense that she was trying to figure out where Gwyn's mother was. "Her Majesty is presently journeying throughout the entirety of West Ikios," she said. "As you well know, delivering a message can take time. We plan to eventually meet with Queen Sloane in the capital itself once Princess Gwyn begins her studies at the academy there. Until that time, however, we know only that Her Majesty is traveling through the various kingdoms and Sovereign Cities, working on establishing diplomatic relations."

Take that.

Lady Batteux responded with a measured nod. "Understandable. It certainly is a considerable amount of travel. We will make sure to include the appropriate information in our regular dispatches throughout the Guild network."

Throughout the exchange, Majordomo Siveril's gaze remained fixed on Taenya. His expression held a hint of skepticism, but he continued to play along with the narrative. "House Reinhart values the support of the Banking Guild. We will make our initial deposit into the house account today."

"Of course. We appreciate your patronage, Ser Siveril. Your Highness," Lady Batteux responded.

Taenya's gaze drifted to Gwyn's handmaiden, who was vigilantly monitoring her charge, ready to step in if needed. Pleased with the young woman's attentiveness, Taenya gestured for her to come over.

"Please fetch some cold milk for the princess. Also, as soon as we've finished here, take her for a stroll around the courtyard. She could use a distraction."

The woman, Emma, gave a subtle nod in acknowledgment. "It will be done, ser," she affirmed. Swiftly, she exited the room, gesturing for a servant to follow her.

Turning her attention back to Gwyn, Taenya noticed she was merely picking at her food. "Your Highness, today is set to be rather busy for us, but I thought it might be enjoyable to take a tour of the city, if you'd be open to it."

Gwyn looked up, her expression lightening with a small smile. "Sure. That sounds fun, Taenya."

Taenya suppressed a sigh, her heart aching for the young princess. She was doing her utmost to support the girl and hoped everything would fall into place eventually. Imagining the whirlwind of emotions coursing through Gwyn's mind was both difficult and heartrending.

CHAPTER THIRTY-ONE

IN THE NAME OF SAFETY

Sabina found herself seated in Majordomo Siveril's office, having spent the night and the better part of the morning completing a litany of tasks. The aging knight had thrown himself into the establishment of the house with an admirable fervor. Even before the princess had retreated to her room to rest, he had dispatched missives and servants across the city before venturing out to meet with various nobles with Taenya. That he and the knight-captain had already orchestrated the alignment of three houses, who even offered their children as retainers to Her Highness, was nothing short of astounding. Sabina couldn't fathom where Lord Iemes had found such a figure as Siveril.

Ever since leaving Castle Larton, she had found the baron's influence to be vastly and impressively far-reaching. Having known only Larton and never having set foot in Strathmore before, she found this side of house business to be brutally swift and competitive. To keep the young princess safe, she would need to adapt quickly.

The door swung open, admitting Taenya and Siveril. Sabina observed their appearance with faint amusement. Both appeared to have concluded their breakfast meeting with the princess on a positive note. They were in high spirits, their satisfaction seeping through their professional demeanors.

Sabina couldn't help but note Taenya's air of measured calm, and the vigilance in her hazel-green eyes, watchful as a hawk's as they flitted over each corner of the room. Her hair, a golden cascade that fell freely to her shoulder blades, sparkled faintly in the morning light. Her short ears were adorned with only a single piercing each, something more common among telv than Loreni, like Sabina or Siveril.

"Ah, Ser Sabina, thank you for your patience," said Siveril as he walked into the room.

As a high elf, the middle-aged Siveril brought an air of dignified gravity into the room. His brown eyes, steeped in wisdom and experience, held an unwavering focus as he looked at her. His hair, once a rich brown, was now peppered with streaks of gray and complemented his clean-shaven face well, in a way that had her curious as to why he was unmarried. His impeccable posture and distinguished appearance suggested a lifetime of navigating the intricate world of house business with both skill and grace.

Sabina responded with a slight nod. "Of course. I believe we're all eager to see House Reinhart firmly established."

Taenya, her expression bright, chimed in. "We're making good headway. The guild account has been set up, the paperwork finalized. Our meeting with the guildmistress was quite productive, which is why we're running a bit late."

"And we've identified three potential ladies-in-waiting," Siveril added, a satisfied smile on his face. "The princess will meet them soon and make her choice. While none of their houses wield significant influence in the broader realm of Aviran politics, they'll serve us well within the duchy. As our house grows, so too will the range of lower nobility at Her Highness's disposal."

Sabina interjected, a skeptical look on her face, "It all seems to be going remarkably smoothly. Almost suspiciously so?"

Taenya nodded in agreement. "I've had the same thought. The process has been far more seamless than I expected."

With a dismissive shake of his head, Siveril countered, "That's precisely why we're moving with such urgency. We have to get established before the scrutiny comes. Her Highness will need to meet with the duke—and soon. That's inevitable. Strathmore is currently the seat of her house. The next few weeks will involve a lot of small things being put together to create a solid foundation. Her Highness is quite likable. It will work to her benefit as she meets the rest of the peerage."

Siveril's tone shifted, becoming more serious. "Now, I need an explanation about her mother and more details about her people, including the one who hardly speaks Common and has been assigned to the guard's quarters."

Caught off guard by the abrupt change of topic, Sabina turned to Taenya. She was better equipped to handle this conversation.

With a resigned sigh, Taenya began. "You must have noticed that the princess belongs to a previously unknown race. They identify as 'humans.'"

"The other one's name is Friedrich, and he is a knight, but he seems to hail from either a different time or place than her," Sabina said. "They both seemed quite confused when they attempted to explain their origins."

"Indeed," Taenya concurred. "According to Gwyn, her people have explored every inch of their world, and she herself has journeyed through numerous nations purely for leisure."

Siveril rubbed his hand through his graying hair, looking somewhat overwhelmed. "I need a drink."

He poured three and passed the women their glasses. "So, what else can you tell me about the princess and these humans? They've been mentioned in rumors throughout the kingdom and Meris. There's even talk that the Republic of Lymtoria has had a few sightings, although they were referred to as 'terrans.'"

"The blue flash that happened at the beginning of the season is responsible for their arrival, including Gwyn and her mother, whom we hope simply ended up somewhere else," began Taenya. "I've pledged to help Gwyn find her."

Sabina took a sip of her drink as Taenya proceeded to explain everything that had happened to them. When the knight mentioned magic, Siveril tipped back his glass, refilled it, and then emptied it again. Sabina refilled his glass for the third time.

"We certainly have our work cut out for us. It's fortunate that we've moved swiftly. The princess has been covering her ears with her hair, which probably led everyone to mistake her for a young telv with unusually short ears. This is something we will need to address—especially with the servants and staff," Siveril stated with a solemn nod, seemingly a bit overwhelmed.

"Ah, there's one more thing," Taenya interjected. "We were required to display Gwyn's Royal Patents at the city gate to a certain Lieutenant Valro upon entry through the gates."

Siveril winced at this revelation, taking a moment to process the implications. "House Valro," he muttered, rubbing his temples. "That's a family of lower nobility, but they're well-known for their steadfast loyalty to the duke. If a Valro saw the patents, it's virtually certain that the duke will hear about it. It's a relief it wasn't one of the other families, but this accelerates our timetable significantly."

His face hardened. "We must act swiftly and surely, for it seems our days of operating in the dark are over. Now that our presence has inevitably been noticed, we need to fortify our position here and ensure the princess is adequately protected. I believe this challenge only adds to the allure of building a house from scratch, don't you agree?"

"I believe we will follow your lead in that, Majordomo," Taenya said. "We'll also need to hire additional staff and perhaps more guards. I want the princess to be thoroughly protected. Given her people's situation, it's vital that no one gets any harmful ideas. Also, we need to find a tutor for her. She has to enroll in the Royal Academy."

"I couldn't agree more. Her status warrants it," Siveril said. "We're going to be extremely occupied. The prospect of building a house from scratch, however, is quite alluring. I'll begin scouting for suitable individuals before the other houses realize they need to spy on us."

Sabina smirked at the thought. "Leave that to me," she volunteered, her protective instincts kicking in. She would diligently root out any threats to the princess or her interests.

With a chuckle that didn't quite hide his anxiety, Siveril raised his glass. "To House Reinhart: may we rise swiftly and securely in the face of our newfound challenges." They clinked their glasses together, the sound echoing through the room, a reminder of the arduous journey that lay ahead of them.

Taenya walked out of the manor several bells later, her mind whirring with thoughts of the challenges they faced and the vast work that still lay ahead. As she moved through the well-maintained grounds, she felt a subtle shift in the air. This was her element. She was in her comfort zone when dealing with real, tangible tasks—people, safety, and the organizational structure that formed the backbone of the house. Something she'd never considered before, but the challenge of it, the duty, called to her like nothing else in her life.

Crossing the manicured lawns, she arrived at the guards' quarters, an imposing stone structure that housed the protectors of the estate. She found Keston standing with Theran as the two spoke with several guards, being briefed on the way things were done within a house guard.

"Ser Theran, Keston, how are things going?" Taenya politely questioned.

The guards all noticed her and straightened, recognizing her as their new house's knight-captain. She had been briefly introduced to the guards as a whole last night after the tour, and so far, she had to say, they at least had a level of professionalism she hadn't expected. Theran would be working to improve their abilities.

"Quite well, Ser Taenya," Theran replied, his tone filled with a mix of satisfaction and anticipation. "The guard here has a solid foundation, which is to be expected from House Iemes. Their dedication is commendable, and they have a good grasp of their duties. With some fine-tuning and modern training practices, I believe we'll have a formidable house guard, similar in quality to the troops of Castle Larton."

Keston nodded in agreement, a small, appreciative smile on his face. "It's been impressive, I must admit. Their commitment to the house and their discipline is something you do not often see in what is essentially a lower noble's vacation home."

"That's encouraging," Taenya said, her hazel-green eyes bright with approval. "Keston, I'm glad you chose to stay with us, I think you'll fit in well here. You bring some experience that I'm sure they'll value. Not to mention, the princess will be very pleased to have you around."

The corners of Keston's mouth tugged upward into a smile. "Of course, I would stay for her. You know me. But I appreciate that, Ser Taenya. I'll do my best to live up to your expectations."

She chuckled. "Thanks, Keston. If there's anything you need, don't hesitate to let me know," Taenya offered, hoping to make his transition as seamless as possible.

"I will, Taenya, and thank you," Keston replied. After a brief pause, he added, "Congratulations again on your knighthood. It is a well-deserved honor. You deserve it, truly."

Taenya thanked him, touched by his sincerity. He patted her on the shoulder in a friendly, comradely gesture, the smile on his face genuine. "Now, if you'll excuse me, I have a few more orientation matters to attend to with the senior guardsmen."

Watching him stride away, Taenya felt a sense of satisfaction. She had faith in Keston and Theran. Having the knight there would indeed help the house guard become a force to be reckoned with. She only wished she had access to more than two knights…

Wait…

"Ser Theran," Taenya began, turning her attention to the high elf knight. "How is Sir Friedrich settling in?"

"Quite well, Ser Taenya, all things considered," Theran responded, gesturing for her to follow him as they began to walk toward one of the private rooms within the guard quarters.

As they walked, Taenya absorbed the sounds of the busy guard quarters. The rhythmic clashing of swords and shields as some of the guards practiced their drills in the small training room, the lower murmurs of discussions, and the occasional bark of laughter. It was a sound that brought her comfort; it was the sound of order and preparation.

"They've been working with him since last night," Theran continued, pushing open the door to a small room. Inside, Friedrich sat at a wooden table, a look of intense concentration on his face as he listened to the soft-spoken words of a woman seated across from him. She was one of the manor's servants, a woman whom Siveril had suggested, a dwarf who would often step in for the baron's children to help with their studies when they were in the city.

Taenya knew that dwarves were a rare sight in the kingdom due to a frosty political relationship. However, the duchy had maintained a decent relationship with the dwarven enclave of Dirn Loduhr, which led to a small number of people venturing into the city in search of opportunities they may not have had back home. Loma and her family were one such instance.

Loma looked up at their entrance, her eyes brightening. "Ser Taenya, Ser Theran," she greeted, her voice filled with warmth. "Welcome. Sir Friedrich has been making excellent progress."

Taenya moved to stand beside the dwarf, studying the scene before her.

Friedrich was indeed engrossed in his lessons, the usually stoic man leaning forward in his chair as he hung on the woman's every word. He was a far cry from the warrior she had first met who had survived weeks in the forests alone. Now, he seemed more like a student eager to absorb knowledge.

"He is quick to grasp new concepts," Friedrich's tutor continued. "His pronunciation still needs a bit of work, but considering the time he's had, I'm very impressed."

Looking at the books and papers strewn about the table, Taenya could see the evidence of Friedrich's efforts. His handwriting, although still clumsy in parts, was significantly improved from when he had first started. She felt a swell of pride for the man's tenacity and dedication.

"He's doing well, then," she asked, giving Friedrich an approving nod. He returned it with a small, almost shy smile. "Good to hear. And how are you holding up? I hope having Friedrich here isn't too much trouble."

"Not at all, Ser Taenya," Loma replied, her smile genuine. "Sir Friedrich is an eager learner. He's very patient and respectful, a real pleasure to teach. I'm eager for him to reach a more conversational level so that we can speak of his world. These… humans are fascinating to me."

Taenya narrowed her eyes slightly. "I hope that you will keep this to yourself. We do not yet know how the public will react to the appearance of a new people. We want to keep him safe. The majordomo will be having a meeting with all staff soon, I believe to discuss this further."

The woman nodded solemnly. "You do not have to worry about me, ser. I will not betray the house's interests. I simply want to help Sir Friedrich and learn more about him in order to help him acclimate easier."

Taenya felt a sense of relief at Loma's words. It was clear that despite his origin, Friedrich was making an effort to integrate into his new surroundings, a fact that brought a measure of peace to her mind.

"Keep up the good work, Friedrich," Taenya encouraged, giving him another nod before turning to leave the room. Her mind was already racing ahead, thinking of the next task at hand. But the image of Friedrich, earnestly learning under Loma's patient guidance, lingered with her. It was a small victory, but a victory nonetheless.

"Your Highness," Emma began, her voice breaking the stillness that hung in the air between them. Emma trailed slightly behind the princess as they walked along the gravel pathways of the estate grounds, strewn with fallen leaves that rustled softly beneath their feet. Occasionally, a distant birdcall punctuated the tranquility of the scene, its farewell song to the day resonating across the expansive gardens. "Your Highness, may I ask from where you hail? I understand it's not exactly my place to ask, but…"

"Hm?" the princess blinked, her attention shifting from the setting sun that bathed the stone edifice of the estate in hues of twilight. Mighty oaks, their leaves aflame with the season's fiery palette, stood scattered around them, their grandeur adding to the noble silhouette of the house. She looked at Emma, a hint of puzzlement coloring her features. "What do you mean by 'hail'?"

Emma blushed. Their progress slowed as they walked amid the last autumn blooms perfuming the crisp evening air. "My apologies for the confusion, Princess," she said, adjusting her inquiry. "I meant to ask about your home. Where is it located?"

"Oh," the princess responded, her voice taking on a distant tone. "I'm... from a place far away." She let her words hang in the air, a veil of silence falling between them once again as she lapsed into quiet contemplation. Emma watched her, her curiosity piqued and heart filled with an inexplicable sense of anticipation.

Seeing an opportunity to clarify another point of interest, Emma ventured, "Is Ser Taenya related to you in some way? The city isn't exactly home to a large number of telv, like yourself."

Stopping in her tracks, the princess turned around to face Emma, her eyes meeting hers with a question. "You haven't been told, have you?"

Emma blinked in confusion. "Told what, Your Highness?" Realizing she might be overstepping her boundaries, she quickly added, "Please, if it's something I shouldn't know, I didn't mean to pry."

Princess Gwyn studied Emma for a moment before gesturing for her to come closer. "You should know, seeing as we're going to be seeing each other a lot. But you must keep it secret."

Emotion swelled within Emma as she realized the weight of trust being placed on her shoulders. "I swear, Your Highness. I won't betray your trust, as is expected in my position."

Seemingly satisfied, the princess gave a small nod and drew her hair back. "You noticed my ears earlier when you brushed my hair, didn't you?"

Alarmed at the potential offense she may have caused, Emma quickly replied, "Princess, I would never speak ill of a birth trait. Perhaps your ears are just taking longer to grow? You're a young girl, still growing. Besides, telv traditionally have shorter ears."

But the princess shook her head. "No, Emma, I'm not a telv."

Emma tilted her head in confusion, her mind whirling with questions. "I'm sorry, Your Highness. I don't understand."

Taking a deep breath, the princess prepared to reveal her secret. "You see, I am a—"

"Your Highness! There you are. I've been searching all over for you."

Startled, both Princess Gwyn and Emma turned to see Sabina striding toward them.

Instantly, Emma took a step back, subtly bowing her head in respect.

"You scared me, Sabina! I was... uhh... just about to tell Emma about myself..." Princess Gwyn interjected, glancing at Emma with a hint of nervousness.

With a respectful inclination of her head, Sabina responded, "I apologize for startling you, Princess. However, Ser Taenya requested a moment of your time for a meeting with the head chef. Moreover, both Ser Taenya and Ser Siveril will soon be addressing the staff to elucidate them about you and House Reinhart. Wouldn't it be prudent to let Emma hear this from them before you reveal more about yourself?"

Understanding seemed to dawn on the young royal's face as she nodded in agreement. "You're right. It's probably best to allow them to handle all of the talking." Her eyes suddenly sparkled with enthusiasm. "Oh! I almost forgot about the chat Taenya and I planned with the chef! I do hope we can work out some tastier food options!"

Emma watched as the princess turned to leave, prepared to follow her charge. But the princess halted abruptly, looking back at her.

"Thank you for joining me on this walk, Miss Emma. See you a bit later?"

"I'll be joining you, Your Highness. It's my responsibility to be by your side at all times."

Sabina gently rested a hand on her shoulder, stopping her. "Wait, Emma. I wish to speak with you." She offered a kind smile. "Emma will join you shortly, Princess. I wish to talk to her for a moment."

With a chirpy response of, "Okay! See you soon, Emma!" the princess hurried off, leaving the two of them alone.

Nervousness permeated Emma's being as she watched the young princess bound off toward the house. Turning toward the knight, she asked in a slightly shaky voice, "What might I assist you with, Ser Sabina?"

As if a weight were pressing down upon her thoughts, Sabina moved closer. Emma felt the force of her penetrating gaze pinning her in place, causing her heart to pound in her chest.

"Anything that girl imparts to you will remain with you. You will not tell a soul. Not your family, not your brother's dog, not even the flower you keep potted by your bed."

A chill of fear snaked down Emma's spine, and she struggled to keep herself from shaking. How did she know that?

Unfazed by Emma's distress, Sabina carried on, her voice unwavering. "There will eventually be spies, and giving away the smallest detail is all they need to cause harm to our house. No matter what you see, you will never mention it to anyone except Ser Taenya or me first. Princess Gwyneth's safety is paramount. We will relay any pertinent information to the majordomo. Do you comprehend?"

Caught in the gravity of the knight's words, Emma stammered, "Y-Yes, milady."

"Remember that you'll be privy to details that most others won't be. Take to heart my words today, as I will not be repeating them."

Mute, Emma merely nodded, still not trusting her voice.

At once, Sabina's stern countenance melted into a smile. "Good! I'm glad we understand each other. Now, let's make our way inside. The majordomo wishes to meet with the staff. You'll take part in a comprehensive briefing, followed by another one specifically designed for those, like you, who will maintain close contact with Her Highness." She fixed Emma with a stare, waiting for her to respond.

"Yes, milady," Emma managed to squeak out.

Nodding, Sabina pivoted on her heel and strode purposefully back toward the house, leaving Emma to follow behind, her body still trembling from the confrontation.

Thoughts swirled in Emma's mind about the implications of the few things Sabina had shared. But almost instinctively, she discarded those thoughts. She never wanted to give the knight any reason to address her in such a manner again. The knight was the most unnerving woman she had ever met, and Emma wasn't sure she could take it again without crying. She decided that from then on, she would follow the knight's instructions explicitly.

Emma stole a glance at Sabina. She could have sworn she detected the hint of a satisfied smile gracing the knight's lips.

CHAPTER THIRTY-TWO

THESE PATHS WE FOLLOW

Under the reddened glow of a midday sun, Sloane, Maud, and Ernald strolled through Vilstaf's market, the crunch of autumn leaves underfoot marking their passage. The marketplace was a vibrant tapestry of color and sound, the shifting hues of the changing season mirrored in the displays of wares on offer.

"Look at this," Maud exclaimed, holding up an intricately embroidered shawl that captured the vibrant reds and golds of autumn. She grinned at Sloane, her excitement infectious. "It's beautiful, isn't it?"

"Yeah, it's nice!" Sloane agreed, smiling as the telv woman instantly turned around and purchased it.

A few stalls over, Ernald was deep in conversation with a burly blacksmith. The pair were locked in a good-natured debate over a dagger with an unusually ornate hilt. As Sloane and Maud approached, the man caught her eye.

"You reckon it's just for show, or could this little beauty hold its own?" Ernald asked, turning to Sloane for her opinion.

She shook her head. "I have no idea. That's a question for Deryk, not me."

"No, you don't need that, Ernald," Maud said quickly. "That's a piece for a noble to have sitting on a mantle."

The sun elf shrugged and handed the dagger back. The blacksmith's expression turned sour.

The three of them took their time to meander through the market, the day unfolding around them as they engaged with various shopkeepers, until they arrived at Reanny and Mulinn's shop. An array of rings and earrings lay neatly arranged on the display table out front, the sun catching the precious gems and metals. Reanny, busy attending to a customer, looked up to see them and flashed a bright smile.

"Sloane! And you brought friends!" she exclaimed, coming around the table to greet them after the customer left.

Sloane introduced Maud and Ernald, both of whom received Reanny's handshake with warmth. The dwarf's eyes sparkled with pleasure at meeting them.

The display of magical wares caught Sloane's attention next. She lifted one of the rings to examine. The craftsmanship was exquisite, a testament to Reanny's skills, and likely to the woman having more time to focus on it after teaching Sloane.

"Oh! I have something to show you," Reanny said excitedly, leading Sloane over to a shelf filled with different-sized crystals and what appeared to be mana cores. "Managed to get these. Thought you might be interested."

Sloane picked up a small teal crystal that seemed to have a slight glow, inspecting it closely. She was impressed. "How much for these?"

Reanny shrugged and shook her head. "Consider them a gift."

After some prompts on the various gem types, Maud was drawn to a pair of diamond earrings that shone with a particular brilliance, and purchased them, hoping they might help strengthen her magic. As the women admired the earrings, Mulinn emerged from the shop, wiping his hands on a cloth.

Reanny's brother was peering curiously at Maud's mace hanging by her side. His eyes twinkled with inquisitiveness and a certain professional hunger. "Aye, now that's a piece of work," he noted, gesturing to the weapon, a silent request for permission to examine it.

Maud, following his gaze, unclipped the weapon from her belt and handed it to him. Mulinn hefted it, noting the weight and balance, his expert eyes taking in every detail.

"Where'd you get this?" he asked, not taking his eyes off the weapon. His fingers traced the large mana core set in the head of the mace, admiration evident in his tone.

"Sloane came up with the core idea and commissioned it from a blacksmith in Valesbeck," Maud explained, watching as Mulinn's respect for the weapon seemed to grow.

Reanny joined her brother, a similar spark of interest in her eyes. "We could do more with this," she mused, her gaze drawn to the hilt of the mace. "Inset some gems. Might be able to fine-tune its capabilities."

Maud looked intrigued. "Do it," she said without hesitation.

Reanny's enthusiastic departure left a momentary lull. Mulinn chatted about their booming business, and the interest their magical wares had generated. He pointed toward a stack of finished items, each adorned with a maker's mark that included Sloane's initial. It was a small but significant detail that filled her with pride.

Mulinn turned to Sloane, rubbing his hands together with an eager glimmer in his eyes. "Now, imagine this," he began, gesturing animatedly with his hands. "Working in collaboration with blacksmiths from all around. We could bring a magical revolution in warfare!"

His words sparked a novel idea in Sloane. She looked at Mulinn, her eyes gleaming with the raw enthusiasm of a new concept. "Not just warfare, Mulinn," she began, capturing everyone's attention. "What about common household items?"

"Household items?" Mulinn echoed, his eyebrows shooting upward.

Just hearing herself say, she knew the concept was so… mundane. Yet it also seemed enticingly lucrative.

"Absolutely," Sloane continued, gesturing widely to encompass their surroundings. "Imagine a spoon enchanted to stir on its own, or a kettle that heats water with a simple rune. Maybe even a large container that keeps food inside cold. The possibilities are endless."

"That's actually genius, Sloane," Maud said. "I'd pay for a pot that heats itself when I'm wanting to cook breakfast."

Ernald chuckled, rubbing his chin thoughtfully. "I can see the appeal. And I can imagine a few items that would be very interesting."

The excitement bubbled up around them as they shared ideas over the next bell. Mulinn, his initial shock fading into thoughtful interest, scratched his fiery beard. "Incorporating gems, mana cores, and crystals into everyday items. I never thought of that… it could revolutionize our everyday lives."

Sloane nodded, her mind racing ahead. "The runes, like those on my watch, could be the key," she suggested, pulling back her sleeve to show them the small intricate engravings. "If I figure out more of them, I'll make sure to share the knowledge with you."

Ernald pointed toward the center of the town. "You could always send your information through the Couriers' Guild. They're reliable and fast."

"Or the Merchant's Guild," Maud said. "They have their own system of fast communication."

"Regardless," Sloane said, "I'll ensure you get any useful information, especially while I'm in Thirdghyll. I'm eager to see where the business goes."

At her words, Reanny emerged from the shop, a grin plastered on her face as she carried the mace. "Oh, you have no idea, Sloane. We're just getting started."

The lively chatter of the marketplace faded into the background as Sloane made her way into the tavern connected to their inn. The warm glow of the hearth, the cozy ambiance, and the quiet murmuring of patrons created an atmosphere much more relaxed than the busy streets outside.

She took a seat on a sturdy wooden stool at the bar and flashed a tired smile at the moon elf bartender, a slender woman with a cascade of silver hair, vibrant purple-hued skin that was common amongst moon elves, and almond-shaped sapphire eyes.

"Could I get some water, please?" Sloane asked, her voice carrying the dust of the day.

With a gentle nod, the elf gracefully filled a wooden cup with cool, refreshing water from a nearby pitcher and placed it in front of Sloane. The chill from the cup seeped into her hands, soothing her muscles that she hadn't realized until then were so tired.

A raithe man slid onto the stool next to her. "Greetings, miss," he started, his voice smooth and calm. "You look like you've had a long day. May I offer you something stronger than water?" His almost-black eyes twinkled in the warm tavern light, presenting a friendly offer.

Sloane frowned faintly and turned to face him, scanning him from head to toe. His pale skin gave him that decidedly vampiric appearance she come to associate with raithe, and his nearly black eyes sparkled mysteriously under the brim of his red hat. His short, neatly trimmed beard framed a handsome face, and he sported an air of confident charisma.

"I'm afraid I don't know you," she said, her tone polite yet firm. She didn't want to appear rude, but she had always been wary of strangers, never mind that she had zero interest in anything that would result in drinking with a man at a bar.

The man's smile didn't waver, and he raised his hands slightly in a gesture of peace. "I mean no harm, miss. Just a humble offer from a stranger. But since we're at it, why don't we drop the 'stranger' bit?" He offered a slight bow from his seat. "Your name, if you don't mind?"

Seeing no harm, Sloane decided to divulge her identity. "Sloane," she started, then paused briefly before continuing, "Baroness of House Reinhart."

The man showed surprise at her revelation, but Sloane caught the subtle flicker in his eyes that betrayed his act.

Unfazed, he responded, "A pleasure to meet you, Lady Reinhart. I am Ser Redding, a member of the Westari Crown Knights." He gestured toward the door. "I've seen you around town with some knights. Made me curious about your presence here."

His words had a ring of truth to them. He seemed to be genuinely curious, and Sloane didn't feel any immediate threat from him.

"We're on our way to Thirdghyll," she responded, a bit more relaxed now.

With a nod, Redding returned to his initial proposal. "Now that introductions are out of the way, might you reconsider that drink?"

Sloane sighed. "Sure, why not." A single drink wouldn't hurt, and she expected the knights to enter any minute.

Ser Redding casually ordered two ales from the bartender.

Sloane looked around the room, observing the patrons and absorbing the pleasant atmosphere, with its soothing murmur of chatter and occasional clinking of dishes. It was dimly lit, the afternoon sun spilling in through small windows casting a warm, reddened hue on the wooden surfaces.

Her gaze fell on a small family seated at a corner table. A young moon elf girl, her face aglow with delight, was eating something with her hands. The sight tugged at Sloane's heartstrings, making a memory flicker in her mind: She and Gwyn sitting on the floor in their living room, happily munching on margherita pizza while they watched a movie that had been recently released. After they'd finished eating, they had snuggled up together with pillows she had propped up against the couch. Her daughter had been utterly engrossed in the movie until a particularly sad scene, which had made empathetic nine-year-old Gwyn start bawling. Sloane had spent a solid half-hour comforting her until she had calmed down… and wanted to continue the movie. *That girl loves sad movies but hates feeling emotional.* The memory was so vivid, it made her heart ache with longing. *She'll be eleven soon.*

A mug of beer set down on the bar disrupted her from her reverie. Sloane quickly composed herself and turned back to Redding. He raised his mug in a small toast before taking a sip. As they drank, he began to open up about himself.

"I'm originally from Grimleah," he shared, his tone taking on a more personal note. He also mentioned he was headed to Thirdghyll to meet with some associates. "Not looking forward to it, to be honest. But duty calls."

Listening to him talk about his journey, Sloane found her thoughts drifting back to her own purpose—finding Gwyn. The lead she'd gotten back in Valesbeck came to mind and she made a mental note to ask Gisele if she'd managed to find anything else.

"How are you adjusting to this new world, milady?" Redding's question caught Sloane so off-guard that she froze for a moment. Her eyes widened in surprise. His words echoed in her mind, bringing forth a multitude of questions.

"Excuse me?"

But Redding didn't even flinch at her surprise, maintaining a calm demeanor as he clarified his thoughts. "I know of your kind. The 'terrans,' as you call yourselves. It's quite evident when you know what to look for. Your people are showing up all over the place."

His straightforwardness, along with the undertone of concern in his voice, left Sloane momentarily stunned. She hesitated, unsure of how to proceed with the conversation.

Redding seemed to soften. "It's alright," he reassured her. "I'm only concerned about your safety. I just want to make sure those knights aren't taking advantage of you."

"They're not," Sloane responded firmly. "I'm quite comfortable with them."

Redding's face brightened at her answer. "Good, good," he said, then gestured to the bartender. When the woman walked over, wiping her hands off on a rag, he ordered some bread and cheese, requesting enough for the two of them.

The food arrived promptly, and they both started to eat in comfortable silence. But Sloane was filled with questions. He had intimated that terrans had been appearing all over the place, so that meant Gwyn could be literally anywhere.

She turned to Redding, "You said my people are popping up everywhere. Have you met any of them?"

Redding took a bite of his cheese before answering. "I haven't met any, personally. But I have been following a lead. There's a group of bandits in this area who've turned to slavery. I have reason to believe they may have terrans among those they have stolen away." His voice had a grim undertone that made Sloane shudder.

He explained his plan to travel to Thirdghyll to gather help, since the local town guard in Vilstaf was not equipped to handle such a large-scale rescue mission. But as he glanced sideways at Sloane, a thought seemed to strike him. "Although," he mused, "you do travel with a large group of knights. If they would be willing to assist... I am certain the Crown would be most grateful."

Sloane was taken aback by the proposition. Her mind raced to understand the implications. It was likely the man was chasing the same slavers they had run into. She knew she had to take the chance, and hoped the knights would not mind her making a decision for them.

"We've had a run-in with some slavers on our journey here. Share what you know, and in return, I'll tell you about our encounter," she proposed.

Redding, his dark eyes flashing with a flicker of anticipation, reached into the weathered leather satchel at his side. With a confident grin spreading across his face, he responded, "Gladly."

Sloane's gaze was focused on her hands, which were nervously fidgeting with the edge of her cloak. Maud and Ismeld's inn room, otherwise filled with the soft glow of an oil lamp, fell into an eerie silence as Sloane shared the details of her conversation with Redding. All six knights either sat or stood there as they listened attentively, their faces illuminated by the warm light.

"You mean to tell us that there are more terrans, potentially even Gwyn, captured by slavers in this region?" Ismeld broke the silence, her voice echoing in the otherwise quiet room. "Possibly the very same slavers we previously encountered?"

"Ser Redding believes so, yes," Sloane affirmed, her eyes darting from one knight to the next. "Not only terrans, but locals as well."

"But how does he know where to find them?" Cristole asked, his eyes filled with worry. "Is there any definitive evidence?"

"He only has a lead. That's why he's heading to Thirdghyll. To get more people to search," Sloane admitted, her voice low but steady. "But it's a lead, perhaps our best yet, and one we can't afford to overlook. We can get there faster than he can."

Ismeld's brow arched in skepticism as she asked, "And what would this Ser Redding be doing while we tackle the slavers head-on?"

Reflecting on her exchange with the Westari knight, Sloane responded, "He intends to rush to Thirdghyll to rally additional support. Once we've dealt with the slavers, he and his team will assist in taking care of the survivors."

Gisele had remained quiet during this exchange. Finally, she spoke. "I uncovered some information that might align with this. A caravan departed for Thirdghyll not too long ago. I couldn't verify, but it's possible that our lead was aboard it."

A jolt of adrenaline surged through Sloane, her heartbeat accelerating. If their lead had indeed joined the caravan, they had no option but to pursue it. There was no telling if it might be Gwyn—or, worse, if the slavers had taken her. The very idea sent a cold shudder racing down her spine.

"We have to follow," she said. "What if the slavers took them? Or worse?"

Maud's face hardened. "You're right. We need to act."

Cristole seemed hesitant. He looked at all of them. "Are we sure this is the right move? It sounds like this knight is getting us to do his dirty work. Worse, what if he is leading us into a trap?"

Gisele and Ismeld exchanged glances. "This is exactly the type of thing we search for in our travels," Gisele reminded them, her voice firm. "To follow leads, to bring justice. Ignoring Ser Redding's information... that would be a greater dishonor."

Ismeld nodded in agreement. "We need to see this through," she said, her voice carrying an undertone of resolution.

After their agreement, the group sat in the room for a while longer, setting plans for the next day. They would rest and replenish their strength that night, and set off at dawn in pursuit of the caravan.

Sloane and Gisele retreated to their shared room. As they prepared for bed, the room was filled with a silence that was not uncomfortable, but pregnant with anticipation and apprehension.

Sloane broke the silence, her voice barely a whisper. "Is it bad... that I hope the lead isn't Gwyn?" She paused, swallowing hard. "The thought that actual slavers could have her... it's too much to bear."

Gisele turned to look at her, her gaze soft in the dim light. "It's not bad to want your child to be safe, Sloane," she responded, her voice comforting. "Every parent would feel the same."

Sleep did not come easily to Sloane. Her mind was haunted by nightmares of Gwyn being taken by cruel men, images that were too distressing to put into words. The night passed in a restless cycle of waking and falling back into fitful slumber.

When morning came, Gisele woke her. The orkun woman was already getting dressed in her armor, looking at Sloane with a determined expression. She asked for Sloane's help to fasten some of the buckles on her back, and Sloane obliged, helping to ensure the armor was snug and secure.

"We are going to put an end to these slavers, Sloane," Gisele said resolutely. "And we're going to save whoever is there... Gwyn or not." Her words echoed in the room, instilling a sense of determination and purpose.

The image of her daughter's smile, a memory she held on to with a desperate hope, filled Sloane's mind. They were going into uncertain danger, but the possibility of finding Gwyn, of ensuring she was safe, drove Sloane forward.

The morning light began to pour through the window. With a deep breath, Sloane prepared herself mentally and emotionally for what lay ahead. She channeled mana through herself, the comforting surge of magic inside steeling her. She grabbed her sword and strapped it to her belt.

Just as Sloane and Gisele made their entrance into the common room, Deryk approached them. His armored form was an imposing presence that was hard to ignore. "The wagon and horses are prepared," he informed Gisele, his voice deep and gravelly.

Gisele nodded, her gaze shifting to the sun elf knight-scholar. "Ernald, you'll be in the wagon," she directed. "Ismeld, you'll handle the reins. Maud, take Ismeld's horse, and Sloane, sit up front with Ismeld. I want all of us who can use magic ready to act at a moment's notice. Sloane, are you ready?"

Sloane exchanged a glance with Maud, seeing the healer's resolve mirrored in her eyes, doing much to help steel her own nerves.

She nodded. "I'm ready."

CHAPTER THIRTY-THREE

THE CALL OF HONOR

The wagon moved steadily along the dirt road. The knights had risen early, their determination driving them forward in pursuit of the lead they'd been given. The last crops of the year in the surrounding farmland were painted a warm hue by the rising red sun, creating a serene backdrop to their departure.

Sloane sat beside Ismeld as the blond knight guided the horses that led the wagon. Maud, riding a horse on their flank, was in sync with their pace, her confident silhouette casting a long shadow in the morning light. Cristole, leading slightly ahead, occasionally turned in his saddle to exchange words with them, while Gisele and Deryk trailed behind, vigilant and watchful.

"I've been trying to use the magic ring, but it's not been working," Ismeld said, her words breaking through the rhythmic clopping of horse hooves. She seemed disheartened. "I feel something, but I cannot cast magic like Gisele, Maud, or you."

Sloane glanced at her, her thoughts drifting back to her own early struggles with magic. "If you remember, I was having a really hard time when I was starting," she began. "It took me quite a while to understand it. My issue was trying to use magic in the same way as Maud, which is not the affinity that I have. Once I figured out what worked for me, it worked. It's possible you may have a different magical affinity than we do, which can make it harder to get the hang of."

Her struggles with magic were different from Ismeld's, yet there was an understanding between them. Sloane could see the spark in Ismeld's eyes, the determination to learn and adapt. She just hoped the woman would figure it out.

As the day progressed, their journey led them through a small hamlet, little more than a clutch of houses gathered around a dusty crossroads. The people there, mostly farmers by the looks of it, were busy with their morning tasks. Children were playing near the houses while their parents worked in the fields or attended to chores outside their homes.

At the sight of the group, activity briefly halted as people stared, curious. Cristole reigned in his horse, approaching an old raithe man who was leaning against a fence, watching their procession with interest.

"Good morning," Cristole greeted politely. The old man shifted his gaze to the young knight. "We're wondering if you've seen any caravans passing through here in the last few days?"

The raithe man, his skin a dark grayish color and his face spotted with sun blemishes, nodded thoughtfully, his pink eyes taking in the group behind Cristole. "Indeed, there was one," he said, his voice a coarse whisper shaped by age and weather. "Passed through here in the evening, day before last. They didn't stop, just moved on through southward."

A wave of relief passed through Sloane, though it was tinged with anxiety. Two days was a significant head start, but at least they were on the right track. She exchanged glances with Ismeld, seeing her own feelings reflected in the moon elf's eyes.

"Thank you, sir," Cristole said respectfully, giving the man a nod. "You've been of great help."

With that, the group moved on, leaving the hamlet behind them. The conversation with the old man had renewed their sense of urgency. They continued their journey at a faster pace, the wagon's wheels crunching on the gravelly road, their eyes set on the horizon, their minds focused on the mission at hand.

As the countryside rolled past them in a tranquil blur, the steady crunching of the wagon wheels on the rough gravel road provided a rhythmic melody to the journey. Maud, maintaining her position alongside the wagon, turned to face Sloan.

"How are you holding up, Sloane?" she asked, her voice cutting through the natural sounds around them.

"I'm fine, thank you," Sloane responded, smiling warmly at Maud. Her body had adjusted to the steady bumping of the wagon, and she found the ride surprisingly comfortable.

"Would you like to try riding for a bit? It could be fun, give you a new perspective. You've only ridden on the wagon since arriving."

Sloane hesitated for a moment before confessing, "I... I don't actually know how to ride a horse."

There was a pause, Maud and Ismeld looking at Sloane with twin expressions of surprise. It was almost comical, the two of them mirroring each other so perfectly.

"You're joking," Ismeld managed to say, her incredulity clear. "You've never ridden a horse?"

"Well, I told you guys what a car was…"

It wasn't that Sloane hadn't wanted to; there had simply never been the opportunity. Life in the twenty-first century didn't really call for horseback riding skills, and she had never thought to learn for recreational purposes.

Sensing Sloane's discomfort, Maud quickly changed the subject to lighten the mood. "Well, when we have a bit of downtime, we'll have to give you a few lessons. It's easier than you might think."

Sloane chuckled, appreciating Maud's attempt to diffuse the awkward situation. A soft sigh escaped her as she returned her gaze to the road stretching out before them.

As the hamlet disappeared behind them, the scenery gradually changed. Fields gave way to an autumnal landscape dotted with clusters of trees leafed in vibrant hues of reds, oranges, and yellows. The road beneath them became rougher, winding between boulders and steep hillocks. The scent of damp earth mingled with the crisp tang of falling leaves, imparting an invigorating freshness that offset the fatigue of their journey.

The sun continued its ascent, casting long shadows behind them. They passed through another hamlet, this one decidedly less active than the previous, before they crossed several streams, the horses splashing through the sparkling water, wagon wheels rumbling over pebble-lined beds. A cool breeze rustled the forest canopy, sending flurries of leaves swirling in their wake, each rustle and crunch whispering tales of distant lands and forgotten paths.

After several more hours of steady travel, Cristole, who was still at the lead, called back to the others, his voice carrying on the wind. "We're not far from the traveler's camp now."

In the late afternoon, as the sun dipped toward the horizon, they finally arrived at the traveler's camp. A simple wooden palisade surrounded the encampment, offering a semblance of safety and structure amid the vast wilderness. But as they entered through the open gate, it became immediately apparent that something was wrong.

Several wagons, their bodies empty and stripped, lay abandoned within the camp. Tents, once a temporary refuge for travelers, stood untouched, their canvas flaps eerily swaying in the evening breeze. The communal fire pit, which Sloane imagined would be normally bustling with laughter and tales, sat cold and dark, its charred wood the only testament to the life that once thrived here.

A shiver ran down Sloane's spine as she took in the eerie silence that now hung over the encampment. It was all too apparent that the slavers had found this camp.

Gisele dismounted. "Everyone," she whispered, her voice barely rising above the evening breeze. "Start looking for clues. They can't have gone far."

Nods met her words and the knights fanned out, their faces set in grim determination. Gisele and Deryk headed for the wagons, their experienced eyes scanning for any sign of the perpetrators or their direction of travel. Cristole and Ernald began a methodical search of the surrounding area, their keen senses attuned to any abnormalities in the landscape.

Ismeld stayed with the wagon, keeping watch, while Maud walked throughout the camp. Left alone, Sloane walked slowly among the tents, her heart heavy at the sight of the deserted camp. The grass beneath her feet was trampled, signifying the hustle and bustle of a previously lively camp, now disturbingly silent. Each tent she passed was a stark reminder of the tragedy that had unfolded here.

With her heart pounding in her chest, Sloane carefully pulled aside the entrance flap of a nearby tent. A gust of cool wind rustled the canvas walls as she stepped inside. The interior was in disarray, possessions scattered in what appeared to be a hurried exit. Among the personal items, a little doll with beaded eyes and a stitched smile lay face-down, a chilling symbol of the innocence lost here.

Sloane paused, her gaze falling on something half-hidden under the rough cot. It was not just any jacket, but a denim one. She reached out, hesitated for a second, and then pulled it free. As the fabric unfolded, she recognized the brand immediately. It was from back home, from Earth.

A human had been here.

Her breath hitched as a wave of panic swept over her. She dropped the doll, the small toy forgotten as she held up the jacket, scrutinizing every inch. Each thread was a stark reminder of the terror she and the others had been pulled from, a terror that was now potentially a reality for others.

She rummaged through the rest of the items in the tent, throwing aside bags and shifting the cot. Maud appeared at the entrance of the tent, her brow furrowed with concern.

"Sloane? What's wrong?" she asked, stepping inside to lend assistance.

But Sloane couldn't find the words to respond, her mind still grappling with the implications of her discovery. As she picked through a pile of clothes, something caught her eye. A piece of fabric, a shirt perhaps. And on it… a hair. Long, curly, and dark brown.

Her heart seized. It was eerily similar to Gwyn's hair. With trembling hands, she picked it up, holding it up against the fading light. She turned to Maud, her voice barely a whisper. "Maud, this… this was Gwyn's, I'm sure of it." Her words hung in the air, heavy with worry and fear.

A sudden yell from outside broke the stifling silence in the tent, causing both women to startle. "We've found something!" The voice unmistakably belonged to Cristole. Maud glanced at Sloane, her eyes mirroring the concern in her friend's.

Sloane tightened her grasp on the strand of hair in her hand as Maud helped her to her feet. Her legs felt wobbly and her mind buzzed with unanswered questions. Together, they moved toward the source of Cristole's shout, the reality of their situation bearing down on them with every step.

The knights had congregated on the edge of the camp, their horses restless with the tension in the air. Cristole was holding a torn satchel. He traced over its ragged edges, a grim expression on his face as he crouched down and turned it over, spilling out its contents to show the others.

Gisele and Ismeld knelt in front of the small pile beside him, their heads bowed over the satchel as they inspected the objects from within. Their faces were grim, hardened with a determination Sloane knew mirrored her own.

Ismeld sifted through the pile, pausing as she found a small cylindrical container. Pulling it free, she carefully pried it open, revealing a tightly rolled parchment inside. Delicately unfurling the scroll, she studied its contents, her lips moving as if murmuring the words to herself. The silence that hung over them was palpable, interrupted only by the occasional rustling of the scroll in Ismeld's hands.

After a moment, Ismeld looked up, her gaze meeting Gisele's. Silently, she passed the scroll to the orkun woman. Gisele scanned the text, her brows furrowed, lips pressed into a thin line. With a final nod of acknowledgment, she rolled the scroll back up and gripped it tightly in her fist. The two women stood.

"The scroll mentions a gathering point. A place where they plan to sell their... merchandise to a prospective buyer. If we go quickly, we'll be able to reach there in time."

Gisele's words hung heavily in the air as the gravity of the situation sank in. Silence echoed throughout the camp, broken only by the soft rustle of wind sweeping through the abandoned tents and wagons. But it was a silence filled with determination and a newfound resolve. They had a lead now, a tangible thread to follow in this vast, complicated maze.

Sloane's hand clenched tighter. *We may find her.*

"What about the wagon?" Ismeld asked. It was a conspicuous vehicle, not easily hidden, and would certainly slow them down in their pursuit.

Gisele nodded and walked over to it. She disappeared inside momentarily, then emerged with a weathered map clutched in her hand. She beckoned the others to gather around as she spread the map out on a nearby flat surface.

"Here," she said, pointing out a spot on the parchment, her tone definitive. "There's a hamlet about five kilometers away in the demesne of a local lord. We'll leave the wagon there. Pay a family to keep it safe."

Her gaze moved over the faces of her companions, meeting each set of eyes, ensuring her plan was understood. "From there, we ride," she concluded, the grim set of her jaw conveying her seriousness. "We have to move swiftly if we want to catch them. Time is of the essence."

* * *

They traveled swiftly, the wagon bumping over the road, the sun dipping behind the distant hills, casting long, ominous shadows across the landscape. By the time they arrived, the hamlet was shrouded in the dim twilight, with only the faintest glow of fires visible from inside the humble dwellings.

They walked down the single main road of the hamlet, passing weather-beaten and worn exteriors. Several people emerged at the sound of their arrival, one of them an old orkun woman with a wary look in her eyes that softened upon seeing Gisele. They conversed briefly, Gisele's tone firm yet respectful. After a few moments, the woman nodded and extended a gnarled hand, accepting the coins Gisele offered. A call from the woman brought out another orkun, a younger man, and the promise of safeguarding their wagon was secured.

With the wagon entrusted to the woman and her son, the knights focused on preparing the two wagon horses for the next leg of their journey. Saddles were fastened, reins adjusted, and stirrups checked for security. The knights worked efficiently, their movements precise and practiced, an undeniable air of urgency in their every action.

A wave of uncertainty washed over Sloane as she watched the knights saddle their horses. She was unaccustomed to riding, and the prospect of joining one of them on horseback was daunting.

As if sensing her apprehension, Gisele approached, a sigh escaping her lips. She extended a hand to Sloane, offering her a reassuring smile. "You're with me," she declared, her voice firm yet gentle.

With Gisele's help, Sloane managed to climb onto the horse. She settled in behind the orkun woman, clinging tightly to her, her knuckles white, her heart pounding as they set off.

The hamlet receded into the distance, its humble lights growing fainter with every stride of their horses. The cool wind whipped past them, a stark contrast to the warmth emanating from Gisele in front of her. Sloane took a deep breath, steeling herself for the task ahead. She closed her eyes momentarily, allowing the rhythmic movement of the horse beneath her to soothe her nerves.

Under the silver veil of the twin moons, the party pressed onward, riding through the rugged wilderness. The cool night breeze tousled their hair and cloaks as they wove through the wild landscape, avoiding craggy rocks and dense patches of undergrowth. Their horses moved swiftly, hooves thudding rhythmically against the earthen ground, yet they maintained a cautious quietness, ensuring their approach went unnoticed.

They navigated around gullies and brooks, always vigilant, searching for any sign of the suspected slavers. The deeper they ventured, the more isolated they became, until all that surrounded them was the untamed wilderness, punctuated only by the distant hooting of an owl or the rustle of nocturnal creatures.

Gradually, the faint flickering of firelight in the distance signaled their nearing destination. Nestled in a wooded area, the campfires gave away the presence of people. Gisele, her face set sternly, gestured for them to halt. Wordlessly, the knights split into two groups, spreading out to cover more ground. Gisele, Ismeld, and Deryk steered their horses toward the northern edge of the wooded area, while the others headed in the opposite direction.

Dismounting, they carefully tethered the animals to sturdy trees, ensuring they were well-hidden from the encampment.

"Sloane, stay close to me. Move quietly," Gisele whispered to her before gesturing to the others.

Sloane nodded and watched as the knights slowly drew their weapons and started forward, each with a slight hunch to their posture. Sloane quietly drew her sword, heart racing, and followed.

They moved in hushed silence, their footfalls muffled by the layer of moist fallen leaves and pine needles underfoot. As they closed in on the camp, the sounds of their surroundings began to shift. The night's natural orchestra was replaced by the low murmur of human voices, occasional harsh laughter, and the distinct clinking of metal. They tread cautiously, using the cover of the undergrowth to their advantage.

The sight that met their eyes as they reached the edge of the camp was harrowing. A significant number of wagons were scattered about, including two that were equipped with cages. Huddled figures of various races were chained together, their faces worn with despair as they were fed a pathetic excuse for a meal.

Slavers moved about the camp, their banter and laughter a stark contrast to the misery they inflicted. One man, in particular, stood out, his cruelty displayed as he kicked a reluctant captive who refused to eat. Sloane's heart clenched at the sight, her breath hitching in her throat. She scanned the captives. There were no terrans; Gwyn was not among the chained.

Despite the absence of her daughter, Sloane couldn't help but feel a profound sadness and anger at the scene unfolding before her eyes. These individuals were victims, their lives reduced to chains and cruelty. As she stood there, tucked away in the shadows with the knights, she made a silent promise to herself—she would do everything in her power to help these people, to bring the slavers to justice.

Mana rushed through her uncalled, and she felt herself want to destroy everything she saw in front of her.

Gisele turned to Sloane, her eyes glinting in the low light of the distant campfires. "Can you create a diversion with your magic?" she whispered, the edges of her words barely carrying to Sloane's ears.

Sloane blinked, taken aback by the suggestion. "What do you mean?" she asked, her eyebrows furrowing.

Gisele paused, her gaze never leaving Sloane's. An odd grin, akin to a wolf closing in on its prey, slowly spread across her face. "I believe you know what to do," she said, her tone full of confidence. She jerked her head slightly.

Sloane followed her gesture. Her eyes widened as she saw the wagons. A grin of her own formed as she turned back to Gisele and nodded.

At Gisele's signal, Ismeld joined Sloane, while Deryk followed the seasoned warrior. Under the cover of darkness, Sloane and Ismeld maneuvered around the camp, their steps quiet, their bodies lowered in a stealthy crouch.

They moved behind the wagons, away from the prying eyes of the slavers. Silently, Ismeld pointed out a group of slavers through a narrow gap between a pair of wagons, and Sloane nodded.

"Are you ready?" she asked, her voice low and steady.

Ismeld narrowed her eyes, her jaw setting in determination as she lifted her sword slightly. "I'm always ready," she affirmed, her voice unwavering.

With a deep breath, Sloane reached within herself, tapping into the core that connected with the mana around them. As the increasingly familiar surge of energy flooded her veins, she focused her intent, shaping the mana into the form of three [**Mana Bolts**].

They pulsed with an arcane energy so vivid, it bathed her in an ethereal purple glow. This magical spectacle was a testament to her control and affinity with the arcane arts.

Hovering above Sloane's outstretched palms, two orbs pulsated in rhythm with her heartbeat, growing in intensity. As she concentrated, they began to crackle with more vigor, sparks of arcane energy dancing around them like celestial bodies around a sun. The subtle hum they emitted filled the quiet space between Sloane and Ismeld, a quiet symphony of power on display.

Then, in a swift and deliberate motion, Sloane brought her hands together, concentrating the crackling energy. Her brow furrowed as she guided the orbs to settle into formation between her hands.

And with a powerful thrust of her hands forward, she unleashed the three [**Mana Bolts**]. Like arrows loosed from a bow, the bolts hurtled through the air, a trio of incandescent missiles that streaked the darkness with their magical glow toward one of the wagons.

The air seemed to ripple around the [**Mana Bolts**] as they sped toward their target. Upon impact, the wagon's walls burst into a dazzling display of arcane energy, the silent night disrupted by the crackling and popping of the unleashed magic. The wagon shuddered under the force of the spell, splinters of wood flying in all directions as the small explosions reverberated through the camp.

The slavers' chatter and laughter were instantly replaced with shouts of surprise and fear, their attention drawn to the sudden and unexplainable phenomenon.

"I meant to hit the slavers! Come on!" the blond knight snapped at her.

Ismeld sprang into action, and with only a moment's hesitation, Sloane followed suit, her blade gripped firmly in her hand. As they maneuvered around the wagons, a scene of chaos unfolded before her.

With a swift and powerful motion, Cristole brought his sword crashing down on an unsuspecting slaver who had his back to the elf knight. Then with a war cry, he ripped his sword back and moved on to the next man, Maud and Ernald yelling their fury alongside him.

A blood-curdling scream on her left tore Sloane's attention away from the scene before her. Ismeld was charging toward two men, her movements as fluid as they were lethal. Sloane turned just in time to see a grim spectacle unfold.

Gisele, her face a mask of cold determination, had impaled a slaver on her gargantuan sword. The man was hoisted off the ground, his body convulsing around the blade that ran through his gut.

Then, in an almost dismissive motion, the imposing orkun woman jerked her blade free, sending the man crumpling to the ground in a lifeless heap. She strode forward, her large figure unyielding and resolute, seemingly unfazed by the gruesome act she had just performed.

Sloane turned, ready to help Ismeld, only to see the two men already on the ground. Overwhelmed and out of her depth, Sloane looked on, a chill of terror and awe creeping up her spine. The knights around her moved with deadly precision and sheer determination, their fury unfurling amid the tumultuous scene. They were forces of nature unleashed, their warrior spirits on full display, a stark contrast to Sloane's hesitation and uncertainty. As they waded through the slavers, a horrifying realization settled within Sloane: she was a spectator in a world she hardly understood, a player struggling to catch up.

And she had to catch up.

Gwyn's safety counted on it.

CHAPTER THIRTY-FOUR

A DOSE OF REALITY

As the echoes of battle faded into the night, the knights pushed forward, their forms moving methodically through the smoldering aftermath of the fight. The scent of blood and burnt wood permeated the air, a grim testament to the events of the evening.

Around the party, the slavers lay strewn about in various states of demise. Some bore the fatal wounds from a knight's blade, while others groaned and writhed from debilitating injuries. The once lively camp had been reduced to a gruesome tableau of carnage and destruction.

While the rest of the knights attended to their immediate surroundings, Cristole and Maud approached the huddled groups of slaves. Sloane observed with an attentive gaze how these beleaguered individuals, previously resigned to their tragic fate, looked upon their saviors with wide, fearful eyes. Sloane wasn't sure she could blame them.

Cristole knelt, speaking quietly, his hands gentle yet firm as he began to remove the chains that bound them. Maud, her face soft with concern, moved from one person to another, her fingers glowing with a soothing green aura of mana as she worked her healing magic.

Among the captured, whispers began to circulate, their voices filled with awe and disbelief. Words of prayer and gratitude hung in the air, their utterances transforming the grim aftermath into a scene of hope and reverence.

After a few moments of observing Cristole and Maud work, Sloane approached the healer. "May I speak to them?" she asked, her voice low.

Maud looked up from the man she was treating, her face lined with weariness, and nodded. "Be gentle, Sloane," she cautioned. "They've been through a lot."

Sloane nodded in understanding and stepped forward to address the group. Their eyes, a mix of fear and nascent hope, met hers as she stood before them. Their bodies bore the weight of their ordeal, exhaustion apparent in their slumped postures. The palpable aura of despair that clung to them was overwhelming.

Gathering her resolve, Sloane drew a deep breath. "Has anyone seen a young girl?" she began, her voice wavering slightly under the weight of her question. "She is ten years old but tall for her age, about one hundred and fifty centimeters with curly dark brown hair—it should have pink tips. She has blue eyes and she is kind."

The small crowd before her stirred, glances exchanged, hushed whispers filling the air. Cristole continued his work, gently freeing the captives from their chains. A man, rubbing his newly freed wrists, spoke up. "She may have been with the others," he said, his voice gravelly with fatigue.

A woman, her face drawn and pale, nodded. "There were more of us," she said, her eyes downcast as if she felt guilty about what she said.

Sloane offered them a small, grateful smile. "Thank you," she said, her voice shaking slightly with emotion. "A knight with the Westari Crown Knights promised that he was on his way to get more help for all of you. You'll see them soon." Her words seemed to breathe new life into the group—Sloane could see a flicker of hope ignite in their eyes.

Turning away, she caught sight of Deryk and Ernald sifting through the slavers' belongings. Near the fire, Gisele was engaged in a terse exchange with a captured man.

Sloane placed a hand on Maud's shoulder, offering her a reassuring smile. "Call if you need any help," she told the healer, her tone sincere.

Maud nodded, her eyes crinkling with a brief smile. "I will," she assured Sloane. She turned to rejoin Cristole, then paused, looking back over her shoulder at Sloane. "We'll find her," she said, her voice full of conviction. In that moment, Sloane found herself wanting to believe Maud's words.

Slowly, Sloane made her way over to Gisele, who was with an injured moon elf. Ismeld stood nearby imperiously. The slaver was lying on his back, his face stained with blood and his eyes flickering with a mix of fear and malice as he scowled up at them.

Gisele towered over the fallen elf. Her hands were planted firmly on her hips, her face a stern mask of authority as she bore down on him. "Where are the others?" she demanded.

When he didn't respond, the orkun knight pressed her boot against his hand, eliciting a sharp scream of pain. Despite the agony, his lips curled into a spiteful sneer. "They're gone, and good riddance," he hissed, sweat beading on his forehead. "That girl wasn't even a real princess anyways."

A princess?

Sloane's breath hitched in her chest and her heart began to beat faster. "What girl?" she demanded, her voice laced with worry.

"Nothing more than a liar," he spat, his eyes sparkling with cruel satisfaction. "Just a girl who tricked some knights and a merchant into believing she was something she's not."

Could it be? Sloane's mind raced. *That sounds like something she'd do.*

"Where is she?" Sloane's voice was steely, but she couldn't keep the panic from creeping into her words. "Where did you take her?"

His sneer widened at her desperation. "We got the jump on them knights good." He looked at Gisele and smirked. "It's why women shouldn't be knights."

Gisele leaned closer. "And yet your people are dead, and I'm the one standing here," she said with a tone that made the man's eyes widen slightly. "Now, answer her. Where is the girl? Tell her now, and I will take you to the Westari Knights alive."

"It's too late, she's gone," he gloated, his eyes drifting closed.

Blind rage filled Sloane as she lashed out, her fists slamming into the man's face three times in rapid succession. "Tell me where you sent her!" she growled, her voice raw with fury.

Gisele pulled her back.

His laugh was wet, blood bubbling at the corners of his mouth. "Some lord bought her. Princess or not..." he managed to choke out between laughs, the pleasure of her anguish evident in his voice. "Said she'd make a good servant."

Sloane froze, her breath hitching as the implications of his words sank in. Her pulse hammered in her ears, a wild crescendo of fear and rage as mana surged through her. Before she knew it, a **[Mana Bolt]** was hovering over her hand.

Suddenly, Gisele was there, gripping Sloane's shoulder with a firm hand. The orkun knight's eyes were hard, a storm of emotions brewing behind the steely facade. She met Sloane's gaze with a nod, a silent pledge. They would find her. They would bring her home. "Enough, Sloane," she said, her voice calm yet firm. "We have what we need."

With that, Gisele rose, leaving the moon elf slaver groaning on the ground, his laughter reduced to a pained wheeze.

Ernald's voice echoed in the camp, effectively drawing everyone's attention. "Come over here," he called out, waving a weathered notebook in his hand. "I've found the slavers' ledger."

Gathered around, the group listened intently as Ernald detailed his find. "It mentions a Lord Marweth, who purchased a group of slaves yesterday," he said, tracing the scribbled lines of text with a grimace.

"Where is this Lord Marweth?" Sloane asked, her tone eager and hopeful.

Ernald shook his head, disappointment etched on his face. "It doesn't say," he admitted, his gaze lingering on the ledger's pages as if willing them to reveal more information. "Just says the amount that the man purchased them for."

"We'll figure it out," Ismeld said. "There are likely other leads here."

Gisele turned to Deryk and Ernald. "Bring the horses," she ordered, her tone leaving no room for debate. "We'll need to move quickly once we find out where we're going."

She beckoned Cristole to join her, and together they approached the freed slaves, their postures a mix of stern resolve and weary compassion.

"There's a traveler's camp along the main road, south of here," Gisele said to the former captives. "Can anyone here take charge of this group? You'll need to take one or two of these wagons and make your way there."

A ripple of uncertainty swept through the people as they exchanged nervous glances and murmured about the knight's instructions.

Suddenly, a woman's voice sliced through the low hum of murmurs. "You're just going to leave us?" she challenged, her voice trembling with a mix of fear and disbelief.

Gisele met her gaze, her expression stern. "Yes. There are others who were taken. We need to free them too. The slavers are dead, so you should be safe. Take any weapons you need and head to the camp. Ser Redding and others of the Royal Knights will meet you there."

The group was silent for a moment. Then, a man gently pushed his way through to the front of the group. He was a raithe, sturdy and strong, with the appearance of a farmer, in Sloane's mind.

"I will lead them," he announced, meeting Gisele's gaze evenly. "I'll make sure we get there safely. We owe you our lives and hope to repay you someday."

Gisele shook her head, a soft smile curving her lips. "Repay it by living a fulfilling life full of happiness," she said. She clapped the man's shoulder in a firm, supportive gesture, then turned to rejoin the others, leaving the newly freed slaves to their path.

A sudden commotion at the edge of the campfire made everyone turn. A woman, one of the freed slaves, was lunging at the leader of the slavers with a large knife, stabbing him over and over in a frenzy. The already injured man let out a strangled gasp and went limp.

"Looks like he won't be going back," Gisele said with a dismissive shrug.

Maud was quick to react, rushing forward and pulling the girl back. The weapon dropped from her hands and she collapsed into the knight's arms, her body wracked with sobs.

As quiet filled the camp, Sloane turned to the slaves. "Does anyone know who Lord Marweth is?"

For a few seconds, silence met her query. Then, a young man stepped forward. "Yeah, I know him," he said. "His castle is nearby."

Sloane turned to share a look with Gisele, her heart pounding in her chest. Marweth, it seemed, was the lord of the very same hamlet where they had left the wagon.

We're coming, Gwyn.

The hamlet was quiet as they returned, the moonlight casting long shadows over the dirt streets. The wagon, left in the care of the orkun woman, was just as they had left it. Her son stood with her, clearly angry at being woken up at the late hour.

Sloane followed as Gisele and Deryk approached the pair, their faces set in stern lines. "Do you know anything about Lord Marweth?" Gisele asked, her voice echoing in the still night air.

The boy glanced at his mother, his eyes wide with fear. "He's a good lord," he stammered, clearly taken aback by their question. "He does everything he can to help us."

His mother scoffed, a bitter sound that cut through the silence. "Stop lying, boy," she spat, her eyes flashing with anger. "He's a horrible man, always holed up in that castle of his. I wish the Crown would come and put him in his place."

Gisele nodded, her gaze thoughtful. "Do you know anything about the castle?" she asked, her tone steady.

The woman glanced at Sloane before shaking her head, her lips pressed into a thin line. "No, only that it's near the main village of Lindale."

"Thank you," Gisele said, her tone softening as she passed a few coins to the woman. She turned back to Deryk and Sloane. "We need to move."

Sloane hopped onto the wagon with Maud, who deftly guided the horses as they began their journey toward Lindale. The rest of the group followed on horseback. The hamlet disappeared behind them into the night.

As they traveled, Sloane's mind wandered back to the events at the slaver camp. The sight of the freed slaves, their faces etched with relief and gratitude, was a stark contrast to the grim scene of the slavers' demise. Before her party had left, they had ensured that the former captives were equipped with whatever they needed from the slavers' stock—food, supplies, and even what remained of their weapons.

They'd locked up the remaining three slavers in one of the caged wagons and gave the key to the raithe man who had stepped forward to lead the group. Determined, he had promised that the slavers would be delivered to the knights under Redding's command to face the justice they deserved.

The thought of the slavers facing justice brought grim satisfaction to Sloane. She hoped that their capture would lead the Westari knights to uncover more of their operations, potentially saving countless others from a similar fate.

The journey to Lindale was quiet, the only sounds the rhythmic clopping of the horses' hooves and grinding of the wagon wheels on the road. The village itself was nestled in the shadow of a looming castle. While small, it was a stone fortress nonetheless, its stone walls bathed in the soft glow of the twin moons.

Just inside the village stood a small, unassuming inn. Its windows were dark, save for a single flickering light on the upper floor. Sloane hopped down from the wagon and caught up to Gisele as she was walking inside. The door creaked open as they entered, revealing a tired-looking innkeeper.

"We need rooms for the night," Gisele said, her voice echoing in the quiet inn.

The innkeeper nodded, his eyes flicking over the two of them. "We have a few rooms available," he said, his voice gruff. "How many of you are there? It's late, but I can get you some food if you're hungry."

Gisele shook her head. "We do not need any food. But there are seven of us. We'll take whatever rooms we can get," she said, her voice firm. "And a place for our wagon."

The innkeeper nodded. "I can arrange that," he said. "It's five silvers per room, and another five for the wagon."

Gisele reached into her pouch and pulled out the required coins, plus a few extra. She handed them over to the innkeeper, her eyes never leaving his. "We'll need some information as well," she added.

The innkeeper raised an eyebrow, pocketing the coins before leaning back against the counter. "What kind of information?" he asked, his eyes wary.

"We're looking for Lord Marweth," Gisele said, her voice low. "We have some business with him."

"Lord Marweth?" the innkeeper echoed, his voice filled with surprise. "He rarely leaves his castle. You'd be better off sending a message."

Gisele shook her head. "We need to see him in person," she said, her tone leaving no room for argument. "How often does he receive visitors? This is the baroness Lady Reinhart, and the rest of us are knights."

The innkeeper sighed, rubbing his forehead. "I really don't want any trouble, ser," he said, his voice resigned. "And I do not want to get in between any spat between noble types. All I know is that Lord Marweth isn't known for his hospitality. So I wouldn't get your hopes up, uhh… milady," he added with an awkward bow toward Sloane.

She waved him off, forcing herself to remain calm. They had come this far, and they wouldn't be deterred now.

"Thank you for your help," Gisele said, her voice softening slightly. She turned to leave, but paused at the door, looking back at the innkeeper. "And if anyone asks, we were never here."

The innkeeper nodded. "Understood," he said quietly, his eyes wide at the unspoken threat.

With the arrangements made, the group moved to the stables behind the inn. The horses were tired, their breaths coming out in heavy puffs in the cool night air. They were led into the stables, their reins untied and saddles removed. The wagon was parked in a corner, its contents secured and covered.

Deryk and Ismeld volunteered to scout out the castle, their faces set in determined lines. Gisele gave them an appreciative look. "Be careful," she warned, her voice low but firm. "We don't know what we're dealing with."

The two knights nodded, their expressions serious. They left the stables, their forms disappearing into the night. Sloane watched them go, her heart heavy with anticipation.

Gisele turned to the rest of the group. "We should get some rest," she said, her voice echoing slightly in the quiet stables. "We'll take shifts. Everyone should sleep in their armor."

After ensuring the horses and wagon were settled, they returned to the inn. The innkeeper had left the keys to their rooms on the counter, and they each picked one up, decided watch shifts, and headed upstairs. The rooms were small but clean, each furnished with a pair of simple beds and a small table.

Sloane found herself sharing a room with Gisele, as she often did, and when they entered, the orkun woman moved to the window, her gaze drawn to the looming silhouette of the castle in the distance. Sloane watched her for a moment and sat on the edge of her bed, her mind still racing with thoughts of the task ahead.

"Are you worried about Ismeld and Deryk?" she asked.

Gisele shook her head, and after a moment of silence, she turned to her, her gaze serious. "I am not. They know what they're doing," she said. "However... Sloane, tomorrow, we will need you to be a baroness."

Sloane blinked, taken aback by her words. "What do you mean?"

"We don't know what we're walking into. We need every advantage we can get. Your title could open doors for us, give us the leverage we need."

Is it even a real title? But... that doesn't matter. Ah... Sloane nodded, understanding dawning on her. "I see. The lord is more likely to welcome a visiting baroness," she said, her voice steady. "That makes sense. Okay, I'll do my best."

Gisele nodded, a small smile curving her lips. "I know you will," she said. She moved to her own bed, settling down with a sigh. "Get some sleep, Sloane. We have a long day ahead."

With that, the room fell into silence, the only sound the distant hoot of an owl and the soft rustle of the wind against the window.

As Sloane lay down, her mind filled with thoughts of the day ahead, and she knew that it would be dangerous, but she was ready to face it.

They were closer to finding Gwyn.

The first rays of dawn were just beginning to filter through the window when Sloane awoke. She sat up, rubbing the remnants of sleep from her eyes, her heart heavy with the weight of the day ahead. Today, she might find her daughter, who had possibly been sold into slavery to a lord.

The thought sent a shiver down her spine, but she steeled herself, determined to face whatever lay ahead.

Gisele was already awake, her figure silhouetted against the window as she gazed out at the distant castle on the hill. Her armor was perfectly in place, her posture rigid and alert. She turned to Sloane, her voice steady but laced with an undercurrent of tension. "Are you ready?" she asked.

Sloane raised an eyebrow, but before she could respond, Gisele let out a small huff of amusement. "You toss and turn just before you wake up," she explained.

"Oh…" Sloane replied, pushing herself to her feet. "Just need to pee first," she added quickly, earning a chuckle from Gisele.

"Take your time," Gisele said, her tone light. "I'll gather the others."

Sloane nodded, strapping her sword to her waist before following Gisele out of the room. After a quick stop to relieve herself, she descended the stairs to find the rest of the group already assembled in the inn's common room, ready for battle. The sight bolstered her confidence.

They left the inn, their steps echoing in the quiet morning. The village was still asleep, the streets empty. Somewhere in the distance a rooster crowed. Sloane walked confidently as she and the knights made their way toward the castle, their gazes focused on the looming structure.

As they approached, the drawbridge was lowered, its heavy chains breaking the silence. Two men-at-arms stood at the entrance, their spears held at the ready. They eyed the group warily, hands tightening on their weapons.

"Halt!" one of them called out, his voice echoing off the stone walls. "State your business."

Gisele stepped forward, her posture straight and her gaze unwavering. "I am Ser Gisele Devereux, and this is Baroness Reinhart of Blightwych," she announced, her voice resonating in the quiet morning air. "We request an audience with Lord Marweth."

The guards looked at each other, their expressions uncertain, but after a moment, one of them nodded and rushed off, his footsteps echoing. The remaining guard kept his spear at the ready, his gaze never leaving their group.

Minutes passed in tense silence, the group remaining stoic and at the ready. Then, the sound of footsteps, growing louder as they approached. A raithe man in plate armor appeared, the other guard behind him.

"What is your business here?" the raithe asked, his voice stern.

"We are traveling through," Gisele said. "But it is only proper for the baroness to greet the lord of the land as she passes. Lady Reinhart seeks an audience with Lord Marweth."

The man narrowed his eyes, studying them for a moment. Then, he nodded, his expression softening slightly. "Very well," he said, stepping aside. "I will escort you to the audience chamber. Lord Marweth will see you there."

The knight turned and led the way into the castle. As they neared a set of imposing double doors, which the knight indicated was their destination, a sense of anticipation bubbled within Sloane.

Time to play the part.

The audience chamber was a spectacle of grandeur. High ceilings, adorned with intricate carvings, towered above them. Rich tapestries that told tales of old lined the walls. At the far end of the room sat Lord Marweth in a high-backed chair, his imposing figure adding to the room's majesty. He was a tall man, his stark white hair contrasting sharply against his dark gray skin. His piercing blue eyes observed their entrance, his face a mask betraying no emotion.

Beside him stood another knight, and as the group reached the center of the room, the one who had guided them moved to stand on the opposite side.

"Lady Reinhart," Lord Marweth said, his voice echoing in the chamber. "Welcome to Lindale. You've traveled far from Blightwych."

Sloane took a quick breath, recalling her etiquette lessons, and straightened. She took a step ahead of the group. "Indeed, Lord Marweth," she replied, her voice steady. "It has been a long journey, filled with many dangers. In fact..." She gestured to Gisele.

"My Lord, if I may," Gisele said, "just last night, we ran across a camp of slavers within your demesne. You'll be pleased to know that they have been handled."

Lord Marweth's face remained impassive, his gaze flickering between Gisele and Sloane. "I am appalled that such fiends were found on my land," he said, his voice controlled. "But I am pleased that you were able to handle them. I am grateful for your assistance to my fief. I will have my people investigate this matter immediately. We cannot allow such atrocities to occur within our borders."

Silence filled out the grand chamber in response to his words, and Sloane found herself locked in a stare with Lord Marweth. Finally, tilting her head inquisitively, her gaze unwavering, she asked, "Tell me, Lord Marweth, where is the girl you purchased from them?"

CHAPTER THIRTY-FIVE

IN DEFENSE OF HOPE

Excuse me?" Lord Marweth ground out as he slowly stood.

On either side of him, his knights' hands went to their hilts. Guards around the room shifted uneasily. Gisele and the others subtly adjusted their positions, ready for any sudden movements. Gisele turned slightly to scowl at Sloane.

Too late now.

"I do believe you heard me," Sloane said. "We already have proof that you did business with them. Where is the girl?"

She [**Focused**] as she watched him, mana flowing into her as her senses dialed up to maximum. Sloane was ready to use her magic at a moment's notice—they needed to get Gwyn.

Lord Marweth's eyes darted to his left, and if it hadn't been for her magically improved senses, she would have missed it. Out of the corner of her eye, she noticed a heavy-looking door peeking out from behind a pillar.

Lord Marweth scowled at her, his gaze filled with defiance. But Sloane was undeterred. They were here for one reason, and she would not leave without Gwyn.

"How dare you enter my home and accuse me of such a heinous act!" Lord Marweth's voice echoed through the chamber, his face contorted in anger. His gaze flicked to his guards, who took a collective step forward, their hands tightening on their spears.

"Door, to the back right," Sloane whispered to Gisele, still watching Marweth.

Gisele gave a subtle nod of understanding before addressing him. "This will not go the way you think it will, Lord Marweth," she said, her voice steady and calm. "We can come to an agreement, but you will release those you took, and we will leave with them."

"You are in the middle of my castle, surrounded by my guards, and you have the audacity to make demands of me?" Lord Marweth replied, his tone incredulous.

Gisele simply nodded. "I do."

A surge of anger rose in Sloane. "Where is she?" she demanded, her voice echoing in the grand chamber.

Lord Marweth raised a hand, and his two knights drew their blades. The sound of steel scraping against scabbards filled the room, and in response, the knights accompanying Sloane pulled out their weapons. Sloane slowly drew her own weapon and shifted it to her left hand as she drew more mana into herself.

"I rescind the right of hospitality, Lady Reinhart," Lord Marweth declared, his voice cold and unyielding. "You either leave my demesne now, or you will be imprisoned for committing acts against a lord of Westaren."

The room fell silent, the tension palpable. Sloane's heart pounded in her chest. She tightened her grip on her sword and glanced at Gisele, who gave her another subtle nod. They were ready for whatever came next.

"Lord Marweth," Sloane said, maintaining the facade of calm. "This need not come to force. Give me the girl, and we will be on our way."

Marweth's gaze hardened, his hands clenched into fists. "I have no knowledge of this child," he retorted, his voice filled with defiance.

"We have evidence that suggests otherwise. We ask you one last time: Where is the girl?"

The room was silent, the tension thick in the air as the guards hefted their spears and shields, their eyes darting between their lord and the group of knights with Sloane.

With a sigh, Lord Marweth gestured to his knights. "Take them," he ordered.

Gisele reacted instantly, her hands moving in a swift motion as she cast her magic. A two-and-a-half-meter-wide shield of red mana materialized between them and Marweth's knights. The knights and the lord let out sounds of surprise as the shield blocked their path.

"Let's go!" Gisele commanded, her voice ringing out in the chamber. The group sprang into action, moving swiftly toward the door Sloane had indicated earlier.

Guards rushed forward to intercept them, but they were met with a force they hadn't anticipated.

Ismeld was the first to engage, her movements were swift and precise, her longsword and shield working in perfect harmony. With a swift parry of her shield, she deflected a guard's attack before her sword found its mark, cutting him down. Another guard rushed at her, but she sidestepped his attack, her sword slicing through the air and landing a fatal blow.

Deryk was right behind her. His longsword and shield were a blur as he moved, his strength and agility surprising for someone of his size. He met the guards head-on, his shield absorbing their blows while his sword cut them down. Within moments, another two guards lay on the ground, their lives extinguished.

Strangely, Maud chose to keep her shield secured on her back. The red-head skillfully wielded her mace, keeping the guards at bay with wide, sweeping strikes. When one guard attempted to block her attack with his shield, she deftly maneuvered around his raised defense. With a swift, powerful punch, she struck him in the face, momentarily stunning him. Seizing the opportunity, she wrenched the shield from the man's forearm with a swift, decisive motion before using it to parry another guard's strike.

Sloane could have sworn the telv knight's entire demeanor changed after that—she looked filled with pride and glee.

As they continued forward, the knights moved with deadly efficiency, their training and experience evident in their actions as Maud, Cristole, and Ernald covered their rear while Gisele stayed close to Sloane. They cut through the guards like a hot knife through butter, their path forward becoming clearer with each fallen enemy.

They reached the door in seconds, and Gisele released her magic, casting another shield to block the pursuing knights. But the door was locked. The knights backed up, their weapons at the ready.

Gisele turned to Sloane. "Take it out," she ordered, her voice steady despite the chaos around them.

Sloane stepped forward, her hands glowing with the familiar warmth of her magic. She focused her energy, her mind clear despite the chaos around her. She extended her hand toward the door, her fingers curled as if holding an invisible sphere.

She formed a [**Mana Bolt**], the crackling arcane mana coalescing into an orb hovering in front of her hand, before she flexed her intent, releasing the first bolt of energy. It shot forward, striking the door with a loud bang. The door shuddered under the impact but held firm.

Undeterred, Sloane cast another bolt, then another. Each one struck the door with increasing force, the wood splintering and cracking under the onslaught. The guards behind them were momentarily forgotten, their attention focused on the door that was slowly giving way.

With a final, determined push, Sloane cast her fourth bolt. It flew forward, the energy crackling around it, and struck the battered door. The impact was deafening, the door bursting inward in a shower of splinters and dust.

Without wasting a moment, they rushed through the door, Gisele casting another shield behind them to block the entrance.

The knights moved swiftly through the narrow hall just inside the doorway, their weapons clashing against those of the guards who dared to stand in their way. They were barely slowed as they quickly passed through another doorway that opened into a larger hallway that wrapped around to the left. There, they found their path blocked by four more guards. Almost immediately, the knights rushed forward and the sounds of renewed battle echoed through the stone corridors, the shouts and clashing of steel filling the air.

Behind them, the shouts of men echoed, their weapons clashing against the red energy shield in a discordant chorus, a strange ethereal noise that reverberated through the air as the guards relentlessly pursued the knights.

Gisele, who had been maintaining her magical shield, suddenly yelled out a warning, "My shield! It's going to collapse soon!"

At her words, three of the knights immediately turned to cover the rear. Gisele called out another warning as the shield dissipated. With that, Sloane turned and shouted for the knights in the rear to get down. She swiftly drew in mana and cast three [**Mana Bolts**] in quick succession, launching them over Maud's and Cristole's heads toward the approaching men.

The bolts flew through the air, their energy crackling as they sped toward their targets. They struck the doorway, exploding on impact and sending a shockwave and crumbling stone down the halls. Shouts of surprise echoed back to them, the pursuing men momentarily halted by the sudden attack.

With the immediate threat gone, the group turned their attention back to the guards blocking their path. They engaged them swiftly, their weapons cutting through the air as they fought. In a matter of moments, the guards were dispatched, their bodies crumpling to the ground.

Ahead of them, a stairwell loomed, leading farther into the castle, and with a shared nod, the knights moved forward, their resolve and commitment unwavering.

As they approached the stairwell, Deryk suddenly veered off to the side, his eyes focused on a large statue of an unknown figure that stood in the hallway. With a grunt, he grabbed the statue and began to drag it toward the stairwell. The others quickly caught on and rushed to help, their combined strength enough to move the heavy statue. Sloane looked back down the hallway to see guards pouring into it after them, two in the front raising crossbows.

"Look out!" she yelled, and not a moment too soon, Maud raised her stolen shield and the two bolts pinged into it. She shoved Sloane into the stairwell.

"We need to go! Now!" she said as she backed through the doorway after Sloane.

With a final push, Deryk and Cristole managed to position the statue in the stairwell, effectively blocking the path. They shut the door and used the statue to bar it, creating a makeshift barricade just as the guards reached it and started slamming their weapons against the door. Sloane knew that it wouldn't hold forever, but hopefully it would buy them some time.

The path behind them secured, the knights charged up the stairs, Gisele and Deryk in the lead as their footsteps echoed in the narrow stairwell. They emerged in a hallway, scanning the area for any signs of danger, and then, seeing none, began to methodically check the rooms.

The first two rooms were empty, their interiors eerily silent. But as they entered the third room, they were met with a surprising sight—two telv women, dressed in simple servant's clothes, were huddled in a corner, their eyes wide with fear.

The knights paused, lowering their weapons slightly as they took in the sight. Maud stepped forward, her face filled with compassion. "We are knights," she said, her voice gentle yet firm. "Are you two here of your own volition? We are rescuing anyone who was taken against their will and forced into Lord Marweth's service. Do you need aid?"

The women quickly shook their heads. They remained silent, their gazes darting between the knights.

Sloane narrowed her eyes, stepping forward to address the women. "There was a young girl who was sold to Lord Marweth. Curly brown hair. Where is she?" she asked, keeping her voice steady despite the urgency she felt.

The women looked terrified, but after a moment, one of them stammered out a response. "The lady's chambers... she was last there. Down the hall, up another flight of stairs."

The other woman's eyes widened in shock, and she raised her hand to slap the one who had spoken, accusing her of betraying their lord. But Maud was quicker. She stepped forward and delivered a punch to the woman's face, knocking her out cold.

Turning back to the remaining woman, Maud asked once more if she wanted to leave. The woman again refused, and Sloane suspected that it was likely out of fear.

Maud nodded, her face filled with understanding. "I hope you stay safe," she said, her voice soft. "The Crown Knights will hopefully soon be arriving after we report what has happened here."

With a sense of urgency propelling them forward, they returned to the hall and sprinted in the direction the woman had indicated, their armor's rattling reverberating off the stone walls. As they neared the other stairwell, they were met with the sight of a group of guards charging down the stairs toward them, their faces set in grim determination.

The knights didn't hesitate.

With lightning-fast reflexes, Gisele and Ismeld shot forward and reached out, their hands closing around two of the guards' shields and weapons. Using their momentum against them, they gave a swift, powerful yank, sending the guards sprawling. The guards tumbled down the stairs, their bodies colliding with each other in a chaotic tumble of armor and limbs.

At the rear of the group, the remaining knights moved in, their movements swift and precise. Their weapons flashed in the dim light, cutting through the air with deadly accuracy. One by one, the guards were dispatched, their bodies falling still on the cold stone stairs.

Behind them, the sound of pounding footsteps echoed ominously, a clear indication that more guards were on their way. Sloane turned, her hands glowing with magic as she launched several **[Mana Bolts]** down the hallway. This time, however, there were no shouts of surprise but, instead, determined yells of "Cover!" echoed back at them.

A moment later, the guards charged out the stairwell with shields in front of them. Sloane raised her hand ready to cast, but Cristole pulled her back. Maud, Cristole, and Ernald stepped in front of her and raised their shields.

"We've got them. Go," Cristole said as he and the others set themselves up, three abreast.

Gisele grabbed Sloane and they rushed up the stairs, the sound of fighting and Maud's fierce war cry resounding up the stairwell as they ascended.

When they emerged on the next level, they were met with the sight of six guards standing in formation in front of a doorway in the center of the hall. Gisele, Ismeld, and Deryk didn't hesitate, immediately rushing forward to engage the guards. In response, the guards charged toward them, their faces set in grim determination.

Just as they were about to clash, Gisele called upon her magic. A shimmering barrier of red mana sprang up between the knights and the guards, effectively splitting the group. Four guards were stranded behind the barrier, their faces filled with surprise and frustration. The remaining two were left to face the knights alone.

Gisele and Ismeld made quick work of the two guards, their weapons cutting through the air with deadly precision. Once the guards were dispatched, Gisele let the magical barrier drop. Deryk immediately rushed forward, his large frame barreling through one of the men. Without even looking back, he grabbed another guard and slammed him against the wall, his strength easily overpowering the man.

Gisele engaged another guard, her large sword beating against his shield relentlessly. With each strike, the wooden shield cracked and splintered until it finally gave way, her sword continuing through to strike the guard.

Meanwhile, Ismeld methodically took down the last guard, her longsword slashing through the air in a series of swift, precise movements. The guard fell, his body slumping to the floor.

Deryk thrust his blade down into the man below him before turning and finishing the man that had fallen.

With the guards dispatched, the knights turned their attention to the doorway. They approached cautiously, weapons at the ready. With a shared nod, Gisele and Sloane pushed the door open and stepped inside.

As they entered the grand bed chamber, their attention was immediately drawn to a lone guard standing protectively in front of a raithe lady. The guard's eyes were wide, his grip on his weapon tightening as he took in their presence.

"Stand down or die!" he barked, his voice echoing in the large room.

Gisele, leading the group, merely scoffed at his threat. "Silence," she commanded, her voice ringing with authority. "You're outnumbered and outmatched."

The raithe lady seemed about to interject, but a sharp look from Ismeld, who had entered the room behind Sloane, silenced her.

In the corner of the room, a small figure caught Sloane's attention. A girl, with long curly dark brown hair like Gwyn's, stood with her back to them, huddled against the chest of another servant. Her body shook. Her face was buried in the servant's dress.

Sloane's heart pounded in her chest, her breath hitching in her throat. She took a hesitant step forward, her voice low and wavering as she called out, "Gwyn?"

The room fell silent, all eyes turning to the girl in the corner. The seconds stretched on, each one feeling like an eternity as Sloane waited for a response. She called out again, louder, "Gwyn, honey? It's me, Mom."

The servant woman seemed confused. She looked down at the girl huddled against her and gently coaxed the child to turn around. Sloane held her breath as the girl slowly turned, her long curly dark brown hair cascading away.

Time seemed to slow as the girl's face came into view. Her features were unfamiliar, her eyes, a different shade of blue, were wide and filled with fear.

It wasn't Gwyn.

The realization hit Sloane like a punch to the gut. This girl, this terrified child, was not her daughter.

The girl's voice trembled as she looked up at Sloane and the knights. "Did my grandfather send you? Are you here to take me home?" she asked quietly, her tone filled with hope.

Sloane's knees buckled beneath her, the cold stone floor meeting her as she fell. Pain shot through her, as if someone had taken a knife and shoved it straight through her heart, leaving only a raw and painful wound in its wake.

All the leads, all the hope, all the desperate searching—it hadn't led to Gwyn. It had led to this girl. And Gwyn wasn't here.

A hollow emptiness consumed Sloane, a void where her hope had once resided. She had been so sure, so certain that she was close to finding her daughter. But now, she was back at the beginning, with no leads, no clues, and no idea where she could be. The weight of her disappointment was crushing, leaving her feeling utterly devastated.

Tears fell down her face, her **[Focus]** destroyed, as she sat there, her mind… blank.

Commotion came from the hallway as footsteps pounded down the hall toward them. She heard words being exchanged, but she couldn't focus.

She could barely breathe.

A voice called out to her, and she recognized it as Maud's, but she didn't even look before a comforting hand was placed on Sloane's shoulder.

Breathing heavily, the healer squeezed gently before nudging her way around Sloane and stepping forward to speak to the girl. Sloane barely registered the words spoken, her mind consumed by a hollow emptiness. She had thought she was so close to finding her daughter, but now she was back to where she had started.

Suddenly, urgent shouting echoed from outside the room, pulling Sloane from her spiraling thoughts and despair. She heard Ernald yell something else, and she knew the knights were fighting more guards.

Gisele grabbed Sloane's arm, forcing her to her feet. "Sloane," she said as she leaned close, her voice urgent. "We need to go."

Sloane nodded, wiping at her eyes as she straightened up. "I know," she said, her voice shaky. "I just… I thought…"

"I know," Gisele said, her voice soft but firm. "We'll find her. But right now, this girl needs us and we have to get out of here. Now. Or none of us will."

With that, they turned and rushed out of the room, Maud keeping the girl and the servant woman close as they followed behind without a second look at the guard or Lady Marweth, who shouted threats of retribution after them.

They returned to the group, Gisele directing the knights as they fought their way back out of the castle. Sloane vaguely recalled Maud healing Cristole as he took a slash to his side, and Deryk, as a crossbow bolt punched into his leg.

Sloane's mind felt hazy, but she managed to keep up with the knights. She barely recalled using her magic to destroy the mechanism keeping the drawbridge locked up, sending it crashing down and allowing the group to escape and nearly straight into a large group of men headed by a man in a red hat.

All she could think about was how she had failed her daughter.

And Sloane had no clue where she was.

"Sloane?" Maud's soft voice echoed through the wagon, pulling Sloane from her thoughts. She turned to see the redhead stepping through the wagon door, her face etched with concern.

Without a word, Maud moved to sit next to Sloane, their shoulders brushing together in a comforting gesture.

"How are you doing?" she finally asked, her voice filled with the compassion Sloane had come to expect from the healer.

"Honestly?" Sloane said, her gaze fixed on her hands. "Not good."

Maud nodded and reached out to gently squeeze Sloane's hand. "I know," she replied. "But we did some good today, Sloane. Ser Redding and his people handled Lord Marweth. They found eleven other people... they're helping them now. And they're taking the young lady back to her house."

"That's good," Sloane said, her voice hollow. "I'm glad she's safe."

Maud was silent for a moment, her gaze focused on Sloane. "She was really scared, Sloane," she said softly. "But she's safe now. You helped do that. Without your magic..."

Sloane turned to look at Maud, her eyes filled with a mix of relief and sadness. "I'm really happy for her, Maud," she said, her voice choked. "I am... but it's not..."

"It's not Gwyn," Maud finished for her, her voice filled with understanding.

Sloane nodded, a tear rolling down her cheek. "Yeah," she whispered. "It's not my Gwyn."

The comfortable silence returned, a quietude wrought from a shared understanding between two people... two friends who had seen and experienced too much.

Sloane was grateful for the woman's presence, even if she couldn't bring herself to say it aloud.

Maud finally broke the silence, her voice firm. "We're going to keep looking, Sloane. We have a long journey ahead of us to Thirdghyll and then to Swanbrook. There's still hope."

Sloane nodded, her gaze distant. "I know," she said. "I just... I thought..."

"I know," Maud interrupted gently. "We all did. But we can't give up. In fact, the others think that what we accomplished today may be reason enough to refocus on our goals for Thirdghyll."

Sloane turned to look at Maud, her brows furrowing in confusion. "What do you mean?"

"Deryk and Ernald," Maud explained. "They expressed that they want to focus almost exclusively on the search for Gwyn in Thirdghyll. They think that we have done what we set out to accomplish here, helping people who needed it. We broke up a slaver ring and saw to it that a corrupt lord was taken down. They think we have a real chance of finding some concrete information in the city. Especially if we manage to make contact with the Westari Order of Secrets."

Sloane was silent for a moment as she collected her thoughts. "I hope they're right," she murmured quietly. "I hope we find her soon."

The sound of footsteps approaching the wagon broke their quiet conversation. The door creaked open and Ismeld poked her head in.

"We're leaving," she announced, but then her voice softened. "Ernald is driving. You two take your time."

Maud nodded. "Thank you, Ismeld."

Not long after Ismeld disappeared from the doorway, the wagon jerked into motion. With the steady rhythm of the wagon's wheels against the road, Sloane finally took a deep breath.

"All of you... you never give up hope, do you?" she asked, her voice hushed and incredulous.

Maud turned to look at her, her eyes filled with a quiet determination. "Never," she replied firmly.

The word hung in the air between them, a promise, a vow.

"Why?" Sloane asked, grasping, hoping for that last bit of reassurance that her path wasn't a lost cause. That she wasn't just a failure of a mother. That her daughter was truly out there, waiting for her to find her.

Maud tilted her head, her eyes glistening as she focused on something just beyond Sloane, something out of reach. "Hope," she started, "is the fuel that drives us, the light that guides us through the darkness. It's the belief that even in the face of the impossible, there's a chance for something better." Her voice was soft, but it carried a strength that resonated within the confines of the wagon. "Hope is the courage to face the unknown, to keep going when all seems lost. It's the conviction that every step we take, every battle we fight, brings us closer to our goal."

She paused, her gaze meeting Sloane's. "And sometimes, hope is all we have to hold on to—it's the thread that keeps us connected to our dreams, to our loved ones, to our sense of who we are and who we want to be. The sole source of resolve that we will find what we are searching for, whether that is a loved one or even ourselves."

Maud gave Sloane's hand a gentle squeeze. "So yes, we never give up hope, because without it, we lose ourselves, and we can't afford to do that. Not when there's still so much left to fight for."

Her words hung in the air, a testament to their shared resolve.

Sloane would keep hoping, keep fighting, until she found Gwyn. Because hope was all she had, and Sloane would cling to it with everything she had.

Slowly, she rested her head against Maud's shoulder, feeling the comforting warmth of her friend's embrace. Sloane's eyes fluttered closed as she let the steady rhythm of the wagon lull her into a sense of calm.

Soon they would be in Thirdghyll, and hopefully... they would find Gwyn. *I have to.*

CHAPTER THIRTY-SIX

A FUTURE FILLED WITH HOPE

Gwyn jolted awake, a blood-curdling scream ripping from her throat as she shot upright in her bed. She was gasping for breath, her eyes wide with terror, as the nightmare clung to her consciousness—images of her mom leaving her, telling her it was her fault. "Mom!" she cried out, her voice choked with sobs. "Come back! Please!"

I didn't mean to let go.

The walls of her chamber seemed to close in on her, the darkness filling her with an inexplicable dread. She lashed out—she needed light, she needed to see.

She didn't leave me.

As if answering her silent plea, a spark ignited within her. Her breath hitched, and without thinking, she let her magic burst forth.

We got split up.

Flames erupted from her hands, illuminating the room in a wash of harsh, unforgiving light. The bright blaze danced across the room, licking the sheets of her bed, scaling the walls, spreading its destructive tendrils in a seething, insatiable hunger.

It was an accident.

Gwyn's panicked cries were swallowed by the roaring of the fire, the mesmerizing flames reflecting in her wide, terror-filled eyes. Within moments, her room was a blazing inferno, the flames feeding on the opulent furnishings, rendering the once comforting space a merciless hellscape.

Before she could comprehend the situation, the door to her chamber burst open, slamming against the wall. A guard clad in the house's colors lunged into the room, his eyes wide with alarm, as he took in the scene. "Fire! Fire!" he shouted urgently.

Hot on his heels was Emma, her face pale with terror. "Your Highness!" she shouted, her voice strained with fear. She scanned the room, searching for Gwyn amid the blaze. But a ring of fire around the bed blocked her path, keeping her away from the young royal.

The chaotic scene quickly attracted more attention. Shouts echoed through the corridors, the clatter of rushed footsteps barely audible over the roar of the flames.

Gwyn's eyes met Emma's through the barrier of flames. There was confusion in her gaze, rapidly morphing into horror as she took in the destruction she'd caused. "No..." she gasped, her voice almost drowned by the consuming inferno.

Closing her eyes, she centered herself and [**Focused**] as she channeled mana into her core. Her will, firm and unwavering, sang in tune with the mana's song of fury and dictated the fire to return to her.

As guards and Sabina burst in with buckets of water, a stunning sight met their eyes. The raging inferno was retracting, drawn in by her [**Pyromancy**], coalescing into a swirling mass of fire around Gwyn before merging with her.

As she sought to contain the magic, flames erupted from her eye sockets, painting a fearsome image.

Sabina sprang into action, commanding a guard to tend to Emma, who had collapsed in shock, before rushing to the princess. Gwyn, seemingly in a trance, turned her flaming gaze toward Sabina as the woman reached her.

"Your Highness?" Sabina asked, her voice wavering as she hesitated only slightly once she looked into Gwyn's burning eyes. "What's happened?"

Like a dam that had overfilled, Gwyn's emotions burst, her concentration lost as all of her magic dissipated back into the song. Tears streamed down her face as her nightmare replayed over and over in her mind. "She's gone, she's gone."

Sabina turned to the guard behind her. "Someone get Taenya!"

The man didn't even make it out of the room before the woman in question burst in. "Gwyn?!" she called out in a panic. "Is she okay? Is the fire out?"

Sabina turned and nodded before moving close to help Gwyn off the charred bed, gently guiding her away from all the damage.

Gwyn looked up at the two women. "I'm sorry..." she said, guilt pouring into her, the fires extinguishing from her eyes. "Is... is Emma okay?"

Sabina and Taenya shared a tense, laden look—the gravity of the situation, the shock, concern, and disbelief swirling in their eyes. They looked at Gwyn.

Taenya turned to a maid who had been watching the ordeal unfold from the relative safety of the door. The woman leaned out of the door to speak quietly with someone before turning back around and nodding quickly at the knight.

"She will be fine," Taenya confirmed, turning back to Gwyn with a small, encouraging smile.

Sabina, wearing a stern yet compassionate expression, broke the silence once more. "What happened, Your Highness?" Her tone was gentle, coaxing, urging her to speak.

As she looked around the charred remains of the furniture around the room, guilt washed over her. She looked down at her hands, once the source of a raging inferno, now trembling slightly in her lap. Her lower lip trembled until she bit it, but she couldn't hide the stream of tears slipping down her cheek.

Sabina leaned closer, and Gwyn looked up through her tear-blurred vision. The knight's voice was soft and quiet so only she could hear. "Your Highness, I cannot aid you if I don't understand what you're feeling. Speak to us. Please," she gently implored. "We want to help."

"It's my mom," Gwyn said slowly, as if every word would bring her more pain. "In my dream, she… she didn't come when I did. She was… happy that I came alone."

Gwyn sniffled, her gaze falling to the floor as she wiped her nose.

"Oh, Gwyn…" Taenya said, her voice filled with compassion.

As though in a daze, Gwyn felt the steady and comforting presence of Taenya and Sabina as they gently encircled her in their arms. They guided her away from the devastated room, their warmth a soothing balm against the cold dread that had settled in her chest. As they moved into the adjacent sitting area, a wave of relief washed over her.

In the midst of the beehive of activity, Siveril stood, an anchor in the storm as he directed the servants in their cleanup efforts. Gwyn noticed the softening of his gaze when it landed on her, a silent gesture of concern that disappeared as quickly as it came, his focus returning to the work at hand.

Theran was stationed nearby, a stoic sentinel ensuring that only designated individuals entered the damaged space. His presence, although quiet, was a reminder of the safety measures that encased her, another layer of protection against the world outside.

Taenya and Sabina guided her to one of the plush seats, and the moment she was seated, she felt them settle on either side of her, their shared silence resonating with reassurance. Despite the distressing occurrence, there was a sense of tranquility found in their unity, as if the two women had formed an unspoken vow. The solidity of their support, their unwavering loyalty, enveloped Gwyn, a warm cloak against the icy remnants of her nightmare, providing her a brief sanctuary from her haunting thoughts.

So, why, then, did she have to start crying again?

Taenya strode into the spacious office that Siveril, as majordomo, used to manage the house in Gwyn's stead. Until Gwyn reached the age of majority at sixteen, this was his domain.

The office was still illuminated despite the late hour, the oil lamps casting their warm glow on the polished mahogany furniture. Long, flickering shadows enlivened the room.

A large desk dominated the center of the room, with meticulously organized piles of scrolls and parchments containing reports, letters, and other pertinent information that had accumulated in the short week since the princess had taken over. Bookshelves, filled to the brim with volumes of history and references of the houses that now pledged fealty to the princess, accounting ledgers for the manor itself, and even tomes of both ducal and crown law, lined the walls, a testament to the scholarly nature of the steward. High vaulted ceilings gave the room an imposing air, while tall, arched windows afford a sweeping view of the estate grounds and allowed in the bright moonlight of the Sisters.

Looking through the window, Taenya saw two of the house guards walking by, one holding a lamp.

Siveril was seated in a small sitting area next to one of those windows, sipping a glass of amber-colored liquor, a grimace on his face. Sabina occupied the chair across from him, and was focusing intently on a series of documents in her hands.

At Taenya's arrival, the majordomo set down his glass and stood, startling Sabina from her work. "Ah, Ser Taenya," he greeted her, a weary smile tugging at his lips. "How fares our young liege?"

With a heavy sigh, Taenya replied, "She's sleeping again, finally."

"That's a relief," Siveril said, sinking back into his chair. But his brows creased with worry. "However, we need to discuss where to go from here, specifically concerning Gwyn's magic. Concealing it won't be a simple task from this point." Siveril fell into his thoughts for a moment before looking from Sabina to Taenya. "Can we restrict her magic somehow?"

Sabina, catching his gaze, shifted her eyes to Taenya, subtly deferring the question to her. Taenya, understanding her role in this conversation, shook her head. "No. Gwyn is fully committed to using it. Any attempt to limit her use of magic will likely backfire." She paused, considering her next words carefully.

"We should provide a safe space for her to learn how to control it responsibly. Training would be beneficial for her, both for her magic and her peace of mind. She has always enjoyed training with the blade, it was a bond she shared with Raafe." At the mention of the deceased guard, a hushed silence filled the room. "Maybe we could increase the frequency of these training sessions, even find a way to integrate magic into them.

"Also, we need to educate our house about magic use. It's likely that they'll witness it more often. If we can create a sense of camaraderie and mutual understanding between Gwyn and the staff, they will be more apt to protect her, even feel pride in her magic, rather than exploit it."

Taenya paused, letting her words hang in the room.

Sabina nodded thoughtfully. "We need to learn more about magic as a whole. This is new, something strange. Additionally, we have to be wary of any reaction from the Church and how it may affect Gwyn. We should educate her on the decrees—we do not want an inquisition to come down on her for any reason. I, for one, do not want to fight off any paladins."

Siveril, absorbing their suggestions, huffed at Sabina's response. "I do not think we will be fighting any paladins, but I agree. We'll put these plans into motion immediately. Gwyn's safety and well-being are our priority, and making sure she feels supported in her magic use is crucial."

Sabina put down the documents she had been perusing and nodded in agreement. "Also, since we are on the subject of members of the house... I've been keeping an eye on the staff, and thus far, I do not believe we should expect any concerns. Of course, there are murmurs and rumors regarding what occurred tonight, but nothing concrete about the origins of the fire. I've spoken with both the guard and Emma and ensured that they will not utter a word about what they witnessed."

"That's good to hear," Siveril responded, though his worry was not entirely alleviated. "We still need to stay ahead of this situation. Any minor slip could lead to significant problems, especially with other houses."

"What about the duke?" Taenya suggested.

Siveril turned to her and quirked a brow. "What do you mean?"

She shrugged. "We all know that the duke is going to want to meet her. Why not skip waiting on him to request the meeting and simply approach him?"

Siveril paused, pondering the proposal. He took a slow sip of his drink, then finally nodded. "That's a sound idea. I can secure us an audience relatively quickly. You'll need to attend with me, Taenya."

Surprise painted itself across Taenya's face. "Me?" she sputtered, her eyes widening with shock. She'd met a baron, but... a duke?

Sabina snorted lightly, a smirk playing on her lips. "Better you than me. Besides, you are the knight-captain."

Siveril chuckled. "She's not wrong, Taenya. You'll need to get used to this, and quickly, especially as the left hand of a princess."

Taenya could only gulp in response, her mind spinning with the gravity of the situation and the newfound responsibilities being thrust upon her.

The majordomo just shook his head. "Do not worry. His Grace and I have had amicable relations for many years now. Before Lord Iemes was bestowed peerage, I was a member of the ducal administration."

Taenya had heard briefly about that, but she didn't know the extent of it. It seemed she would soon find out.

As Taenya and Siveril approached the majestic Tiloral Palace, a sense of anticipation filled the air. The carriage, hastily adorned with the heraldry of House Reinhart—with its flying reptilian creature that Gwyn had requested—rolled steadily along the cobblestone path that led to the grand entrance of the palace.

Taenya's keen eyes took in the picturesque scene that unfolded before them. Lush gardens, meticulously maintained, stretched out on either side of the pathway, filled with colorful blooms and vibrant foliage, their fragrant scents wafting through the air. She couldn't help but appreciate the care that had gone into creating such a splendid setting.

As the carriage drew nearer to the palace, the grandeur of the ancestral seat of a former kingdom became apparent. Towering stone walls rose majestically, their imposing presence a testament to the might and influence of the Tiloral dynasty. Intricate statues and ornate carvings adorned the facade, depicting tales of valor and conquest. Taenya's gaze lingered on these artistic details, silently acknowledging the history and power they represented. She couldn't help but feel small.

Stained-glass windows in vibrant hues caught her attention. The sunlight seemed to make them glow, and she wished she were inside to see the assault of colors that was surely there. The soothing sounds of fountains reached her ears as they drew up, their cascading waters adding a tranquil harmony to the scene.

As the carriage came to a halt, Taenya felt a mixture of excitement and responsibility. Siveril had helped her prepare for the upcoming meeting with the duke all morning but she couldn't help but feel her anxiety rise as she considered the seriousness of the encounter. Never before had she even witnessed a family of such immense influence and prominence—in fact, it was a rare opportunity for a commoner born to even be in their presence, let alone engage with them directly. Granted, she was a knight-captain of a royal House now. So, perhaps she was letting her nerves get away from her. Breathing deeply, Taenya adjusted her armor and ensured her sword was securely fastened at her side. She stepped out of the carriage, ready to do what was necessary to help lay a strong foundation for House Reinhart.

The palace, in all its opulence and grandeur, was a sharp contrast to the quiet, understated elegance of House Reinhart. Every surface gleamed with wealth and power, from the priceless artifacts adorning the walls to the elaborate mosaics inlaid in the marble floors. The air was thick with the scent of exotic flowers, a heady aroma that spoke of lands far beyond their borders.

A servant led them through the labyrinthine corridors of the palace, his polished boots clicking against the stone floor in rhythm with Taenya's pounding heart. Her palms were sweaty against the hilt of her sword, and she had to consciously resist the urge to fidget in her armor. She had faced battle-hardened enemies without flinching, yet the thought of this meeting set her nerves on edge.

At last, they arrived at an ornate door to a private office where they would meet the duke, and were promptly abandoned by their guide. A second servant stepped forward, his face as emotionless as the marble statues that lined the hallway. "His Grace will attend to you shortly," he intoned before disappearing into an adjoining room.

As Taenya and Siveril sat on a small bench set beneath a window in the hallway, she felt a pit of unease growing in her stomach. House Reinhart's majordomo gave her a reassuring smile.

Eventually, she heard the distant chime of the city bells ring, signaling how long they had waited. The door to the office opened and a young girl emerged.

She was a high elf, with flowing blond hair and vibrant violet eyes, who appeared to be roughly the same age as Gwyn. But there was a different kind of maturity about her, as if she felt the weight of the world on her shoulders.

Her eyes narrowed slightly as they landed on Siveril. A flash of recognition sparked in her eyes, but without uttering a word, she simply nodded and continued on her way, her silken gown rustling softly against the marble floor and leaving Taenya bewildered.

Siveril leaned close and whispered in her ear, his voice low as to not carry. "His Grace's granddaughter. She will be duchess one day."

The sound of the door opening interrupted them. The servant from before returned, standing stiffly, with an air of formality. "His Grace will see you now," he said, gesturing for them to follow him.

Taenya and Siveril exchanged a glance and stepped into the room. The duke's office was surprisingly modest compared to the rest of the palace. There was a sense of homely charm to it, a place where one could escape from the constant pressures of ruling a duchy. The most prominent feature was an ornate desk, but the Duke of Tiloral himself was not behind it. Instead, he was standing in front of a marble fireplace, a small fire crackling cheerily within. A cozy arrangement of chairs was set up before the fire, and a small table with a bottle of fine liquor was placed strategically between them.

Upon seeing his guests, the duke broke into a warm smile. He moved to greet Siveril, pulling the majordomo into a hearty embrace. "Siveril, my old friend," he said, his voice deep and rich. "It is good to see you."

Taenya's mind went blank. *What?* She didn't know whether or not she should bow. Or just watch the two… hug.

Siveril returned the smile, pulling away from the embrace to bow slightly. "Thank you for seeing us at such short notice, Your Grace," he said, gratitude evident in his tone. "Allow me to introduce Ser Taenya Shavyre, recently knighted by Lord Iemes before passing along her service to another." His gaze briefly flicked toward Taenya, and she suddenly became quite nervous as the attention was turned toward her.

The Duke of Tiloral warmly extended his hand to her. "Ser Taenya Shavyre," he said. "Lord Iemes is a man I hold in high esteem, and for him to bestow such an honor is no small service. The passing of a knight's service is a significant event. You carry a considerable responsibility now."

"Thank you, Your Grace," Taenya replied, curtsying before taking his hand in a firm shake. The duke's grip was strong, his fingers enveloping hers in a reassuring manner. She could feel her nerves starting to ease.

A chuckle escaped the duke as he released her hand, stepping back to appraise her. "Your humility does you credit, Ser Taenya. But do not forget that your position demands a certain level of confidence. You have earned your knighthood, and with it, the right to stand tall among your peers."

Taenya nodded, taking the duke's words to heart. "I appreciate your counsel, Your Grace," she replied earnestly.

"Well then," the duke said, clapping his hands together and turning his attention back to Siveril. "I trust there is a significant matter at hand that has brought you both here. Shall we discuss it over a drink?" He gestured at the bottle on the table, his eyebrows raised invitingly.

Siveril shared a glance with Taenya before nodding. "A drink would be appreciated, Your Grace. The matter we need to discuss... It is rather complex."

The duke simply nodded, turning his attention to pouring a generous measure of liquor into the three glasses. His movements were smooth and deliberate, suggesting a man who was no stranger to such rituals.

"Complex matters are best tackled with a friend and a full glass," he commented, passing the drinks to his guests. "I suspect this has something to do with the princess that Valro boy in the Guard informed me of. Now, my old friend, tell me everything."

Taenya felt her breath hitch as Siveril heaved a deep sigh, his grip tightening around the glass in his hand. She watched as he drained a significant portion of his drink in a single gulp. A knot of anticipation tightened in her stomach as the room fell silent except for the crackling of the fire.

Siveril set his glass down on the table and turned to face the duke, a determined expression on his face. He began to speak, his voice steady as he recounted the tale of House Reinhart and Princess Gwyneth, pausing to allow Taenya to interject as required for further detail.

The duke's expression was serious, his gaze fixed intently on the two of them as he absorbed the tale being laid before him.

Finally, the duke nodded, a deep understanding reflected in his eyes. He looked at Siveril and said firmly, "I will give my acknowledgment, my friend. At court. And I look forward to meeting this princess from another world."

Taenya let out a quiet sigh of relief, the knot in her stomach finally unraveling. A wave of gratitude toward the duke filled her. She knew that the duchy's support was going to make a world of difference for Gwyn and their house.

They continued their discussion for another bell, but as the meeting drew to a close, Taenya couldn't help but find herself caught in a whirlwind of thoughts. The future, as ever, remained uncertain, and the path that House Reinhart was to tread had suddenly become a lot more stable, and yet more complicated, especially as knowledge of Gwyn's magic came to light.

She found herself thinking about the young princess, who had been thrust into a world she barely understood and was expected to seamlessly transition into. Gwyn, with her fiery magic and an equally fiery determination, was an anomaly in their world, a wild card that had the potential to change everything. Would the nobility see her as a threat, or would they embrace her unique abilities?

Taenya knew they were on the cusp of something big, something that could potentially change the very fabric of their society. As the weight of her thoughts pressed on her, she felt a renewed sense of determination. She would stand by Gwyn's side, guiding and supporting her as she navigated through the turbulent waters of nobility and magic.

She looked at Siveril, who was finishing up his conversation with the duke. The man had been an unexpectant boon for their nascent house, and his guidance and advice would be greatly needed in the days to come.

The future was uncertain, yes, but as long as they stayed together, as long as they faced whatever came their way as a united front, Taenya believed they could weather any storm. They could guide House Reinhart and Gwyn to a future filled with hope and prosperity.

And hopefully, the knight-captain thought, *we'll reunite her with her mother along the way.*

MACHINATIONS

In the bustling city of Drakensburg, Crown Prince Kerrell reclined in his plush, velvet-lined carriage. The coach jostled slightly as it trundled along the cobblestone streets, though the interior was as quiet as a sanctuary, insulating him from the clamor outside before it slowed to a stop.

After a moment, the door to the carriage swung open, and Lord Angwin, a marquess and one of his "agents" within the Duchy of Tiloral, stepped inside. His dark eyes briefly surveyed the interior before settling on the prince. He took the seat across from Kerrell and bowed in greeting. "Your Royal Highness," the marquess addressed him formally.

Kerrell dismissed the formalities with a casual wave of his hand as the carriage resumed its motion. "What news of the Tilorals, Angwin?" he asked, his eyes filled with a curious yet calculating gaze.

"The Tilorals are grooming their granddaughter to take a more active role in their affairs," Angwin replied. "They intend to send her to the Royal Academy next year."

A dismissive snort escaped Kerrell's lips. "Of course they are—she's the heir to one of the duchies. But children are of no concern to me, Angwin," he said, irritation creeping into his voice. "I want to know if they are indeed seeking to expand their influence."

"Signs point to yes, Sir," Angwin said, a slight grimace twisting his features. "In fact, I have it on good authority that the duke has recently met with the dwarves of Dirn Loduhr."

A dark cloud seemed to pass over Kerrell's features, his previously relaxed posture tightening. "They would meet with him but refuse my overtures?" he growled. He had tried for years to court the dwarven mountain enclave positioned in the center of the kingdom away from the icy relations they had shared for nearly a century, but to no avail.

And yet, the Tilorals had been afforded this gesture… another sign that the so-called neutral house was seeking to undermine the Crown.

Wisely, Angwin chose to remain silent on the matter rather than fan the prince's ire.

"That's not all, Sir," he said, his voice taking on a more solemn tone. "There's been some commotion within the Grand Temple. I've learned that the duke has also met with the archpriestess. From my sources, it appears to concern the Flash and the people who arrived with it, the terrans."

The carriage fell silent, the words hanging heavy in the air. Prince Kerrell looked out of the carriage window, his mind whirling with this new information. If the Tilorals were truly expanding their influence—even aligning with other nations and meddling in religious affairs—it could only mean one thing. The balance of power was shifting, and he needed to respond.

He nodded slowly, contemplating the new information. "Within the season, I will be enacting a royal decree with my father's approval regarding these… magical… anomalies brought by the Flash. However, the kingdom needs to gather more information before we can move forward. If it comes to it, Angwin, I will require your utmost cooperation. You will hold a central position in my plans within the duchy and the decree's enforcement."

Angwin bowed his head respectfully. "I am humbled by your trust, Sir," he said earnestly.

The prince dismissed his gratitude with a wave of his hand. "You are simply the highest-ranking noble within the Crown's sphere in the duchy—no other would suffice. Now, you will work to disrupt the Tilorals in any way you can. We cannot afford for them to garner more power and influence."

The marquess nodded. "It will be done. There is… one last thing, Sir."

Prince Kerrell gestured impatiently for Angwin to speak, his hesitance annoying.

"Several smaller houses are looking to improve their standing, Sir," Angwin reported. "Some of their actions are cause for concern. I have heard whispers of a terran princess aligning herself with an upstart baron with outsized influence who holds ties with the duke."

Prince Kerrell's eyebrows drew together in a scowl. "A princess? In my kingdom?" he questioned, his tone incredulous. "Angwin, you are to find more information on this princess immediately. If she is seeking power or aligning herself with the duchy, disrupt her plans. I don't care how you do it."

Angwin bowed his head again, his voice steady as he responded, "I will need to include others in this, Your Royal Highness."

Prince Kerrell's eyes narrowed, causing the marquess to hastily add, "I will oversee it personally."

"Good." With that, the prince banged on the carriage wall, signaling the driver to halt. One of his royal knights immediately opened the carriage door. "Now, leave me," he instructed the marquess.

Angwin exited the carriage swiftly. Kerrell took pleasure seeing the marquess standing at attention as the carriage moved on. He settled back into his seat, lost in his thoughts, planning his next move.

Amanda Levings stepped out of the carriage, her eyes wide as she took in the luxurious facade of the noble manor before her. The woman who had saved her life, Lady Racine, offered her a reassuring smile as they made their way toward the entrance. As she walked, Amanda couldn't help but reflect on the crazy events that had brought her to this point.

She had woken up in a world that was a far cry from the Toronto she knew. It wasn't even the same year anymore. It was more like the fifteenth century than eighty-four and it was so… different than anything she knew.

How can anyone be prepared for something like this?.

Instead, she found herself in a place called Eona, a world that seemed to be straight out of medieval times, complete with elves and magic. The shock had been overwhelming, to say the least.

Her journey had begun near a road, and after almost a day of traveling on foot, she had been attacked by a bear. She would have been a goner if it hadn't been for a man who had come to her rescue. He had introduced himself as a terran, a term she had found hard to believe at first. But they traveled together for several weeks, passing through quaint villages filled with people who shouldn't have been real. Amanda had been taken aback by the sight of the first elf she saw, his pointed ears and ethereal beauty unlike anything she had ever seen.

Then, as she traveled, it was in the vast landscapes that she had come to accept the reality of her situation.

Their journey together had come to an abrupt end when they were attacked by some creatures in the middle of the night. Amanda had never even seen them, but when she woke up to find her companion gone and the signs of their large claw marks, she had felt a sense of despair wash over her.

Just when she thought all was lost, she had come across Lady Racine's carriage.

Amanda's salvation had come in the form of a group of knights and guards who had spotted her stumbling along the road. Among them was a tall knight with the most captivating green eyes she had ever seen.

He had introduced her to Lady Racine, a telv countess, and her husband, Lord Alec, who was an actual elf.

The countess had been pleasantly surprised to learn that Amanda was a human, seemingly unfazed by the notion of a woman from another world.

From that moment on, the countess had taken Amanda under her wing, engaging her in endless conversations as they journeyed toward the city of Strathmore. The older woman was a fountain of knowledge, and taught Amanda about the customs, cultures, and creatures of this strange new world.

Lord Alec, though more reserved, had been equally kind, offering Amanda words of comfort and reassurance whenever she felt overwhelmed. Together, they had made her feel welcome, easing her transition into this fantasy world.

Upon their arrival in Strathmore, Amanda had been awestruck by the city's grandeur. The stone buildings, the bustling markets, the people in their medieval attire—it was like stepping into a history book. Yet, amid the unfamiliarity, she had found a sense of comfort, a feeling of home.

As they entered the manor, Amanda couldn't help but feel a sense of gratitude toward Lady Racine. Despite the circumstances, she was determined to make the most of her new life in Eona.

With a warm smile, Lady Racine led Amanda into the manor's library, a grand room filled with shelves upon shelves of books. The scent of old parchment filled the air, a comforting aroma that reminded Amanda of the libraries back home.

"It's time you learned about the true nobility of the kingdom," Lady Racine said, her voice echoing softly in the quiet room. She gestured toward a large table in the center of the room, where several books were already laid out. "These texts will give you a good understanding of our nation's true history and the tyranny of kings."

Amanda nodded. *That sounds horrible. They have to suffer under tyranny? These poor people.*

"Once we're finished here, perhaps we could discuss your world," Lady Racine continued, her eyes twinkling with curiosity. "I've arranged for one of my retainers to join us. He's quite interested in learning about other worlds."

Lady Racine paused, her gaze thoughtful as she looked at Amanda. "You spoke of the man who was with you. You know, it's possible there are even more like you out there," she mused. "People from worlds like yours who have found themselves here on Ikios."

Amanda blinked, she hadn't really thought about it since... that night.

"And if that's the case," the countess continued, her tone betraying her excitement, "then your knowledge could be invaluable. You could help us understand your world better, and perhaps we could use that understanding to improve the lives of our people. To fight back against the tyranny that oppresses us."

Amanda felt a surge of hope at the countess's words. Maybe she could make a difference here, after all.

＊　＊　＊

Count Sylvain Kayser sat in his study, the room filled with the scent of old books and polished wood. He was a man of stature, with sharp features and a gaze that could pierce through the toughest of men. His eyes were focused on Captain Lars, one of his most trusted subordinates within the Thirdghyll City Guard.

"Have you received any word from Lord Marweth?" Kayser asked, his voice echoing in the quiet room.

Captain Lars shook his head, his expression serious. "No, my lord. But the... mercenaries... they have brought another group to the city."

A slow smile spread across Kayser's face. "Excellent. We must learn all we can about these new 'terrans' and the magic they wield. Bring the group to the castle. I will have them... debriefed."

Lars nodded, but his expression remained troubled. "There is one other problem, my lord. Mister Rowe has been making moves in the slums. He has been collecting people, and seems to be trying to ascertain a way to utilize the terran magic himself."

Kayser's smile faded, replaced by a scowl. "Pass along information regarding Mister Rowe and his gangs to one of the other captains. Let them deal with this nuisance. Perhaps we can kill two wynvers with one stone."

"I will pass it to Captain Jorin of the Eastern Garrison," Lars suggested.

Kayser nodded, his gaze thoughtful. "Yes, that will keep him away from our interests and focused on those who work against such. We cannot afford any distractions at this crucial time."

As Captain Lars left the room, Kayser leaned back in his chair, his mind already spinning with plans and strategies. His gaze drifted to a letter on his desk, the seal of the baron Lord Bolton still visible on the parchment.

It was thanks to this man, this terran baron, that he had learned about the witches and their magic. The baron had been surprisingly forthcoming, perhaps even naive, in his eagerness to establish relations and share knowledge. Kayser had seized upon this opportunity, gleaning as much information as he could about the terrans and their strange abilities.

He picked up the letter, his fingers tracing over the seal. The baron had proved to be a useful tool, a conduit through which he could learn more about these new arrivals. But Kayser was not a man to rest on his laurels. He saw potential in the baron, a possibility for further manipulation and control.

"Perhaps," he mused aloud. "the baron could be persuaded to bring more of his kind under my influence."

He could already see the benefits of such a move. More terrans meant more magic, more power. And with that power, he could solidify his control over Thirdghyll and expand his influence throughout Westaren. The other lords would have no choice but to acknowledge his supremacy.

But first, he needed to ensure the baron remained loyal and useful. Kayser had no illusions about the man's character. He was ambitious, yes, but also honorable to a fault even as he spoke of his strange single god that his world worshipped.

Another peculiarity: How did a single god rise?

What he would give to see the Goddess of Night, Tenera, and the patron of his people, the moon elves, rise to her rightful place at the mantle of the Family.

He sighed as his thoughts returned to the terran noble. He would need to be handled carefully, manipulated subtly. But Kayser was confident in his abilities. After all, he had been playing this game for a long time.

The arrival of the terrans and their magic was a game-changer, and he intended to use it to his advantage. The city of Thirdghyll, and all of Westaren, would soon see the true power of Count Sylvain Kayser.

The agents of the Westaren Order of Secrets adhered to a strict code of silence when on assignment, speaking to other agents only when ordered or absolutely necessary. This protocol was designed to maintain the organization's veil of secrecy and avoid attracting unwanted attention. The man in the yellow hat leaned back in his seat, reflecting on the series of events that had led him to this point.

The existence of the Westaren Order of Secrets was a poorly kept secret among those in the know. These individuals, influential figures within their respective nations or organizations, were aware of the order's existence, but the full extent of its operations remained a mystery. Everyone had their suspicions, of course. Paranoia was a common trait among those in their line of work, and in Westaren, it had been honed into a weapon. This was precisely why the order had chosen to establish its secondary headquarters in Ghyll.

Ghyll was a hotbed of political intrigue, the only place where the Crown had sanctioned its agents, spies, and assassins to operate against its own people. The city was a cesspool, teeming with corruption, and not just of the insect variety. Despite numerous attempts to cleanse the city of its filth, it always returned.

The citizens had even turned it into a perverse form of entertainment. They reveled in the "Big Ones," the events that threatened to wipe the city off the map. Yet, they turned a blind eye to the smaller, localized purges. Whether it was a business here, a gang there, or an entire noble line elsewhere, all were fair game in the twisted spectacle enjoyed by the city's masochistic inhabitants.

The man had recently adopted a new alias following a positively delightful conversation with a terran named Giacomo. As was customary in the order, each member assumed a different identity for each assignment. His current persona was named Giallo, a nod to the color of the hat he wore, which in Giacomo's native language meant yellow. He found the name appealing, as it bore a phonetic resemblance to the Tene'loreni word for darkness. As a moon elf, he found the association fitting.

The city teetered on the brink of open unrest, a situation the Crown could ill afford. The order had been compelled to adopt a more proactive approach since the Flash, the event that had seen a new race of people magically appear across the kingdom. As the Hand of the Crown for Thirdghyll, it was his responsibility to manage this crisis. However, the task was proving increasingly challenging without resorting to... drastic measures. His upcoming meeting would likely determine the extent of the "plague" he would need to eradicate from the kingdom.

His gaze shifted as a group of raithe and moon elves entered the tavern where he was seated. He was still in search of a man, a man he was determined to find. "Jorne" was a common name within the kingdom, and it was the alias currently used by the asset he sought. His assignment was to investigate the connection between the gang that owned the tavern where Giallo was currently seated and Count Kayser, the ruling noble of Thirdghyll.

The group of thugs who had entered the tavern comprised four raithe and three moon elves. Giallo had learned that despite employing individuals of any race, Mister Rowe reserved his inner circle for the two races that favored the night. Giallo himself didn't discriminate as many of the other nobles tended to do within the kingdom.

As the seven men moved past him, he slowly rose from his seat, picked up his drink, and trailed behind them.

He paused as they approached a door in an open room at the back of the tavern. Two of the raithe turned to stand on either side of the door. Giallo took a large gulp of the watered-down ale and staggered toward the two men.

"Oi! Is the privy back there? Feels like this swill I'm drinkin' is 'bout to make a reappearance, mate," he slurred, stumbling toward the men.

The man on the left raised a hand. "Hold up. This area's off-limits. The privy's... outside. Get out of here, you sot."

Giallo slurred as he responded, "Aw, come on, mate! I just need to drain the..." He mimicked a retching sound and leaned forward, continuing the act.

The man on the right made a disgusted face and moved forward to push him away.

Just as Giallo was grabbed, he plunged the dagger he kept concealed under his long sleeves into the man's armpit. The man stumbled forward with a grunt.

"Oh! Sorry, mate. Here, let me help you," Giallo said. He grabbed the man and pulled him close, turning him around. As he did so, he stabbed the base of his neck from behind and shoved him forward into the other man. In two swift steps, he had stabbed the stumbling man trying to catch his companion three times before he could do more than grunt.

He positioned the men on either side of the door and quietly checked the handle. Sensing that it was barred, he knocked on it and moved to the side. He drew a longer dagger from beneath his coat and waited.

The door was unlatched and swung open. A telv man he hadn't noticed earlier opened it. "What? The boss said not to let anyone disturb—Ungh!" The man collapsed into a fit of coughs that were quickly silenced by the second blade.

He moved into the hallway, his eyes narrowing as he instantly noticed the stairs. *Those aren't supposed to be there.*

Giallo slowly and quietly descended the stairwell that spiraled down two levels before opening up into a warehouse-like area supported by pillars and filled with wooden boxes and crates.

He heard talking and listened in as he stealthily moved closer to the source of the voices.

"That's the third terran this week we haven't been able to get before the count has," the first voice said.

A deeper, more suave voice spoke up. "None of you has figured out what the count wants with the terrans?"

"No, boss. It's like they disappear once taken," a third voice said.

There were some muffled curses before the man who seemed to be the boss spoke again. "Do we have anything?"

"No, boss."

A door opened on the far side. Giallo peeked around a corner and watched a raithe man rush in.

"Boss!"

The group turned toward the lone man and the boss made a sound of displeasure. "What the hell are you doing here?"

"There's another terran noble, and she and some knights made some waves in Lindale against Lord Marweth."

The raithe launched into an explanation of all that he had heard, mentioning a Ser Redding, which piqued Giallo's interest.

Sounds like one of my colleagues.

"Here's the thing, though, boss! She can use magic! Damaged entire parts of the castle." The raithe's voice was filled with a mix of fear and excitement. The room fell silent, the implications of his words hanging heavily in the air.

Giallo's eyebrows shot up in surprise. The Flash had been a source of constant headaches for him. However, it had brought one unexpected benefit: physical changes. After resolving his first few disputes, he had barely noticed it. But now, after dispatching enough foes, he could feel the improvements. Something had happened during the Flash, and it seemed to bring physical enhancements the more active he was.

This was something the order was actively investigating. Another point of interest was the various small phenomena that seemed to be popping up around the kingdom and nearby Sovereign Cities.

He sighed quietly. His priorities had just shifted once again. A terran performing magic took precedence over anything going on with Mister Rowe's gang.

Giallo listened long enough to gather information about when the raithe suspected the terran would arrive, then slipped back into the shadows and made his way out of the structure and into the night.

It seems that things are about to get interesting.

ACKNOWLEDGMENTS

I could not have finished this first book without the support of my family. And the super-late-night tea my wife would make as I tired away at a chapter that took longer than I'd thought. "You da MVP, babe."

I would also like to thank my beta readers: you guys are the reason this story has taken the shape that it has. The comments, advice, and brainstorming were well received and beneficial to helping me mold this into a coherent and hopefully plothole-free story!

Lastly, I'd like to thank the authors who provided mentorship in this journey, particularly Ivan Kal and JLMullins. You guys were unbelievably patient and supportive, and I definitely appreciate the time you gave.

ABOUT THE AUTHOR

Travis Albrecht spends his days working and traveling the globe for the US Air Force. When he's not doing that, you can usually find him reading fantasy or science fiction stories or playing a plethora of PC games. You may also find him struggling to figure out how his young daughter keeps destroying him without remorse in *Mario Kart*. After living abroad for some time, Travis currently lives in California with his wife and daughter. This is his first novel in the Manabound series.

Podium
DISCOVER
STORIES UNBOUND
PodiumAudio.com

www.ingramcontent.com/pod-product-compliance
Lightning Source LLC
Chambersburg PA
CBHW020645120726

47906CB00001B/129